STAR TREK

THE NEXT GENERATION®

THE SPACE BETWEEN

SPACE... THE FINAL FRONTIER.

THESE ARE THE VOYAGES OF
THE STARSHIP ENTERPRISE.

ITS CONTINUING MISSION:
TO EXPLORE STRANGE
NEW WORLDS,

TO SEEK OUT NEW LIFE AND
NEW CIVILIZATIONS,

TO BOLDLY GO WHERE NO ONE
HAS GONE BEFORE.

CONTENTS and CREDITS

IDW PUBLISHING IS:
TED ADAMS, PRESIDENT
ROBBIE ROBBINS, EVP/SR. GRAPHIC ARTIST
CLIFFORD METH, EVP OF STRATEGIES/EDITORIAL
CHRIS RYALL, PUBLISHER/EDITOR-IN-CHIEF
ALAN PAYNE, VP OF SALES
NEIL UYETAKE, ART DIRECTOR
DAN TAYLOR, EDITOR
JUSTIN EISINGER, ASSISTANT EDITOR
TOM WALTZ, ASSISTANT EDITOR
CHRIS MOWRY, GRAPHIC ARTIST
AMAURI OSORIO, GRAPHIC ARTIST
MATTHEW RUZICKA, CPA, CONTROLLER
ALONZO SIMON, SHIPPING MANAGER
KRIS OPRISKO, EDITOR/FOREIGN LIC. REP.

978-1-60010-116-8

Collection Edits by Justin Eisinger
Collection Design by Chris Mowry

9 08 07   1 2 3 4

® STAR TREK created by Gene Roddenberry
Special thanks to Paula Block of CBS Consumer Products
for her invaluable assistance.

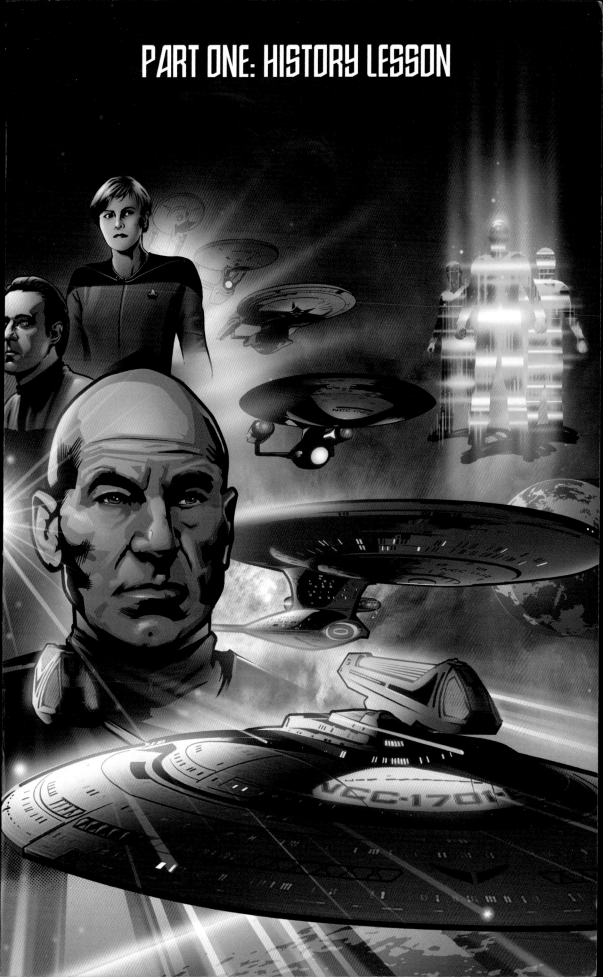

PART ONE: HISTORY LESSON

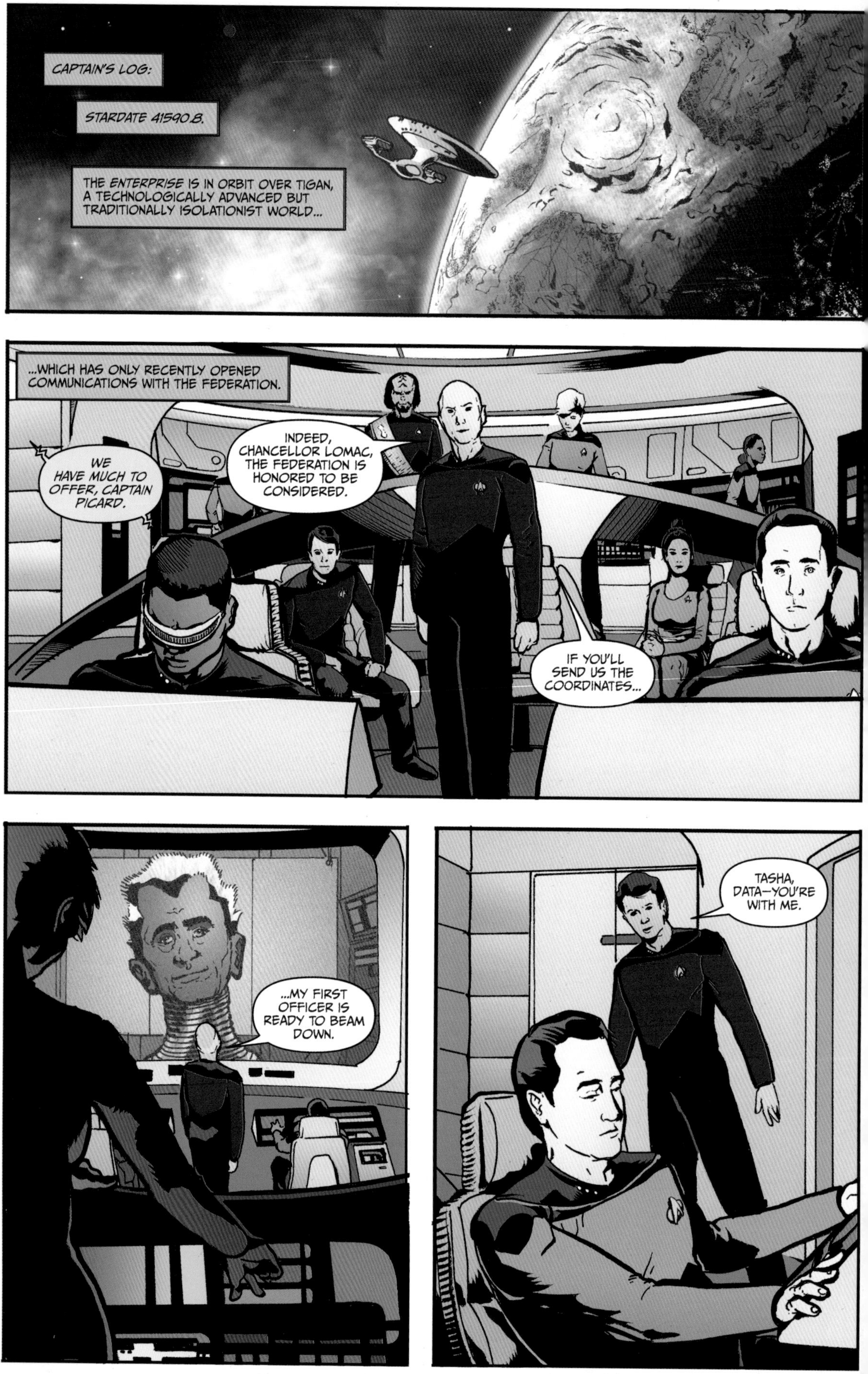
CAPTAIN'S LOG:
STARDATE 41590.8.
THE *ENTERPRISE* IS IN ORBIT OVER TIGAN, A TECHNOLOGICALLY ADVANCED BUT TRADITIONALLY ISOLATIONIST WORLD...
...WHICH HAS ONLY RECENTLY OPENED COMMUNICATIONS WITH THE FEDERATION.
WE HAVE MUCH TO OFFER, CAPTAIN PICARD.
INDEED, CHANCELLOR LOMAC, THE FEDERATION IS HONORED TO BE CONSIDERED.
IF YOU'LL SEND US THE COORDINATES...
...MY FIRST OFFICER IS READY TO BEAM DOWN.
TASHA, DATA—YOU'RE WITH ME.

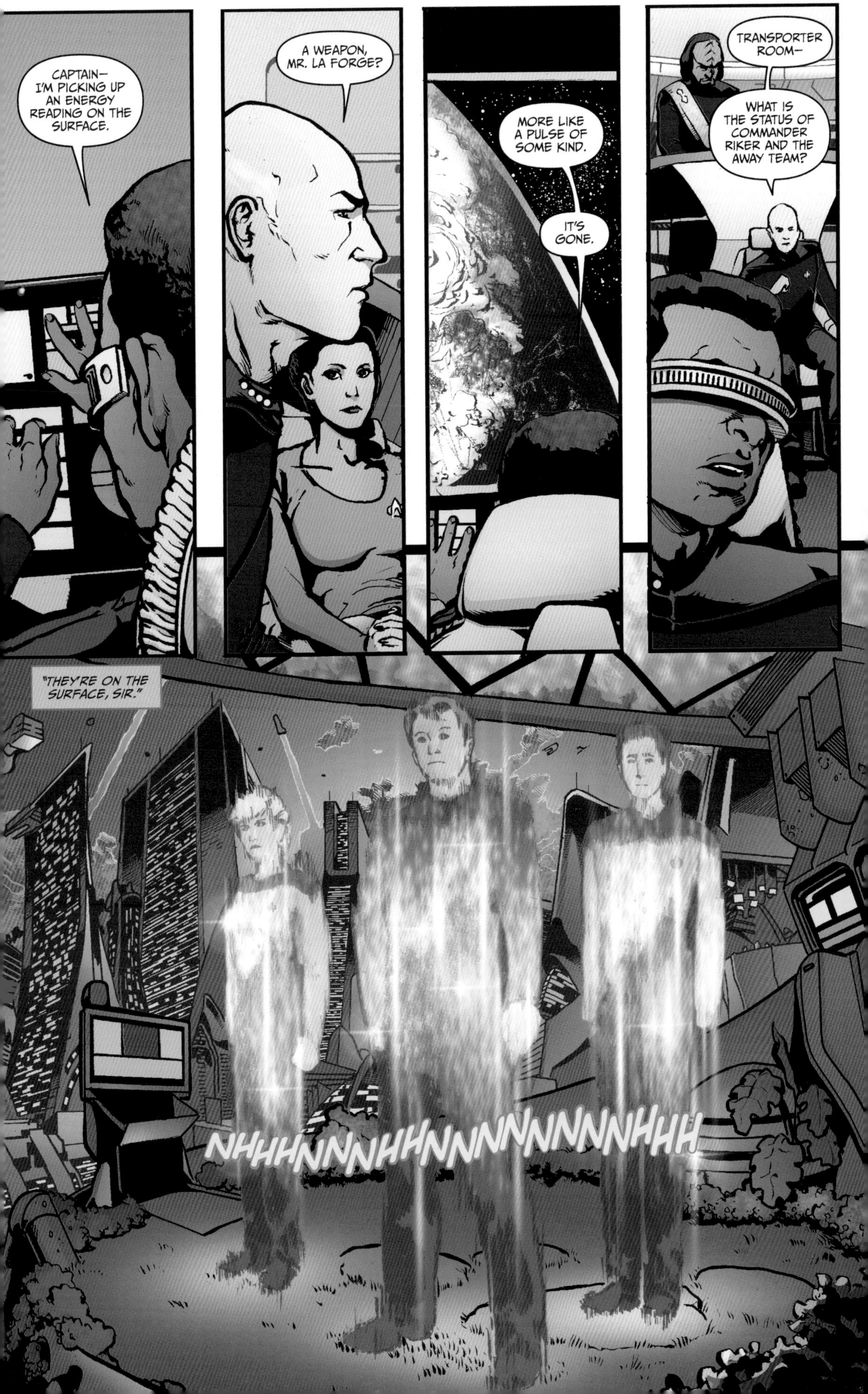
CAPTAIN— I'M PICKING UP AN ENERGY READING ON THE SURFACE.
A WEAPON, MR. LA FORGE?
MORE LIKE A PULSE OF SOME KIND.
IT'S GONE.
TRANSPORTER ROOM—
WHAT IS THE STATUS OF COMMANDER RIKER AND THE AWAY TEAM?
"THEY'RE ON THE SURFACE, SIR."
NHHHNNNHHNNNNNNNNNHHH

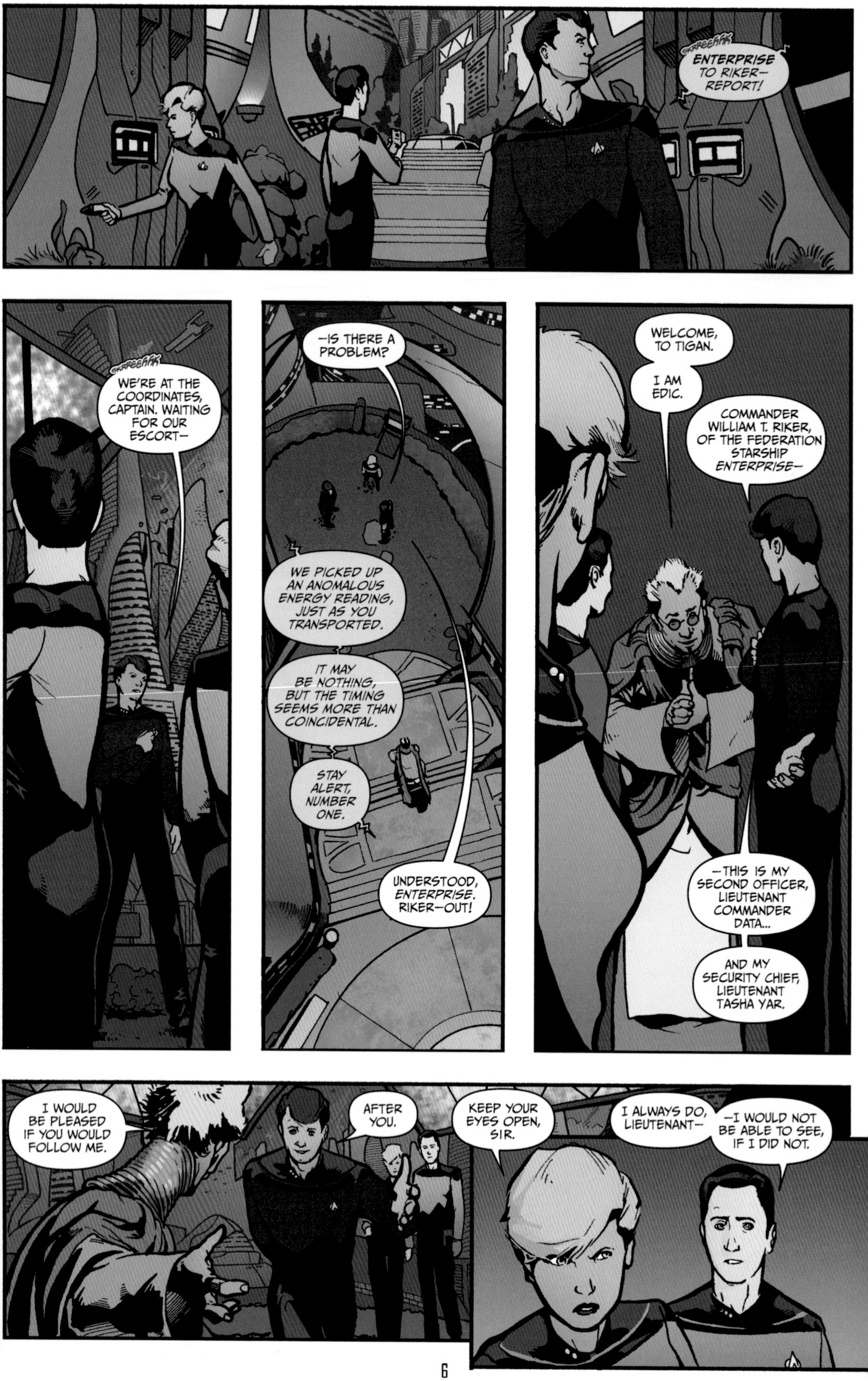

SKRREEEKK
ENTERPRISE TO RIKER— REPORT!
SKRREEEKK
WE'RE AT THE COORDINATES, CAPTAIN. WAITING FOR OUR ESCORT—
—IS THERE A PROBLEM?
WE PICKED UP AN ANOMALOUS ENERGY READING, JUST AS YOU TRANSPORTED.
IT MAY BE NOTHING, BUT THE TIMING SEEMS MORE THAN COINCIDENTAL.
STAY ALERT, NUMBER ONE.
UNDERSTOOD, ENTERPRISE. RIKER—OUT!
WELCOME, TO TIGAN.
I AM EDIC.
COMMANDER WILLIAM T. RIKER, OF THE FEDERATION STARSHIP ENTERPRISE—
—THIS IS MY SECOND OFFICER, LIEUTENANT COMMANDER DATA...
AND MY SECURITY CHIEF, LIEUTENANT TASHA YAR.
I WOULD BE PLEASED IF YOU WOULD FOLLOW ME.
AFTER YOU.
KEEP YOUR EYES OPEN, SIR.
I ALWAYS DO, LIEUTENANT—
—I WOULD NOT BE ABLE TO SEE, IF I DID NOT.

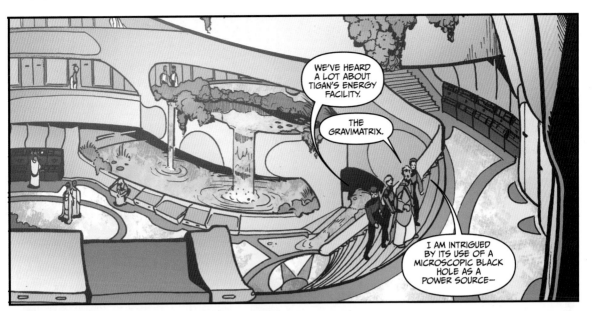

WE'VE HEARD A LOT ABOUT TIGAN'S ENERGY FACILITY.

THE GRAVIMATRIX.

I AM INTRIGUED BY ITS USE OF A MICROSCOPIC BLACK HOLE AS A POWER SOURCE—

—STARFLEET HAS BEEN UNABLE TO CREATE A STABLE CONTAINMENT FIELD TO MAKE ITS APPLICATION SAFE.

TIGAN'S GEOTHERMIC ENERGY POWERS THE CONTAINMENT FIELD—

—AS LONG AS THE PLANET STANDS, THE STAR CAN BE HARNESSED.

DATA—?

YOU'RE STARING.

I AM SORRY, EDIC—MY INTENTION WAS NOT TO BE RUDE.

AHHHH—

—YOU NOTICED MY INTERFACE.

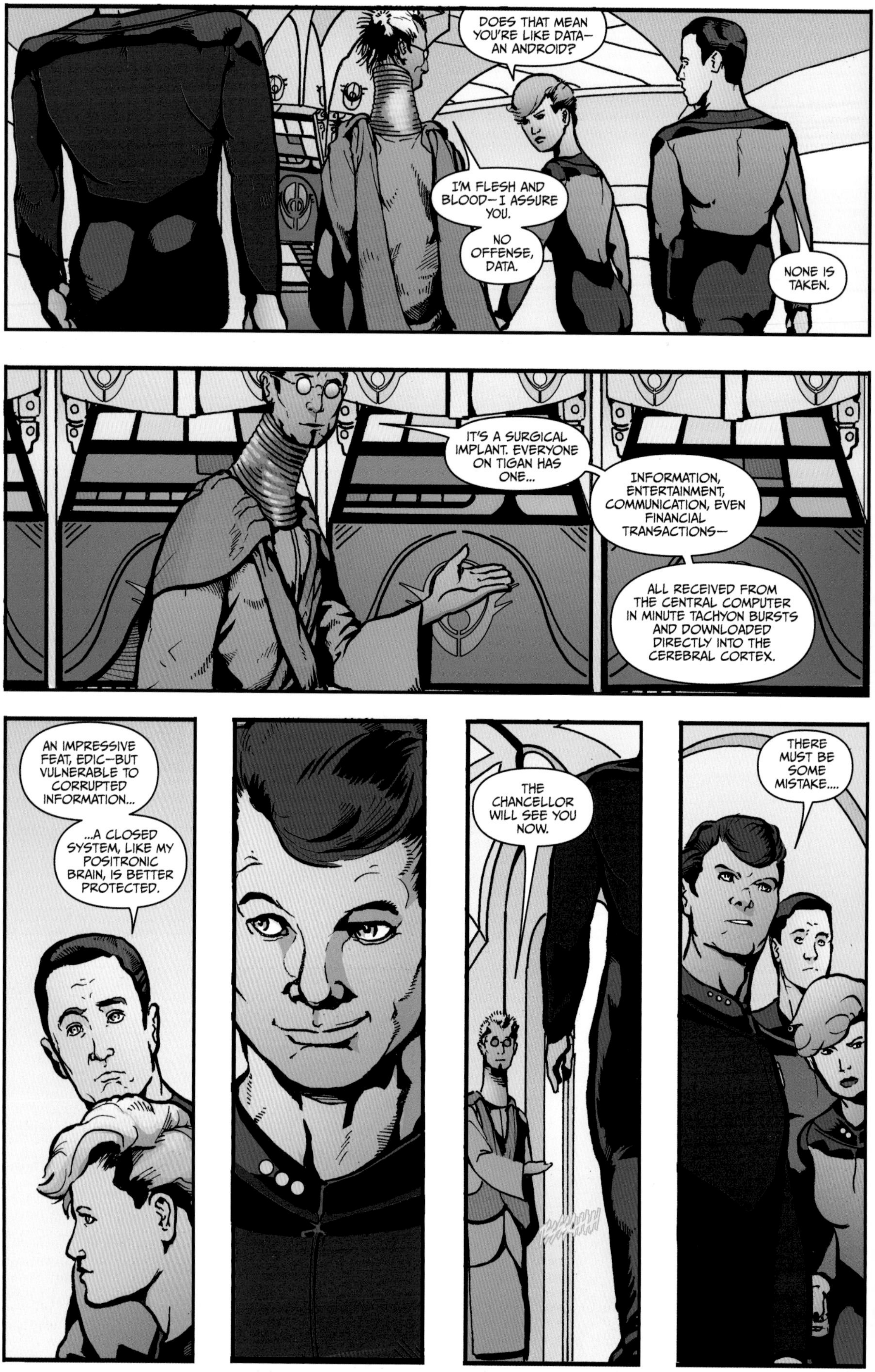
DOES THAT MEAN YOU'RE LIKE DATA— AN ANDROID?
I'M FLESH AND BLOOD—I ASSURE YOU.
NO OFFENSE, DATA.
NONE IS TAKEN.
IT'S A SURGICAL IMPLANT. EVERYONE ON TIGAN HAS ONE...
INFORMATION, ENTERTAINMENT, COMMUNICATION, EVEN FINANCIAL TRANSACTIONS—
ALL RECEIVED FROM THE CENTRAL COMPUTER IN MINUTE TACHYON BURSTS AND DOWNLOADED DIRECTLY INTO THE CEREBRAL CORTEX.
AN IMPRESSIVE FEAT, EDIC—BUT VULNERABLE TO CORRUPTED INFORMATION...
...A CLOSED SYSTEM, LIKE MY POSITRONIC BRAIN, IS BETTER PROTECTED.
THE CHANCELLOR WILL SEE YOU NOW.
THERE MUST BE SOME MISTAKE....

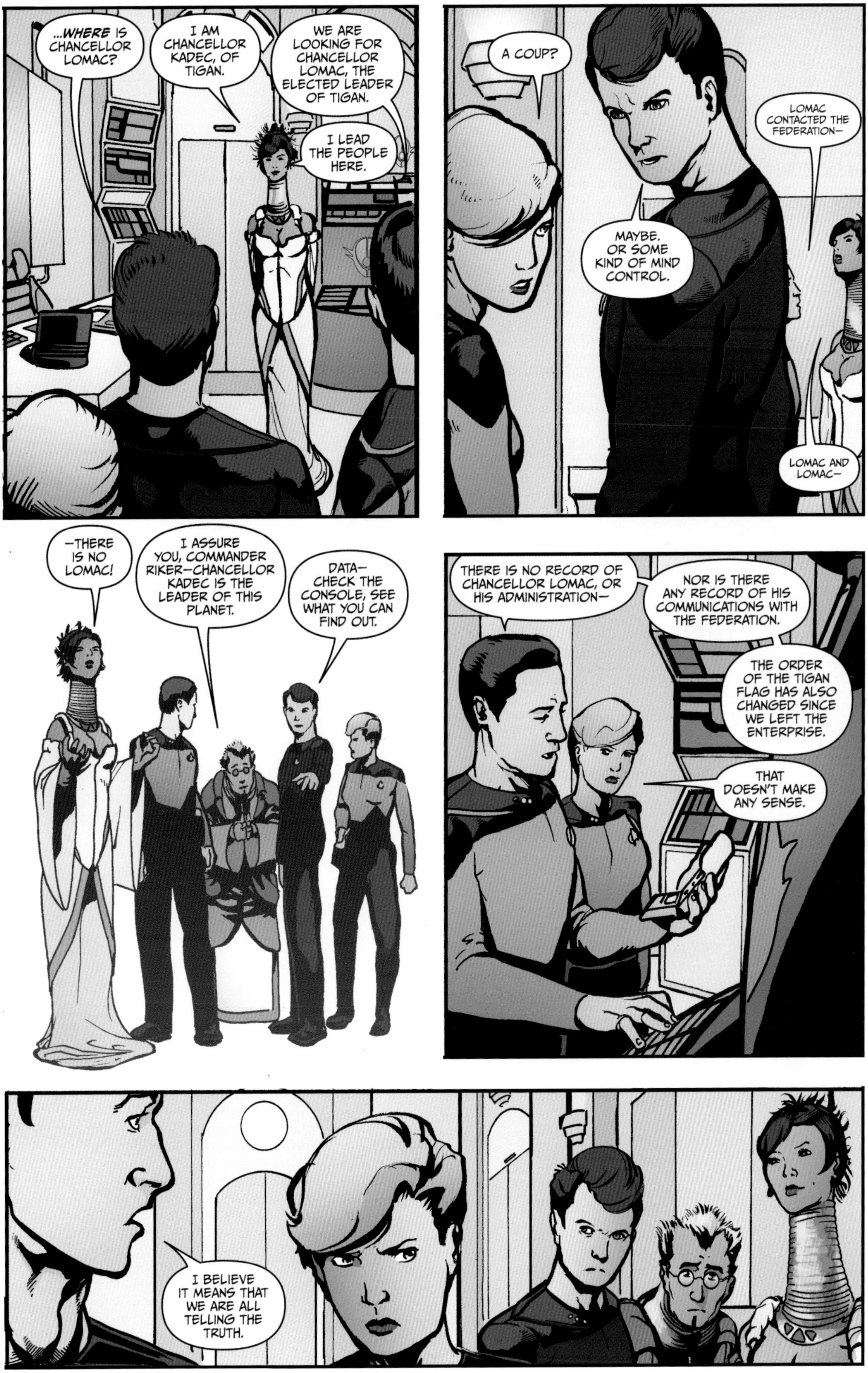

...WHERE IS CHANCELLOR LOMAC?
I AM CHANCELLOR KADEC, OF TIGAN.
WE ARE LOOKING FOR CHANCELLOR LOMAC, THE ELECTED LEADER OF TIGAN.
I LEAD THE PEOPLE HERE.
A COUP?
LOMAC CONTACTED THE FEDERATION—
MAYBE. OR SOME KIND OF MIND CONTROL.
LOMAC AND LOMAC—
—THERE IS NO LOMAC!
I ASSURE YOU, COMMANDER RIKER—CHANCELLOR KADEC IS THE LEADER OF THIS PLANET.
DATA— CHECK THE CONSOLE, SEE WHAT YOU CAN FIND OUT.
THERE IS NO RECORD OF CHANCELLOR LOMAC, OR HIS ADMINISTRATION—
NOR IS THERE ANY RECORD OF HIS COMMUNICATIONS WITH THE FEDERATION.
THE ORDER OF THE TIGAN FLAG HAS ALSO CHANGED SINCE WE LEFT THE ENTERPRISE.
THAT DOESN'T MAKE ANY SENSE.
I BELIEVE IT MEANS THAT WE ARE ALL TELLING THE TRUTH.

THERE'S A SECOND ENERGY READING, CAPTAIN.

ANOTHER PULSE?

WEAPONS HAVE BEEN FIRED!

WE ARE UNDER ATTACK!

SHIELDS UP—!

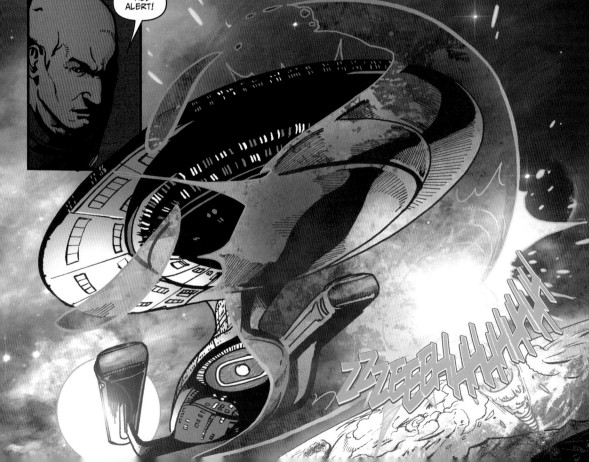

—RED ALERT!

ZZEEBHHHHH

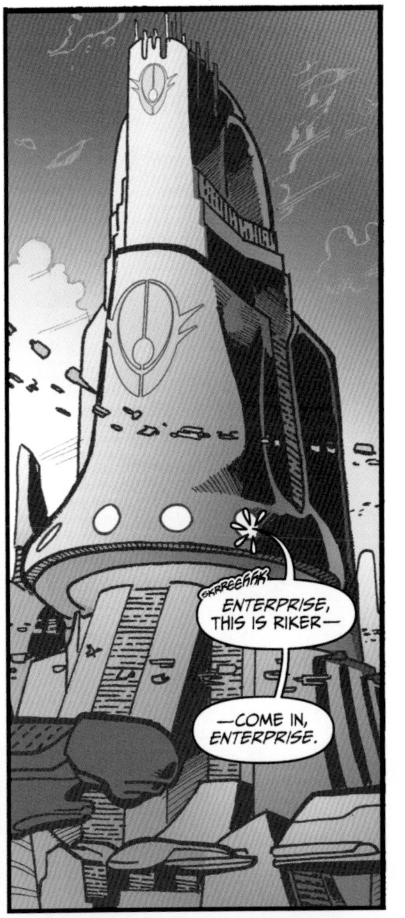
SKRREEAAK
ENTERPRISE, THIS IS RIKER—
—COME IN, *ENTERPRISE*.

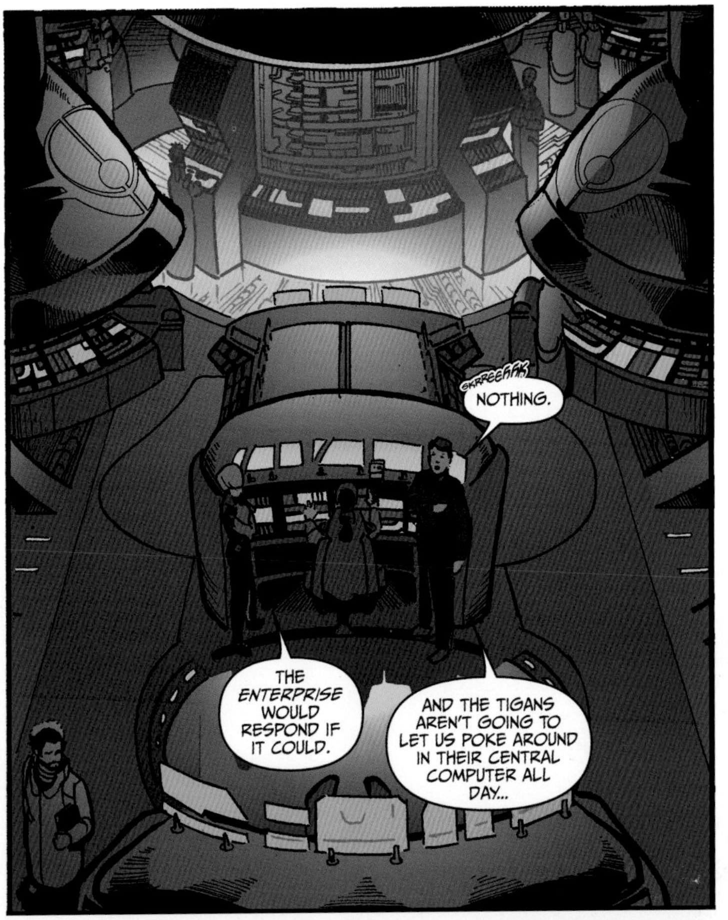
SKRREEAAK
NOTHING.
THE *ENTERPRISE* WOULD RESPOND IF IT COULD.
AND THE TIGANS AREN'T GOING TO LET US POKE AROUND IN THEIR CENTRAL COMPUTER ALL DAY...

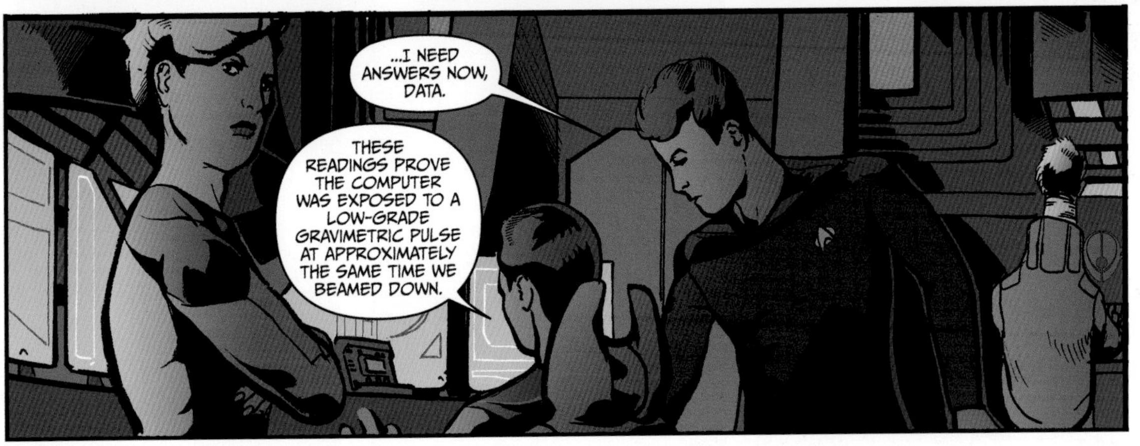
...I NEED ANSWERS NOW, DATA.
THESE READINGS PROVE THE COMPUTER WAS EXPOSED TO A LOW-GRADE GRAVIMETRIC PULSE AT APPROXIMATELY THE SAME TIME WE BEAMED DOWN.

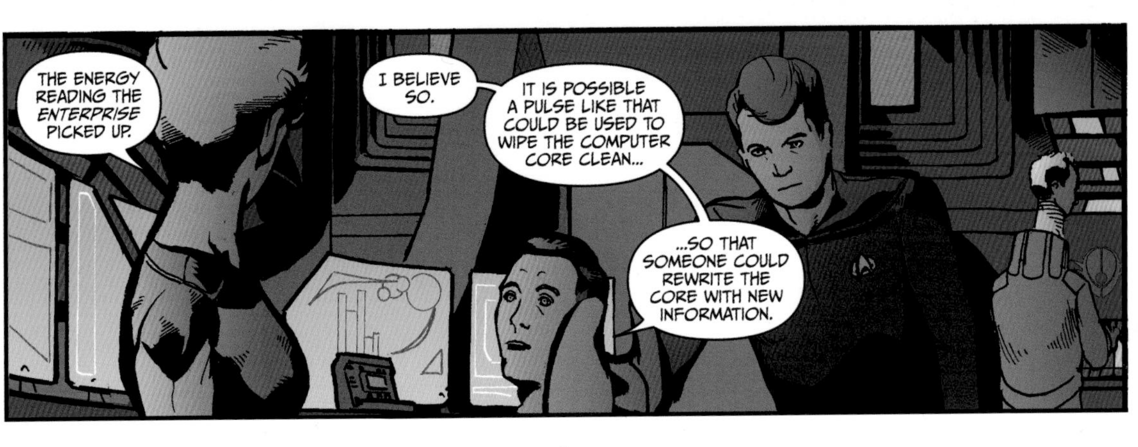
THE ENERGY READING THE *ENTERPRISE* PICKED UP.
I BELIEVE SO.
IT IS POSSIBLE A PULSE LIKE THAT COULD BE USED TO WIPE THE COMPUTER CORE CLEAN...
...SO THAT SOMEONE COULD REWRITE THE CORE WITH NEW INFORMATION.

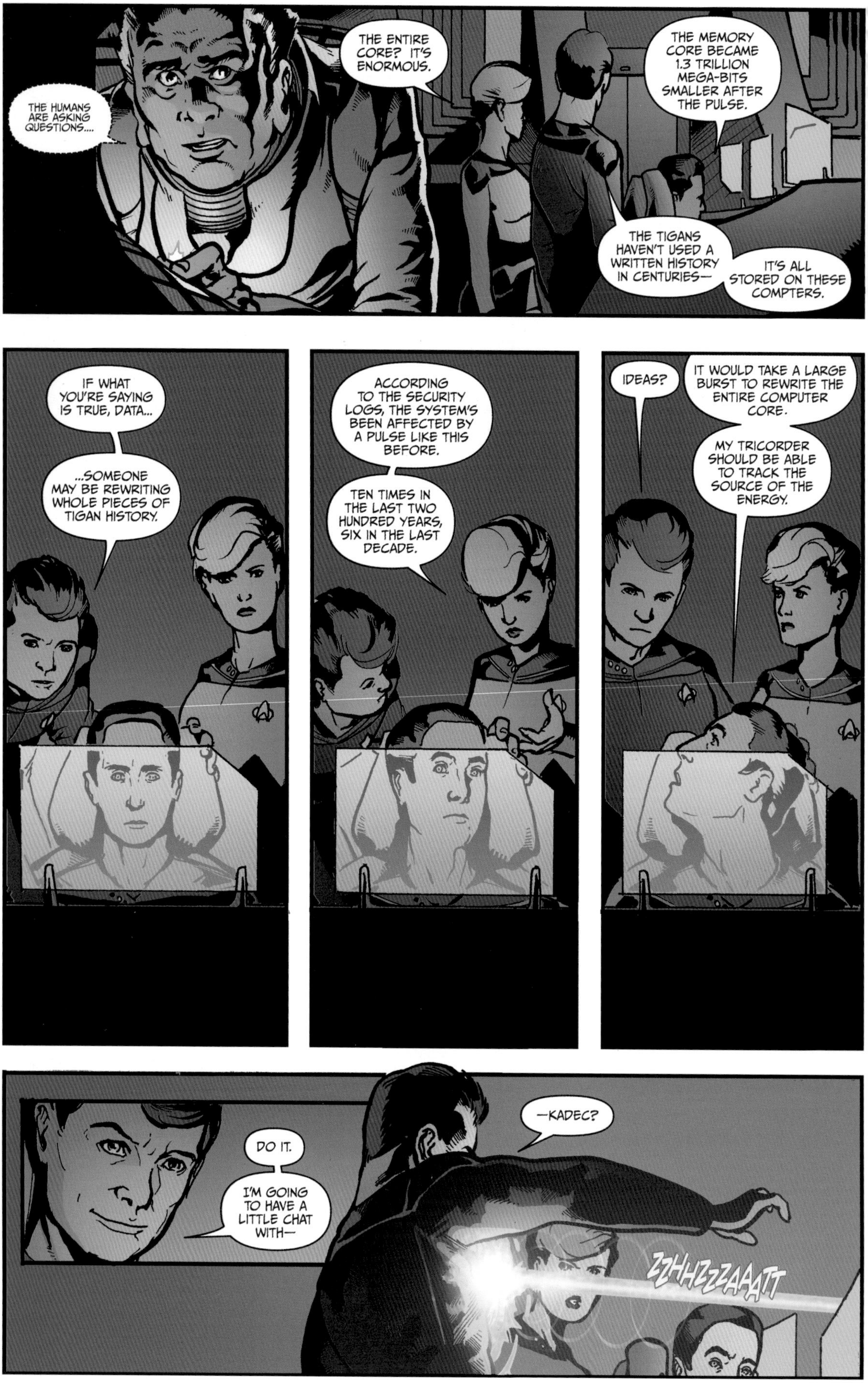

THE HUMANS ARE ASKING QUESTIONS....
THE ENTIRE CORE? IT'S ENORMOUS.
THE MEMORY CORE BECAME 1.3 TRILLION MEGA-BITS SMALLER AFTER THE PULSE.
THE TIGANS HAVEN'T USED A WRITTEN HISTORY IN CENTURIES—
IT'S ALL STORED ON THESE COMPTERS.
IF WHAT YOU'RE SAYING IS TRUE, DATA...
...SOMEONE MAY BE REWRITING WHOLE PIECES OF TIGAN HISTORY.
ACCORDING TO THE SECURITY LOGS, THE SYSTEM'S BEEN AFFECTED BY A PULSE LIKE THIS BEFORE.
TEN TIMES IN THE LAST TWO HUNDRED YEARS, SIX IN THE LAST DECADE.
IDEAS?
IT WOULD TAKE A LARGE BURST TO REWRITE THE ENTIRE COMPUTER CORE.
MY TRICORDER SHOULD BE ABLE TO TRACK THE SOURCE OF THE ENERGY.
DO IT.
I'M GOING TO HAVE A LITTLE CHAT WITH—
—KADEC?
ZZHHZZZAAATT

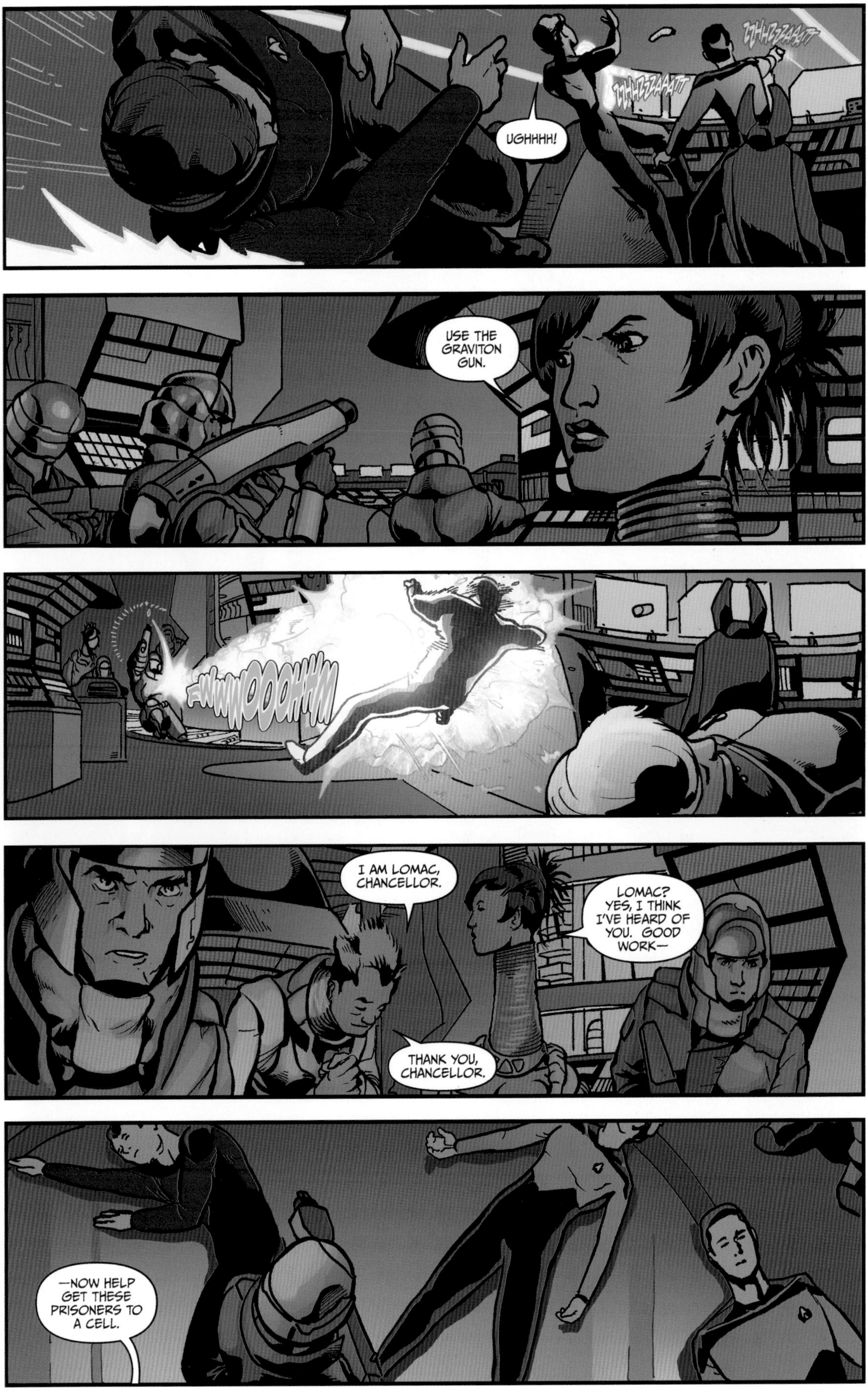
ZZHHZZAAATT
ZZHHZZAAATT
UGHHHH!
USE THE GRAVITON GUN.
FWWWOOOHHM
I AM LOMAC, CHANCELLOR.
LOMAC? YES, I THINK I'VE HEARD OF YOU. GOOD WORK—
THANK YOU, CHANCELLOR.
—NOW HELP GET THESE PRISONERS TO A CELL.

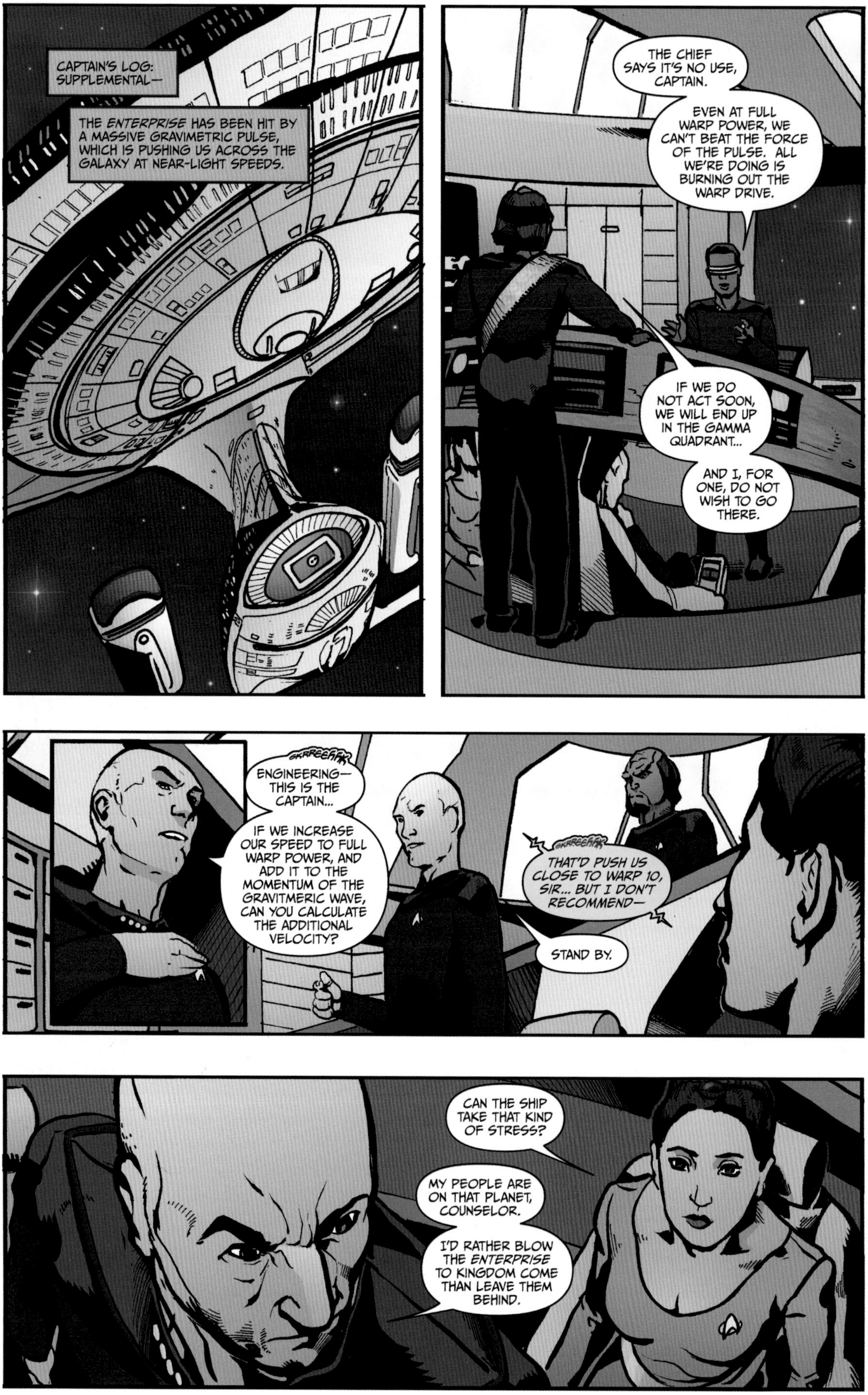
CAPTAIN'S LOG: SUPPLEMENTAL—
THE *ENTERPRISE* HAS BEEN HIT BY A MASSIVE GRAVIMETRIC PULSE, WHICH IS PUSHING US ACROSS THE GALAXY AT NEAR-LIGHT SPEEDS.
THE CHIEF SAYS IT'S NO USE, CAPTAIN.
EVEN AT FULL WARP POWER, WE CAN'T BEAT THE FORCE OF THE PULSE. ALL WE'RE DOING IS BURNING OUT THE WARP DRIVE.
IF WE DO NOT ACT SOON, WE WILL END UP IN THE GAMMA QUADRANT...
AND I, FOR ONE, DO NOT WISH TO GO THERE.
SKRREEEAAK
ENGINEERING— THIS IS THE CAPTAIN...
IF WE INCREASE OUR SPEED TO FULL WARP POWER, AND ADD IT TO THE MOMENTUM OF THE GRAVITMERIC WAVE, CAN YOU CALCULATE THE ADDITIONAL VELOCITY?
SKRREEAAK
THAT'D PUSH US CLOSE TO WARP 10, SIR... BUT I DON'T RECOMMEND—
STAND BY.
CAN THE SHIP TAKE THAT KIND OF STRESS?
MY PEOPLE ARE ON THAT PLANET, COUNSELOR.
I'D RATHER BLOW THE *ENTERPRISE* TO KINGDOM COME THAN LEAVE THEM BEHIND.

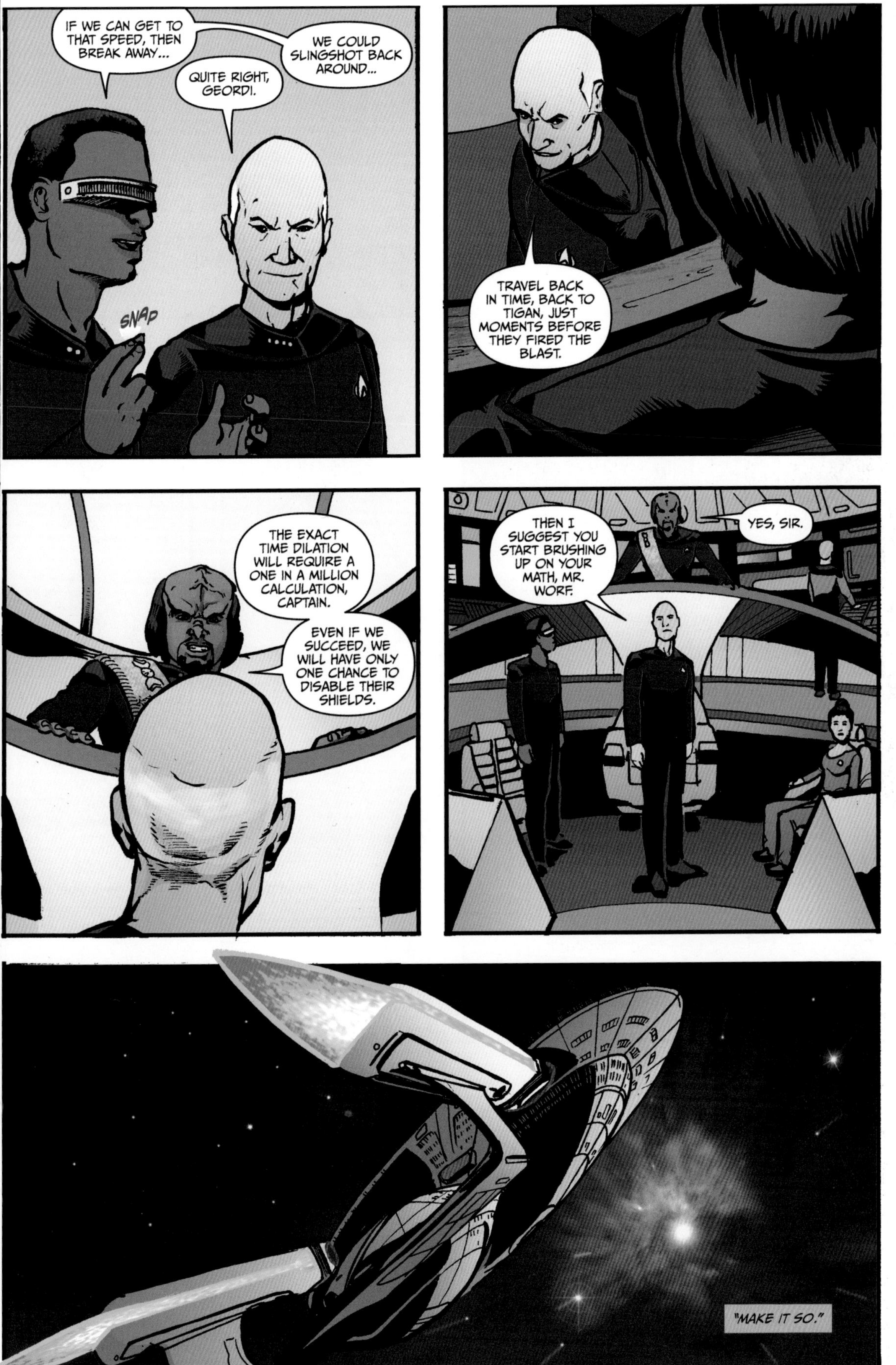
IF WE CAN GET TO THAT SPEED, THEN BREAK AWAY...
WE COULD SLINGSHOT BACK AROUND...
QUITE RIGHT, GEORDI.
SNAP
TRAVEL BACK IN TIME, BACK TO TIGAN, JUST MOMENTS BEFORE THEY FIRED THE BLAST.
THE EXACT TIME DILATION WILL REQUIRE A ONE IN A MILLION CALCULATION, CAPTAIN.
EVEN IF WE SUCCEED, WE WILL HAVE ONLY ONE CHANCE TO DISABLE THEIR SHIELDS.
THEN I SUGGEST YOU START BRUSHING UP ON YOUR MATH, MR. WORF.
YES, SIR.
"MAKE IT SO."

20227869

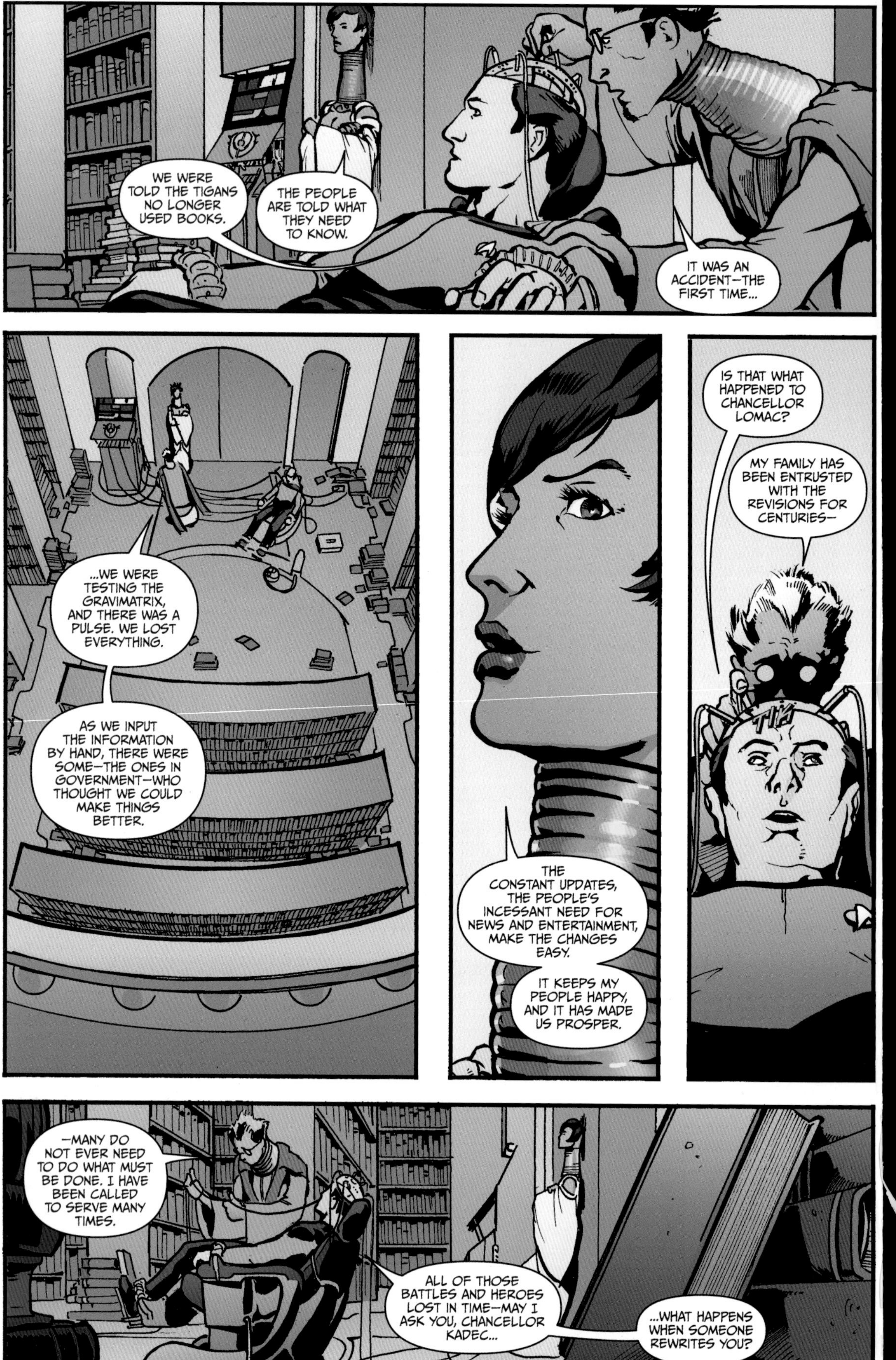
WE WERE TOLD THE TIGANS NO LONGER USED BOOKS.
THE PEOPLE ARE TOLD WHAT THEY NEED TO KNOW.
IT WAS AN ACCIDENT—THE FIRST TIME...
...WE WERE TESTING THE GRAVIMATRIX, AND THERE WAS A PULSE. WE LOST EVERYTHING.
AS WE INPUT THE INFORMATION BY HAND, THERE WERE SOME—THE ONES IN GOVERNMENT—WHO THOUGHT WE COULD MAKE THINGS BETTER.
THE CONSTANT UPDATES, THE PEOPLE'S INCESSANT NEED FOR NEWS AND ENTERTAINMENT, MAKE THE CHANGES EASY.
IT KEEPS MY PEOPLE HAPPY, AND IT HAS MADE US PROSPER.
IS THAT WHAT HAPPENED TO CHANCELLOR LOMAC?
MY FAMILY HAS BEEN ENTRUSTED WITH THE REVISIONS FOR CENTURIES—
—MANY DO NOT EVER NEED TO DO WHAT MUST BE DONE. I HAVE BEEN CALLED TO SERVE MANY TIMES.
ALL OF THOSE BATTLES AND HEROES LOST IN TIME—MAY I ASK YOU, CHANCELLOR KADEC...
...WHAT HAPPENS WHEN SOMEONE REWRITES YOU?

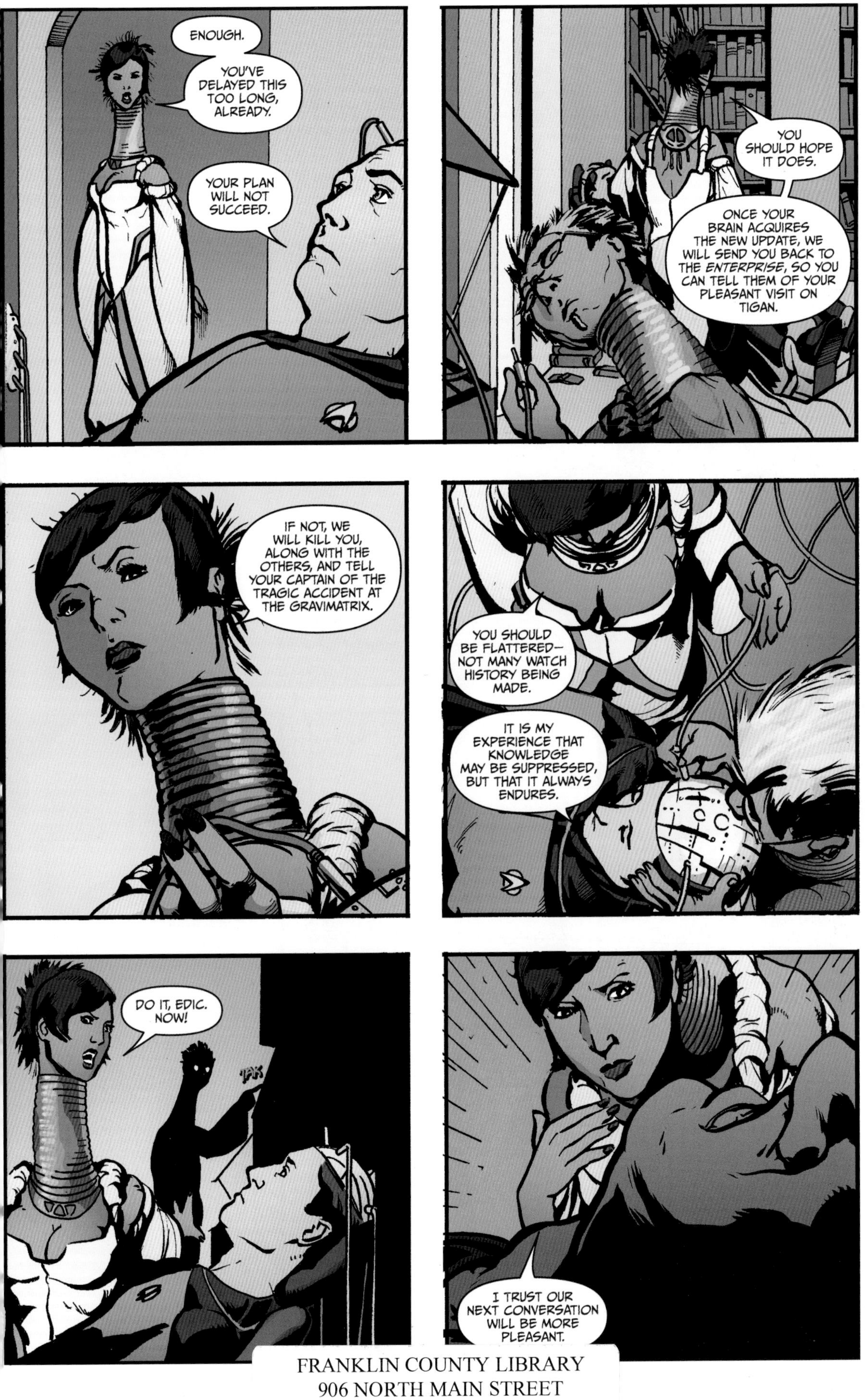
ENOUGH.
YOU'VE DELAYED THIS TOO LONG, ALREADY.
YOUR PLAN WILL NOT SUCCEED.
YOU SHOULD HOPE IT DOES.
ONCE YOUR BRAIN ACQUIRES THE NEW UPDATE, WE WILL SEND YOU BACK TO THE *ENTERPRISE*, SO YOU CAN TELL THEM OF YOUR PLEASANT VISIT ON TIGAN.
IF NOT, WE WILL KILL YOU, ALONG WITH THE OTHERS, AND TELL YOUR CAPTAIN OF THE TRAGIC ACCIDENT AT THE GRAVIMATRIX.
YOU SHOULD BE FLATTERED— NOT MANY WATCH HISTORY BEING MADE.
IT IS MY EXPERIENCE THAT KNOWLEDGE MAY BE SUPPRESSED, BUT THAT IT ALWAYS ENDURES.
DO IT, EDIC. NOW!
TAK
I TRUST OUR NEXT CONVERSATION WILL BE MORE PLEASANT.

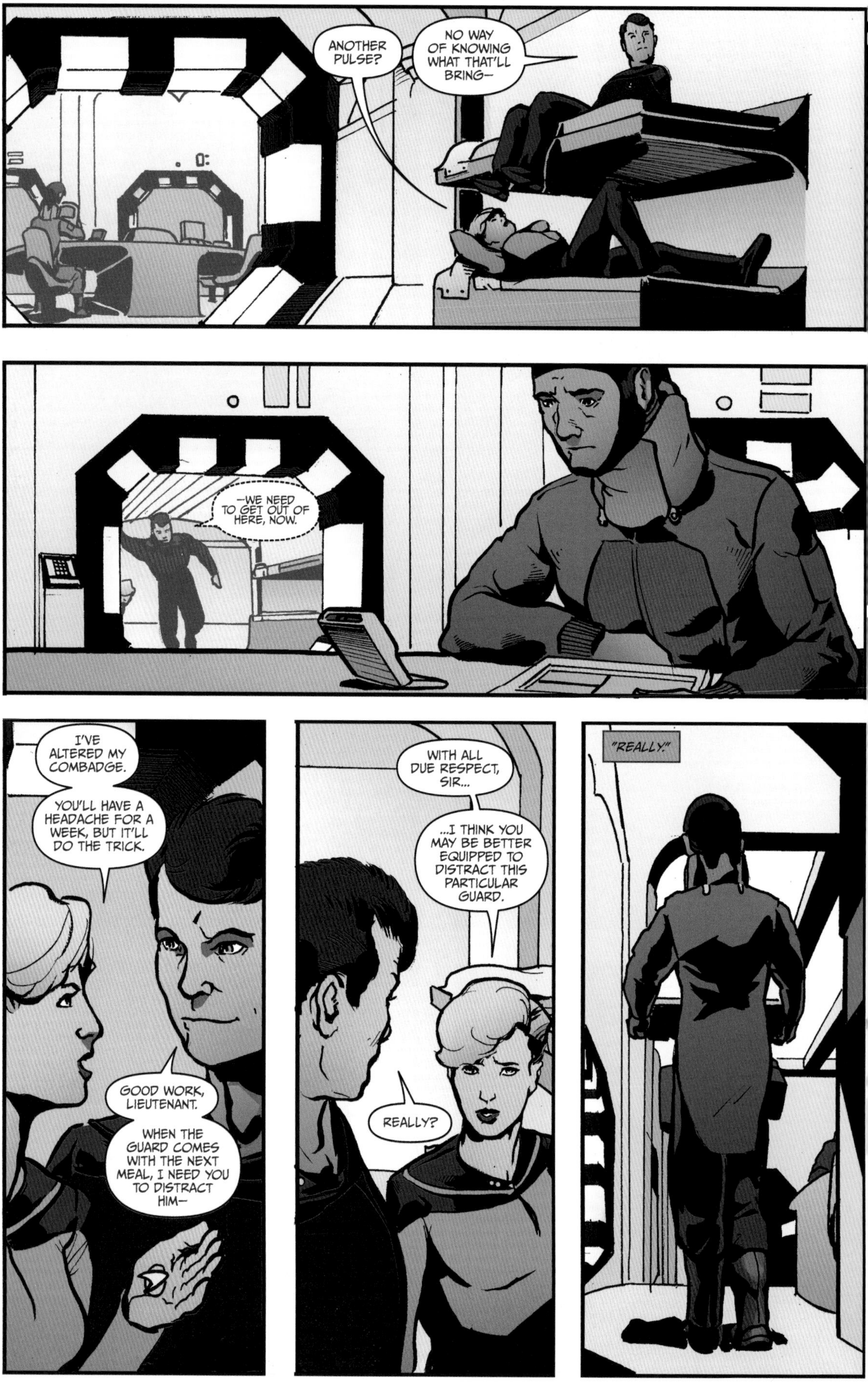
ANOTHER PULSE?
NO WAY OF KNOWING WHAT THAT'LL BRING—
—WE NEED TO GET OUT OF HERE, NOW.
I'VE ALTERED MY COMBADGE.
YOU'LL HAVE A HEADACHE FOR A WEEK, BUT IT'LL DO THE TRICK.
GOOD WORK, LIEUTENANT.
WHEN THE GUARD COMES WITH THE NEXT MEAL, I NEED YOU TO DISTRACT HIM—
WITH ALL DUE RESPECT, SIR...
...I THINK YOU MAY BE BETTER EQUIPPED TO DISTRACT THIS PARTICULAR GUARD.
REALLY?
"REALLY."

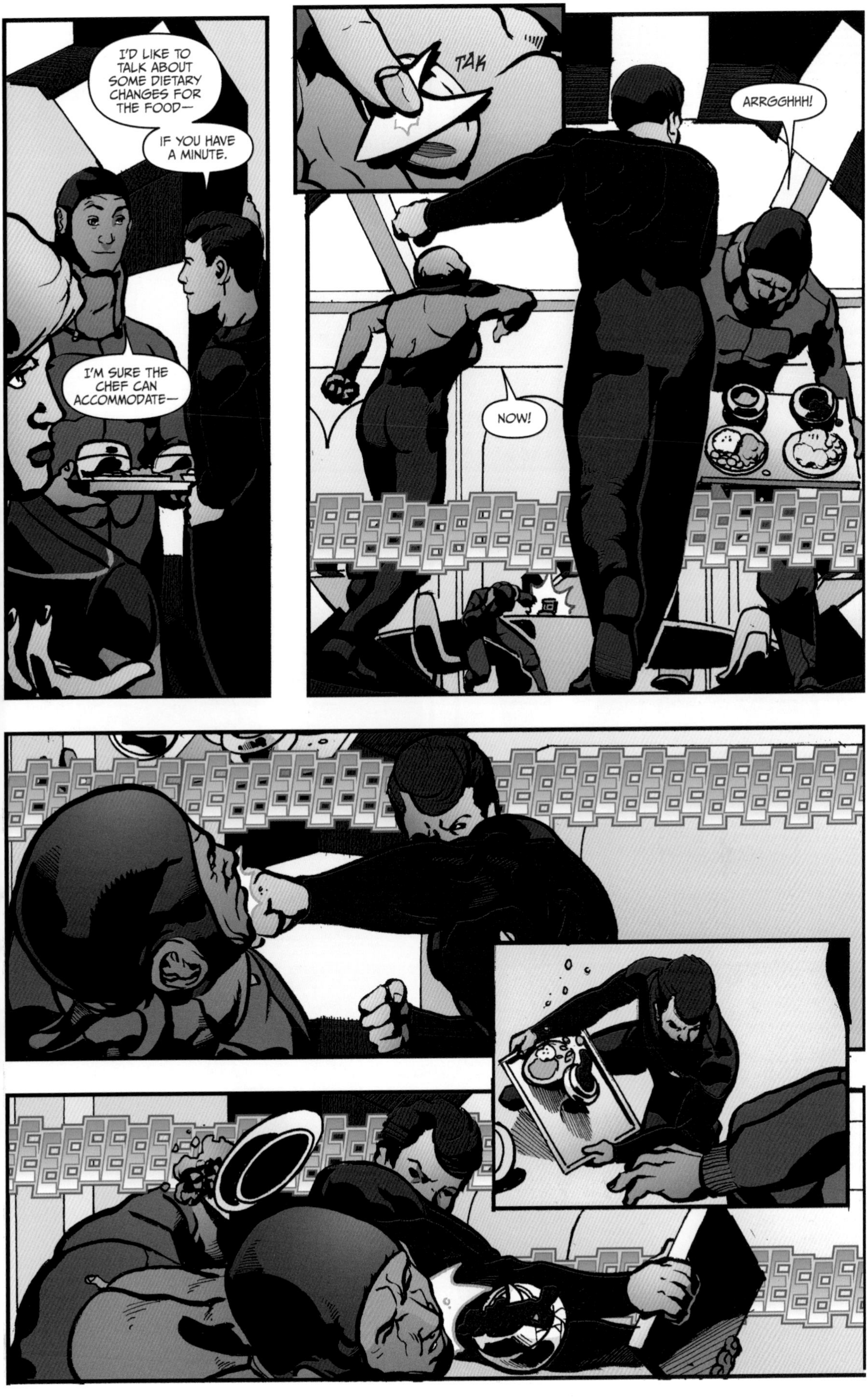
I'D LIKE TO TALK ABOUT SOME DIETARY CHANGES FOR THE FOOD—
IF YOU HAVE A MINUTE.
I'M SURE THE CHEF CAN ACCOMMODATE—
TAK
ARRGGHHH!
NOW!

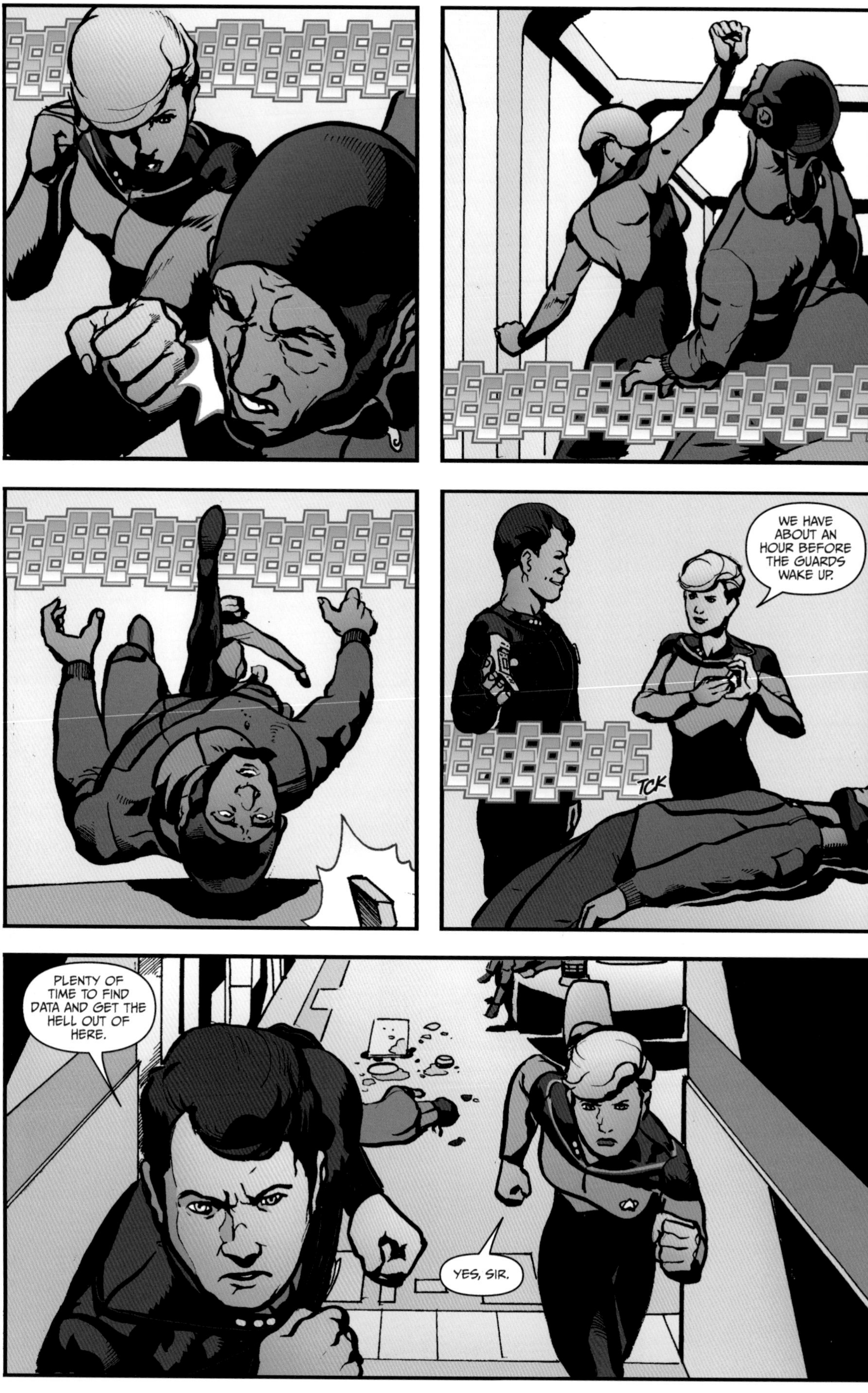

WE HAVE ABOUT AN HOUR BEFORE THE GUARDS WAKE UP.
TCK
PLENTY OF TIME TO FIND DATA AND GET THE HELL OUT OF HERE.
YES, SIR.

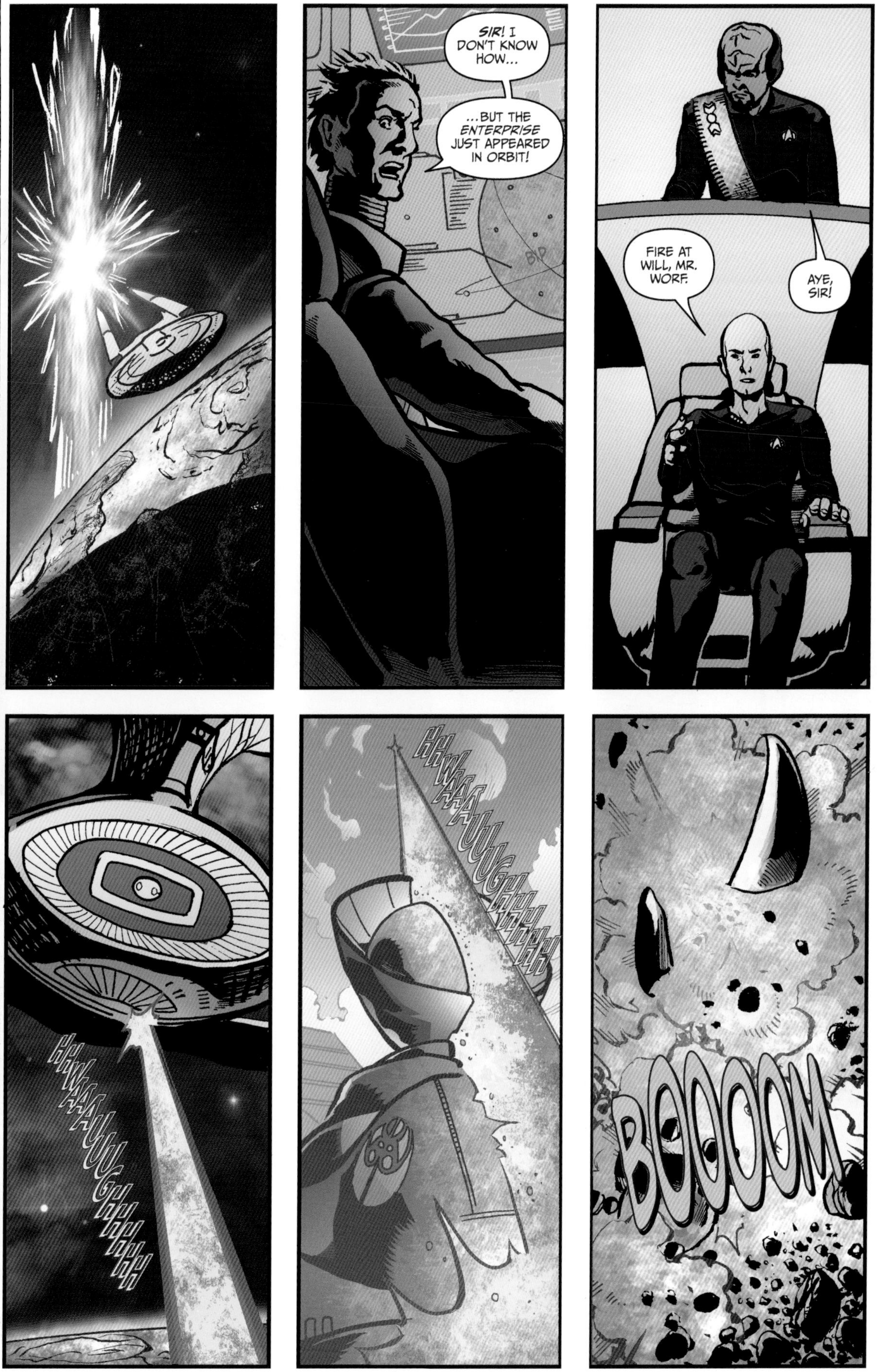
SIR! I DON'T KNOW HOW...
...BUT THE ENTERPRISE JUST APPEARED IN ORBIT!
FIRE AT WILL, MR. WORF.
AYE, SIR!
HHWAAUUGHHHHH
HHWAAUUGHHHHH
BOOOOM

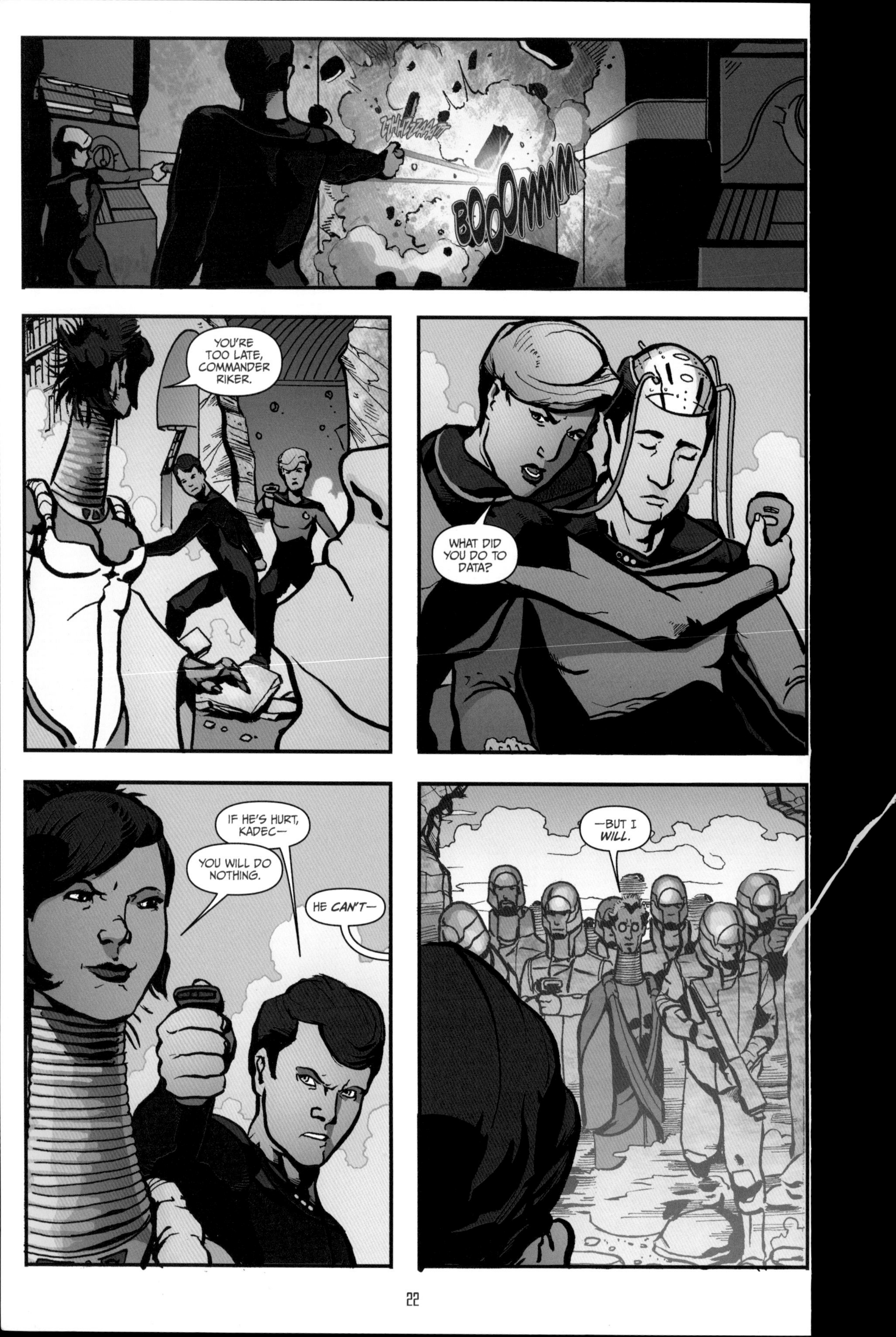
BOOOMMM
YOU'RE TOO LATE, COMMANDER RIKER.
WHAT DID YOU DO TO DATA?
IF HE'S HURT, KADEC—
YOU WILL DO NOTHING.
HE CAN'T—
—BUT I WILL.

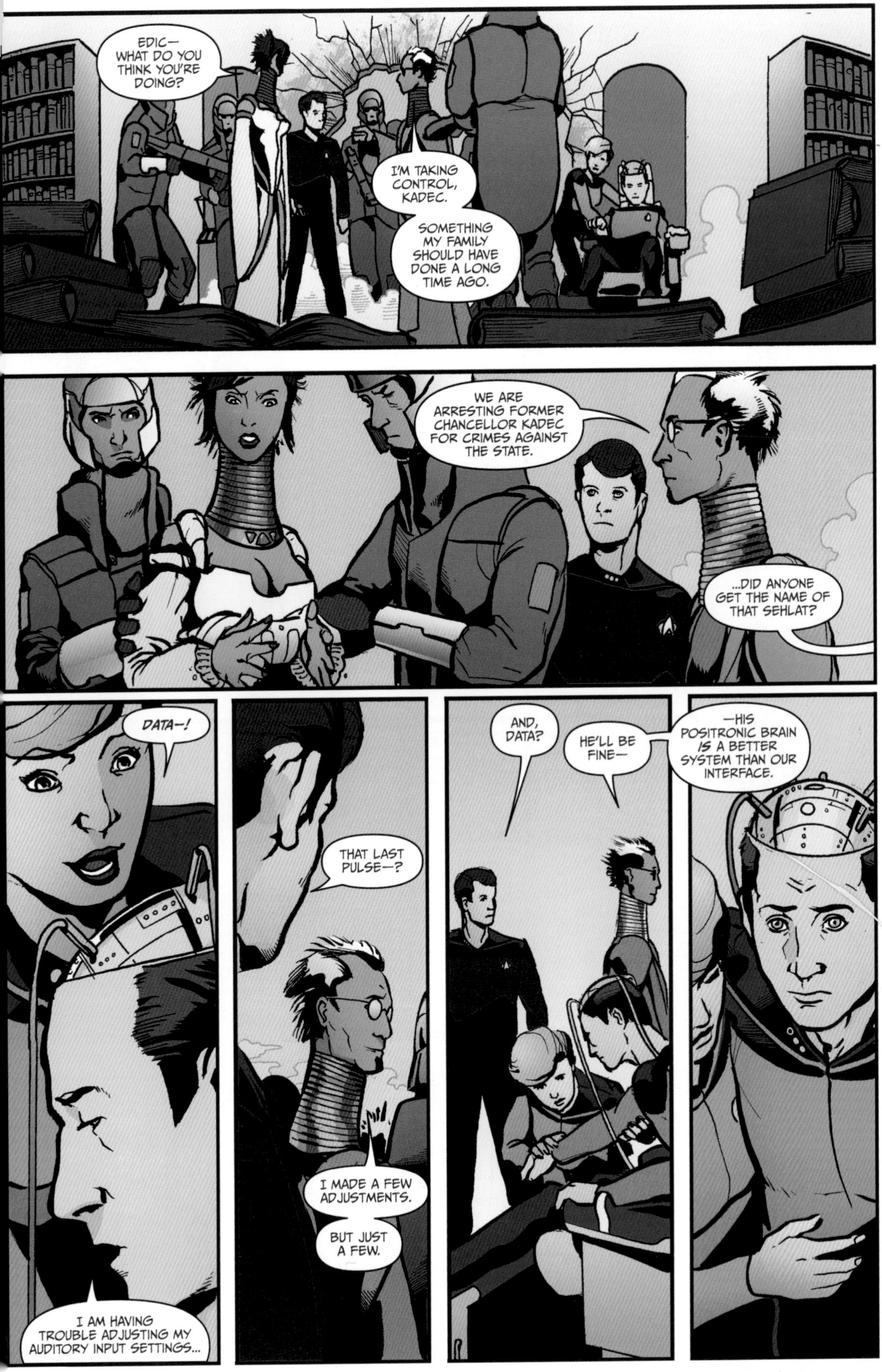
EDIC— WHAT DO YOU THINK YOU'RE DOING?
I'M TAKING CONTROL, KADEC.
SOMETHING MY FAMILY SHOULD HAVE DONE A LONG TIME AGO.
WE ARE ARRESTING FORMER CHANCELLOR KADEC FOR CRIMES AGAINST THE STATE.
...DID ANYONE GET THE NAME OF THAT SEHLAT?
DATA—!
I AM HAVING TROUBLE ADJUSTING MY AUDITORY INPUT SETTINGS...
THAT LAST PULSE—?
I MADE A FEW ADJUSTMENTS.
BUT JUST A FEW.
AND, DATA?
HE'LL BE FINE—
—HIS POSITRONIC BRAIN *IS* A BETTER SYSTEM THAN OUR INTERFACE.

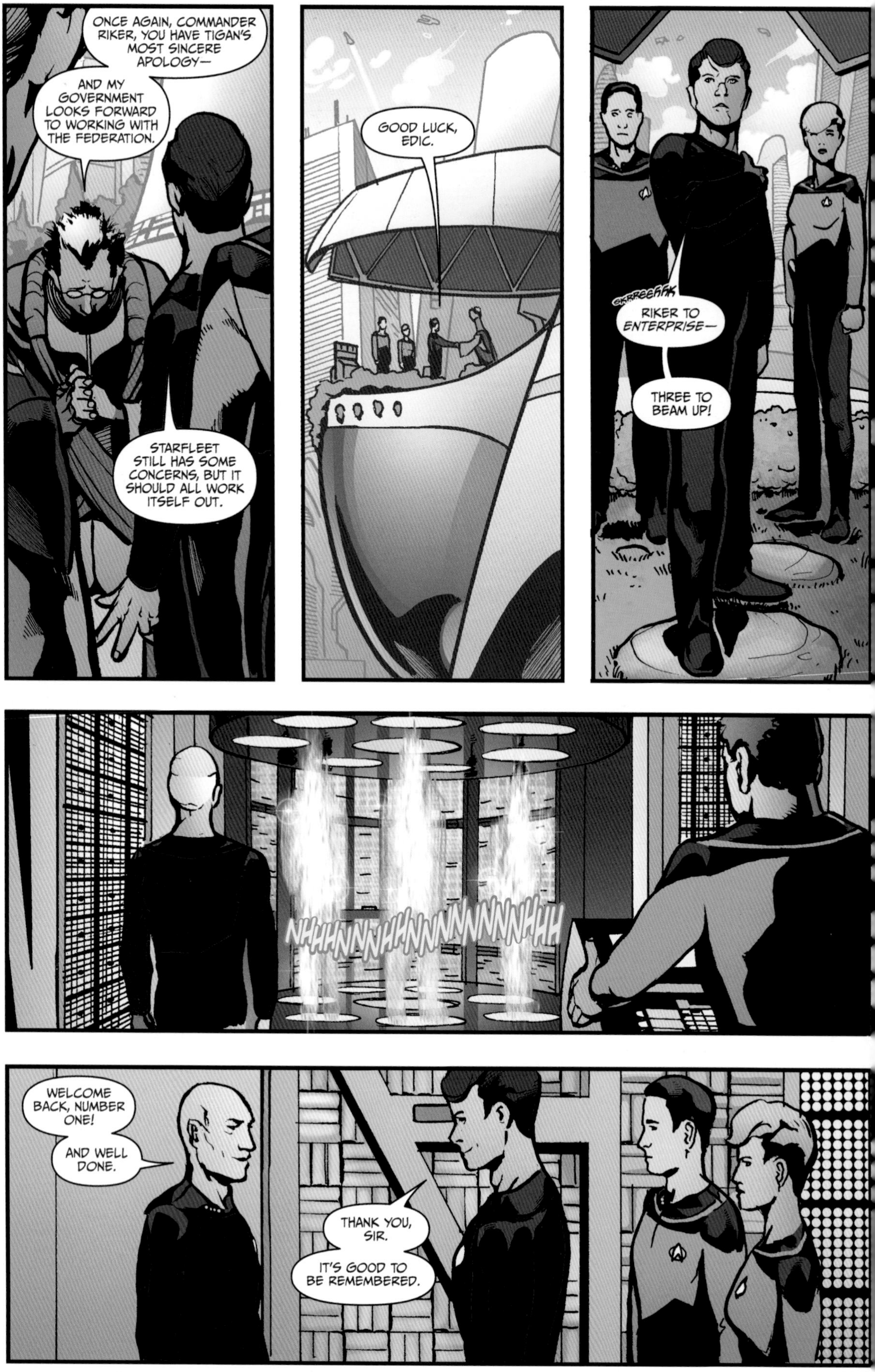
ONCE AGAIN, COMMANDER RIKER, YOU HAVE TIGAN'S MOST SINCERE APOLOGY—
AND MY GOVERNMENT LOOKS FORWARD TO WORKING WITH THE FEDERATION.
STARFLEET STILL HAS SOME CONCERNS, BUT IT SHOULD ALL WORK ITSELF OUT.
GOOD LUCK, EDIC.
SKRREEEKK
RIKER TO *ENTERPRISE*—
THREE TO BEAM UP!
NHHHNNNNHHNNNNNNNNHHH
WELCOME BACK, NUMBER ONE!
AND WELL DONE.
THANK YOU, SIR.
IT'S GOOD TO BE REMEMBERED.

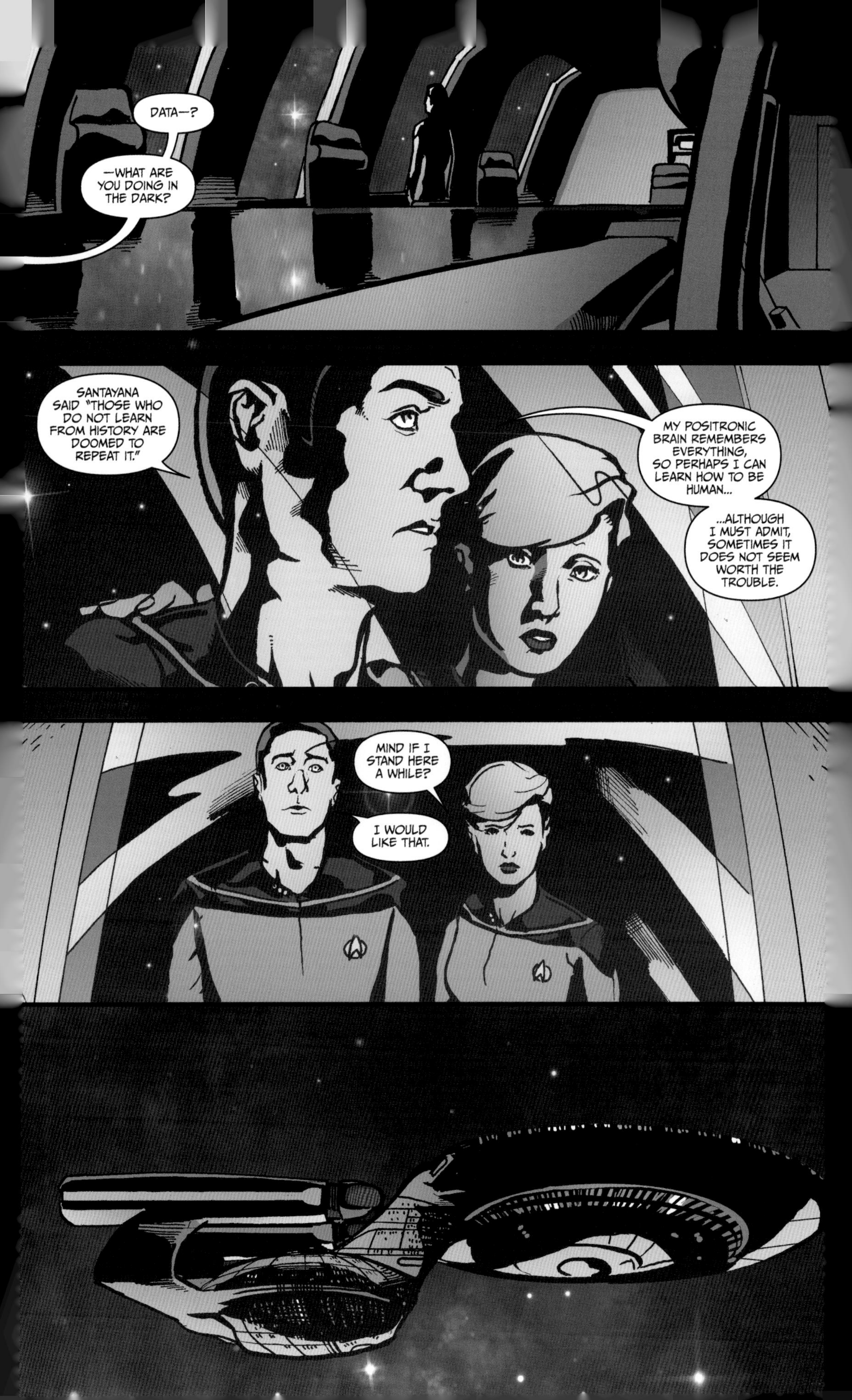
DATA—?
—WHAT ARE YOU DOING IN THE DARK?
SANTAYANA SAID "THOSE WHO DO NOT LEARN FROM HISTORY ARE DOOMED TO REPEAT IT."
MY POSITRONIC BRAIN REMEMBERS EVERYTHING, SO PERHAPS I CAN LEARN HOW TO BE HUMAN...
...ALTHOUGH I MUST ADMIT, SOMETIMES IT DOES NOT SEEM WORTH THE TROUBLE.
MIND IF I STAND HERE A WHILE?
I WOULD LIKE THAT.

PART TWO: CAPTAIN'S PLEASURE

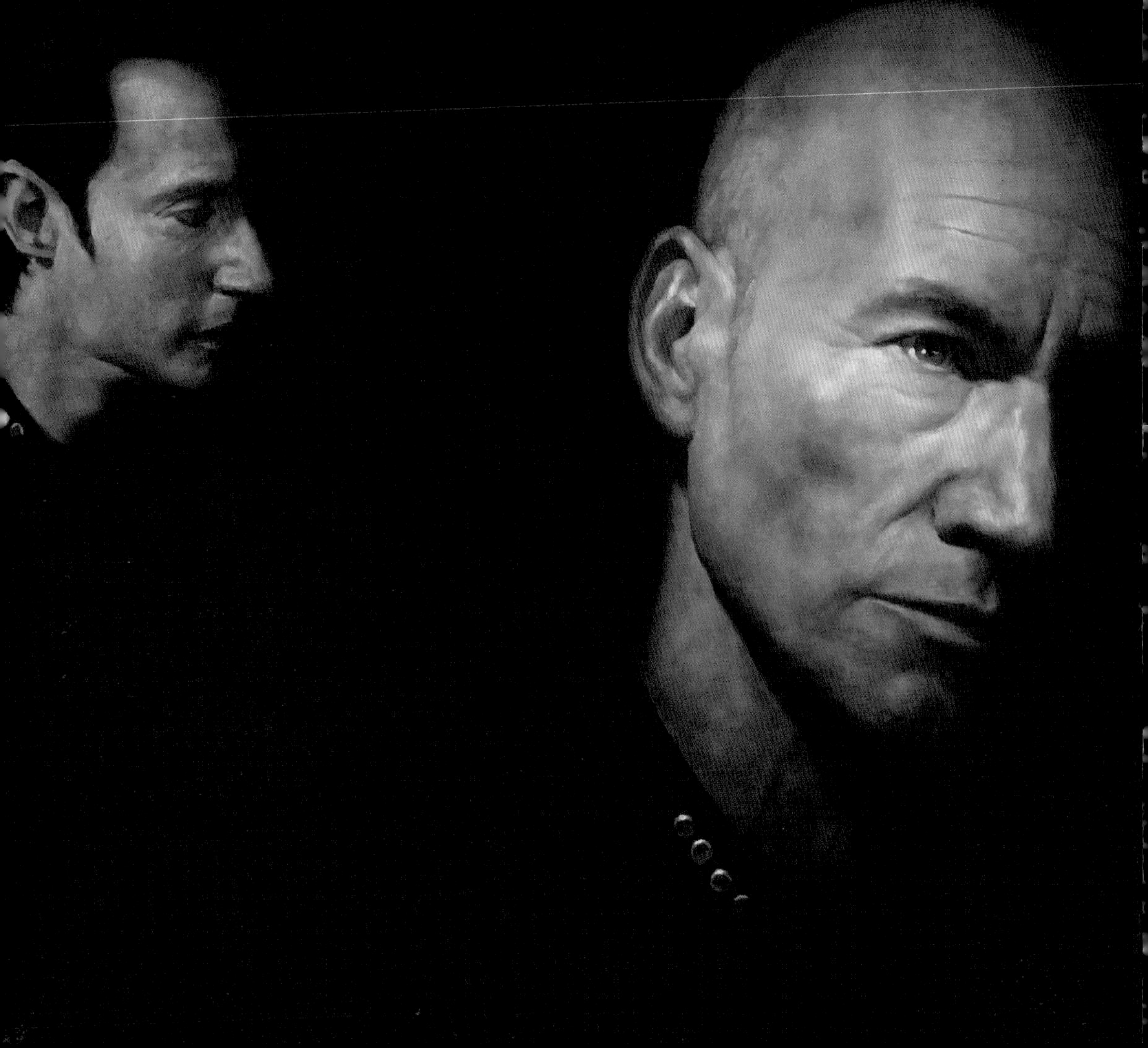

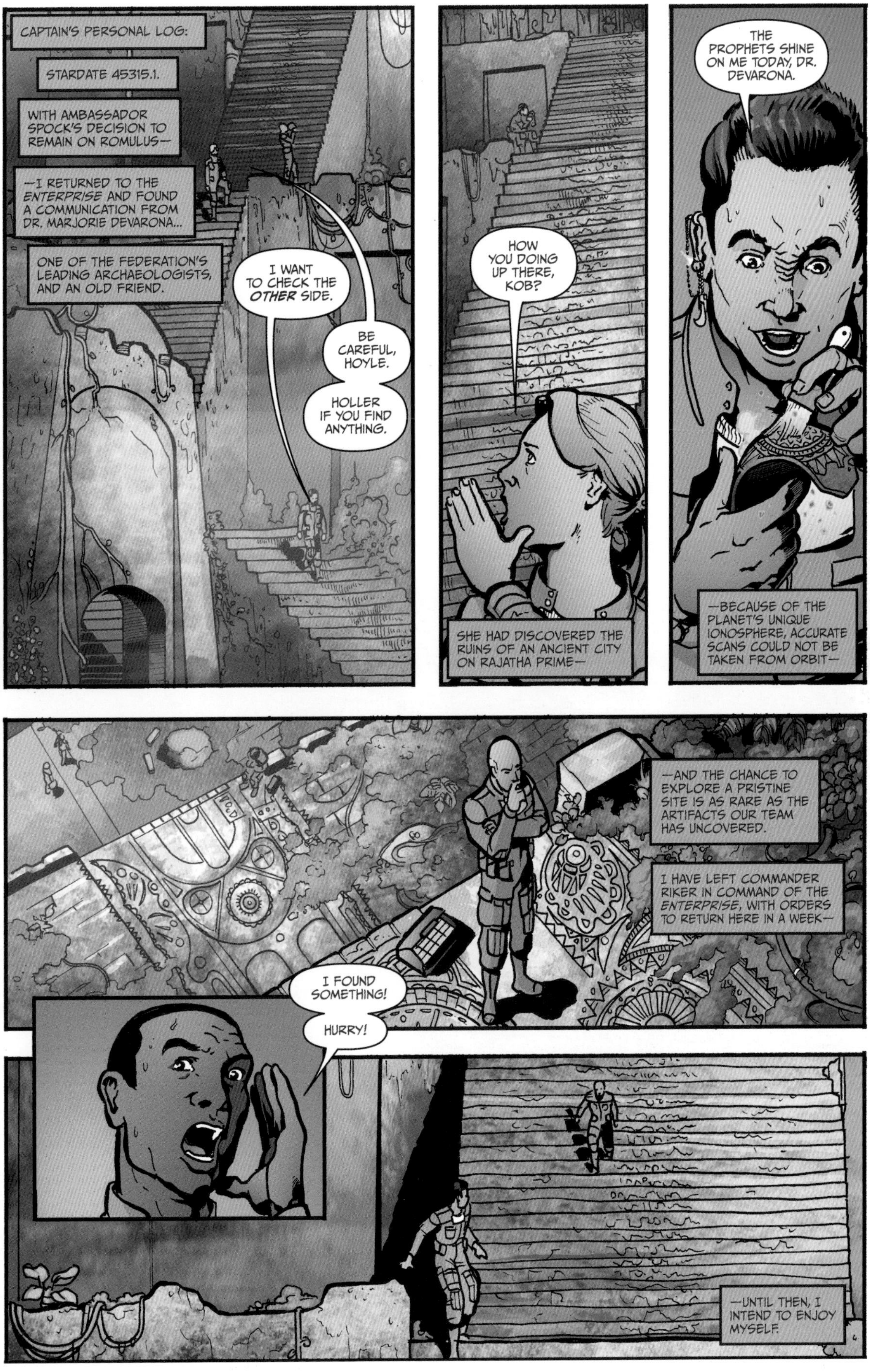
CAPTAIN'S PERSONAL LOG:
STARDATE 45315.1.
WITH AMBASSADOR SPOCK'S DECISION TO REMAIN ON ROMULUS—
—I RETURNED TO THE ENTERPRISE AND FOUND A COMMUNICATION FROM DR. MARJORIE DEVARONA...
ONE OF THE FEDERATION'S LEADING ARCHAEOLOGISTS, AND AN OLD FRIEND.
I WANT TO CHECK THE OTHER SIDE.
BE CAREFUL, HOYLE.
HOLLER IF YOU FIND ANYTHING.
HOW YOU DOING UP THERE, KOB?
SHE HAD DISCOVERED THE RUINS OF AN ANCIENT CITY ON RAJATHA PRIME—
THE PROPHETS SHINE ON ME TODAY, DR. DEVARONA.
—BECAUSE OF THE PLANET'S UNIQUE IONOSPHERE, ACCURATE SCANS COULD NOT BE TAKEN FROM ORBIT—
—AND THE CHANCE TO EXPLORE A PRISTINE SITE IS AS RARE AS THE ARTIFACTS OUR TEAM HAS UNCOVERED.
I HAVE LEFT COMMANDER RIKER IN COMMAND OF THE ENTERPRISE, WITH ORDERS TO RETURN HERE IN A WEEK—
I FOUND SOMETHING!
HURRY!
—UNTIL THEN, I INTEND TO ENJOY MYSELF.

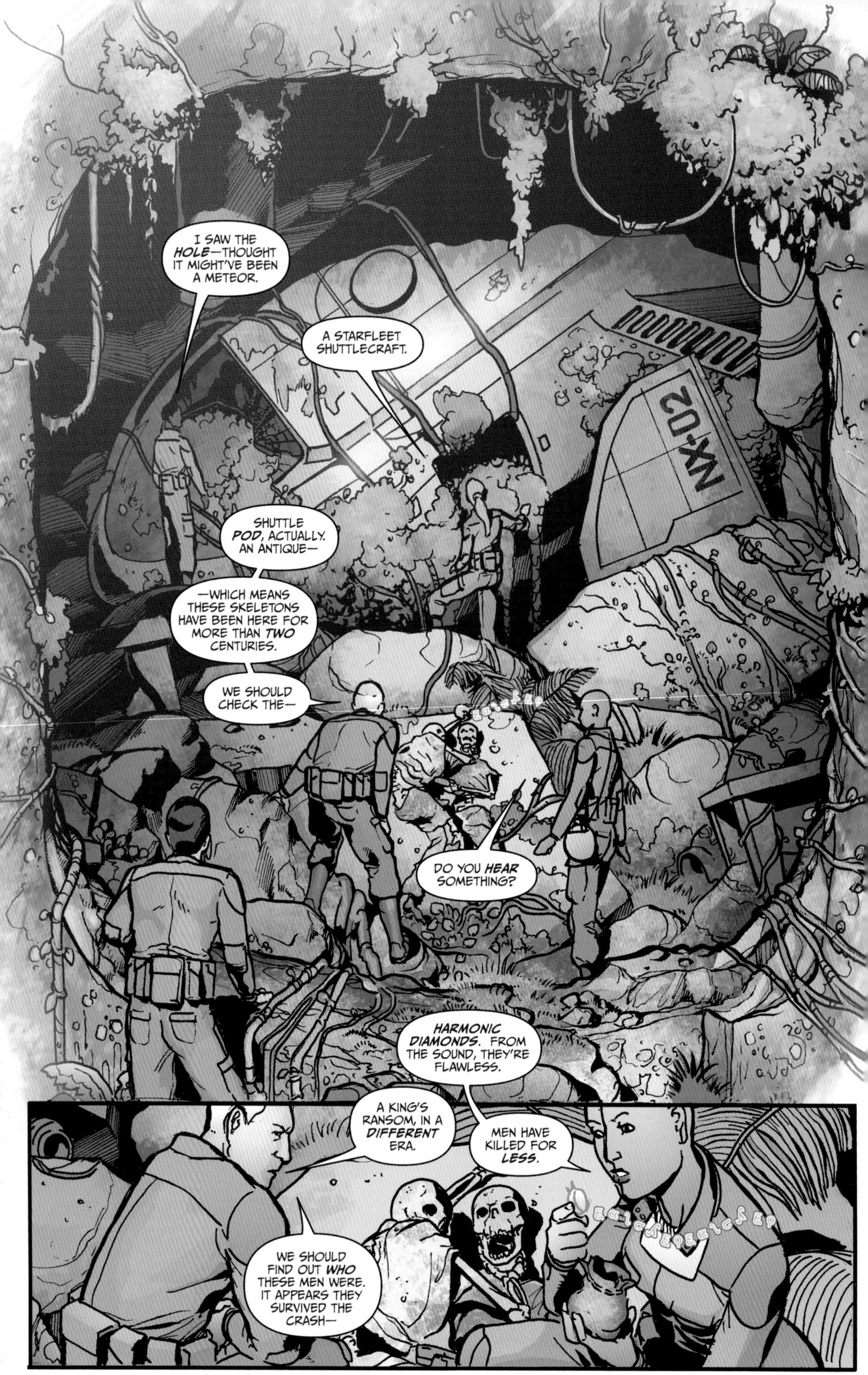
I SAW THE HOLE—THOUGHT IT MIGHT'VE BEEN A METEOR.
A STARFLEET SHUTTLECRAFT.
NX-02
SHUTTLE POD, ACTUALLY. AN ANTIQUE—
—WHICH MEANS THESE SKELETONS HAVE BEEN HERE FOR MORE THAN TWO CENTURIES.
WE SHOULD CHECK THE—
DO YOU HEAR SOMETHING?
HARMONIC DIAMONDS. FROM THE SOUND, THEY'RE FLAWLESS.
A KING'S RANSOM, IN A DIFFERENT ERA.
MEN HAVE KILLED FOR LESS.
WE SHOULD FIND OUT WHO THESE MEN WERE. IT APPEARS THEY SURVIVED THE CRASH—

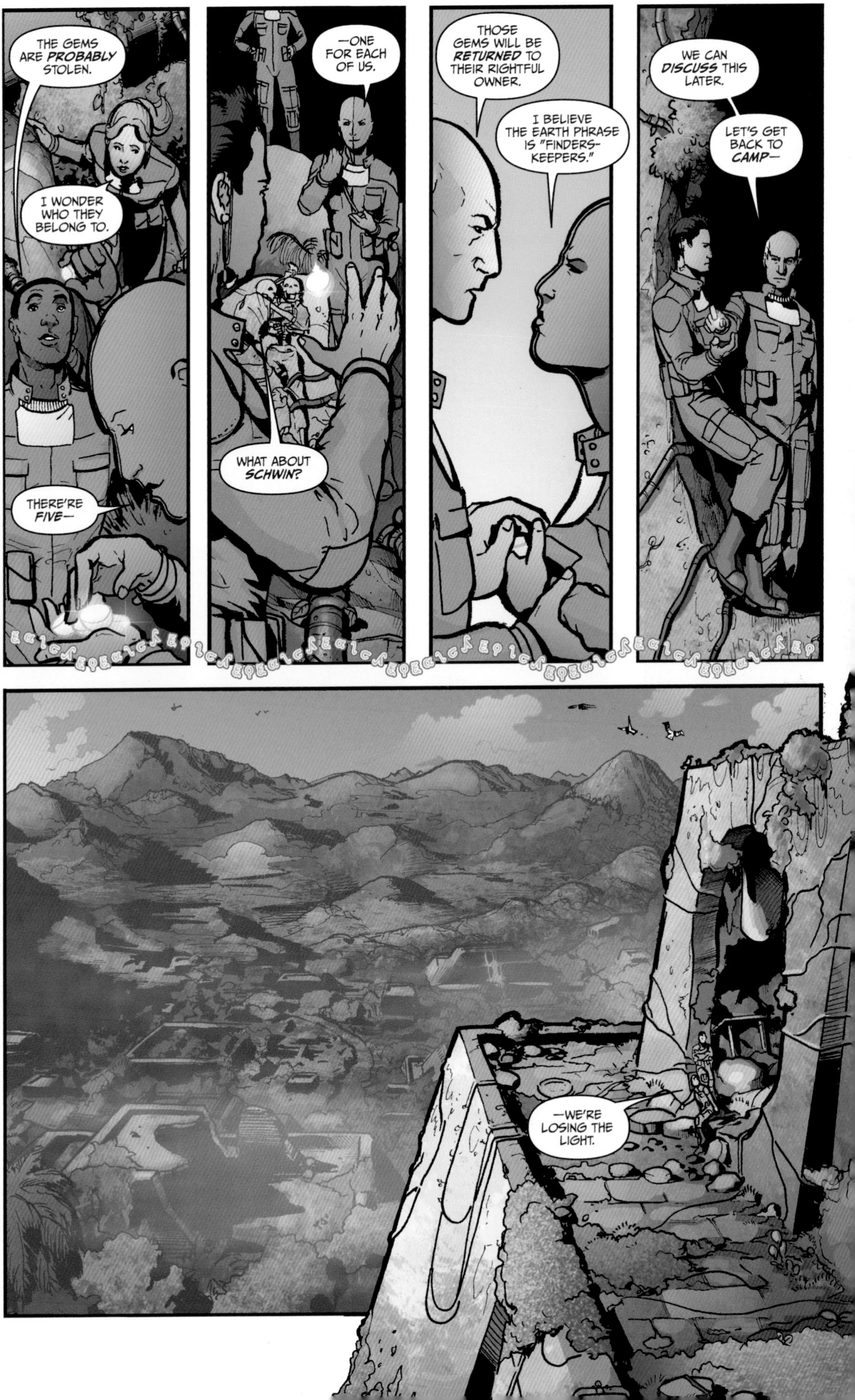
THE GEMS ARE *PROBABLY* STOLEN.
I WONDER WHO THEY BELONG TO.
THERE'RE *FIVE*—
—ONE FOR EACH OF US.
WHAT ABOUT *SCHWIN?*
THOSE GEMS WILL BE *RETURNED* TO THEIR RIGHTFUL OWNER.
I BELIEVE THE EARTH PHRASE IS "FINDERS-KEEPERS."
WE CAN *DISCUSS* THIS LATER.
LET'S GET BACK TO *CAMP*—
—WE'RE LOSING THE LIGHT.

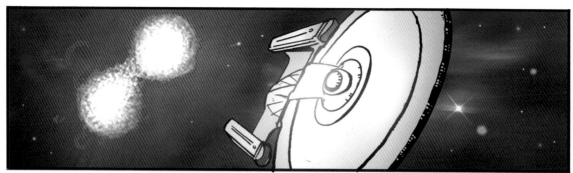

COMPUTER— OPEN DOOR TO PROGRAM, *CRUSHER 54.*

OH, MY—

CHOOOOOSHH!

IT'S ANOTHER *DISCO* SATURDAY NIGHT, HERE AT THE BRIDGE CLUB...

SO LET'S GIVE IT UP FOR BROOKLYN'S BEST—

COMPUTER... WHAT YEAR IS THIS?

THE YEAR IS 1975.

MIKEY AND *BEVERLY!*

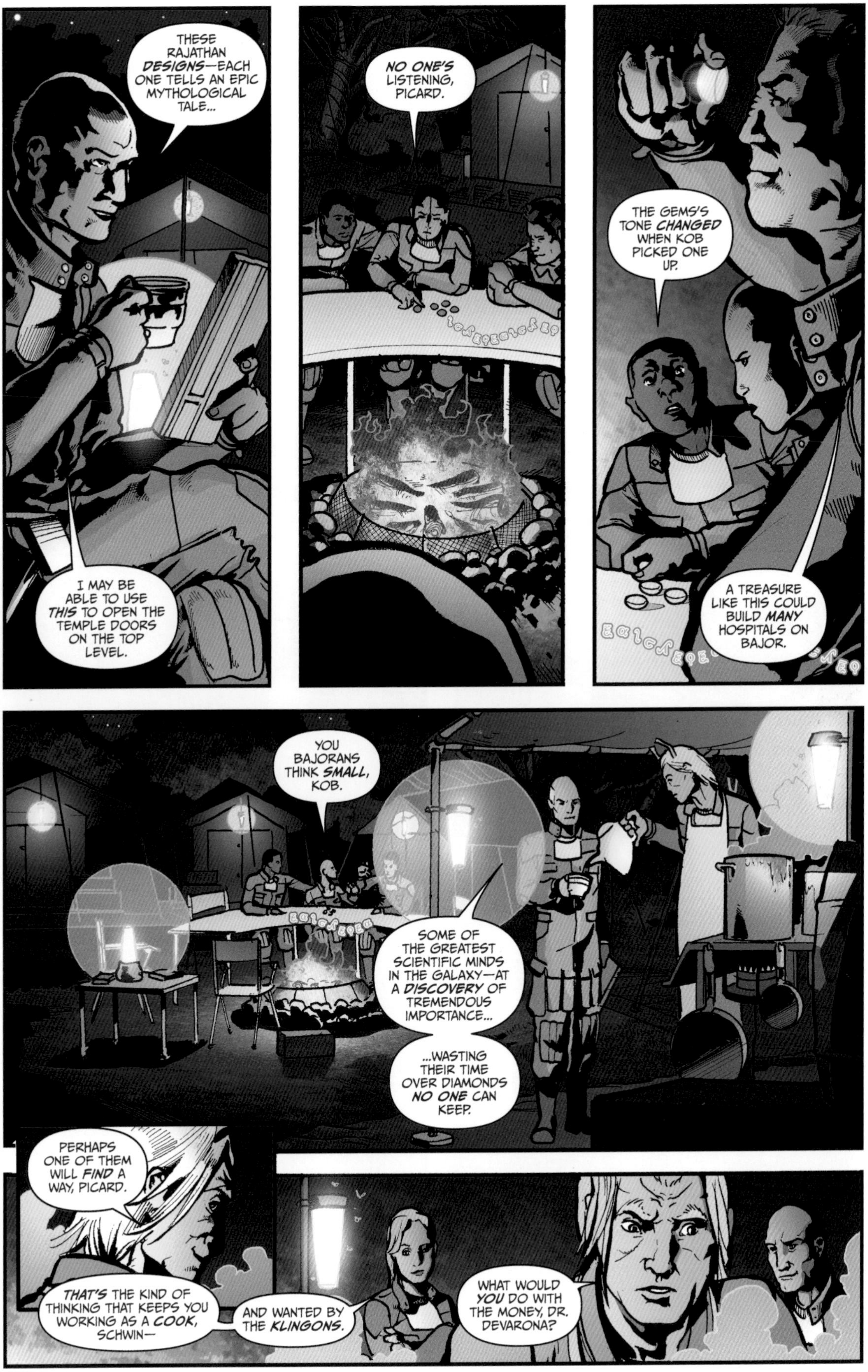

THESE RAJATHAN DESIGNS—EACH ONE TELLS AN EPIC MYTHOLOGICAL TALE...
I MAY BE ABLE TO USE THIS TO OPEN THE TEMPLE DOORS ON THE TOP LEVEL.
NO ONE'S LISTENING, PICARD.
THE GEMS'S TONE CHANGED WHEN KOB PICKED ONE UP.
A TREASURE LIKE THIS COULD BUILD MANY HOSPITALS ON BAJOR.
YOU BAJORANS THINK SMALL, KOB.
SOME OF THE GREATEST SCIENTIFIC MINDS IN THE GALAXY—AT A DISCOVERY OF TREMENDOUS IMPORTANCE...
...WASTING THEIR TIME OVER DIAMONDS NO ONE CAN KEEP.
PERHAPS ONE OF THEM WILL FIND A WAY, PICARD.
THAT'S THE KIND OF THINKING THAT KEEPS YOU WORKING AS A COOK, SCHWIN—
AND WANTED BY THE KLINGONS.
WHAT WOULD YOU DO WITH THE MONEY, DR. DEVARONA?

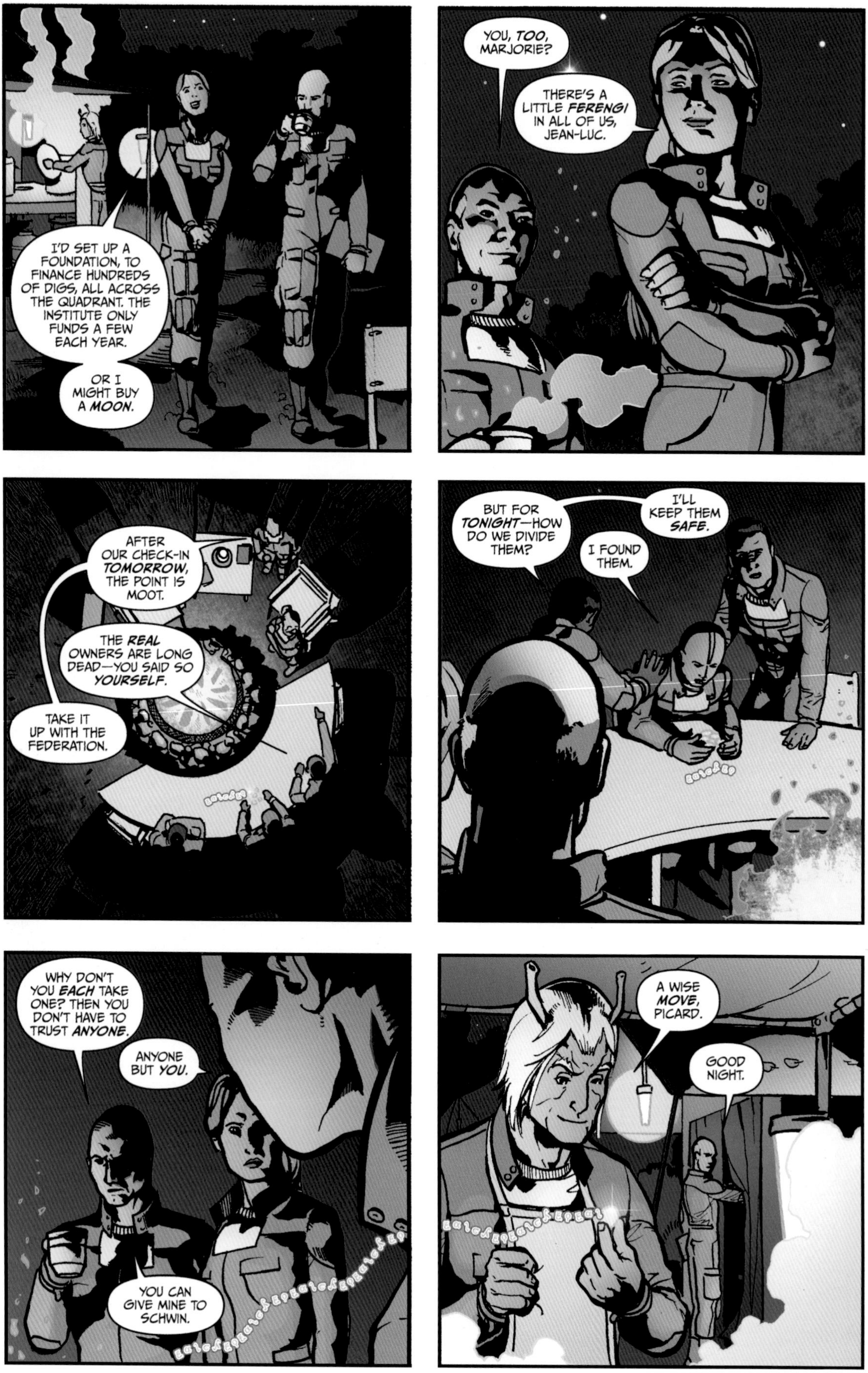
I'D SET UP A FOUNDATION, TO FINANCE HUNDREDS OF DIGS, ALL ACROSS THE QUADRANT. THE INSTITUTE ONLY FUNDS A FEW EACH YEAR.
OR I MIGHT BUY A MOON.
YOU, TOO, MARJORIE?
THERE'S A LITTLE FERENGI IN ALL OF US, JEAN-LUC.
AFTER OUR CHECK-IN TOMORROW, THE POINT IS MOOT.
THE REAL OWNERS ARE LONG DEAD—YOU SAID SO YOURSELF.
TAKE IT UP WITH THE FEDERATION.
BUT FOR TONIGHT—HOW DO WE DIVIDE THEM?
I'LL KEEP THEM SAFE.
I FOUND THEM.
WHY DON'T YOU EACH TAKE ONE? THEN YOU DON'T HAVE TO TRUST ANYONE.
ANYONE BUT YOU.
YOU CAN GIVE MINE TO SCHWIN.
A WISE MOVE, PICARD.
GOOD NIGHT.

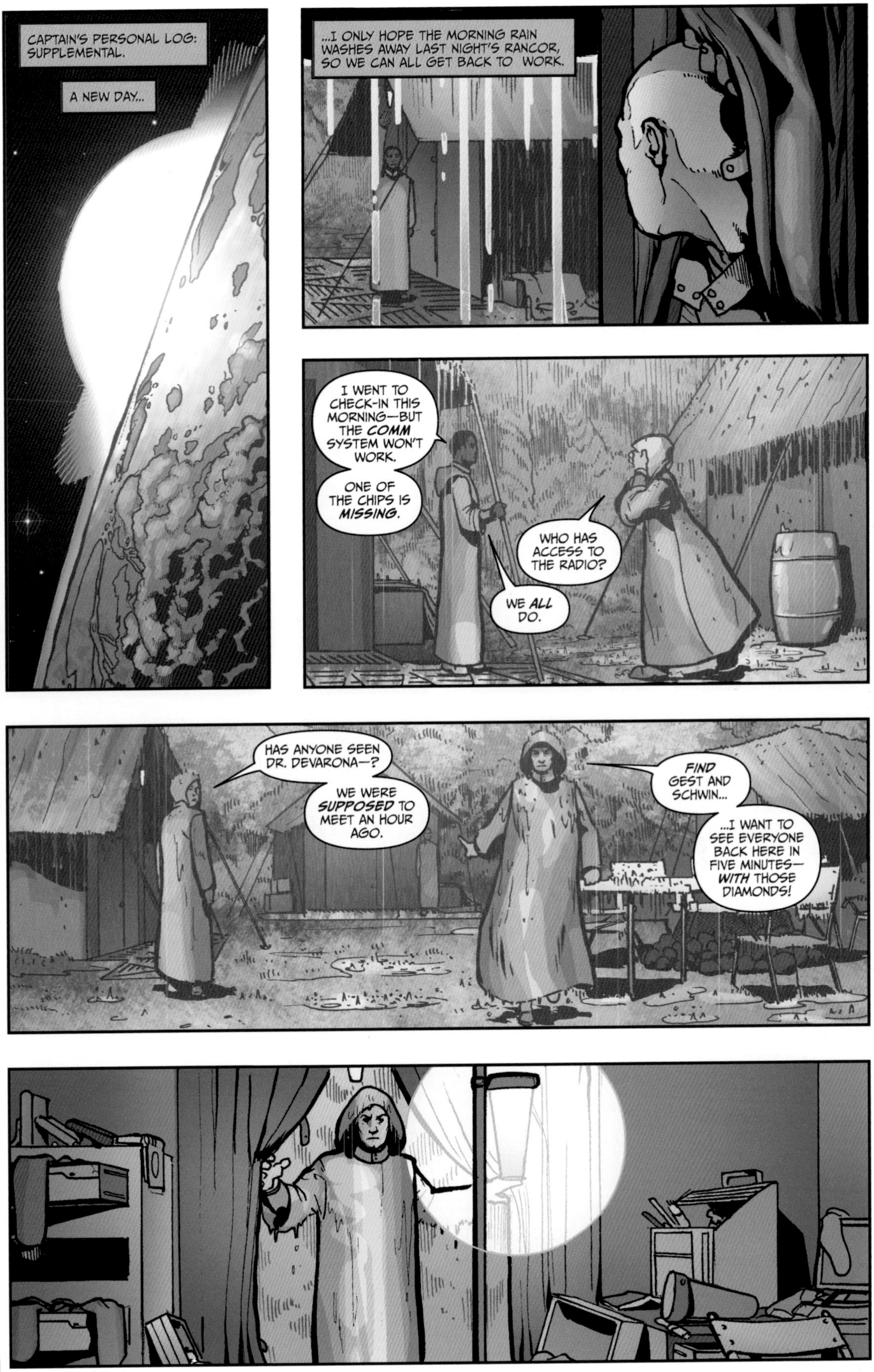
CAPTAIN'S PERSONAL LOG: SUPPLEMENTAL.
A NEW DAY...
...I ONLY HOPE THE MORNING RAIN WASHES AWAY LAST NIGHT'S RANCOR, SO WE CAN ALL GET BACK TO WORK.
I WENT TO CHECK-IN THIS MORNING—BUT THE COMM SYSTEM WON'T WORK.
ONE OF THE CHIPS IS MISSING.
WHO HAS ACCESS TO THE RADIO?
WE ALL DO.
HAS ANYONE SEEN DR. DEVARONA—?
WE WERE SUPPOSED TO MEET AN HOUR AGO.
FIND GEST AND SCHWIN...
...I WANT TO SEE EVERYONE BACK HERE IN FIVE MINUTES—WITH THOSE DIAMONDS!

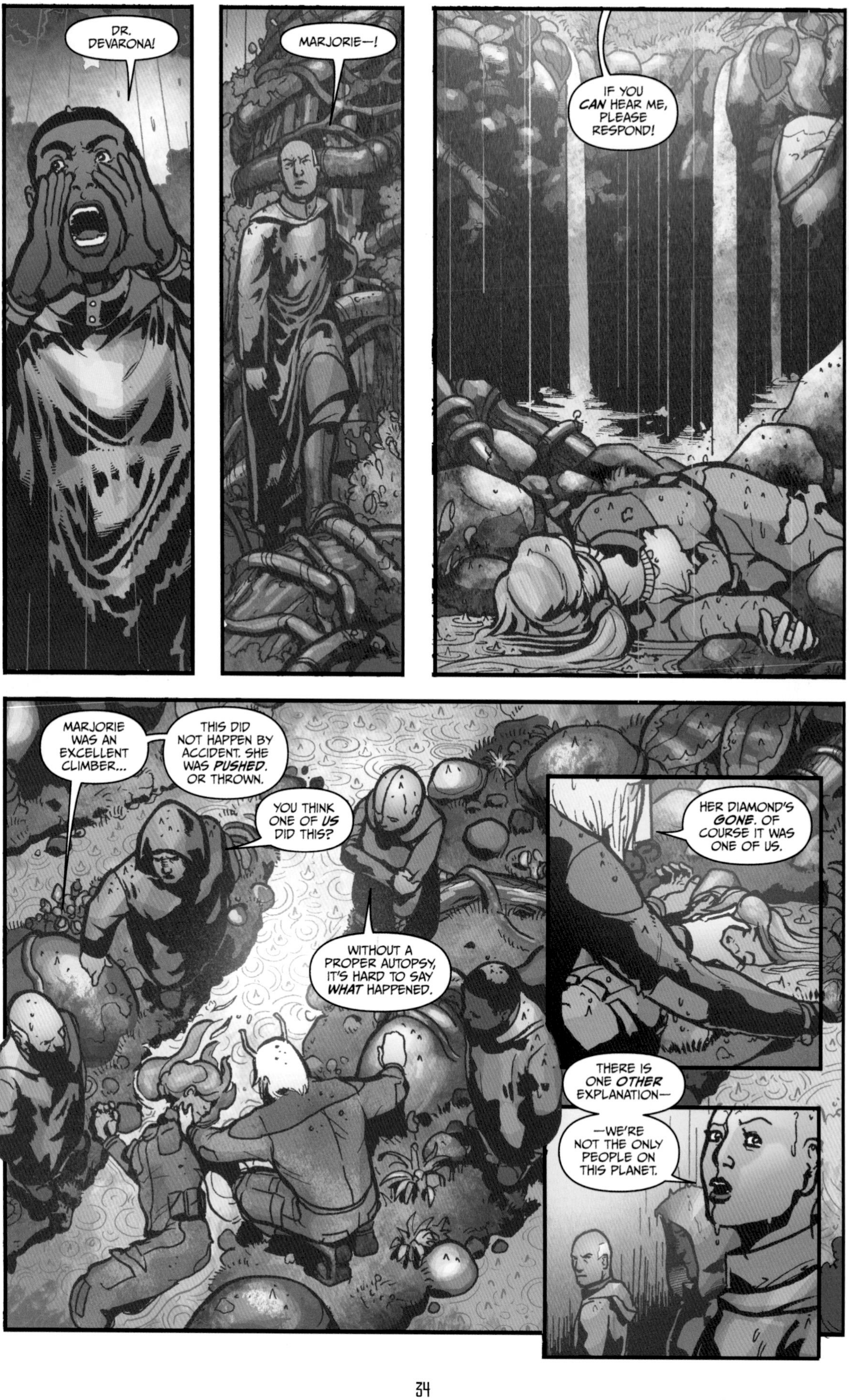
DR. DEVARONA!
MARJORIE—!
IF YOU CAN HEAR ME, PLEASE RESPOND!
MARJORIE WAS AN EXCELLENT CLIMBER...
THIS DID NOT HAPPEN BY ACCIDENT. SHE WAS PUSHED. OR THROWN.
YOU THINK ONE OF US DID THIS?
WITHOUT A PROPER AUTOPSY, IT'S HARD TO SAY WHAT HAPPENED.
HER DIAMOND'S GONE. OF COURSE IT WAS ONE OF US.
THERE IS ONE OTHER EXPLANATION—
—WE'RE NOT THE ONLY PEOPLE ON THIS PLANET.

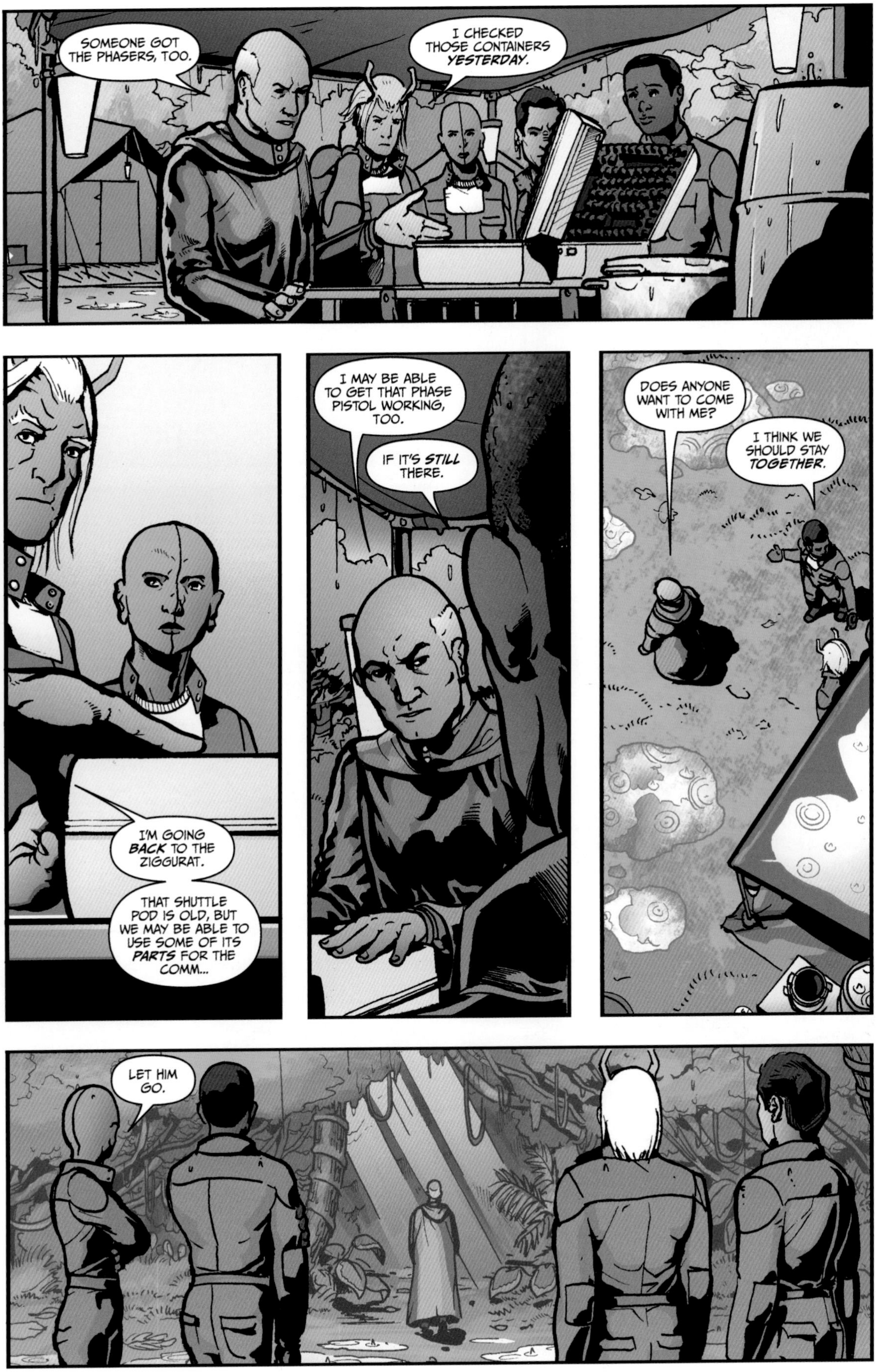
SOMEONE GOT THE PHASERS, TOO.
I CHECKED THOSE CONTAINERS YESTERDAY.
I'M GOING BACK TO THE ZIGGURAT.
THAT SHUTTLE POD IS OLD, BUT WE MAY BE ABLE TO USE SOME OF ITS PARTS FOR THE COMM...
I MAY BE ABLE TO GET THAT PHASE PISTOL WORKING, TOO.
IF IT'S STILL THERE.
DOES ANYONE WANT TO COME WITH ME?
I THINK WE SHOULD STAY TOGETHER.
LET HIM GO.

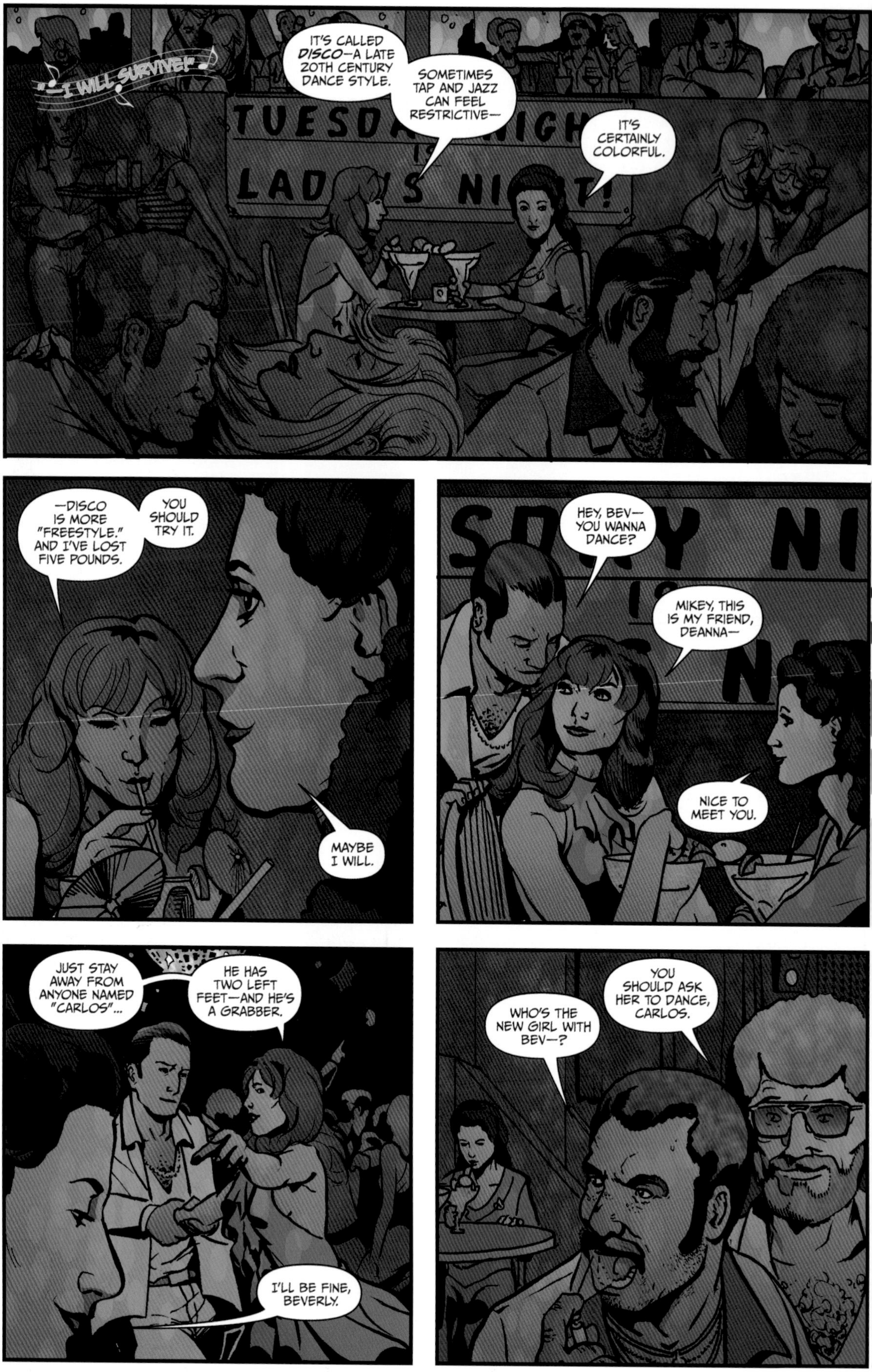
"I WILL SURVIVE!"
IT'S CALLED DISCO—A LATE 20TH CENTURY DANCE STYLE.
SOMETIMES TAP AND JAZZ CAN FEEL RESTRICTIVE—
IT'S CERTAINLY COLORFUL.
TUESDA NIGH IS LAD S NI T!
—DISCO IS MORE "FREESTYLE." AND I'VE LOST FIVE POUNDS.
YOU SHOULD TRY IT.
MAYBE I WILL.
HEY, BEV— YOU WANNA DANCE?
MIKEY, THIS IS MY FRIEND, DEANNA—
NICE TO MEET YOU.
JUST STAY AWAY FROM ANYONE NAMED "CARLOS"...
HE HAS TWO LEFT FEET—AND HE'S A GRABBER.
I'LL BE FINE, BEVERLY.
WHO'S THE NEW GIRL WITH BEV—?
YOU SHOULD ASK HER TO DANCE, CARLOS.

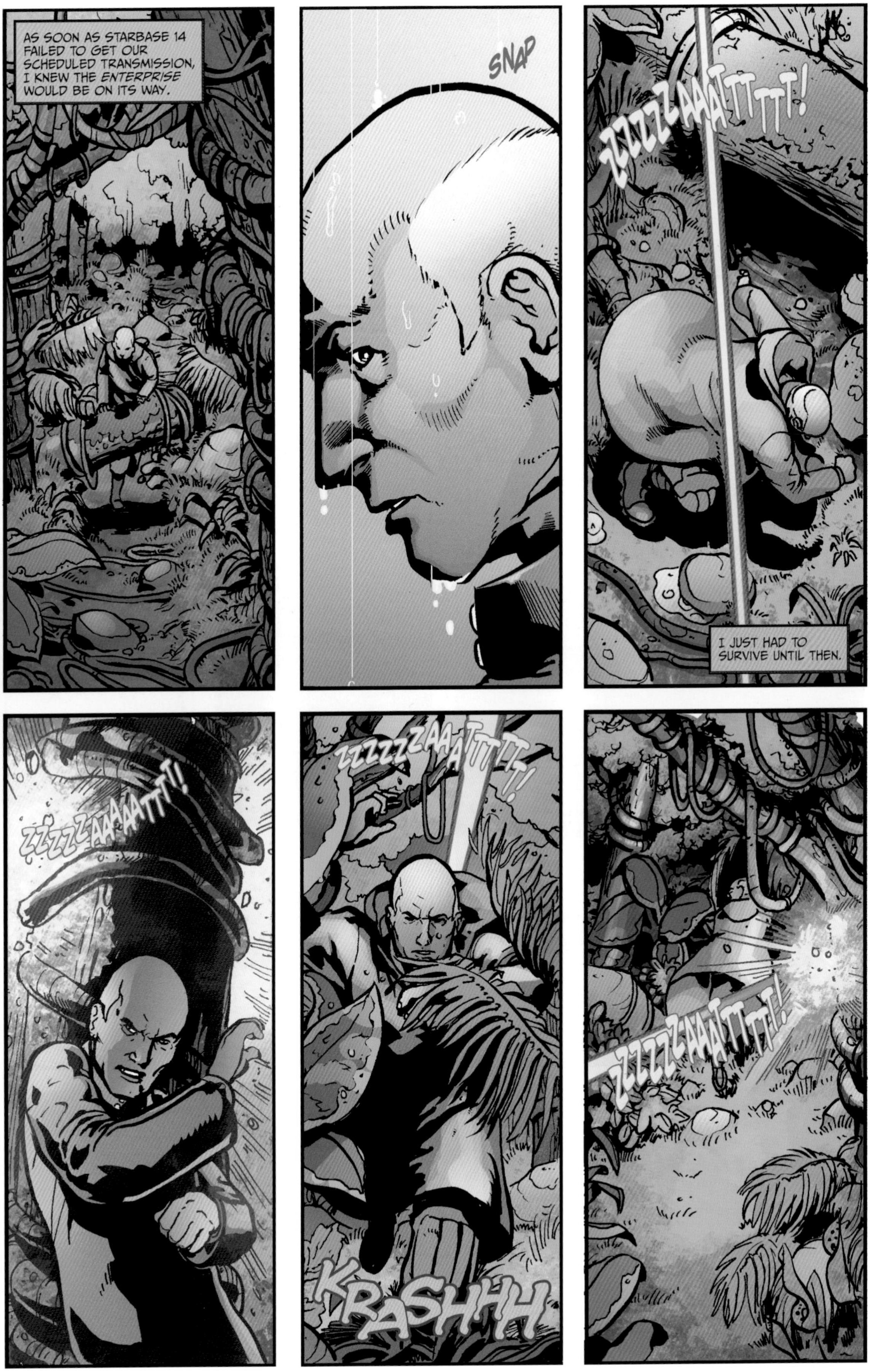
AS SOON AS STARBASE 14 FAILED TO GET OUR SCHEDULED TRANSMISSION, I KNEW THE *ENTERPRISE* WOULD BE ON ITS WAY.
SNAP
ZZZZZZAAAATTTTT!
I JUST HAD TO SURVIVE UNTIL THEN.
ZZZZZAAAAATTTT!
ZZZZZZAAAATTTTT!
KRASHHH
ZZZZZZAAAATTTTT!

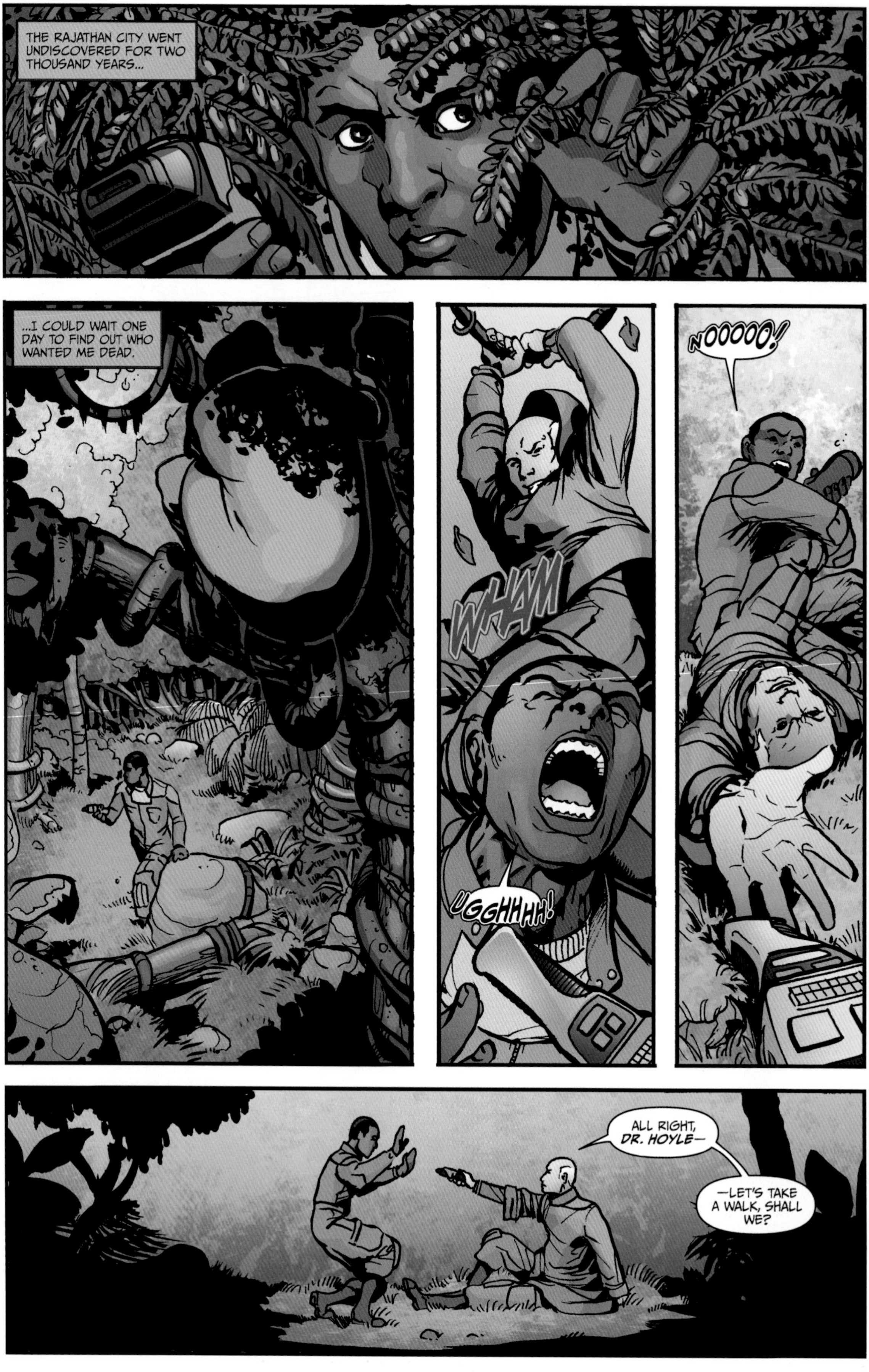

THE RAJATHAN CITY WENT UNDISCOVERED FOR TWO THOUSAND YEARS...
...I COULD WAIT ONE DAY TO FIND OUT WHO WANTED ME DEAD.
WHAM
UGGHHHH!
NOOOOO!
ALL RIGHT, DR. HOYLE—
—LET'S TAKE A WALK, SHALL WE?

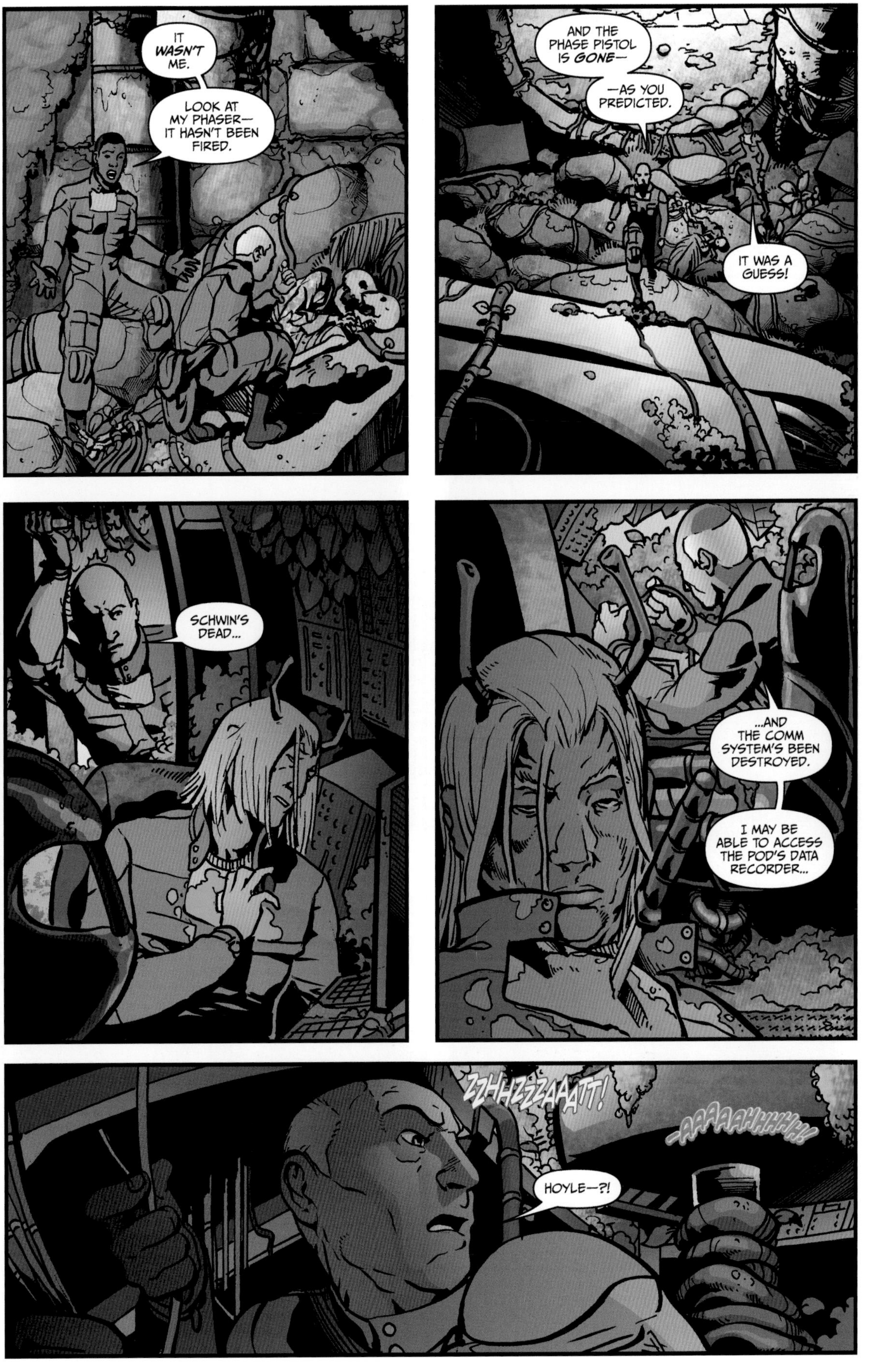
IT WASN'T ME.
LOOK AT MY PHASER— IT HASN'T BEEN FIRED.
AND THE PHASE PISTOL IS GONE—
—AS YOU PREDICTED.
IT WAS A GUESS!
SCHWIN'S DEAD...
...AND THE COMM SYSTEM'S BEEN DESTROYED.
I MAY BE ABLE TO ACCESS THE POD'S DATA RECORDER...
ZZHHZZZAAATT!
—AAAAAHHHHH!
HOYLE—?!

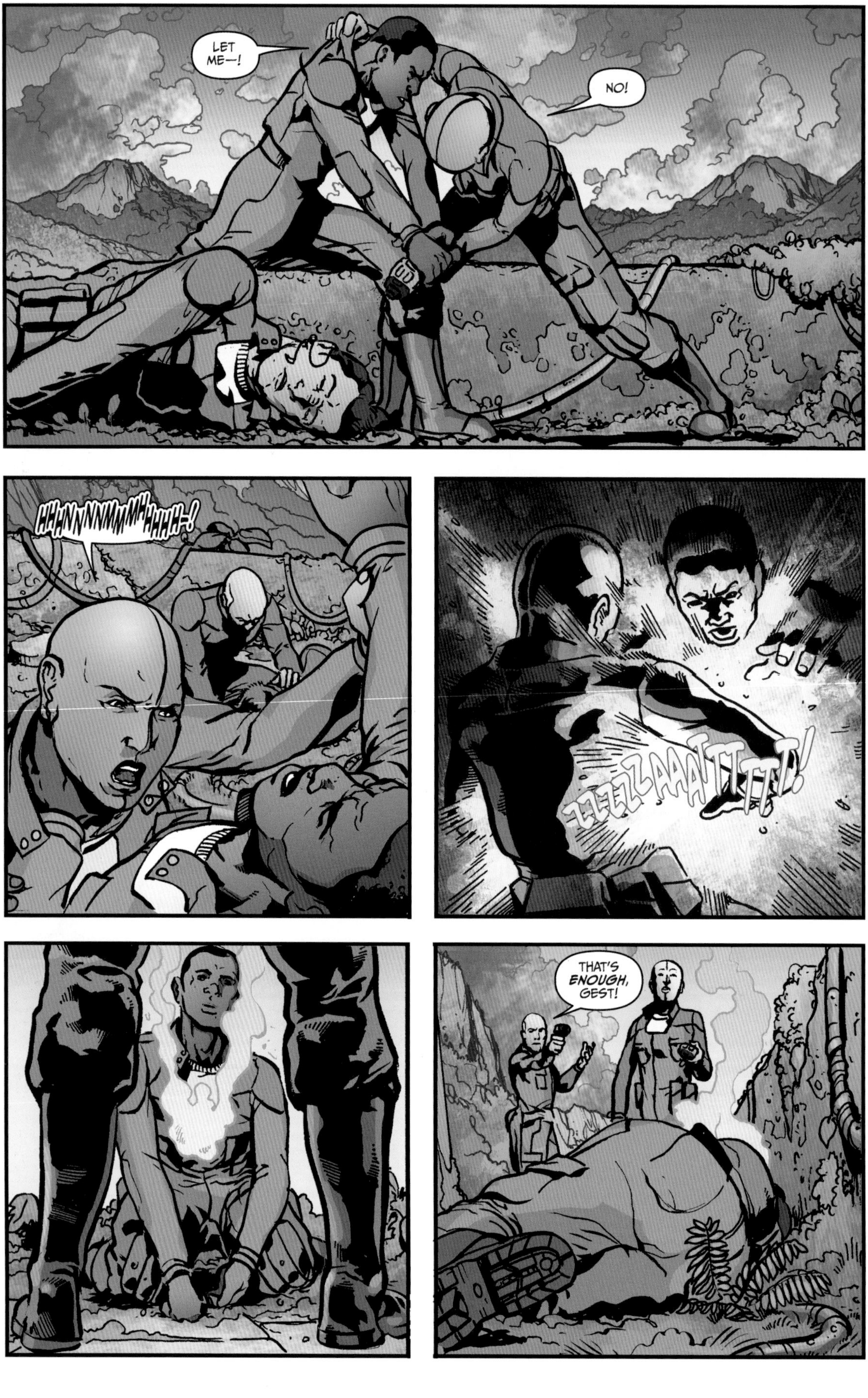
LET ME—!
NO!
HHHNNNNMMMHHHHH—!
ZZZZZAAATTTTTT!
THAT'S ENOUGH, GEST!

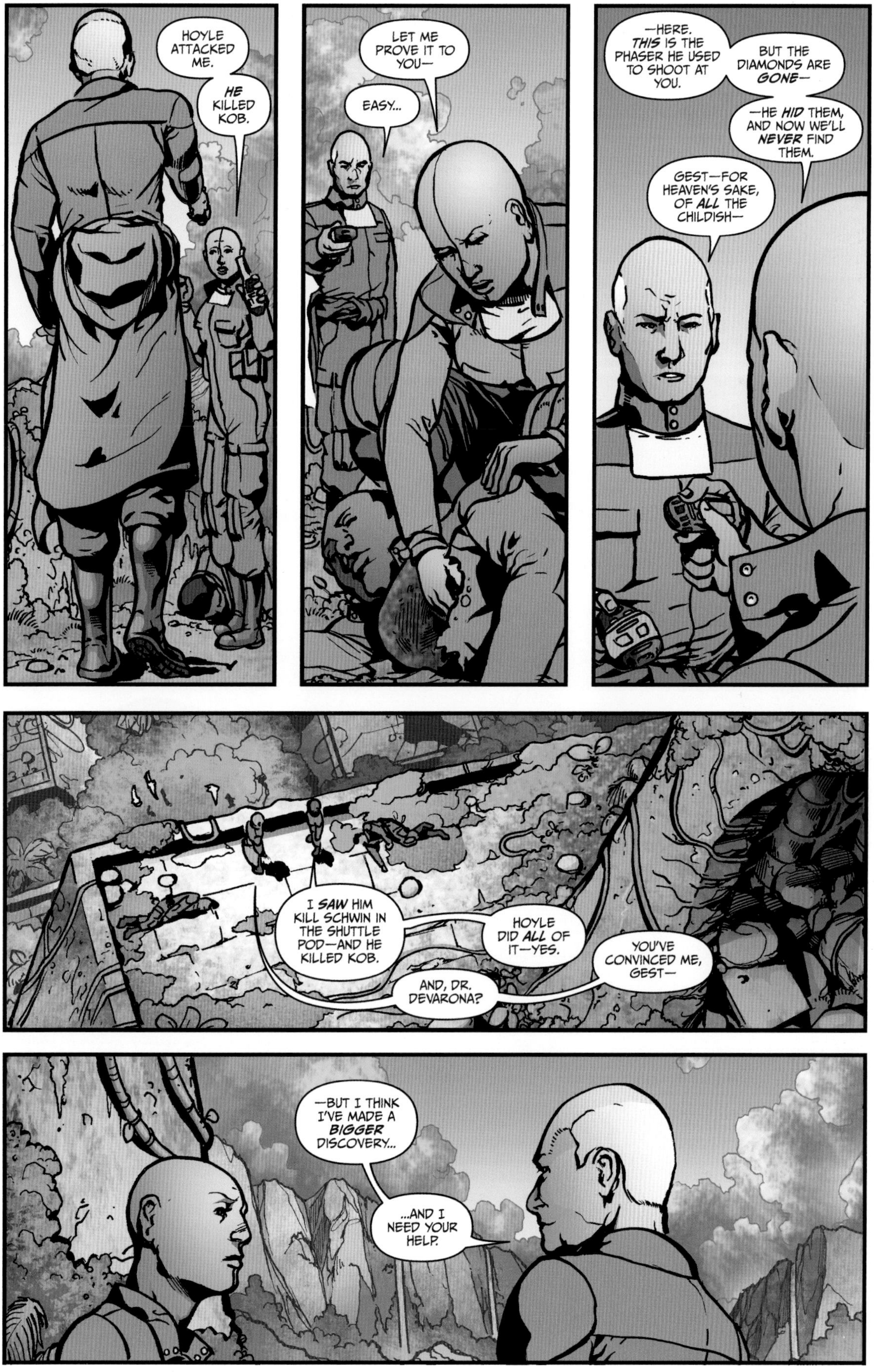
HOYLE ATTACKED ME.
HE KILLED KOB.
LET ME PROVE IT TO YOU—
EASY...
—HERE. THIS IS THE PHASER HE USED TO SHOOT AT YOU.
BUT THE DIAMONDS ARE GONE—
—HE HID THEM, AND NOW WE'LL NEVER FIND THEM.
GEST—FOR HEAVEN'S SAKE, OF ALL THE CHILDISH—
I SAW HIM KILL SCHWIN IN THE SHUTTLE POD—AND HE KILLED KOB.
HOYLE DID ALL OF IT—YES.
AND, DR. DEVARONA?
YOU'VE CONVINCED ME, GEST—
—BUT I THINK I'VE MADE A BIGGER DISCOVERY...
...AND I NEED YOUR HELP.

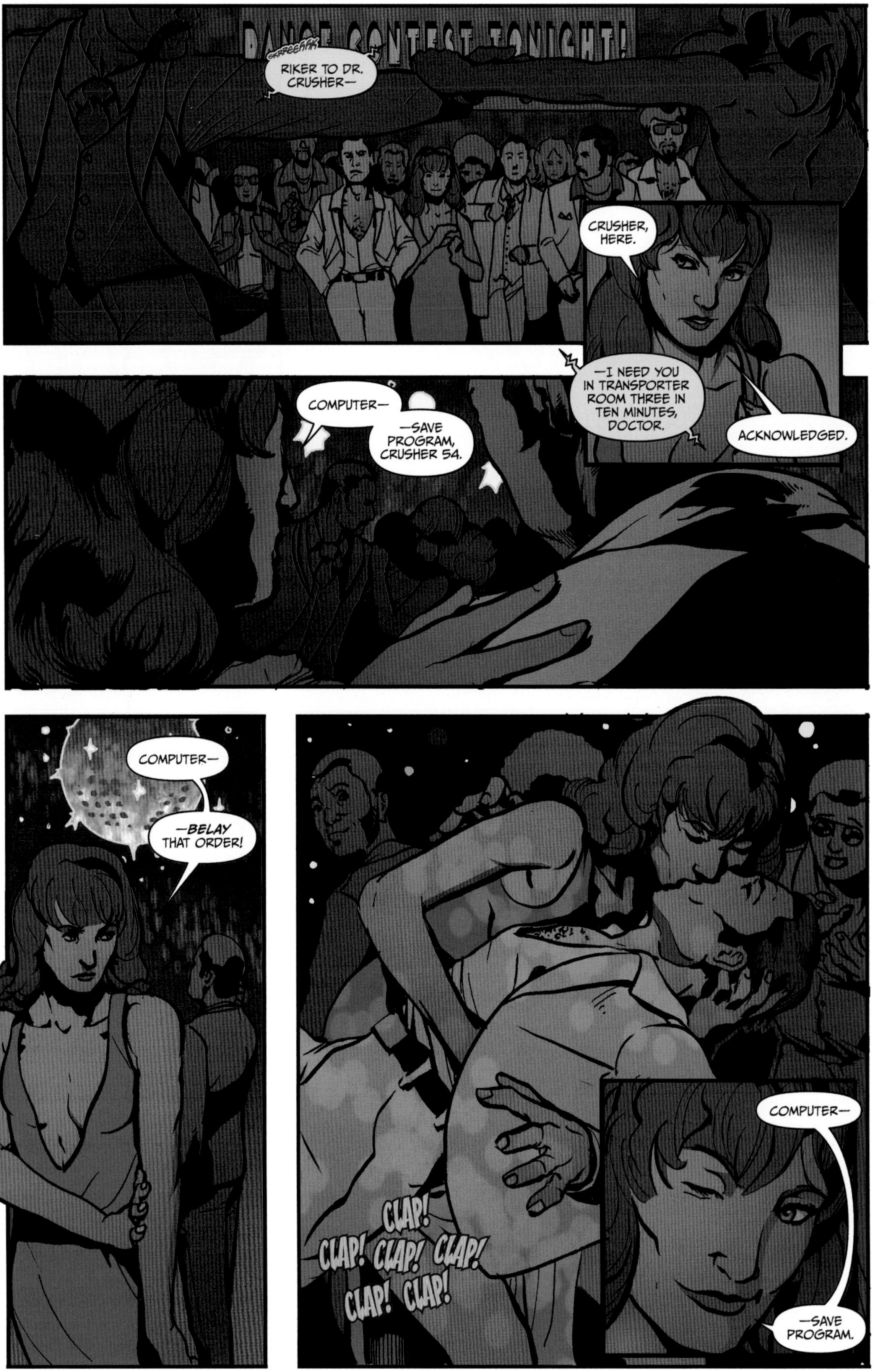
DANCE CONTEST TONIGHT!
RIKER TO DR. CRUSHER—
CRUSHER, HERE.
—I NEED YOU IN TRANSPORTER ROOM THREE IN TEN MINUTES, DOCTOR.
ACKNOWLEDGED.
COMPUTER—
—SAVE PROGRAM, CRUSHER 54.
COMPUTER—
—*BELAY* THAT ORDER!
CLAP! CLAP! CLAP! CLAP! CLAP! CLAP!
COMPUTER—
—SAVE PROGRAM.

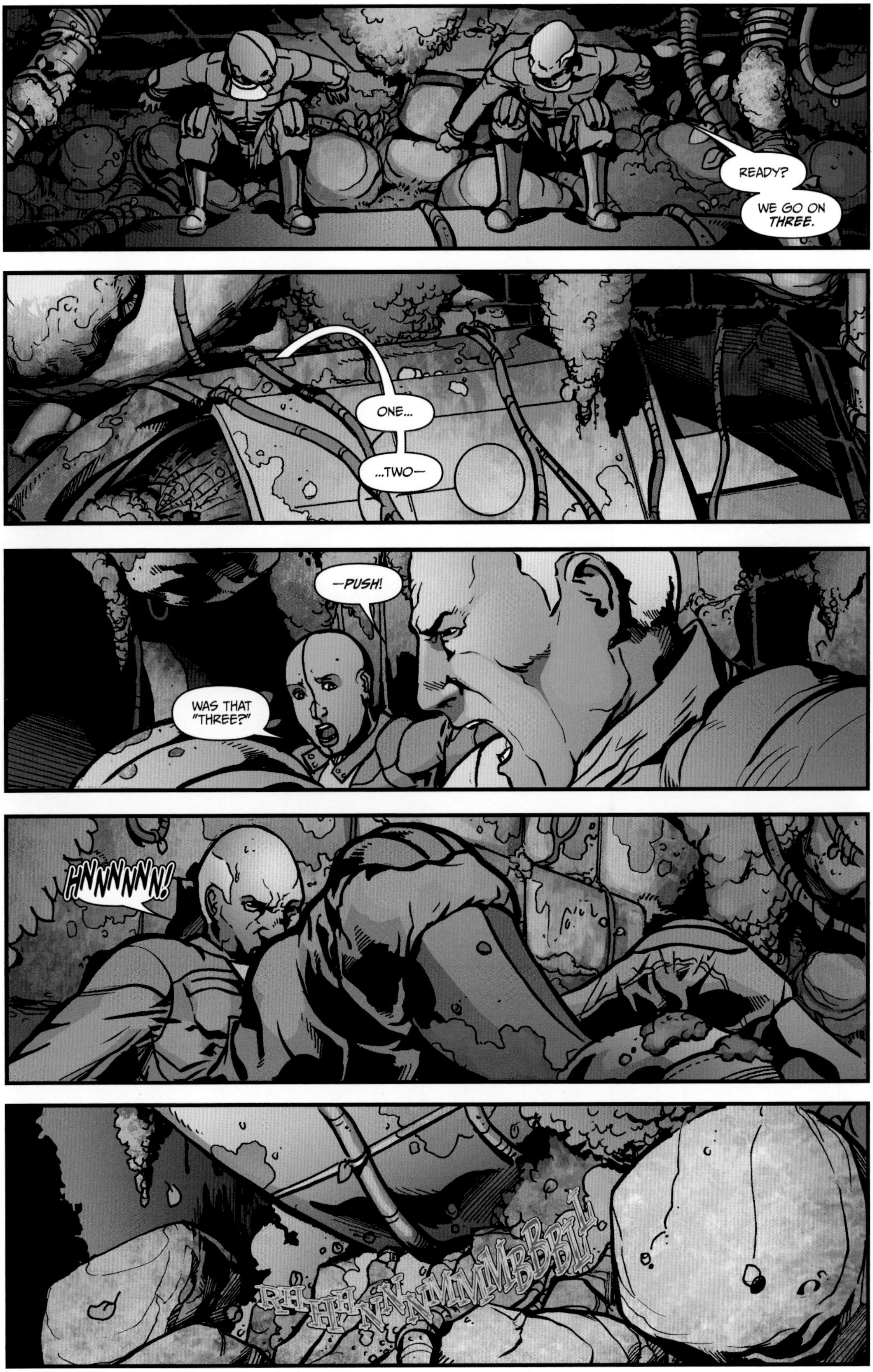
READY?
WE GO ON THREE.
ONE...
...TWO—
—PUSH!
WAS THAT "THREE?"
HNNNNNN!
RHHHNNNMMMMBBBLL

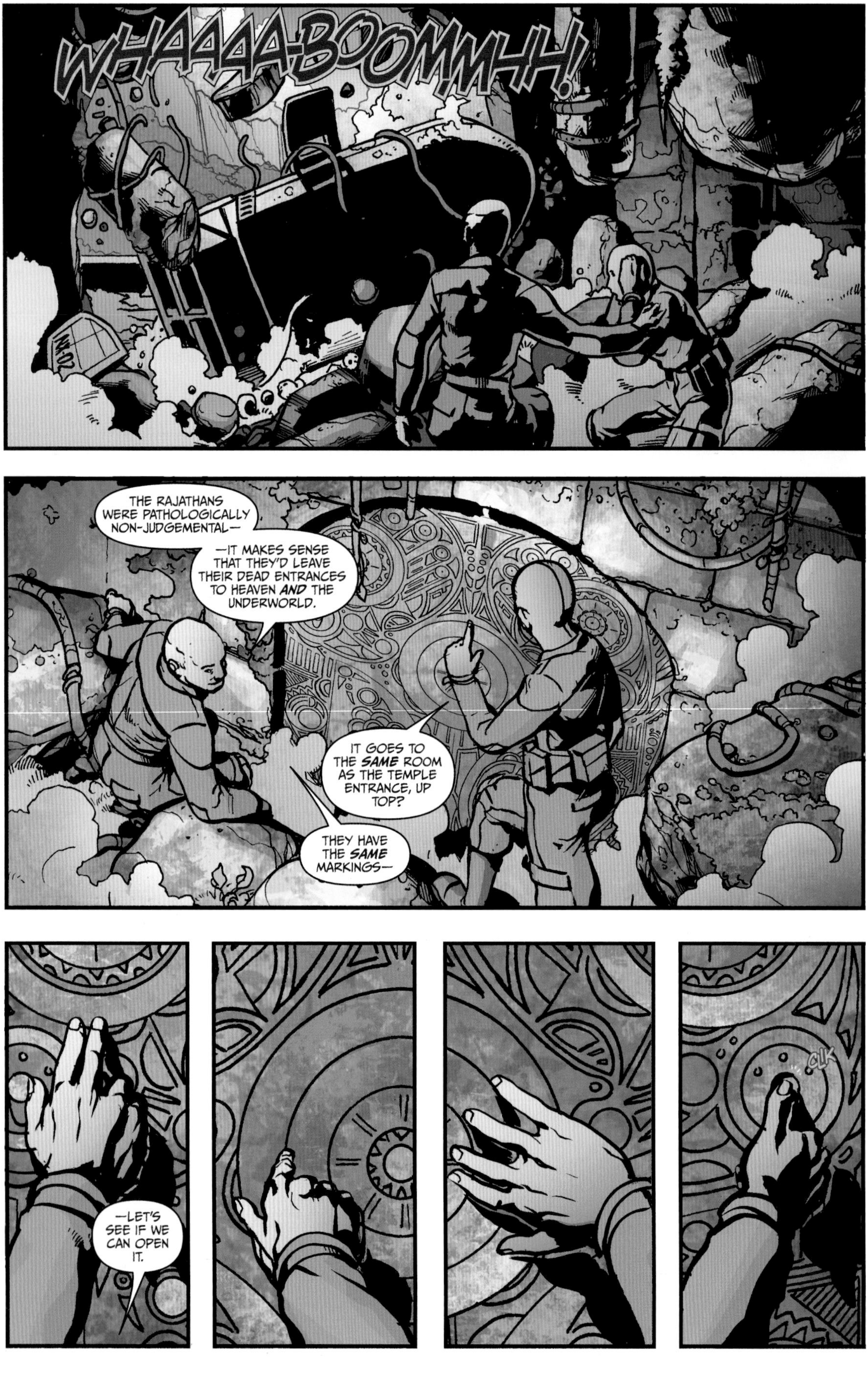
WHAAAA-BOOMMHH!
THE RAJATHANS WERE PATHOLOGICALLY NON-JUDGEMENTAL—
—IT MAKES SENSE THAT THEY'D LEAVE THEIR DEAD ENTRANCES TO HEAVEN AND THE UNDERWORLD.
IT GOES TO THE SAME ROOM AS THE TEMPLE ENTRANCE, UP TOP?
THEY HAVE THE SAME MARKINGS—
—LET'S SEE IF WE CAN OPEN IT.
CLIK

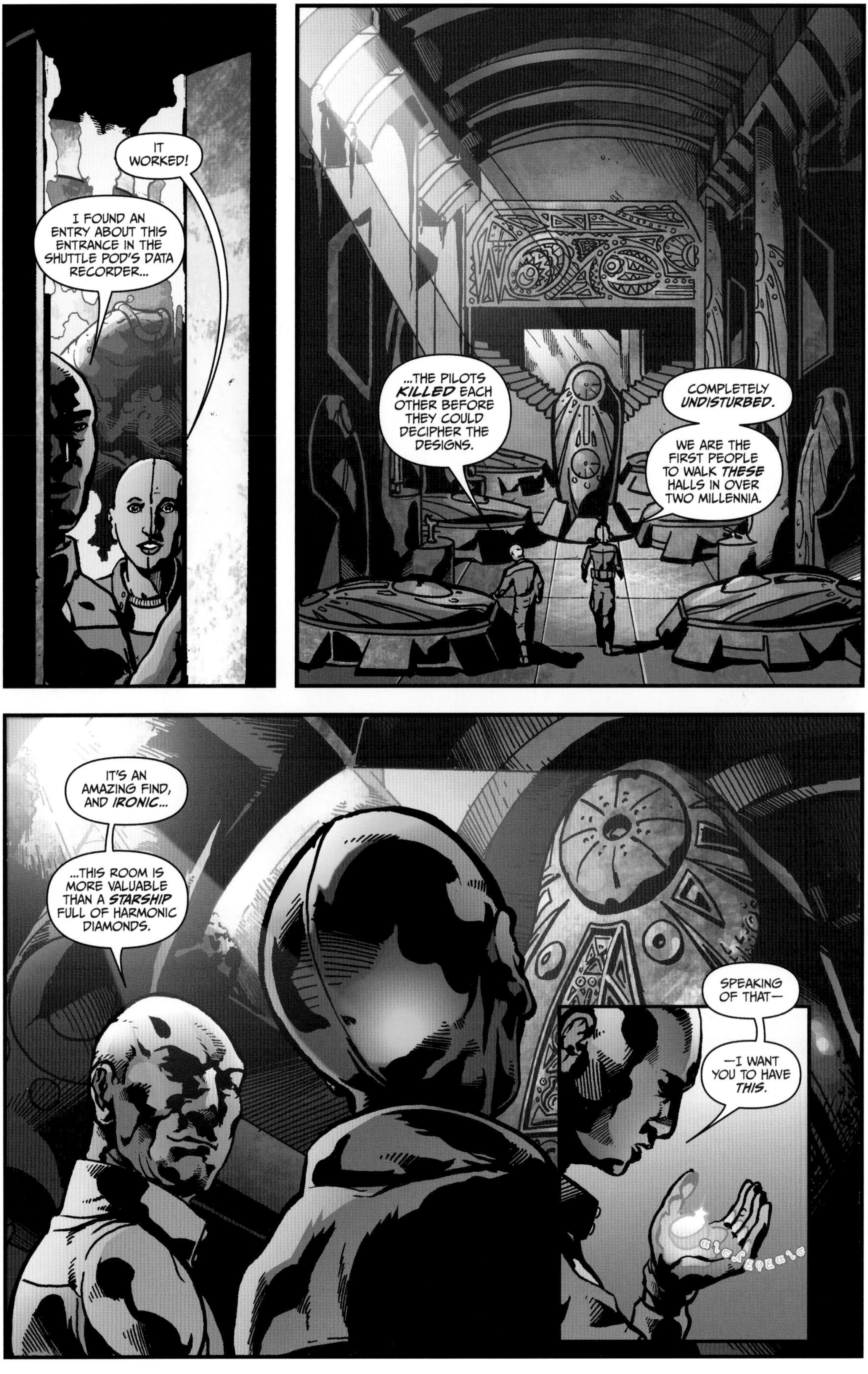
IT WORKED!
I FOUND AN ENTRY ABOUT THIS ENTRANCE IN THE SHUTTLE POD'S DATA RECORDER...
...THE PILOTS *KILLED* EACH OTHER BEFORE THEY COULD DECIPHER THE DESIGNS.
COMPLETELY *UNDISTURBED.*
WE ARE THE FIRST PEOPLE TO WALK *THESE* HALLS IN OVER TWO MILLENNIA.
IT'S AN AMAZING FIND, AND *IRONIC*...
...THIS ROOM IS MORE VALUABLE THAN A *STARSHIP* FULL OF HARMONIC DIAMONDS.
SPEAKING OF THAT—
—I WANT YOU TO HAVE *THIS.*

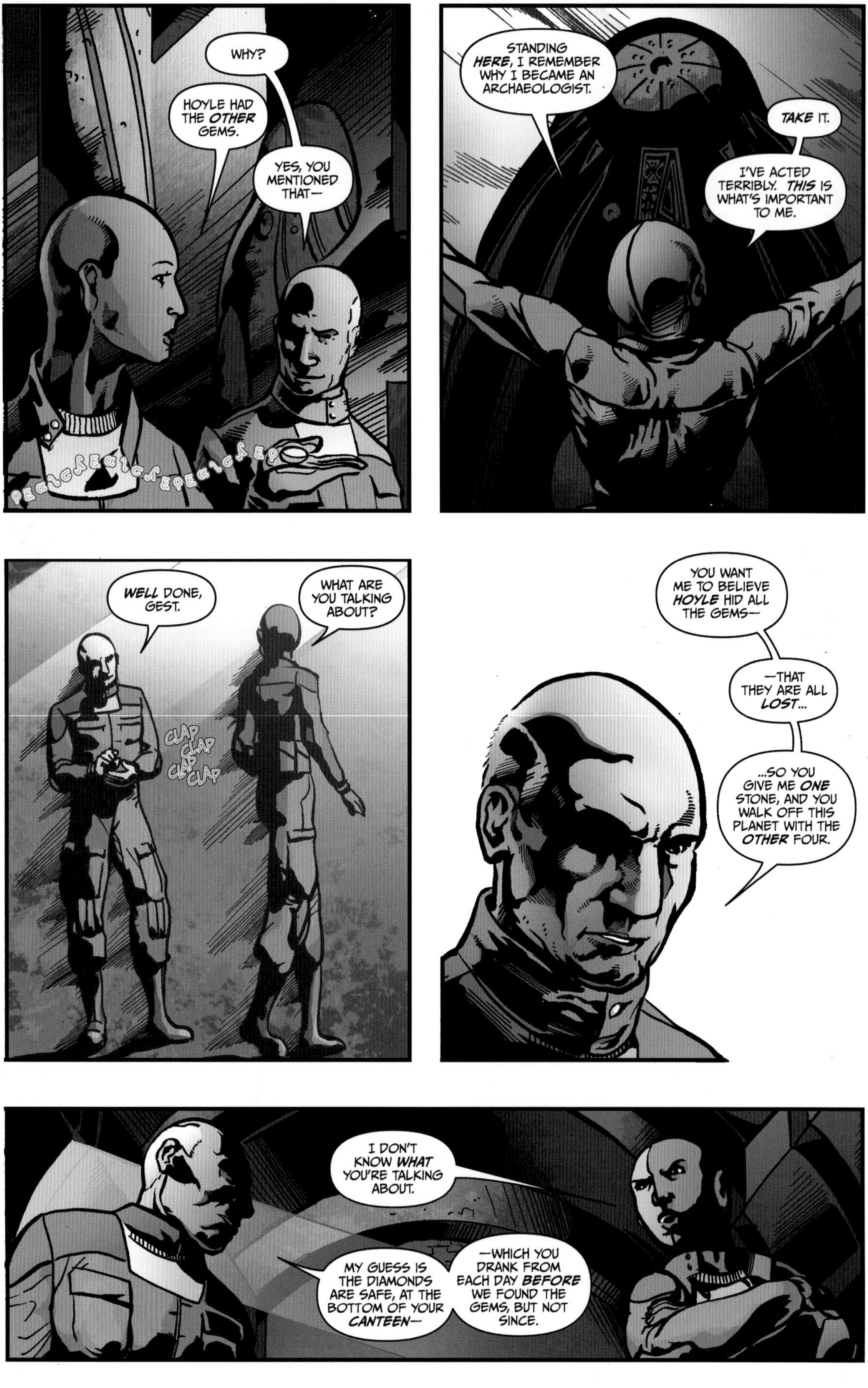
WHY?
HOYLE HAD THE *OTHER* GEMS.
YES, YOU MENTIONED THAT—
STANDING *HERE*, I REMEMBER WHY I BECAME AN ARCHAEOLOGIST.
TAKE IT.
I'VE ACTED TERRIBLY. *THIS* IS WHAT'S IMPORTANT TO ME.
WELL DONE, GEST.
WHAT ARE YOU TALKING ABOUT?
CLAP CLAP CLAP CLAP
YOU WANT ME TO BELIEVE *HOYLE* HID ALL THE GEMS—
—THAT THEY ARE ALL *LOST*...
...SO YOU GIVE ME *ONE* STONE, AND YOU WALK OFF THIS PLANET WITH THE *OTHER* FOUR.
I DON'T KNOW *WHAT* YOU'RE TALKING ABOUT.
MY GUESS IS THE DIAMONDS ARE SAFE, AT THE BOTTOM OF YOUR *CANTEEN*—
—WHICH YOU DRANK FROM EACH DAY *BEFORE* WE FOUND THE GEMS, BUT NOT SINCE.

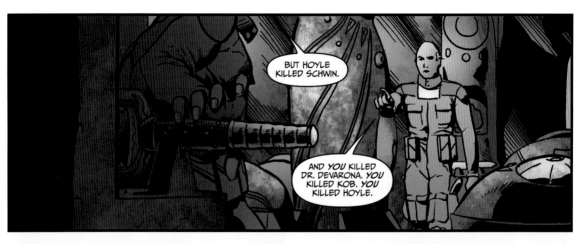

BUT HOYLE KILLED SCHWIN.

AND *YOU* KILLED DR. DEVARONA. *YOU* KILLED KOB. *YOU* KILLED HOYLE.

WOULD YOU LIKE THE PHASER?

DON'T *MOVE.*

WHERE WILL YOU GO?

I CONTACTED MY SHIP BEFORE I DISABLED THE COMM SYSTEM—

—THEY'LL BE HERE BEFORE THE *ENTERPRISE...*

...WHO WILL NEVER FIND YOU TRAPPED IN THIS TOMB.

ENJOY THE RELICS, PICARD.

CAN WE *HELP* YOU WITH SOMETHING, DR. GEST?

CAPTAIN'S LOG:

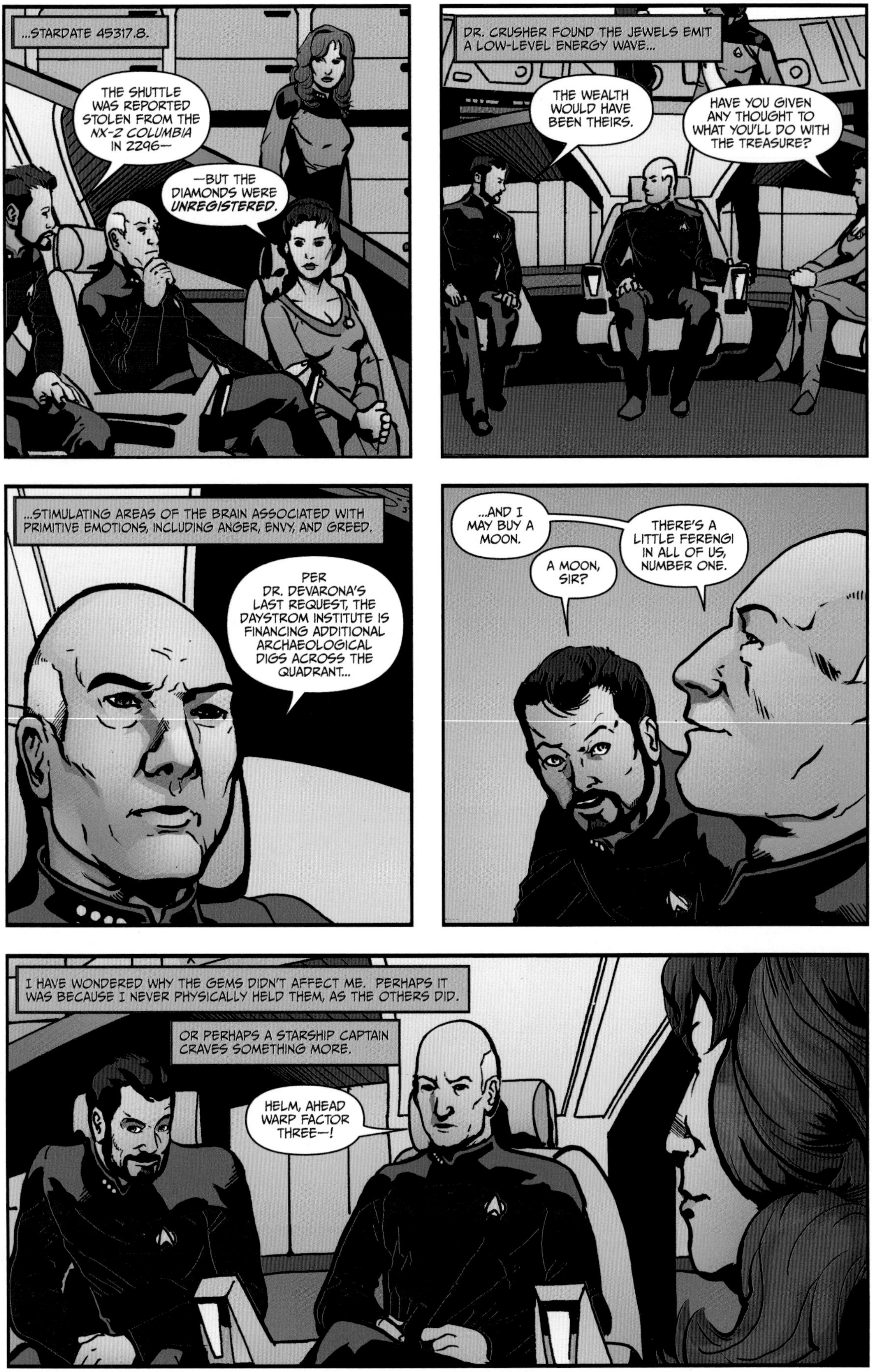
...STARDATE 45317.8.
THE SHUTTLE WAS REPORTED STOLEN FROM THE *NX-2 COLUMBIA* IN 2296—
—BUT THE DIAMONDS WERE *UNREGISTERED.*
DR. CRUSHER FOUND THE JEWELS EMIT A LOW-LEVEL ENERGY WAVE...
THE WEALTH WOULD HAVE BEEN THEIRS.
HAVE YOU GIVEN ANY THOUGHT TO WHAT YOU'LL DO WITH THE TREASURE?
...STIMULATING AREAS OF THE BRAIN ASSOCIATED WITH PRIMITIVE EMOTIONS, INCLUDING ANGER, ENVY, AND GREED.
PER DR. DEVARONA'S LAST REQUEST, THE DAYSTROM INSTITUTE IS FINANCING ADDITIONAL ARCHAEOLOGICAL DIGS ACROSS THE QUADRANT...
...AND I MAY BUY A MOON.
A MOON, SIR?
THERE'S A LITTLE FERENGI IN ALL OF US, NUMBER ONE.
I HAVE WONDERED WHY THE GEMS DIDN'T AFFECT ME. PERHAPS IT WAS BECAUSE I NEVER PHYSICALLY HELD THEM, AS THE OTHERS DID.
OR PERHAPS A STARSHIP CAPTAIN CRAVES SOMETHING MORE.
HELM, AHEAD WARP FACTOR THREE—!

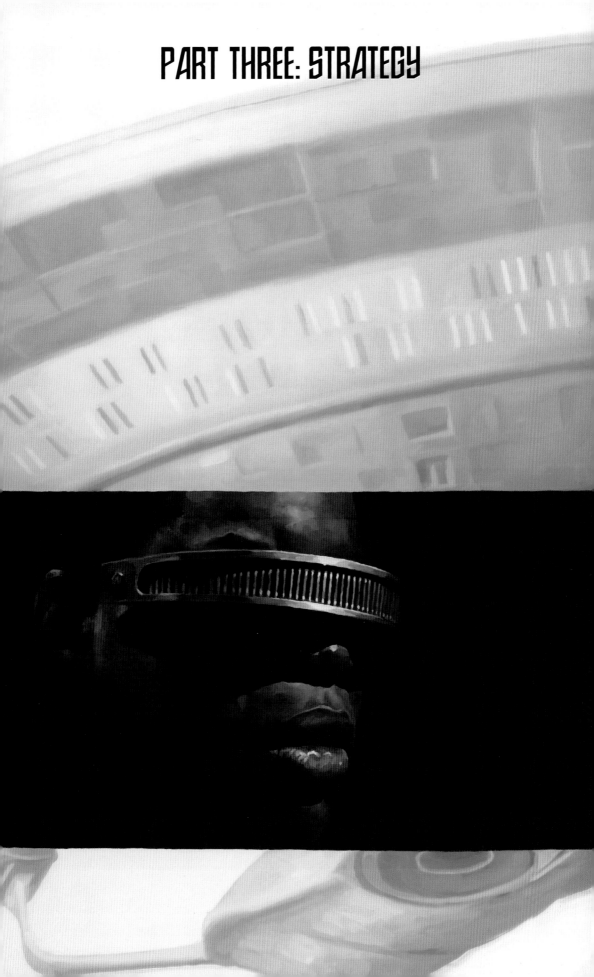

PART THREE: STRATEGY

TSSSSHHHH

LIEUTENANT.

ENSIGN.

BooOomm

WUUHRRHHHRRRR WUUHRRHHHRRRR

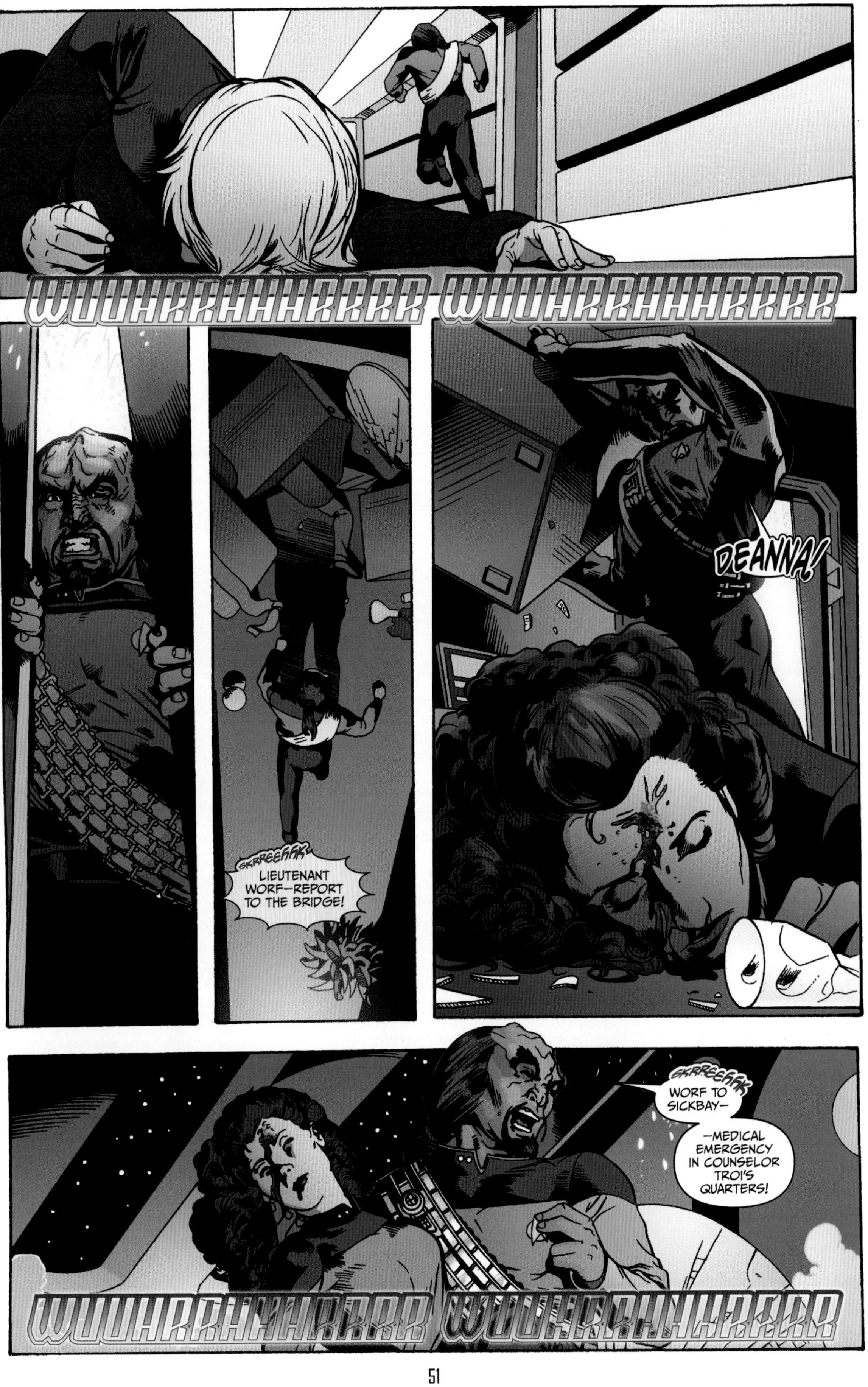
WUUHRRHHHRRRR WUUHRRHHHRRRR
DEANNA!
SKRREEFFK
LIEUTENANT WORF—REPORT TO THE BRIDGE!
SKRREEFFK
WORF TO SICKBAY—
—MEDICAL EMERGENCY IN COUNSELOR TROI'S QUARTERS!
WUUHRRHHHRRRR WUUHRRHHHRRRR

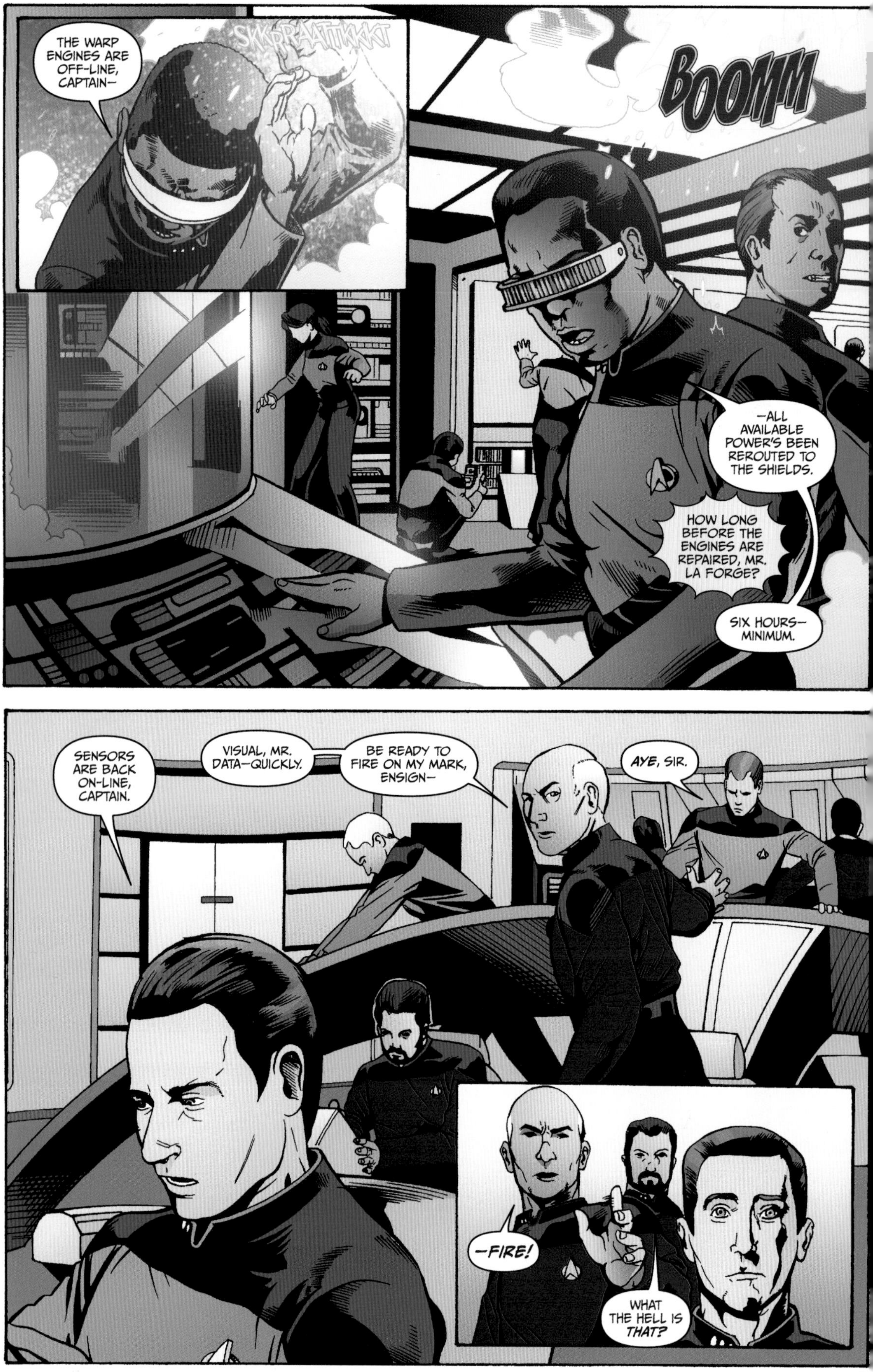
SKKRRAATTKKKT
THE WARP ENGINES ARE OFF-LINE, CAPTAIN—
BOOMM
—ALL AVAILABLE POWER'S BEEN REROUTED TO THE SHIELDS.
HOW LONG BEFORE THE ENGINES ARE REPAIRED, MR. LA FORGE?
SIX HOURS—MINIMUM.
SENSORS ARE BACK ON-LINE, CAPTAIN.
VISUAL, MR. DATA—QUICKLY.
BE READY TO FIRE ON MY MARK, ENSIGN—
AYE, SIR.
—FIRE!
WHAT THE HELL IS THAT?

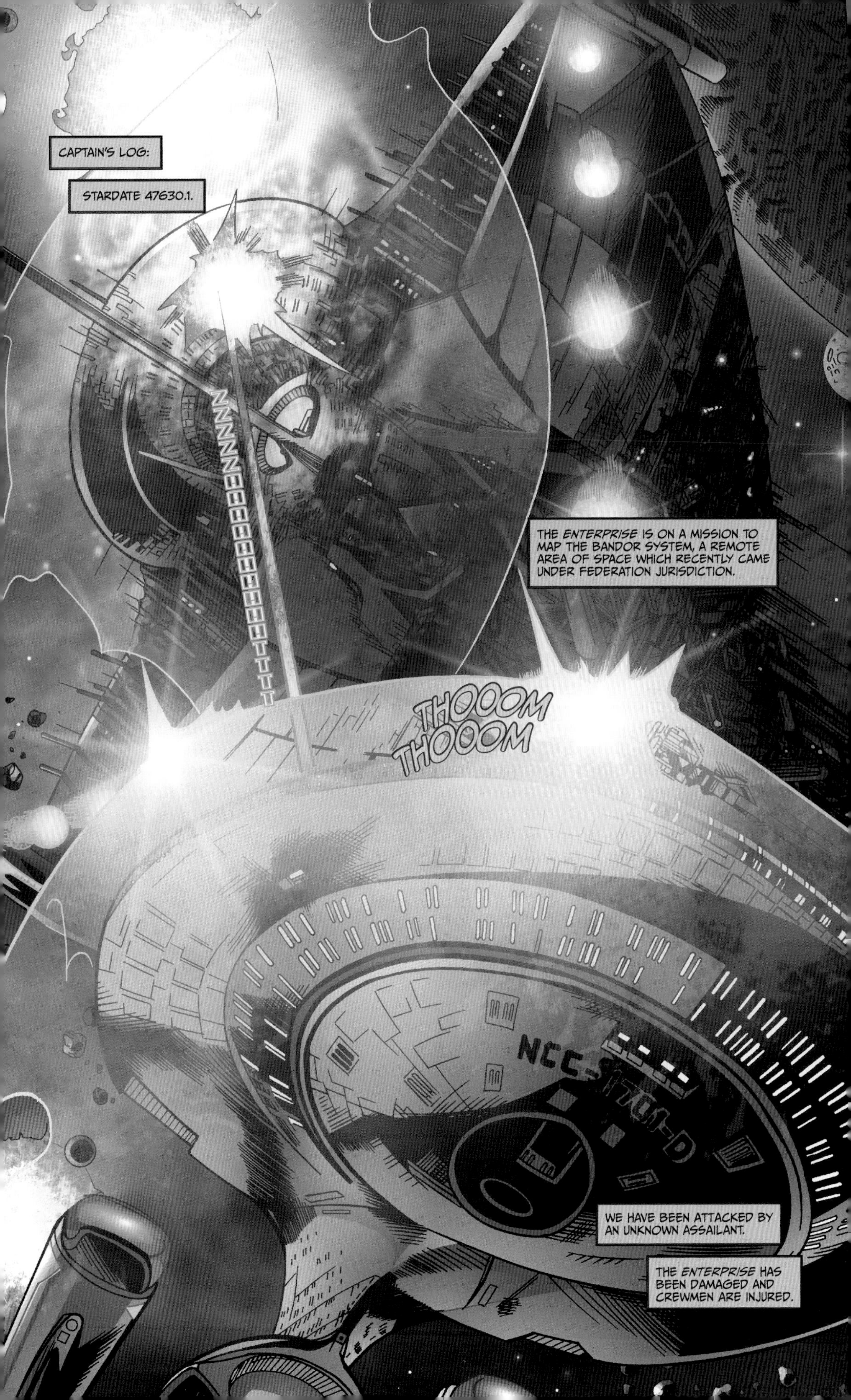
CAPTAIN'S LOG:
STARDATE 47630.1.
ZZZZZZOOOOOOOOOOOOOTTTTT
THE *ENTERPRISE* IS ON A MISSION TO MAP THE BANDOR SYSTEM, A REMOTE AREA OF SPACE WHICH RECENTLY CAME UNDER FEDERATION JURISDICTION.
THOOOM THOOOM
NCC-1701-D
WE HAVE BEEN ATTACKED BY AN UNKNOWN ASSAILANT.
THE *ENTERPRISE* HAS BEEN DAMAGED AND CREWMEN ARE INJURED.

BRING US AROUND, MR. KARP.

YOU'RE LATE, MR. WORF—

—TAKE YOUR STATION.

GGRRRRR—!

THRUNNNCHT
THRUNNNCHT

FIRE!

ZZZZZOMMAAAHUUUTTT

54

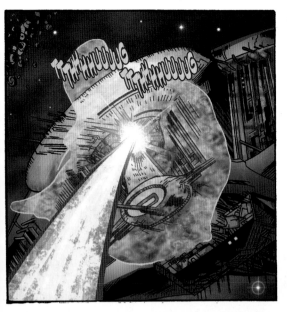

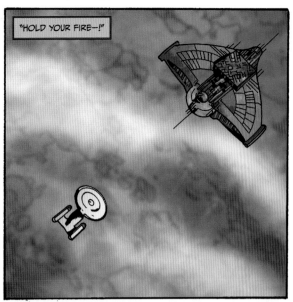

TTTHHHOUUUG
TTTHHHOUUUG
"HOLD YOUR FIRE--!"
OPEN A HAILING FREQUENCY.
CAPTAIN, THE ALIEN VESSEL IS POWERING ENGINES...
ZZZZZHHHHHMMMMMM

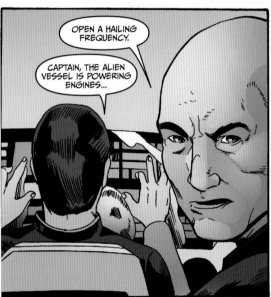

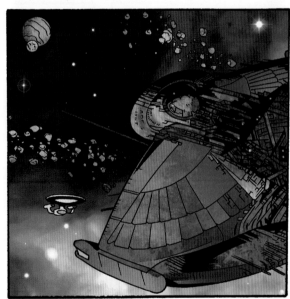

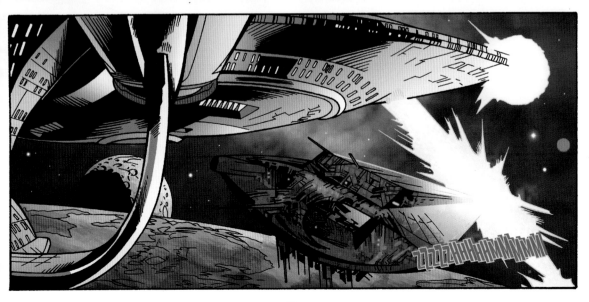

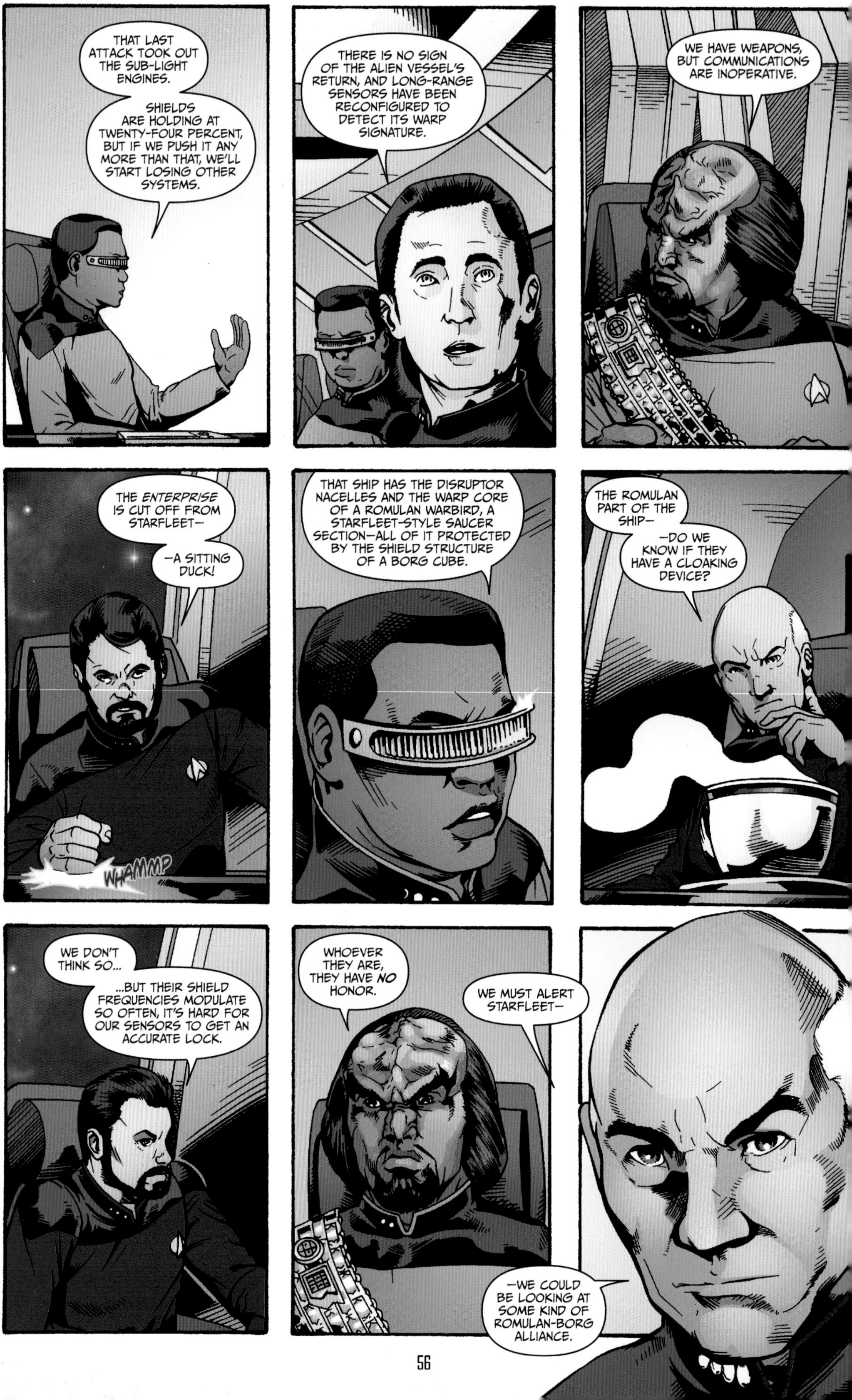
THAT LAST ATTACK TOOK OUT THE SUB-LIGHT ENGINES.
SHIELDS ARE HOLDING AT TWENTY-FOUR PERCENT, BUT IF WE PUSH IT ANY MORE THAN THAT, WE'LL START LOSING OTHER SYSTEMS.
THERE IS NO SIGN OF THE ALIEN VESSEL'S RETURN, AND LONG-RANGE SENSORS HAVE BEEN RECONFIGURED TO DETECT ITS WARP SIGNATURE.
WE HAVE WEAPONS, BUT COMMUNICATIONS ARE INOPERATIVE.
THE *ENTERPRISE* IS CUT OFF FROM STARFLEET—
—A SITTING DUCK!
WHAMMP
THAT SHIP HAS THE DISRUPTOR NACELLES AND THE WARP CORE OF A ROMULAN WARBIRD, A STARFLEET-STYLE SAUCER SECTION—ALL OF IT PROTECTED BY THE SHIELD STRUCTURE OF A BORG CUBE.
THE ROMULAN PART OF THE SHIP—
—DO WE KNOW IF THEY HAVE A CLOAKING DEVICE?
WE DON'T THINK SO...
...BUT THEIR SHIELD FREQUENCIES MODULATE SO OFTEN, IT'S HARD FOR OUR SENSORS TO GET AN ACCURATE LOCK.
WHOEVER THEY ARE, THEY HAVE *NO* HONOR.
WE MUST ALERT STARFLEET—
—WE COULD BE LOOKING AT SOME KIND OF ROMULAN-BORG ALLIANCE.

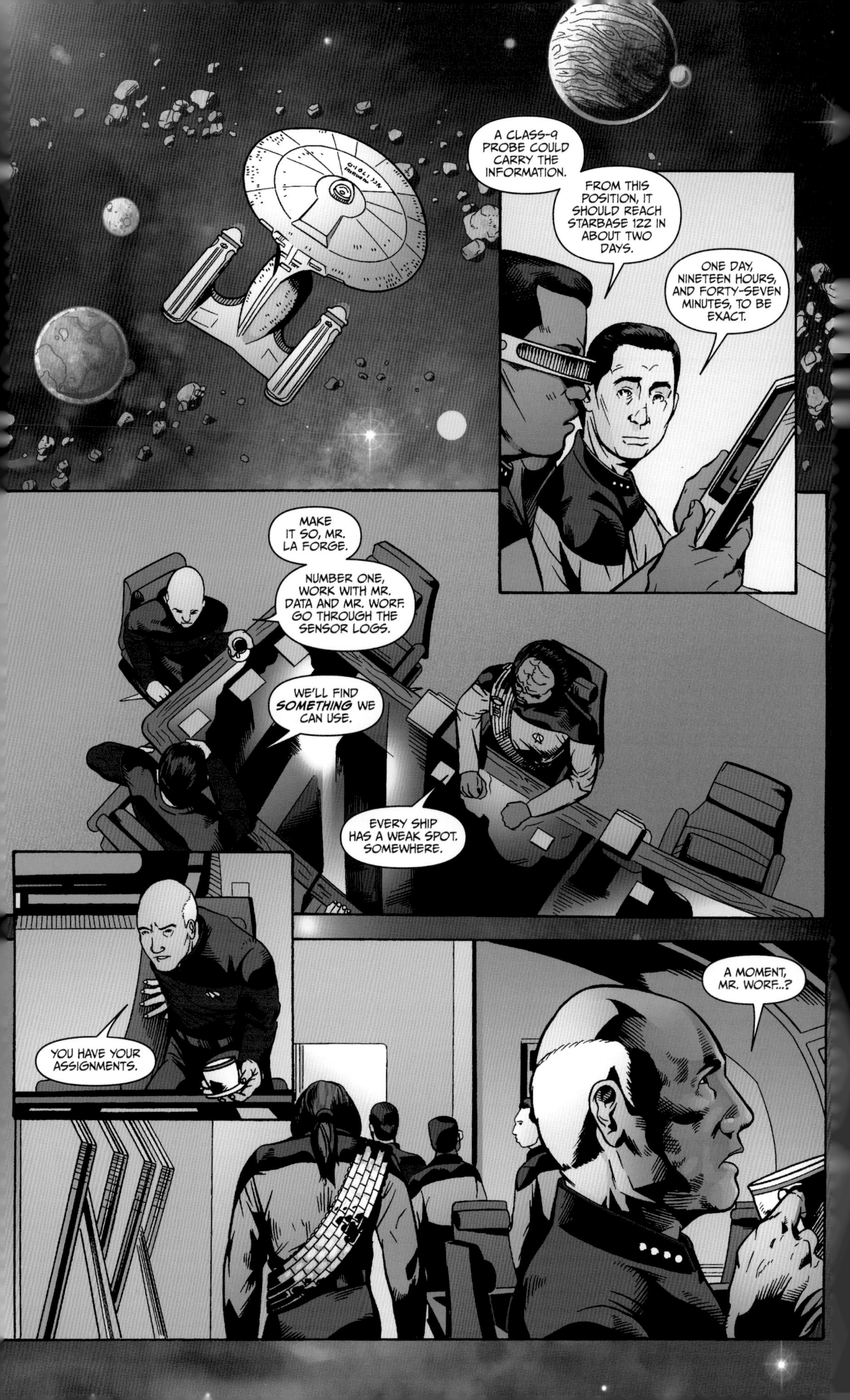
A CLASS-9 PROBE COULD CARRY THE INFORMATION.
FROM THIS POSITION, IT SHOULD REACH STARBASE 122 IN ABOUT TWO DAYS.
ONE DAY, NINETEEN HOURS, AND FORTY-SEVEN MINUTES, TO BE EXACT.
MAKE IT SO, MR. LA FORGE.
NUMBER ONE, WORK WITH MR. DATA AND MR. WORF. GO THROUGH THE SENSOR LOGS.
WE'LL FIND *SOMETHING* WE CAN USE.
EVERY SHIP HAS A WEAK SPOT. SOMEWHERE.
YOU HAVE YOUR ASSIGNMENTS.
A MOMENT, MR. WORF...?

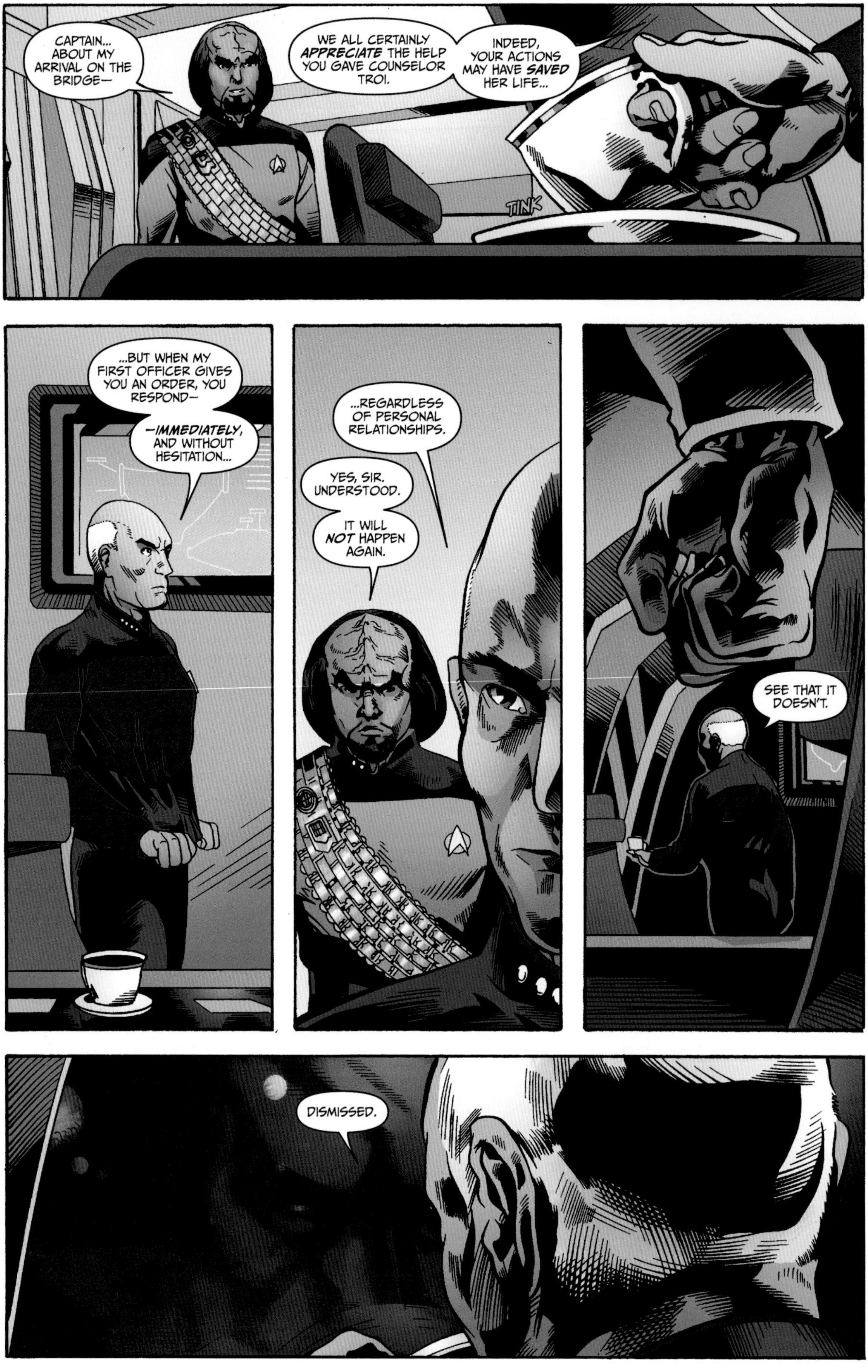
CAPTAIN... ABOUT MY ARRIVAL ON THE BRIDGE—
WE ALL CERTAINLY APPRECIATE THE HELP YOU GAVE COUNSELOR TROI.
INDEED, YOUR ACTIONS MAY HAVE SAVED HER LIFE...
TINK
...BUT WHEN MY FIRST OFFICER GIVES YOU AN ORDER, YOU RESPOND—
—IMMEDIATELY, AND WITHOUT HESITATION...
...REGARDLESS OF PERSONAL RELATIONSHIPS.
YES, SIR. UNDERSTOOD.
IT WILL NOT HAPPEN AGAIN.
SEE THAT IT DOESN'T.
DISMISSED.

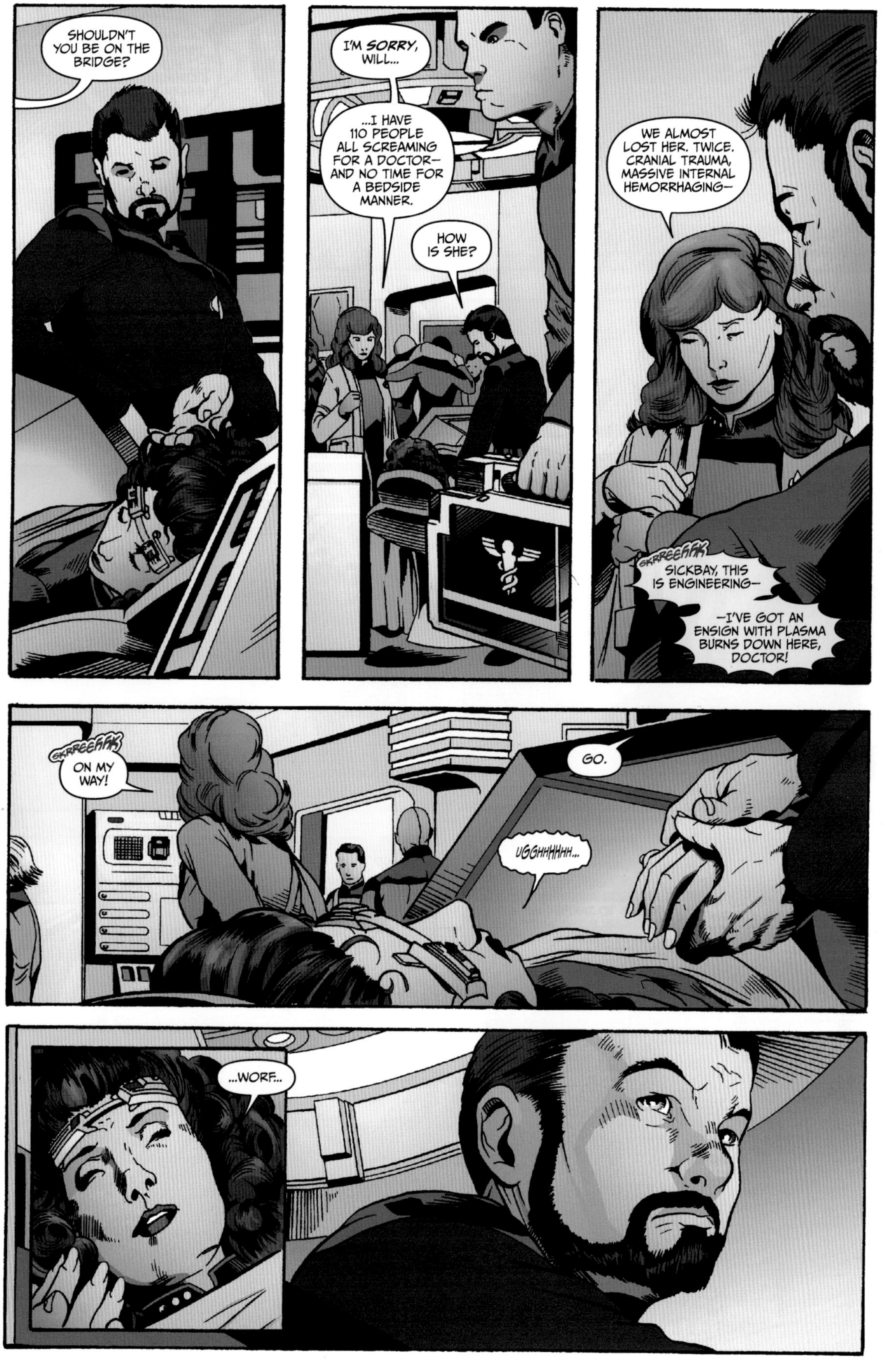
SHOULDN'T YOU BE ON THE BRIDGE?
I'M SORRY, WILL...
...I HAVE 110 PEOPLE ALL SCREAMING FOR A DOCTOR— AND NO TIME FOR A BEDSIDE MANNER.
HOW IS SHE?
WE ALMOST LOST HER. TWICE. CRANIAL TRAUMA, MASSIVE INTERNAL HEMORRHAGING—
SKRREEFFFK
SICKBAY, THIS IS ENGINEERING—
—I'VE GOT AN ENSIGN WITH PLASMA BURNS DOWN HERE, DOCTOR!
SKRREEFFFK
ON MY WAY!
GO.
UGGHHHHHH...
...WORF...

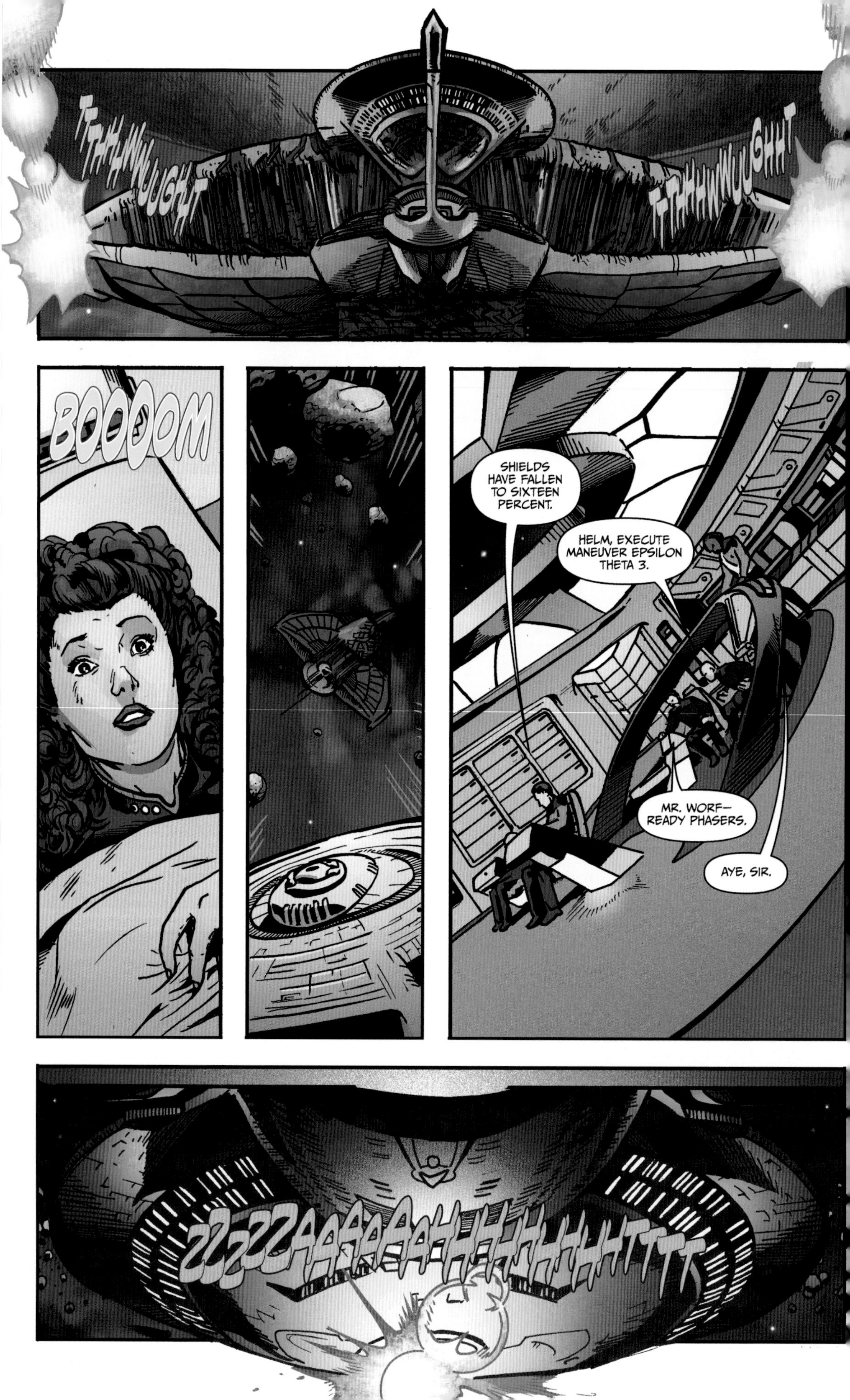
TTTHHWNUUGHHT
TTTHHWNUUGHHT
BOOOOM
SHIELDS HAVE FALLEN TO SIXTEEN PERCENT.
HELM, EXECUTE MANEUVER EPSILON THETA 3.
MR. WORF— READY PHASERS.
AYE, SIR.
ZZZZAAAAAHHHHHHHHHTTTTT

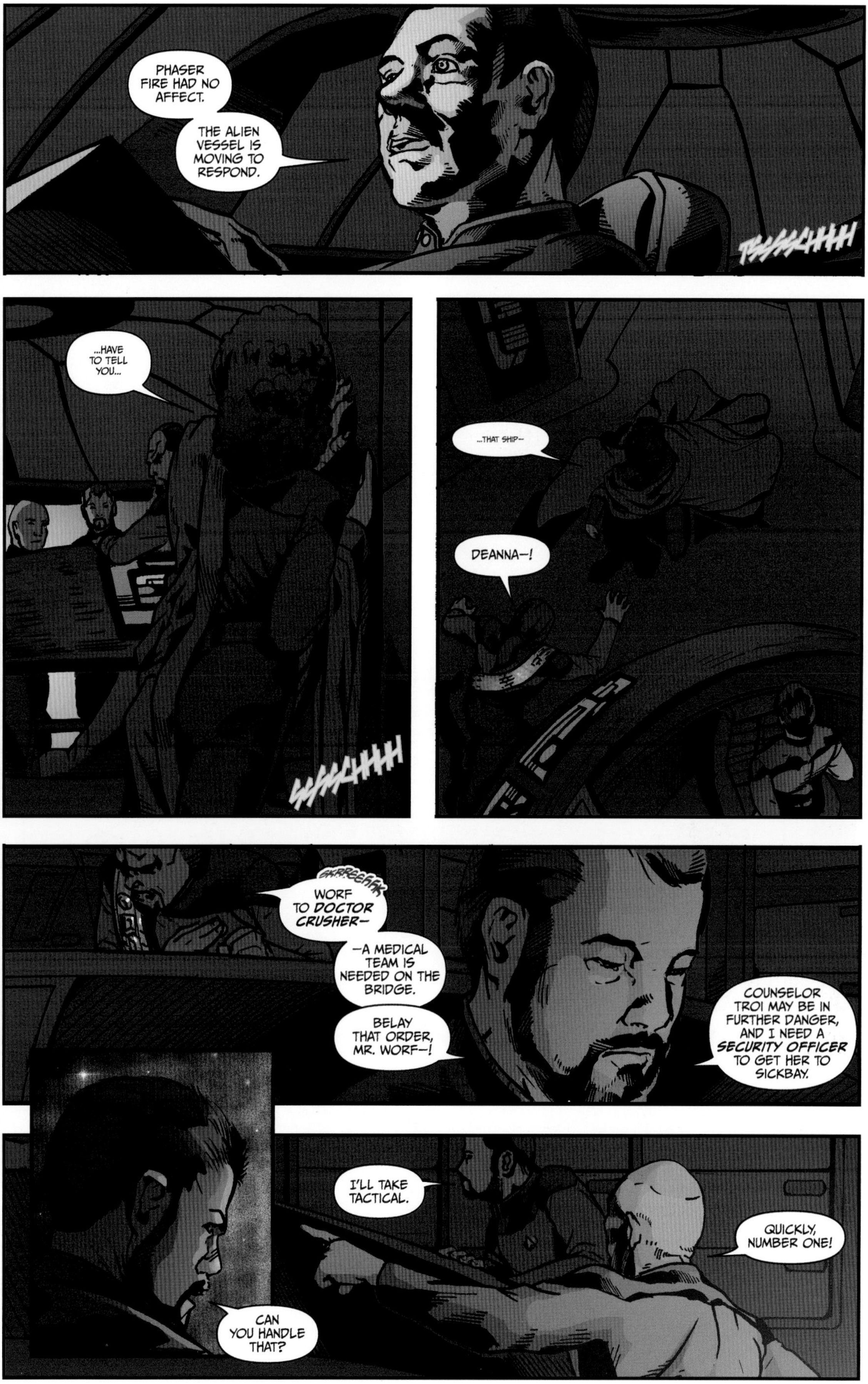
PHASER FIRE HAD NO AFFECT.
THE ALIEN VESSEL IS MOVING TO RESPOND.
TSSSSCHHHH
...HAVE TO TELL YOU...
SSSSCHHHH
...THAT SHIP--
DEANNA--!
SKRREEEEK
WORF TO DOCTOR CRUSHER--
--A MEDICAL TEAM IS NEEDED ON THE BRIDGE.
BELAY THAT ORDER, MR. WORF--!
COUNSELOR TROI MAY BE IN FURTHER DANGER, AND I NEED A SECURITY OFFICER TO GET HER TO SICKBAY.
I'LL TAKE TACTICAL.
QUICKLY, NUMBER ONE!
CAN YOU HANDLE THAT?

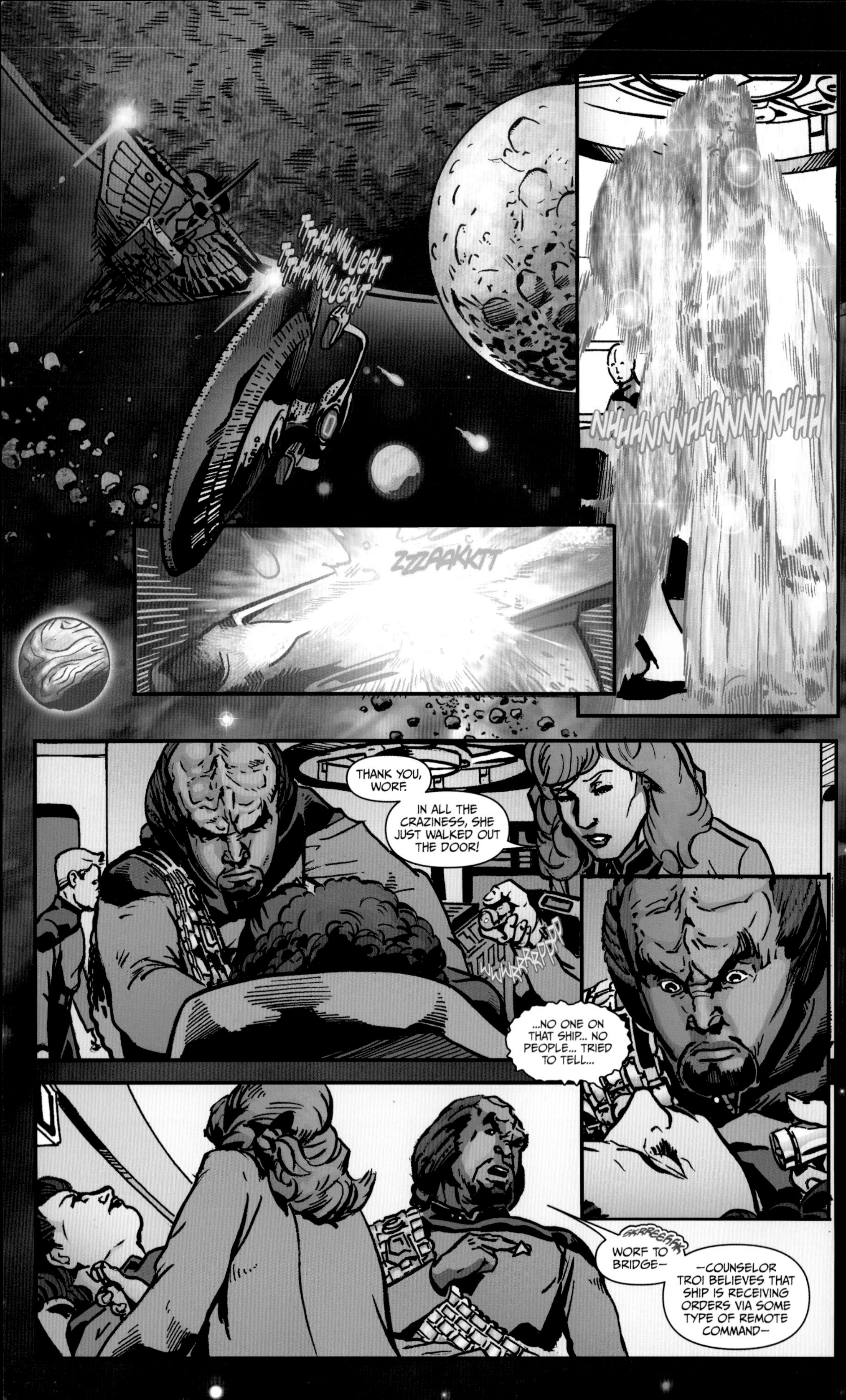
TTTHHWNNUUGHT
TTTHHWNNUUGHT
NHHHNNNHHNNNNNNHHH
ZZZAAKKTT
THANK YOU, WORF.
IN ALL THE CRAZINESS, SHE JUST WALKED OUT THE DOOR!
WWWRRRRPPP
...NO ONE ON THAT SHIP... NO PEOPLE... TRIED TO TELL...
SKRREEEHK
WORF TO BRIDGE—
—COUNSELOR TROI BELIEVES THAT SHIP IS RECEIVING ORDERS VIA SOME TYPE OF REMOTE COMMAND—

—THERE IS *NO ONE* ABOARD.

IF THAT'S TRUE, ALL WE NEED TO DO IS DISRUPT THE SIGNAL.

THE LIEUTENANT SAID THE SHIP RECEIVED SEVERAL COMMUNICATIONS DURING OUR FIRST ENCOUNTER.

MR. DATA, WHAT IS THE *MOST* EFFECTIVE METHOD OF SEVERING SUB-SPACE COMMUNICATIONS?

SEVERAL TYPES OF RADIATION—

THE *MOST* EFFECTIVE, DATA.

—AN INTER-RECEPTIVE NETWORK OF SUB-SPACE BEACONS STRATEGICALLY PLACED AT POINTS AROUND THE SHIP'S EXTERIOR WOULD BE BEST...

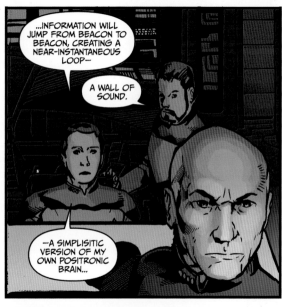

...INFORMATION WILL JUMP FROM BEACON TO BEACON, CREATING A NEAR-INSTANTANEOUS LOOP—

A WALL OF SOUND.

—A SIMPLISITIC VERSION OF MY OWN POSITRONIC BRAIN...

...POWERFUL ENOUGH TO STOP ANY EXTERIOR COMMUNICATIONS FROM REACHING THE SHIP—

—BUT THE BEACONS NEED TO BE PRECISELY POSITIONED. TO ACCOMPLISH THAT, WE SHOULD GET AS CLOSE TO THE SHIP AS POSSIBLE.

SKRREEAAK

MR. LA FORGE! CAN YOU GIVE ME *MANEUVERING* THRUSTERS?

THAT'S ALL WE'VE GOT LEFT, CAPTAIN.

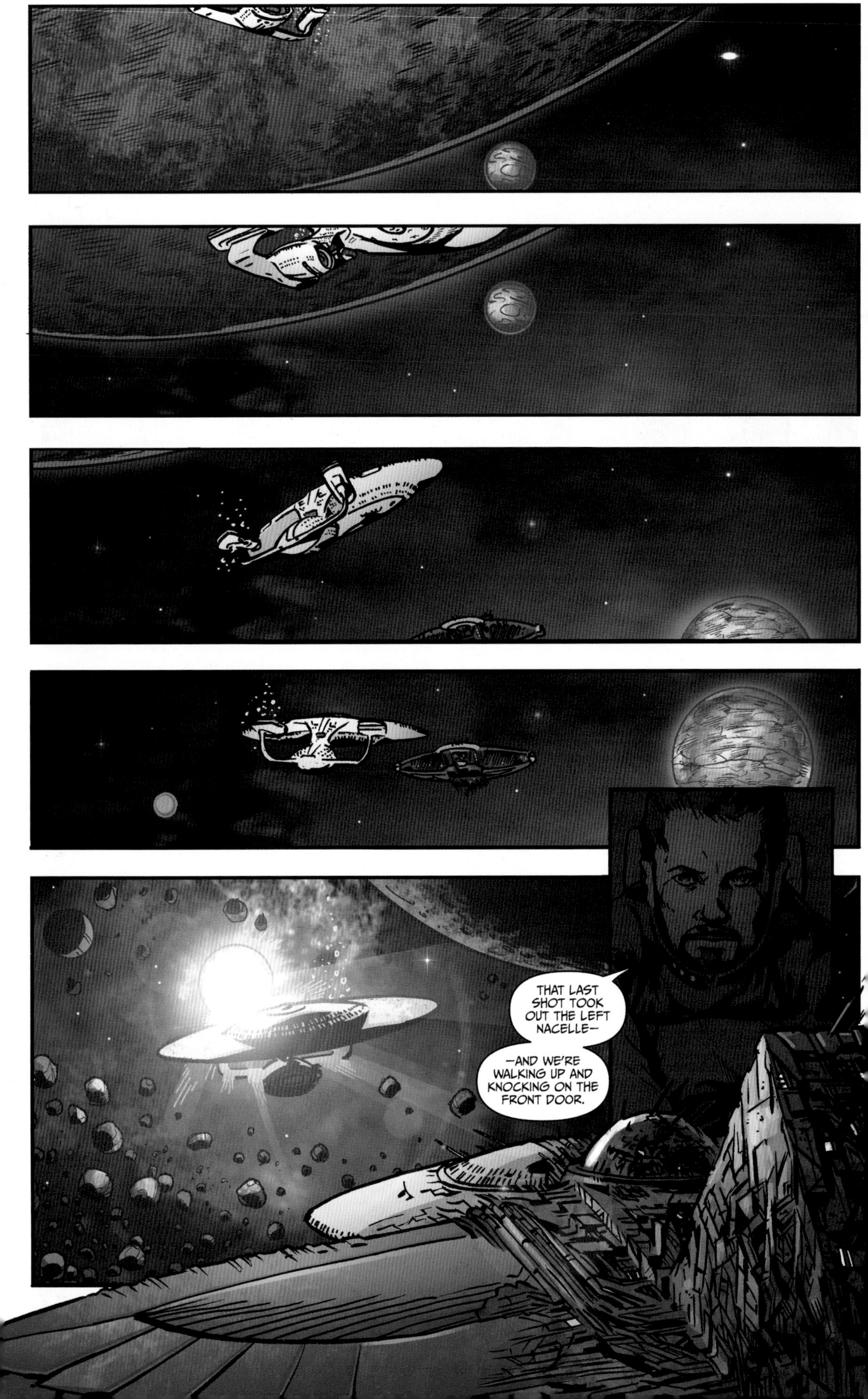
THAT LAST SHOT TOOK OUT THE LEFT NACELLE—
—AND WE'RE WALKING UP AND KNOCKING ON THE FRONT DOOR.

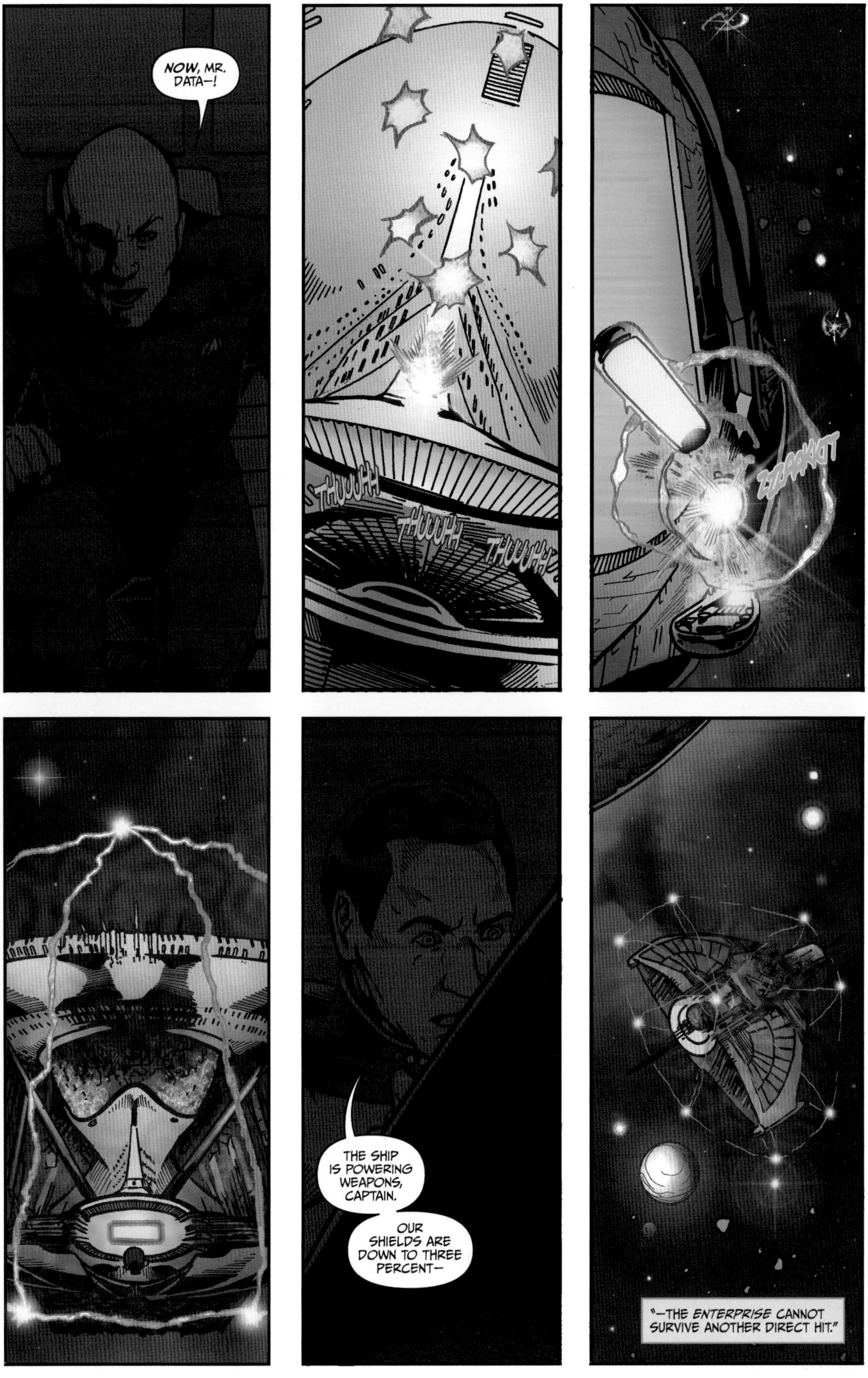
NOW, MR. DATA—!
THUUUHH
THUUUHH
THUUUHH
ZZZAAKKTT
THE SHIP IS POWERING WEAPONS, CAPTAIN.
OUR SHIELDS ARE DOWN TO THREE PERCENT—
"—THE *ENTERPRISE* CANNOT SURVIVE ANOTHER DIRECT HIT."

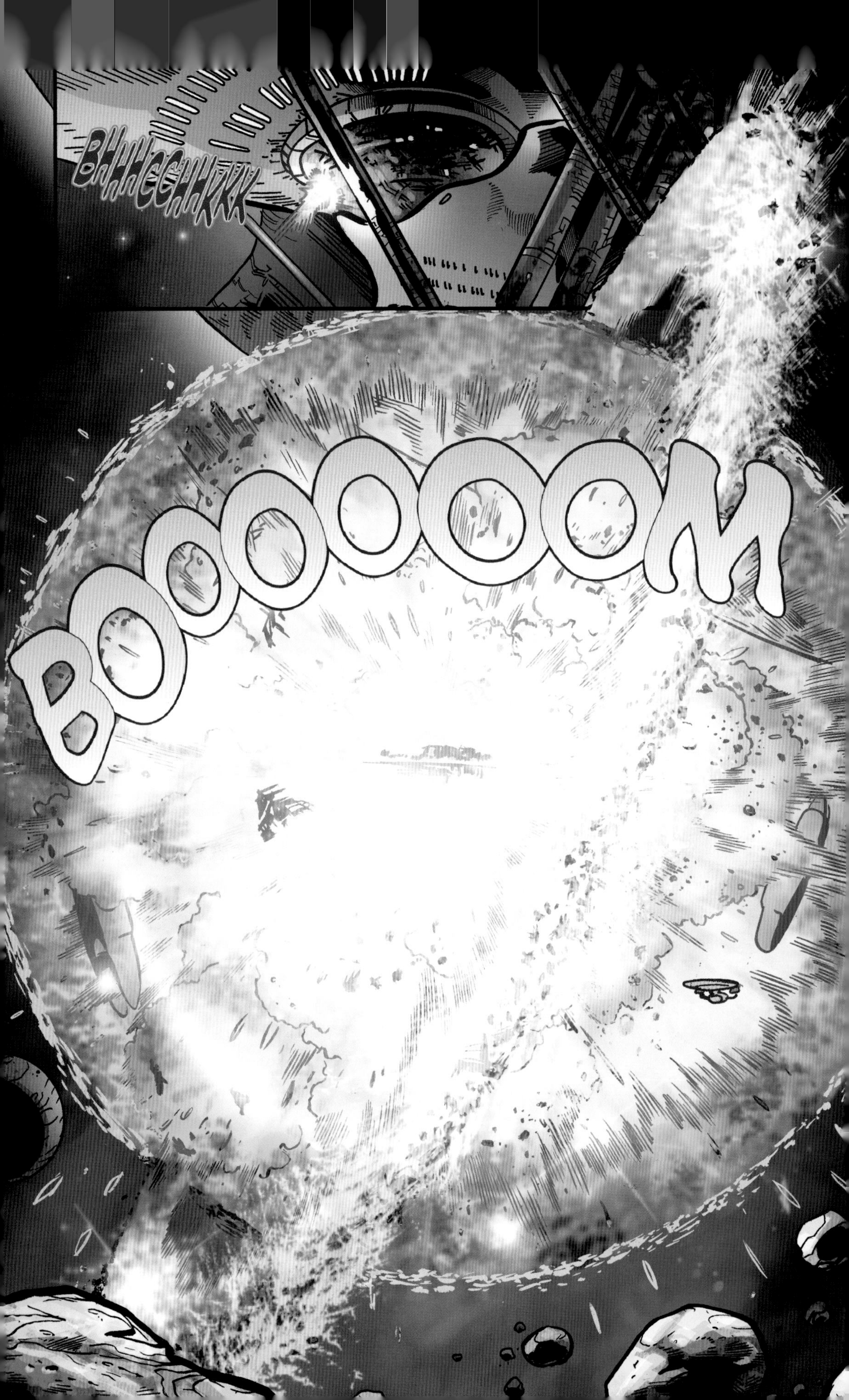
BHHHCCHHKKK
BOOOOOOM

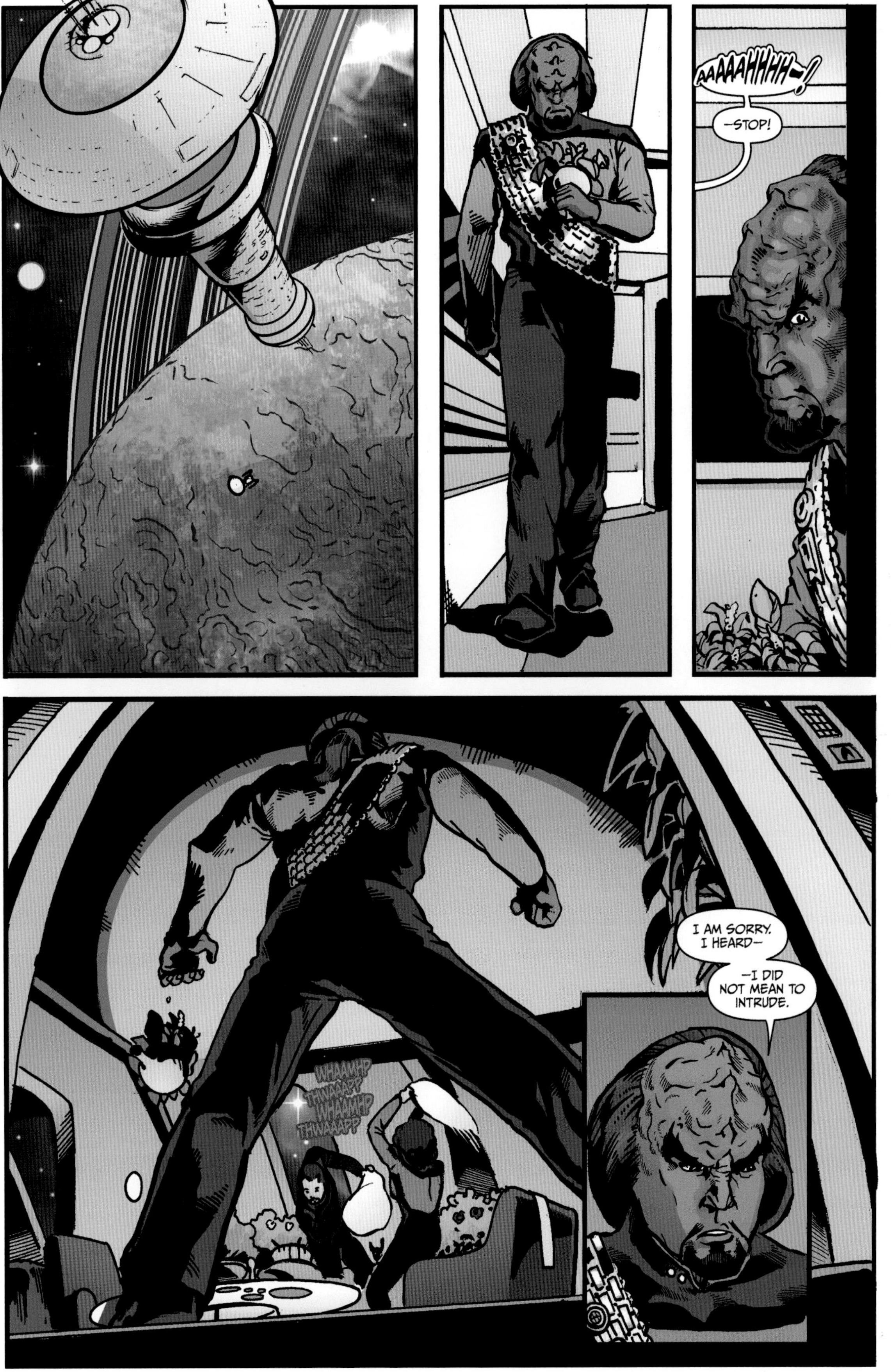
AAAAAHHHH—!
—STOP!
I AM SORRY. I HEARD—
—I DID NOT MEAN TO INTRUDE.
WHAAMHP
THWAAAPP
WHAAMHP
THWAAAPP

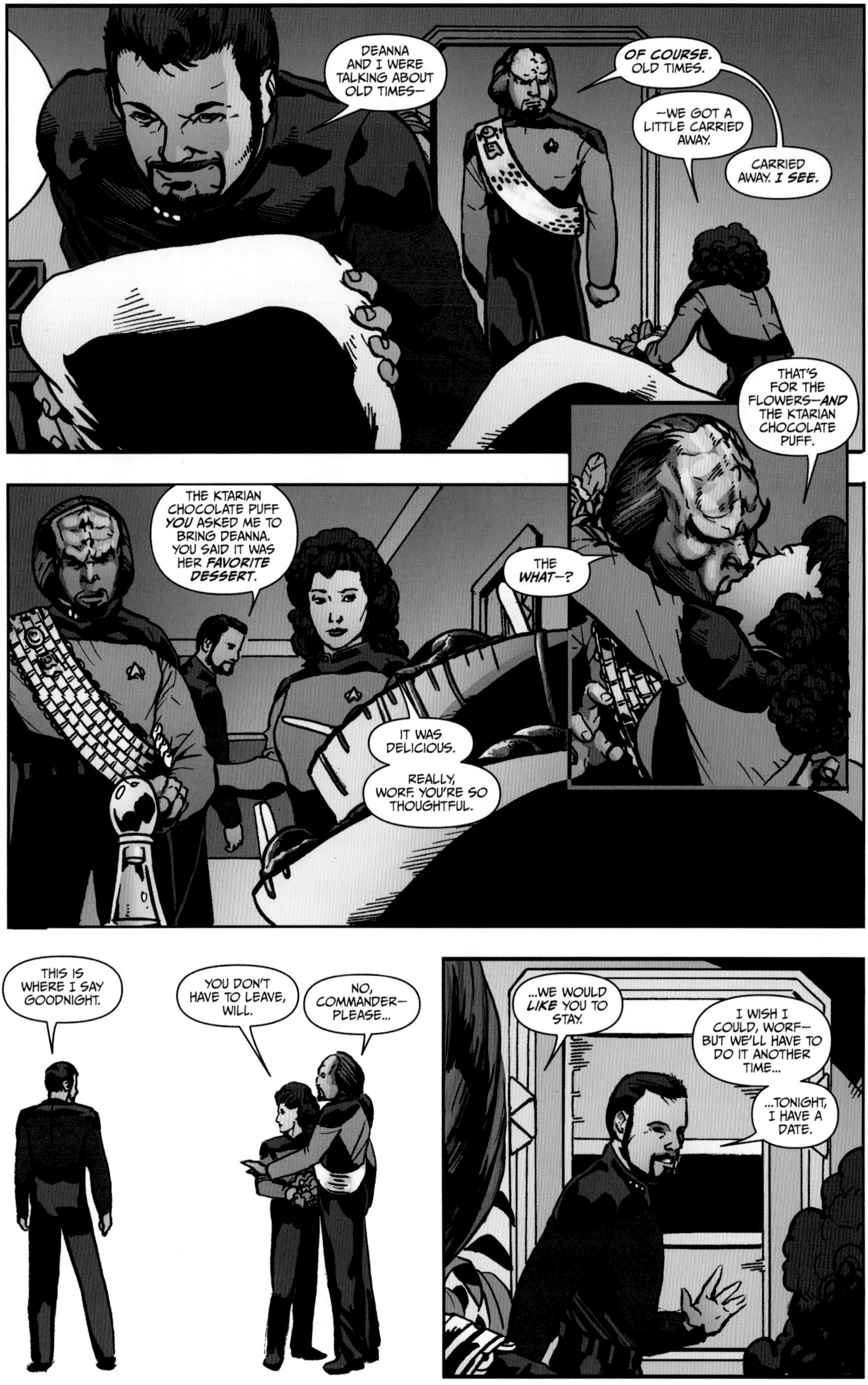
DEANNA AND I WERE TALKING ABOUT OLD TIMES—
OF COURSE. OLD TIMES.
—WE GOT A LITTLE CARRIED AWAY.
CARRIED AWAY. I SEE.
THAT'S FOR THE FLOWERS—AND THE KTARIAN CHOCOLATE PUFF.
THE WHAT—?
THE KTARIAN CHOCOLATE PUFF YOU ASKED ME TO BRING DEANNA. YOU SAID IT WAS HER FAVORITE DESSERT.
IT WAS DELICIOUS.
REALLY, WORF. YOU'RE SO THOUGHTFUL.
THIS IS WHERE I SAY GOODNIGHT.
YOU DON'T HAVE TO LEAVE, WILL.
NO, COMMANDER— PLEASE...
...WE WOULD LIKE YOU TO STAY.
I WISH I COULD, WORF— BUT WE'LL HAVE TO DO IT ANOTHER TIME...
...TONIGHT, I HAVE A DATE.

I WAS SO BUSY WORRYING ABOUT A *CLOAKING DEVICE*—I FORGOT THE ROMULANS ALSO HAVE A HISTORY WITH REMOTE-CONTROLLED VESSELS.

WE CAN ONLY SURMISE THE VESSEL HAD A SELF-DESTRUCT PROTOCOL, IN THE EVENT CONTACT WITH ITS CREATOR WAS EVER BROKEN.

AND STARFLEET HAS NO KNOWLEDGE OF ANY VESSEL OF THIS TYPE?

NONE THAT I HAVE BEEN ABLE TO REVEAL.

THAT SHIP WAS DESIGNED TO DESTROY THE *ENTERPRISE*—

—WE GOT *LUCKY*, DATA.

BUT WE STILL DON'T KNOW WHO OUR ENEMY IS...

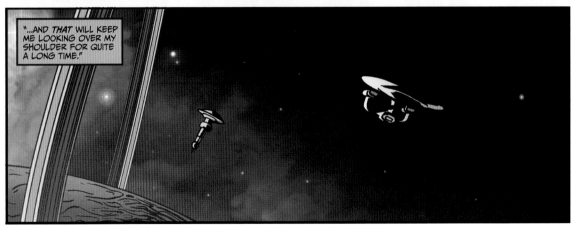

"...AND *THAT* WILL KEEP ME LOOKING OVER MY SHOULDER FOR QUITE A LONG TIME."

PART FOUR: LIGHT OF THE DAY

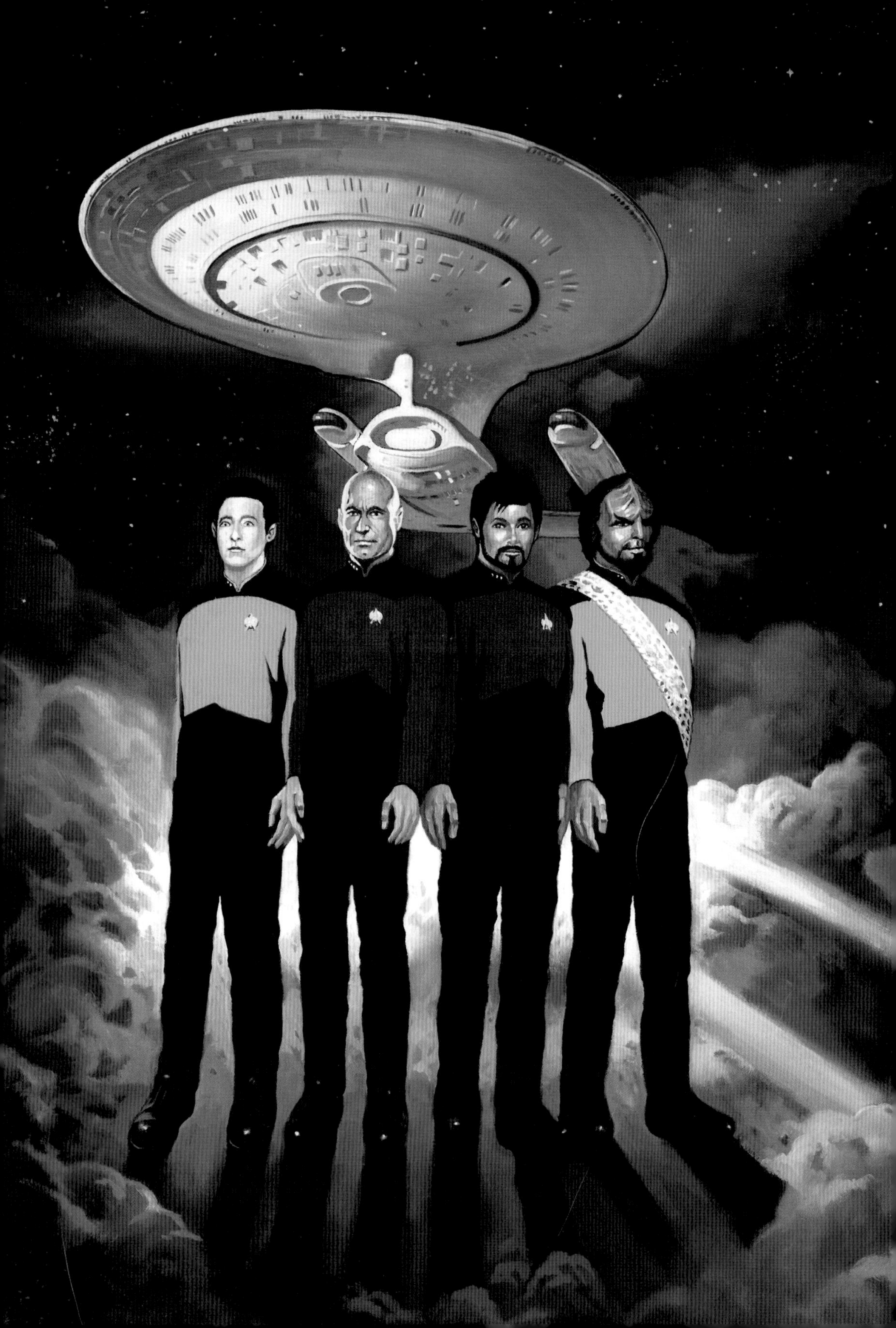

"IT WILL BE *GOOD* TO RETURN TO THE *ENTERPRISE*."

NCC-1701-D

GODDARD

I'M SURE *CAPTAIN PICARD* WILL BE EAGER TO HEAR YOUR REPORT ON OUR STARFLEET BRIEFINGS.

OF COURSE. AS SECURITY CHIEF, IT IS MY *DUTY—*

WORF, I THINK ENSIGN RO'S HAVING A LITTLE *FUN* AT YOUR EXPENSE.

WARNING— INCREASED SOLAR FLARE ACTIVITY.

I'M TAKING US OUT OF WARP.

PICKING UP A *MASSIVE* WAVE—!

ODARD

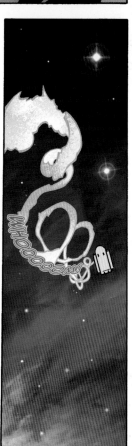

WHOOOOOM

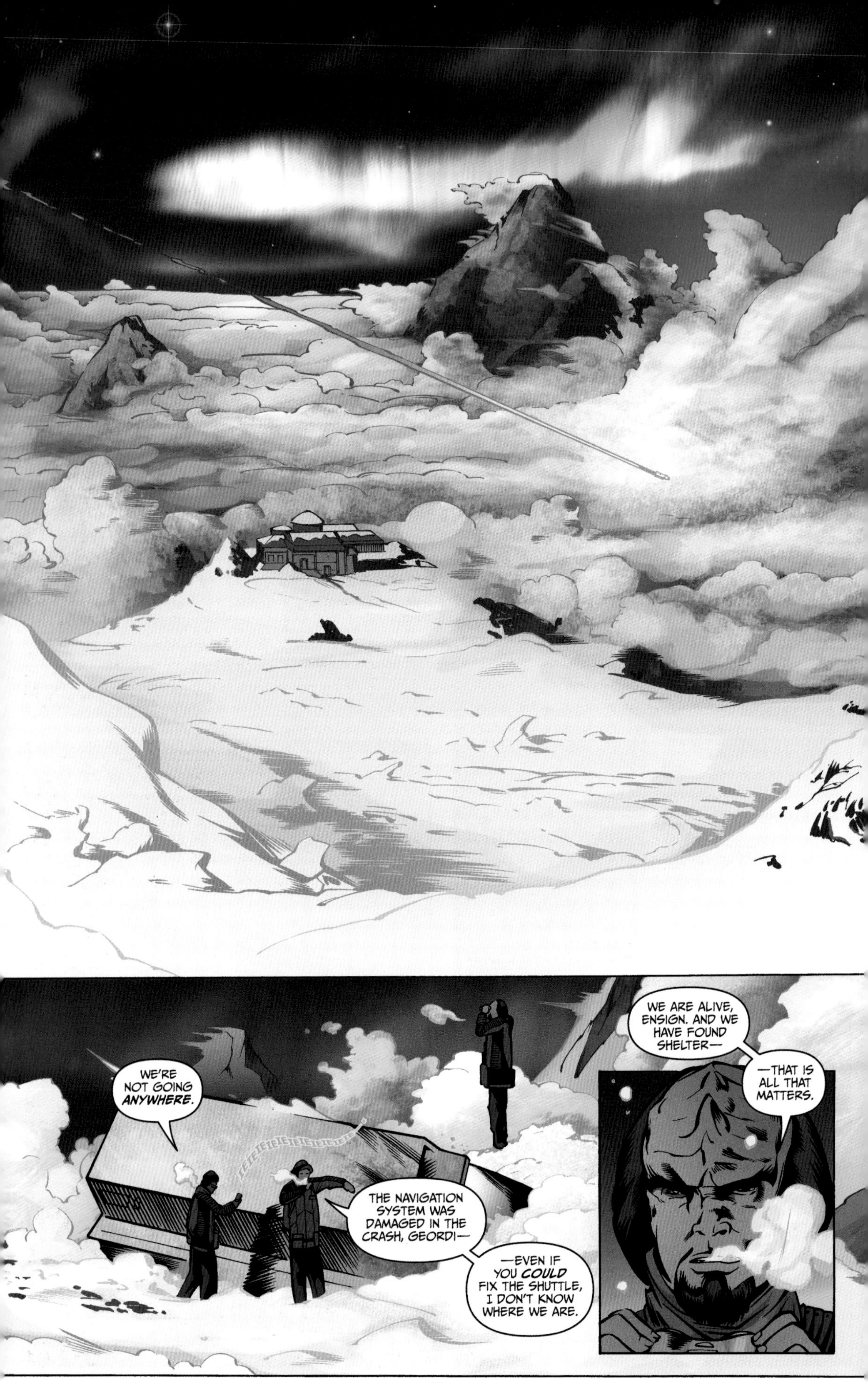
WE'RE NOT GOING *ANYWHERE.*
THE NAVIGATION SYSTEM WAS DAMAGED IN THE CRASH, GEORDI—
—EVEN IF YOU *COULD* FIX THE SHUTTLE, I DON'T KNOW WHERE WE ARE.
WE ARE ALIVE, ENSIGN. AND WE HAVE FOUND SHELTER—
—THAT IS ALL THAT MATTERS.

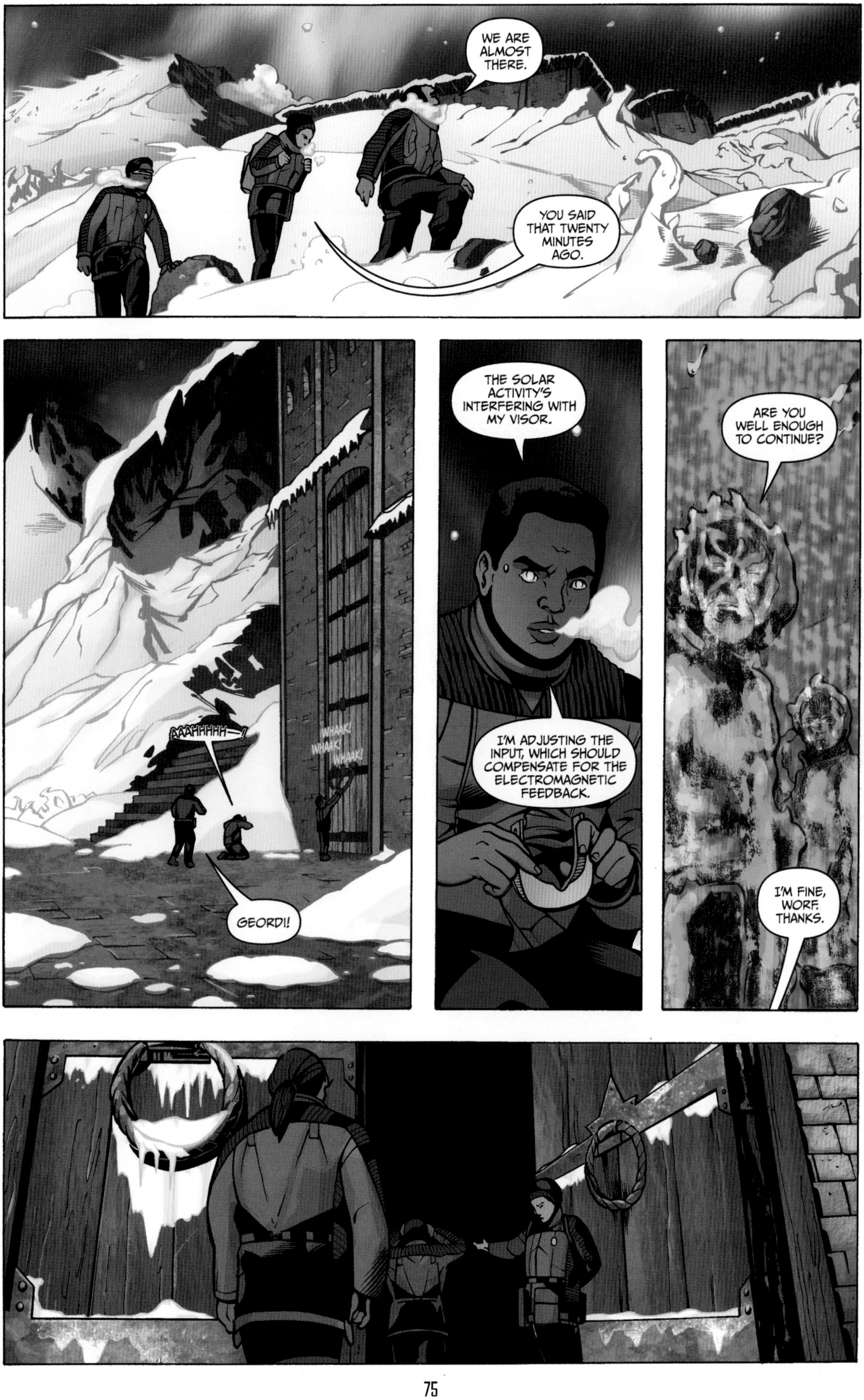
WE ARE ALMOST THERE.
YOU SAID THAT TWENTY MINUTES AGO.
AAAHHHHH—!
WHAAK! WHAAK! WHAAK!
GEORDI!
THE SOLAR ACTIVITY'S INTERFERING WITH MY VISOR.
I'M ADJUSTING THE INPUT, WHICH SHOULD COMPENSATE FOR THE ELECTROMAGNETIC FEEDBACK.
ARE YOU WELL ENOUGH TO CONTINUE?
I'M FINE, WORF. THANKS.

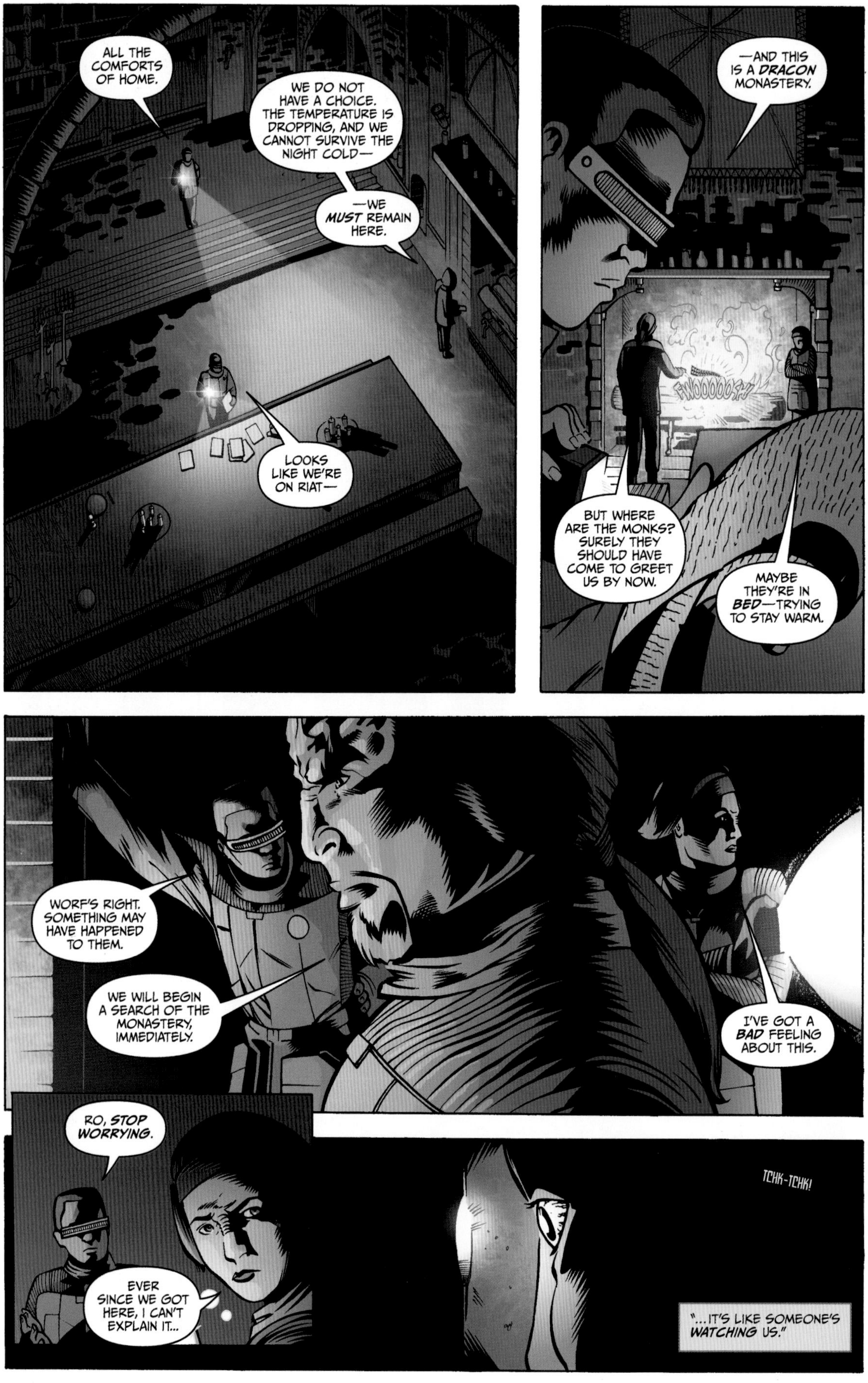
ALL THE COMFORTS OF HOME.
WE DO NOT HAVE A CHOICE. THE TEMPERATURE IS DROPPING, AND WE CANNOT SURVIVE THE NIGHT COLD—
—WE MUST REMAIN HERE.
LOOKS LIKE WE'RE ON RIAT—
—AND THIS IS A DRACON MONASTERY.
FWOOOOOSH
BUT WHERE ARE THE MONKS? SURELY THEY SHOULD HAVE COME TO GREET US BY NOW.
MAYBE THEY'RE IN BED—TRYING TO STAY WARM.
WORF'S RIGHT. SOMETHING MAY HAVE HAPPENED TO THEM.
WE WILL BEGIN A SEARCH OF THE MONASTERY, IMMEDIATELY.
I'VE GOT A BAD FEELING ABOUT THIS.
RO, STOP WORRYING.
EVER SINCE WE GOT HERE, I CAN'T EXPLAIN IT...
TCHK-TCHK!
"...IT'S LIKE SOMEONE'S WATCHING US."

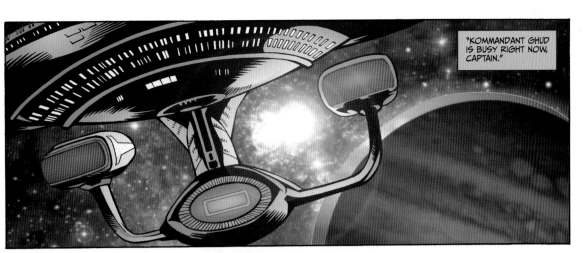

"KOMMANDANT GHUD IS BUSY RIGHT NOW, CAPTAIN."

HIS NAME IS PRONOUNCED "HUD," ENSIGN. ON *WYATH*, THE "G" IS SILENT...

YES, *SIR!*

AND, FRANKLY, I DOUBT ANYONE WOULD ACCUSE HIM OF BEING "*GOOD*."

...MAY THE LIGHT SHINE ON US ALL.

YOU *KNOW* ME?

KOMMANDANT GHUD, THE *SCIENTIST* WHO TOOK CONTROL OF THE PLANET WYATH—

—AND DESTROYED THE ECOLOGY OF A DEVELOPING WORLD FOR HIS OWN PROFIT...

...WHEN THE PEOPLE ROSE UP, YOU *FLED* THE SYSTEM, FUELING A CIVIL WAR.

AND FOR MY RETURN, MY PEOPLE REQUESTED *THESE* ACCOMMODATIONS?

INDEED, KOMMANDANT. THEY *INSISTED*.

I AM NOT THE SELFISH DESPOT MY PEOPLE THINK I AM.

I HAVE FOUND *THE LIGHT*.

I AM NOT HERE TO JUDGE.

AND YET YOU HAVE ALREADY MADE UP YOUR MIND.

SKREEEET—!

RIKER TO CAPTAIN PICARD—

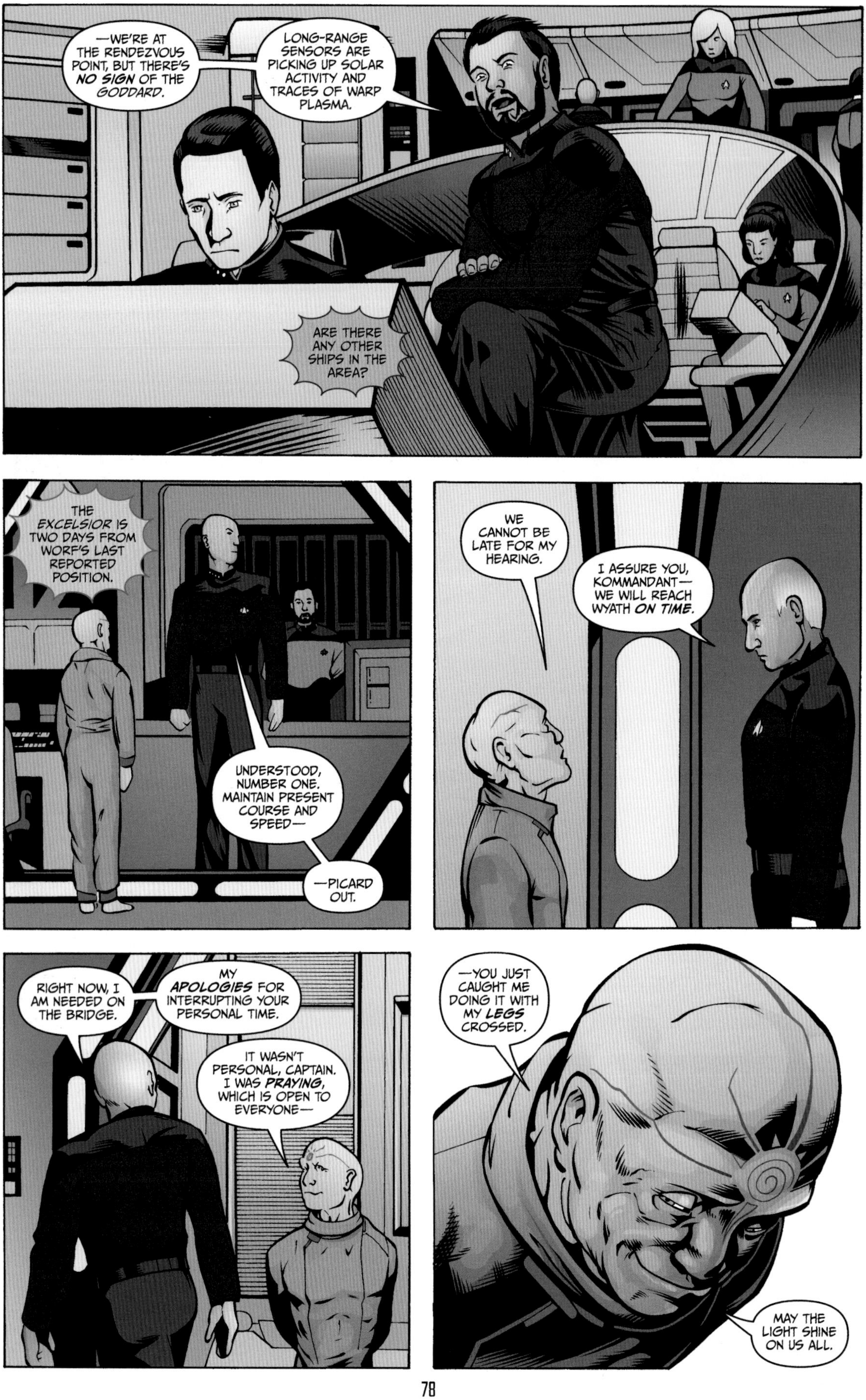
—WE'RE AT THE RENDEZVOUS POINT, BUT THERE'S NO SIGN OF THE GODDARD.
LONG-RANGE SENSORS ARE PICKING UP SOLAR ACTIVITY AND TRACES OF WARP PLASMA.
ARE THERE ANY OTHER SHIPS IN THE AREA?
THE EXCELSIOR IS TWO DAYS FROM WORF'S LAST REPORTED POSITION.
UNDERSTOOD, NUMBER ONE. MAINTAIN PRESENT COURSE AND SPEED—
—PICARD OUT.
WE CANNOT BE LATE FOR MY HEARING.
I ASSURE YOU, KOMMANDANT—WE WILL REACH WYATH ON TIME.
RIGHT NOW, I AM NEEDED ON THE BRIDGE.
MY APOLOGIES FOR INTERRUPTING YOUR PERSONAL TIME.
IT WASN'T PERSONAL, CAPTAIN. I WAS PRAYING, WHICH IS OPEN TO EVERYONE—
—YOU JUST CAUGHT ME DOING IT WITH MY LEGS CROSSED.
MAY THE LIGHT SHINE ON US ALL.

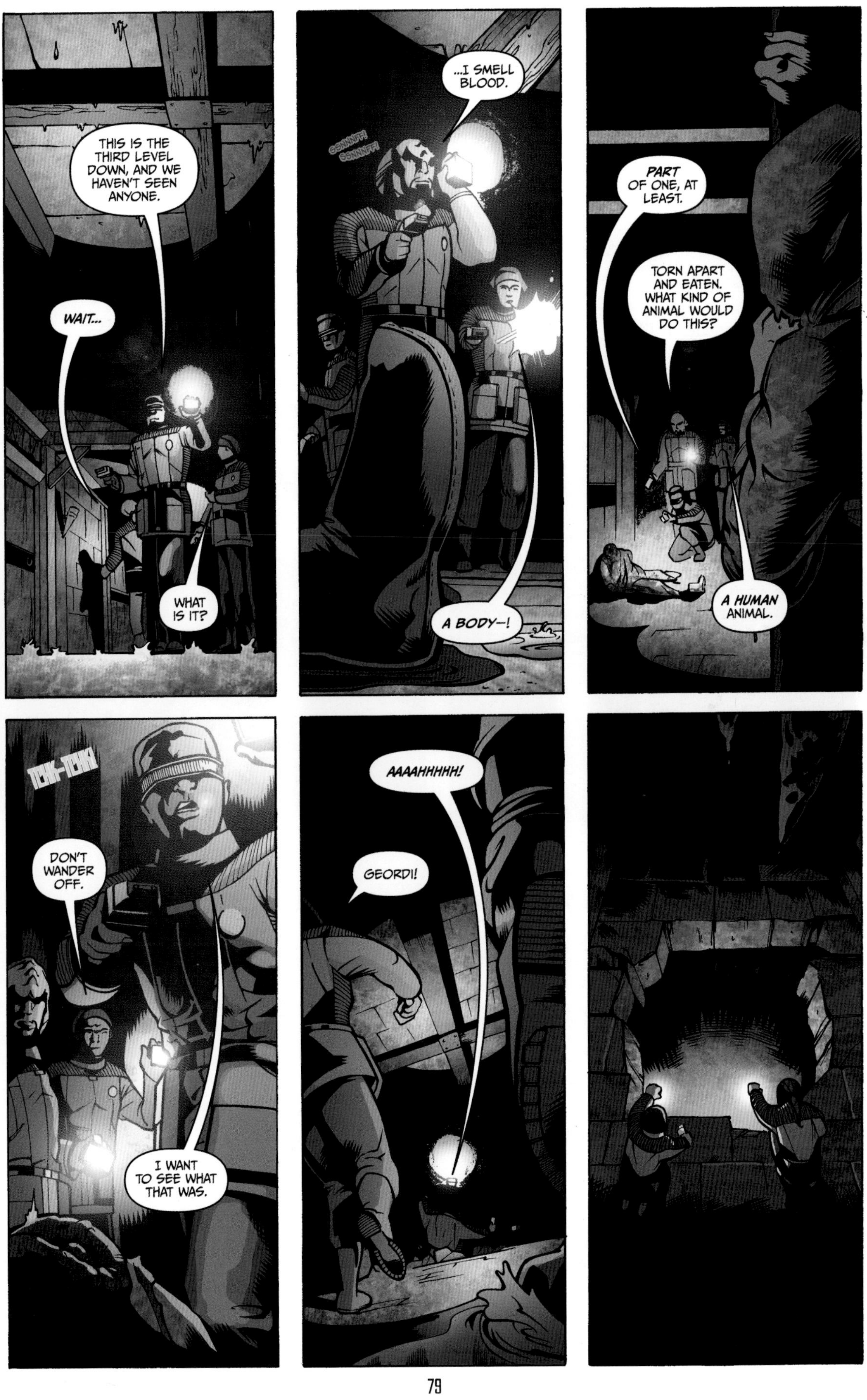
THIS IS THE THIRD LEVEL DOWN, AND WE HAVEN'T SEEN ANYONE.
WAIT...
WHAT IS IT?
SSNNFF! SSNNFF!
...I SMELL BLOOD.
A BODY--!
PART OF ONE, AT LEAST.
TORN APART AND EATEN. WHAT KIND OF ANIMAL WOULD DO THIS?
A HUMAN ANIMAL.
TCHK-TCHK
DON'T WANDER OFF.
I WANT TO SEE WHAT THAT WAS.
AAAAHHHHH!
GEORDI!

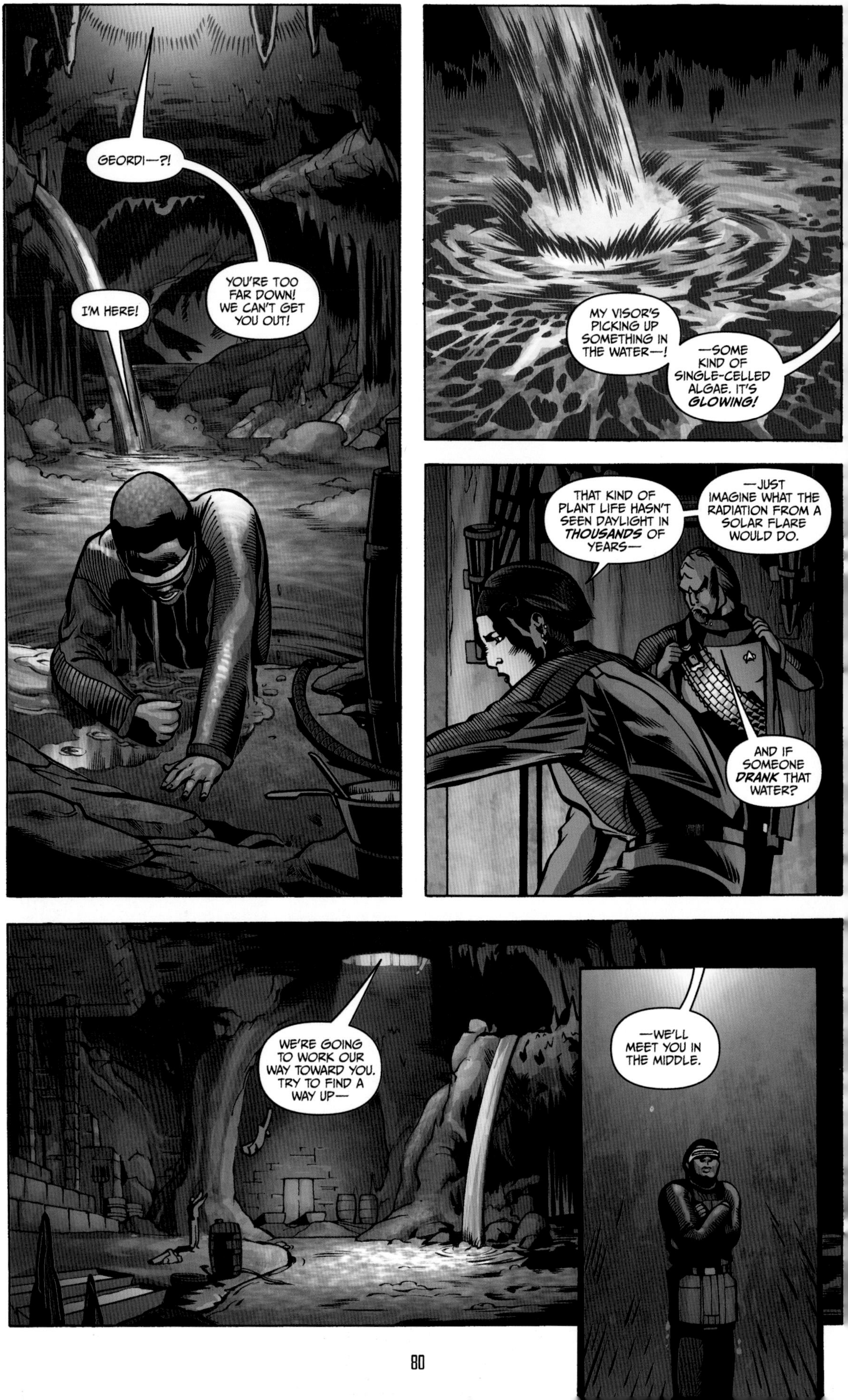
GEORDI—?!
YOU'RE TOO FAR DOWN! WE CAN'T GET YOU OUT!
I'M HERE!
MY VISOR'S PICKING UP SOMETHING IN THE WATER—!
—SOME KIND OF SINGLE-CELLED ALGAE. IT'S *GLOWING!*
THAT KIND OF PLANT LIFE HASN'T SEEN DAYLIGHT IN *THOUSANDS* OF YEARS—
—JUST IMAGINE WHAT THE RADIATION FROM A SOLAR FLARE WOULD DO.
AND IF SOMEONE *DRANK* THAT WATER?
WE'RE GOING TO WORK OUR WAY TOWARD YOU. TRY TO FIND A WAY UP—
—WE'LL MEET YOU IN THE MIDDLE.

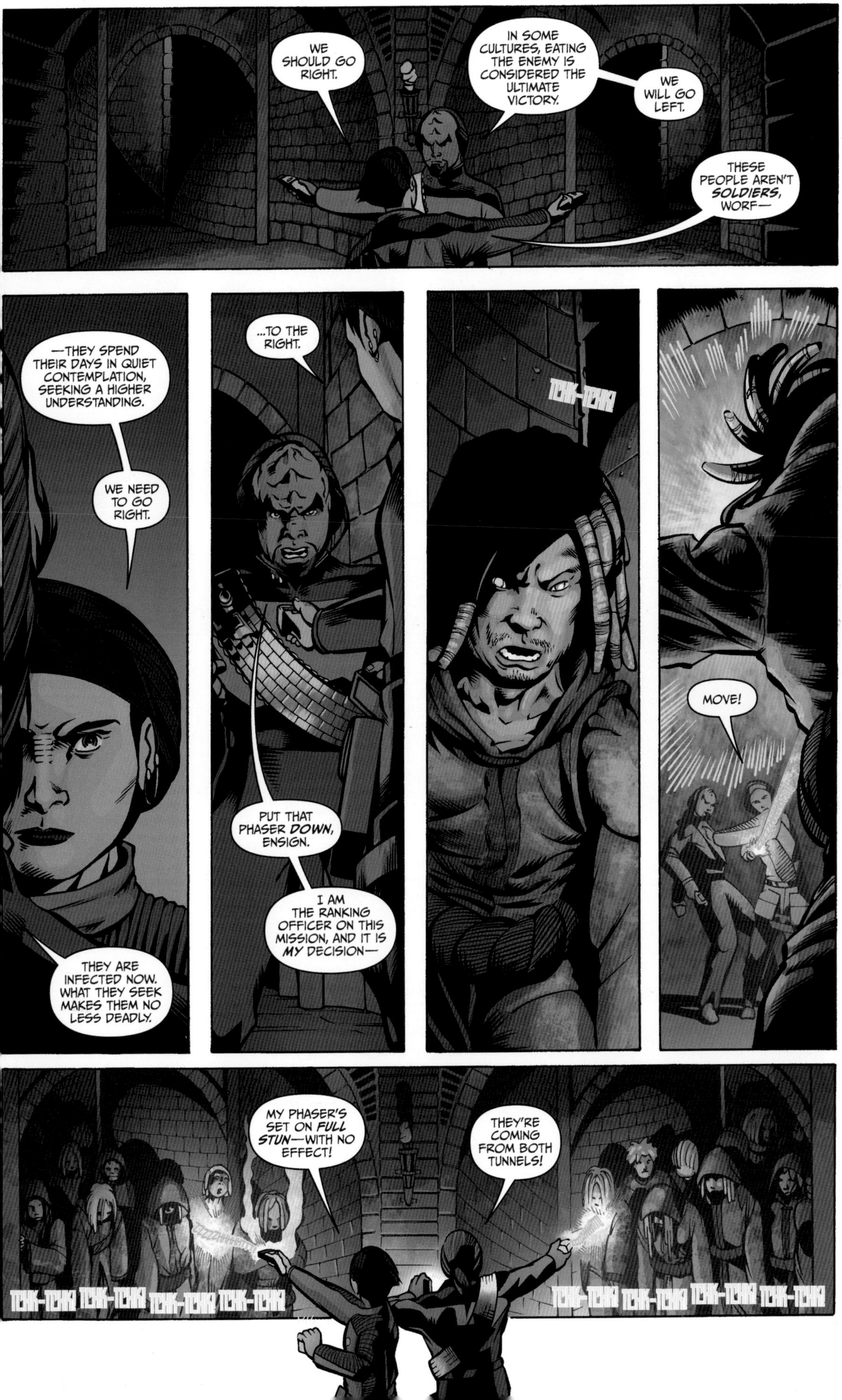
WE SHOULD GO RIGHT.
IN SOME CULTURES, EATING THE ENEMY IS CONSIDERED THE ULTIMATE VICTORY.
WE WILL GO LEFT.
THESE PEOPLE AREN'T SOLDIERS, WORF—
—THEY SPEND THEIR DAYS IN QUIET CONTEMPLATION, SEEKING A HIGHER UNDERSTANDING.
WE NEED TO GO RIGHT.
THEY ARE INFECTED NOW. WHAT THEY SEEK MAKES THEM NO LESS DEADLY.
...TO THE RIGHT.
PUT THAT PHASER DOWN, ENSIGN.
I AM THE RANKING OFFICER ON THIS MISSION, AND IT IS MY DECISION—
TCHK-TCHK!
MOVE!
MY PHASER'S SET ON FULL STUN—WITH NO EFFECT!
THEY'RE COMING FROM BOTH TUNNELS!
TCHK-TCHK! TCHK-TCHK! TCHK-TCHK! TCHK-TCHK!
TCHK-TCHK! TCHK-TCHK! TCHK-TCHK! TCHK-TCHK!

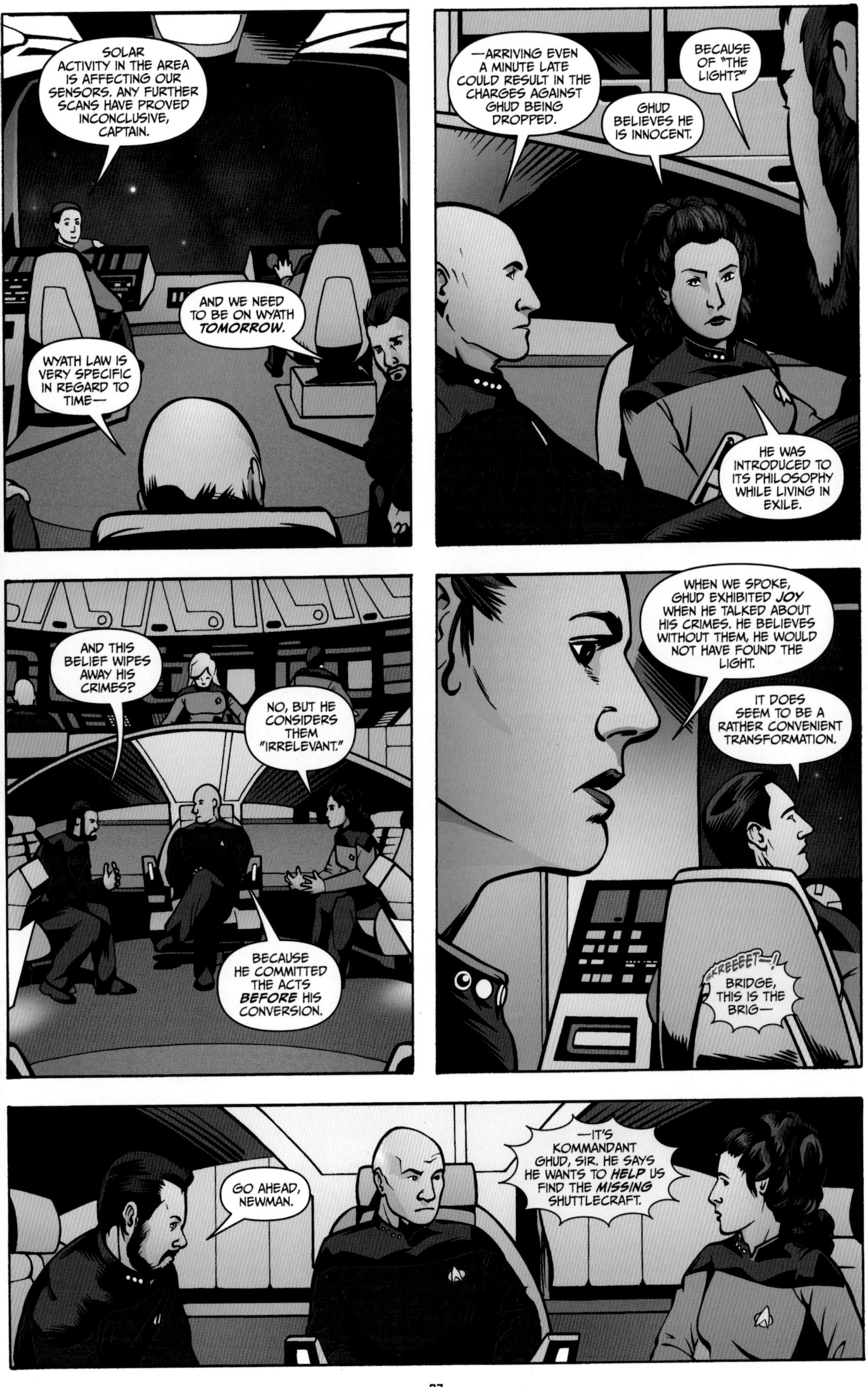
SOLAR ACTIVITY IN THE AREA IS AFFECTING OUR SENSORS. ANY FURTHER SCANS HAVE PROVED INCONCLUSIVE, CAPTAIN.
AND WE NEED TO BE ON WYATH TOMORROW.
WYATH LAW IS VERY SPECIFIC IN REGARD TO TIME—
—ARRIVING EVEN A MINUTE LATE COULD RESULT IN THE CHARGES AGAINST GHUD BEING DROPPED.
GHUD BELIEVES HE IS INNOCENT.
BECAUSE OF "THE LIGHT?"
HE WAS INTRODUCED TO ITS PHILOSOPHY WHILE LIVING IN EXILE.
AND THIS BELIEF WIPES AWAY HIS CRIMES?
NO, BUT HE CONSIDERS THEM "IRRELEVANT."
BECAUSE HE COMMITTED THE ACTS BEFORE HIS CONVERSION.
WHEN WE SPOKE, GHUD EXHIBITED JOY WHEN HE TALKED ABOUT HIS CRIMES. HE BELIEVES WITHOUT THEM, HE WOULD NOT HAVE FOUND THE LIGHT.
IT DOES SEEM TO BE A RATHER CONVENIENT TRANSFORMATION.
SKREEEET—!
BRIDGE, THIS IS THE BRIG—
GO AHEAD, NEWMAN.
—IT'S KOMMANDANT GHUD, SIR. HE SAYS HE WANTS TO HELP US FIND THE MISSING SHUTTLECRAFT.

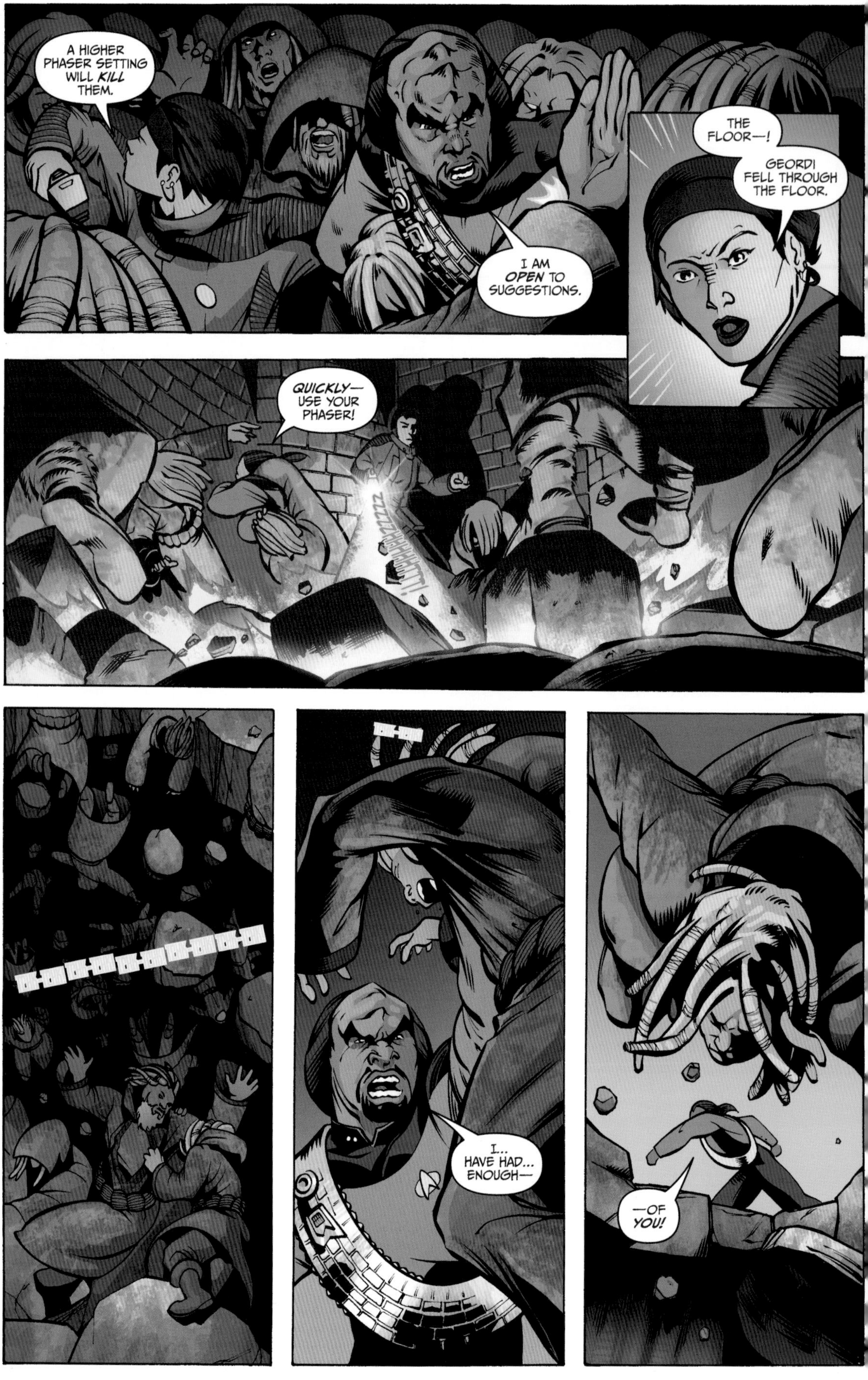
A HIGHER PHASER SETTING WILL *KILL* THEM.
I AM *OPEN* TO SUGGESTIONS.
THE FLOOR—!
GEORDI FELL THROUGH THE FLOOR.
QUICKLY— USE YOUR PHASER!
I... HAVE HAD... ENOUGH—
—OF *YOU!*

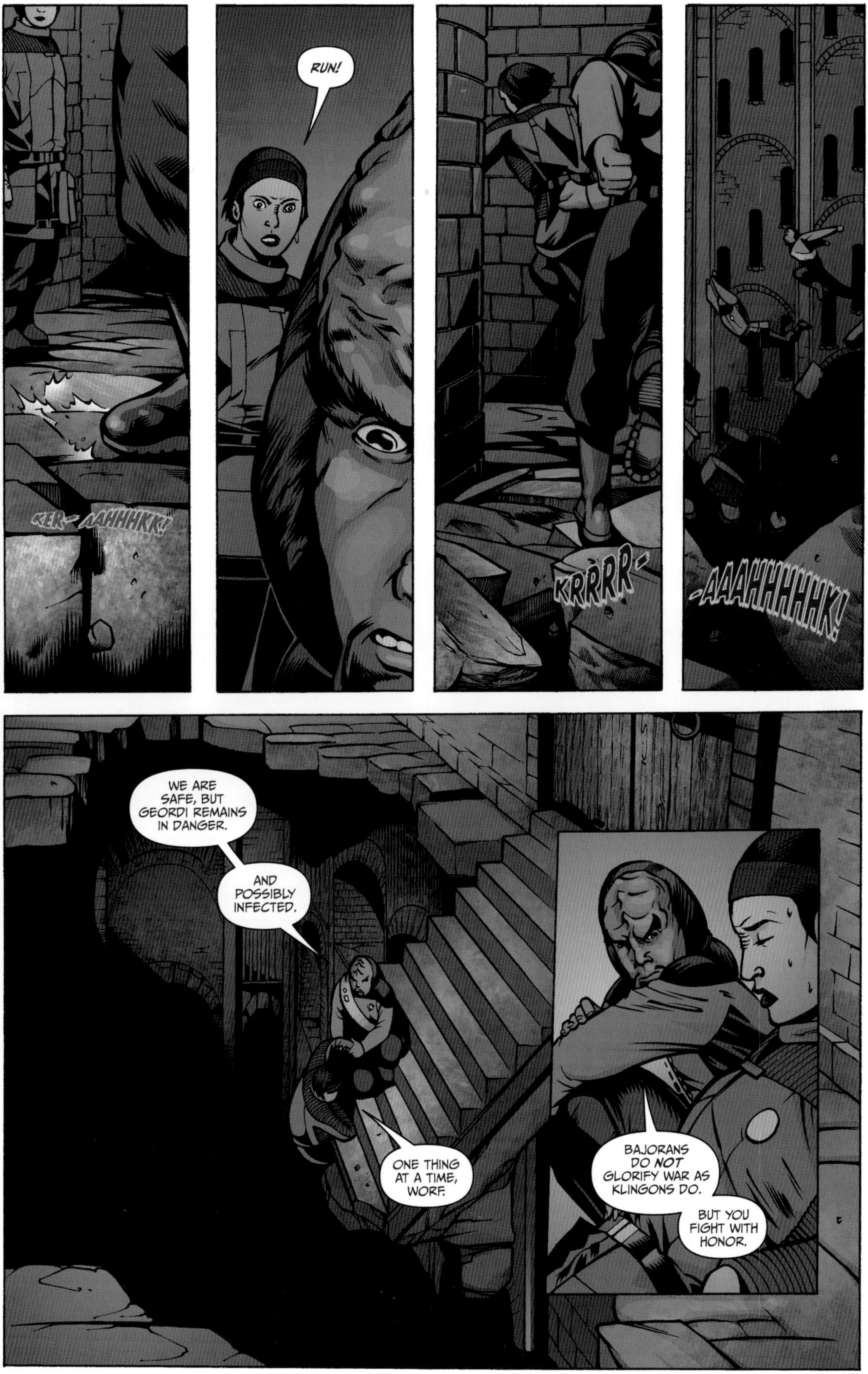
RUN!
KER-AAHHHKK!
KRRRR-
-AAAHHHHHK!
WE ARE SAFE, BUT GEORDI REMAINS IN DANGER.
AND POSSIBLY INFECTED.
ONE THING AT A TIME, WORF.
BAJORANS DO NOT GLORIFY WAR AS KLINGONS DO.
BUT YOU FIGHT WITH HONOR.

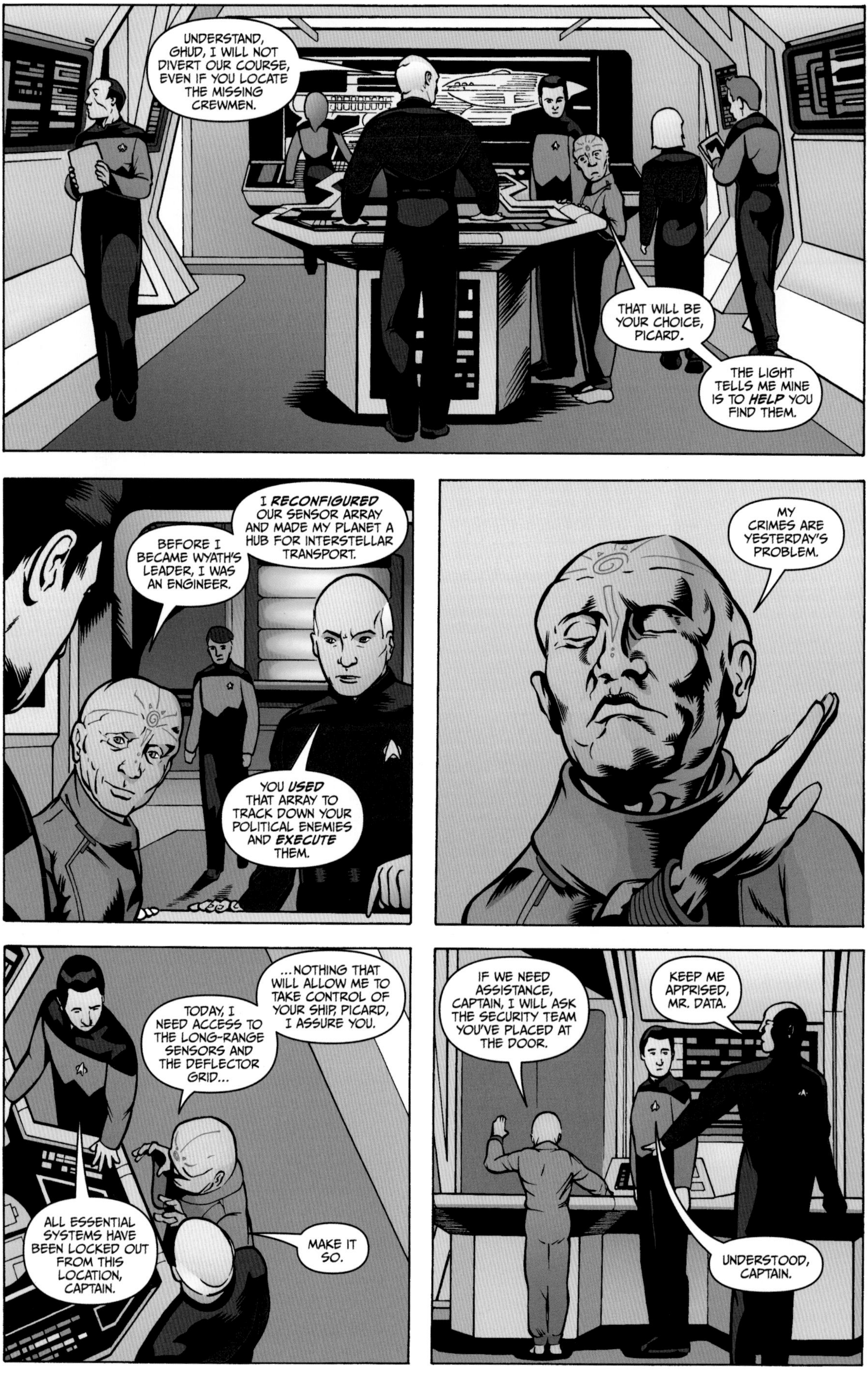
UNDERSTAND, GHUD, I WILL NOT DIVERT OUR COURSE, EVEN IF YOU LOCATE THE MISSING CREWMEN.
THAT WILL BE YOUR CHOICE, PICARD.
THE LIGHT TELLS ME MINE IS TO HELP YOU FIND THEM.
BEFORE I BECAME WYATH'S LEADER, I WAS AN ENGINEER.
I RECONFIGURED OUR SENSOR ARRAY AND MADE MY PLANET A HUB FOR INTERSTELLAR TRANSPORT.
YOU USED THAT ARRAY TO TRACK DOWN YOUR POLITICAL ENEMIES AND EXECUTE THEM.
MY CRIMES ARE YESTERDAY'S PROBLEM.
TODAY, I NEED ACCESS TO THE LONG-RANGE SENSORS AND THE DEFLECTOR GRID...
...NOTHING THAT WILL ALLOW ME TO TAKE CONTROL OF YOUR SHIP, PICARD, I ASSURE YOU.
ALL ESSENTIAL SYSTEMS HAVE BEEN LOCKED OUT FROM THIS LOCATION, CAPTAIN.
MAKE IT SO.
IF WE NEED ASSISTANCE, CAPTAIN, I WILL ASK THE SECURITY TEAM YOU'VE PLACED AT THE DOOR.
KEEP ME APPRISED, MR. DATA.
UNDERSTOOD, CAPTAIN.

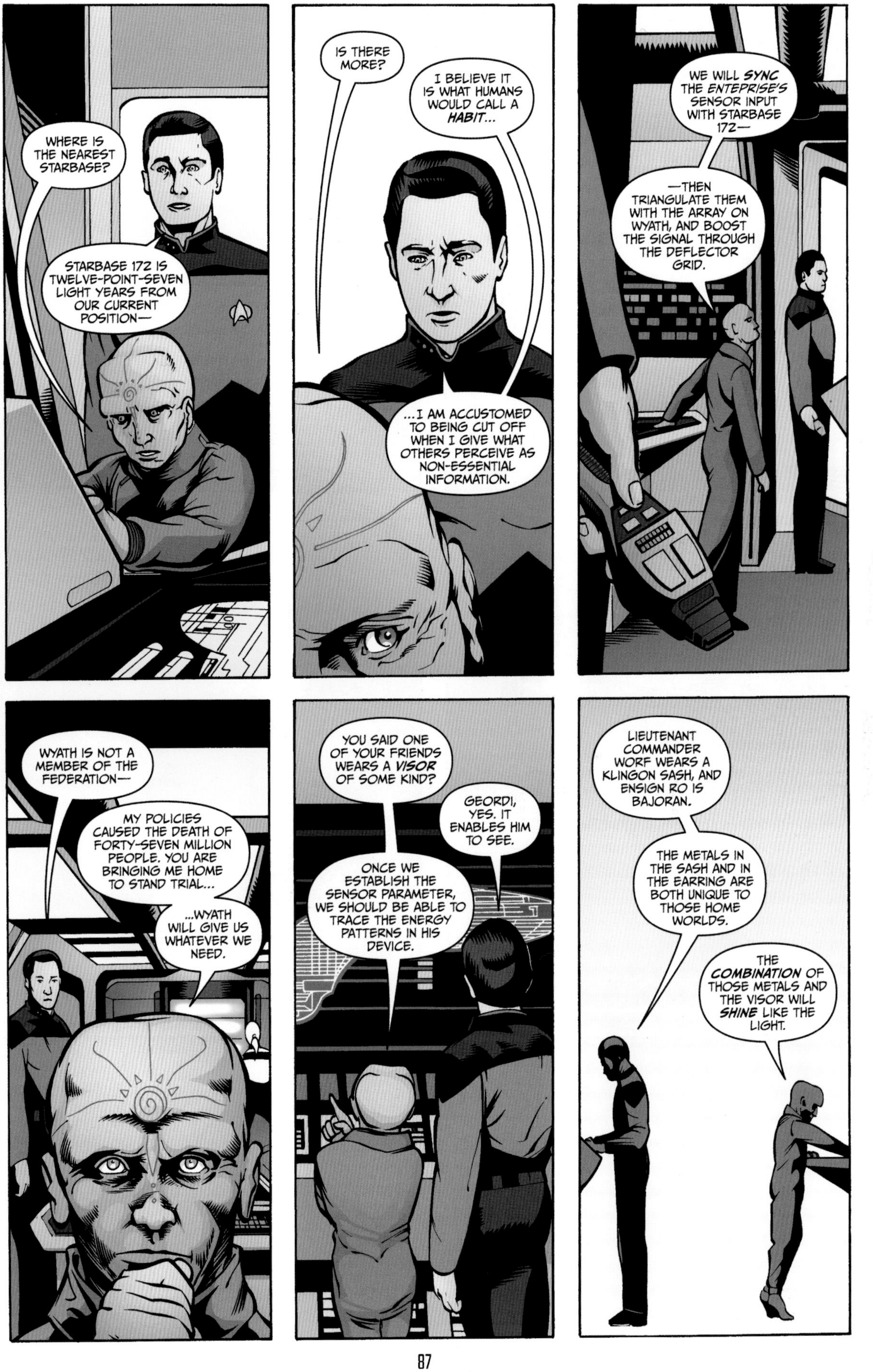
WHERE IS THE NEAREST STARBASE?
STARBASE 172 IS TWELVE-POINT-SEVEN LIGHT YEARS FROM OUR CURRENT POSITION—
IS THERE MORE?
I BELIEVE IT IS WHAT HUMANS WOULD CALL A *HABIT*...
...I AM ACCUSTOMED TO BEING CUT OFF WHEN I GIVE WHAT OTHERS PERCEIVE AS NON-ESSENTIAL INFORMATION.
WE WILL ***SYNC*** THE *ENTEPRISE'S* SENSOR INPUT WITH STARBASE 172—
—THEN TRIANGULATE THEM WITH THE ARRAY ON WYATH, AND BOOST THE SIGNAL THROUGH THE DEFLECTOR GRID.
WYATH IS NOT A MEMBER OF THE FEDERATION—
MY POLICIES CAUSED THE DEATH OF FORTY-SEVEN MILLION PEOPLE. YOU ARE BRINGING ME HOME TO STAND TRIAL...
...WYATH WILL GIVE US WHATEVER WE NEED.
YOU SAID ONE OF YOUR FRIENDS WEARS A ***VISOR*** OF SOME KIND?
GEORDI, YES. IT ENABLES HIM TO SEE.
ONCE WE ESTABLISH THE SENSOR PARAMETER, WE SHOULD BE ABLE TO TRACE THE ENERGY PATTERNS IN HIS DEVICE.
LIEUTENANT COMMANDER WORF WEARS A KLINGON SASH, AND ENSIGN RO IS BAJORAN.
THE METALS IN THE SASH AND IN THE EARRING ARE BOTH UNIQUE TO THOSE HOME WORLDS.
THE ***COMBINATION*** OF THOSE METALS AND THE VISOR WILL ***SHINE*** LIKE THE LIGHT.

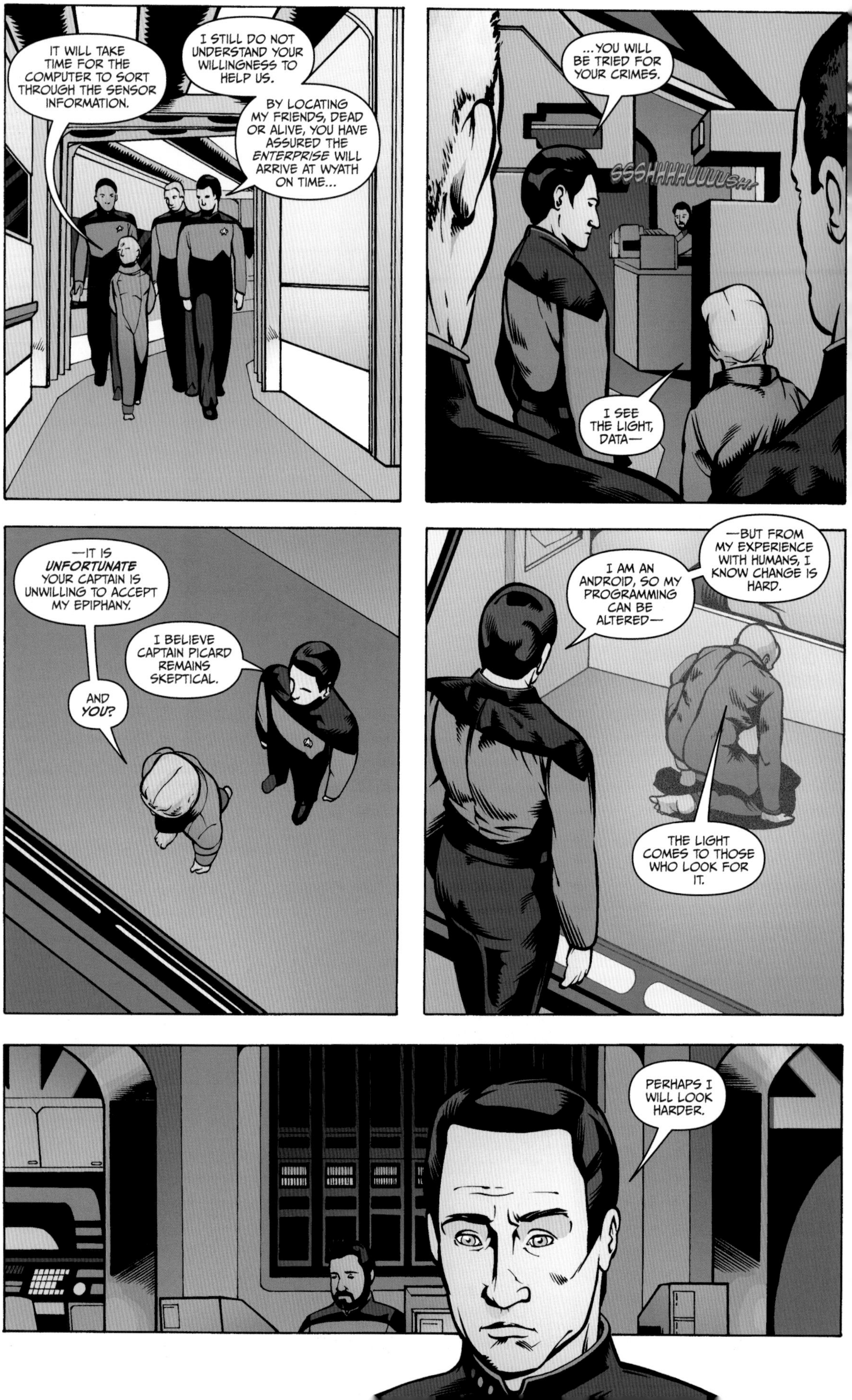
IT WILL TAKE TIME FOR THE COMPUTER TO SORT THROUGH THE SENSOR INFORMATION.
I STILL DO NOT UNDERSTAND YOUR WILLINGNESS TO HELP US.
BY LOCATING MY FRIENDS, DEAD OR ALIVE, YOU HAVE ASSURED THE *ENTERPRISE* WILL ARRIVE AT WYATH ON TIME...
...YOU WILL BE TRIED FOR YOUR CRIMES.
SSSHHHHUUUUSH!
I SEE THE LIGHT, DATA—
—IT IS ***UNFORTUNATE*** YOUR CAPTAIN IS UNWILLING TO ACCEPT MY EPIPHANY.
I BELIEVE CAPTAIN PICARD REMAINS SKEPTICAL.
AND ***YOU?***
I AM AN ANDROID, SO MY PROGRAMMING CAN BE ALTERED—
—BUT FROM MY EXPERIENCE WITH HUMANS, I KNOW CHANGE IS HARD.
THE LIGHT COMES TO THOSE WHO LOOK FOR IT.
PERHAPS I WILL LOOK HARDER.

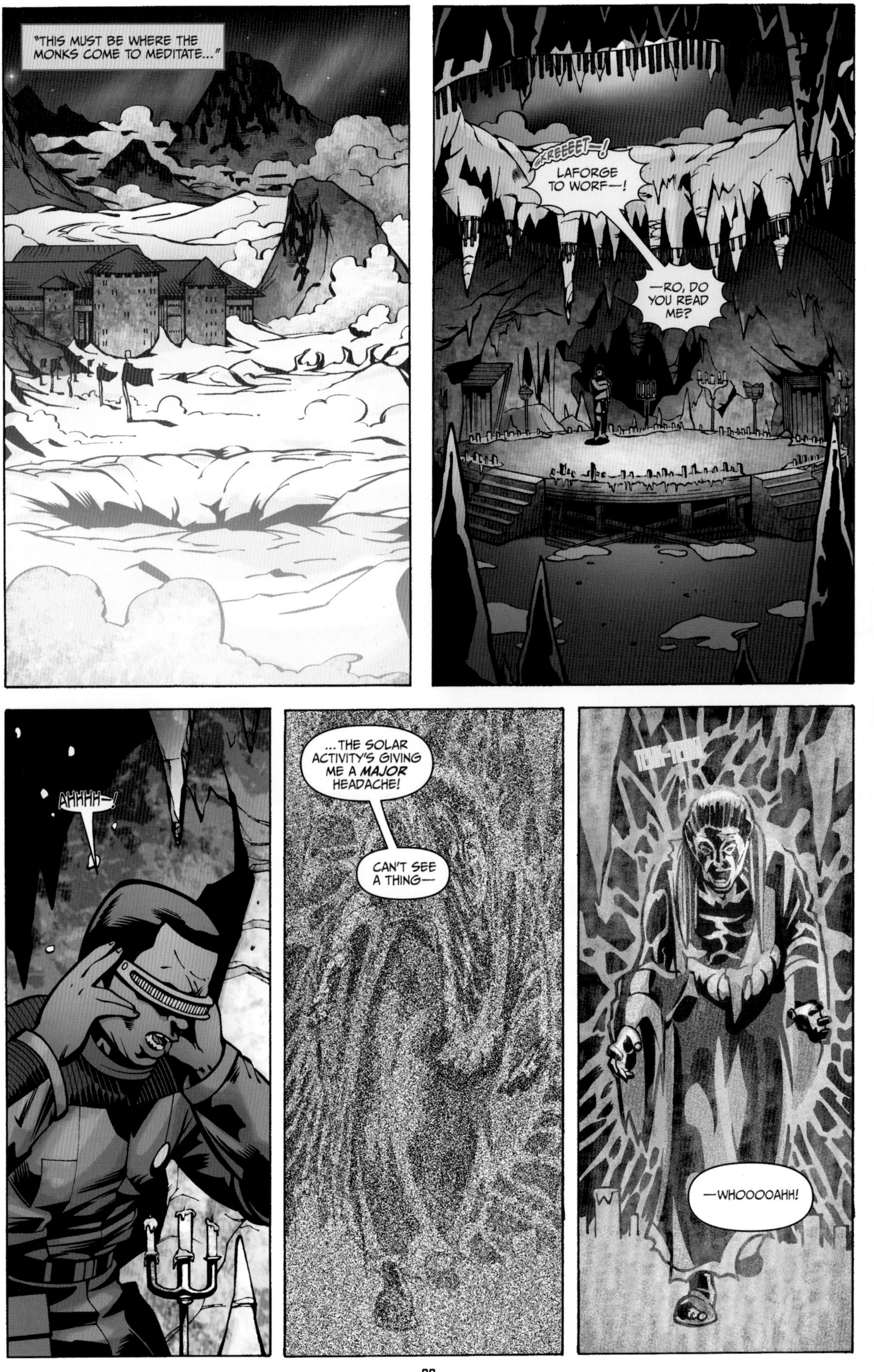
"THIS MUST BE WHERE THE MONKS COME TO MEDITATE..."
SKREEEEET—!
LAFORGE TO WORF—!
—RO, DO YOU READ ME?
AHHHH—!
...THE SOLAR ACTIVITY'S GIVING ME A ***MAJOR*** HEADACHE!
CAN'T SEE A THING—
TCHK-TCHK!
—WHOOOOAHH!

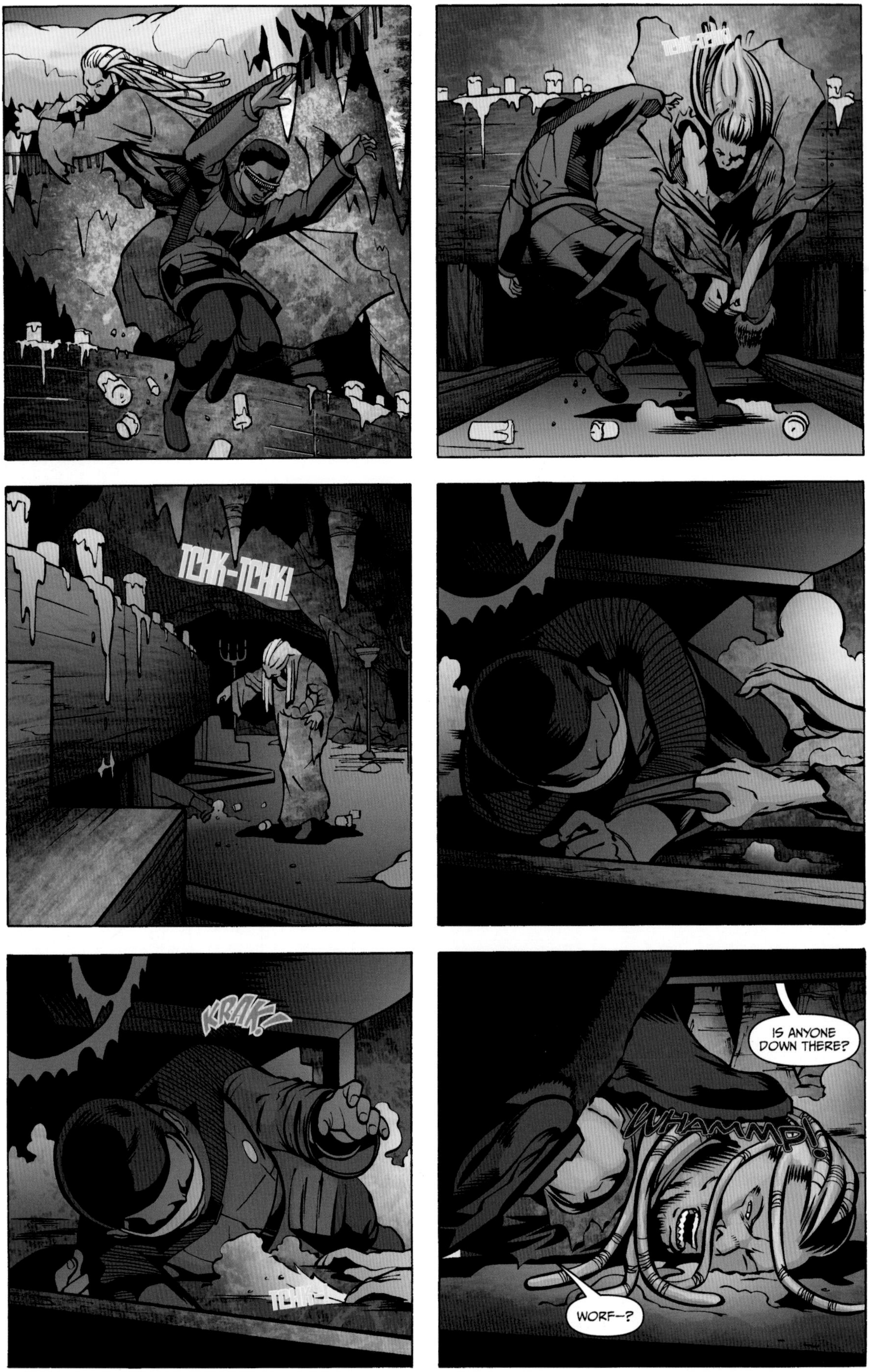
TCHK-TCHK!
KRAK!
IS ANYONE DOWN THERE?
WHAMMP!
WORF—?

PHASERS DO NOT STOP THEM, BUT ENSIGN RO AND I WERE ABLE TO *PHYSICALLY* SUBDUE ONE OF THE MONKS.

WE WERE WORRIED YOU'D BEEN INFECTED.

MY EXPOSURE PROBABLY WASN'T HIGH ENOUGH TO TRIGGER THE MUTATION.

I AM GLAD YOU ARE SAFE.

FOR THE MOMENT. THERE ARE MORE MONKS IN THESE TUNNELS, AND WE *STILL* NEED TO FIND A WAY OUT.

IF THIS MUTATION IS FUELED BY THE *EXCESS* SOLAR ACTIVITY, ITS EFFECTS MAY ONLY BECOME ACTIVE AT *NIGHT*.

SO WE JUST HAVE TO STAY ALIVE UNTIL MORNING, IS THAT WHAT YOU'RE SAYING?

TONK-TONK

IT'S JUST A THEORY—

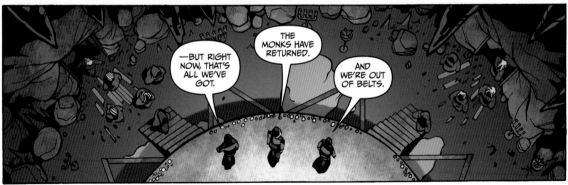

—BUT RIGHT NOW, THAT'S ALL WE'VE GOT.

THE MONKS HAVE RETURNED.

AND WE'RE OUT OF BELTS.

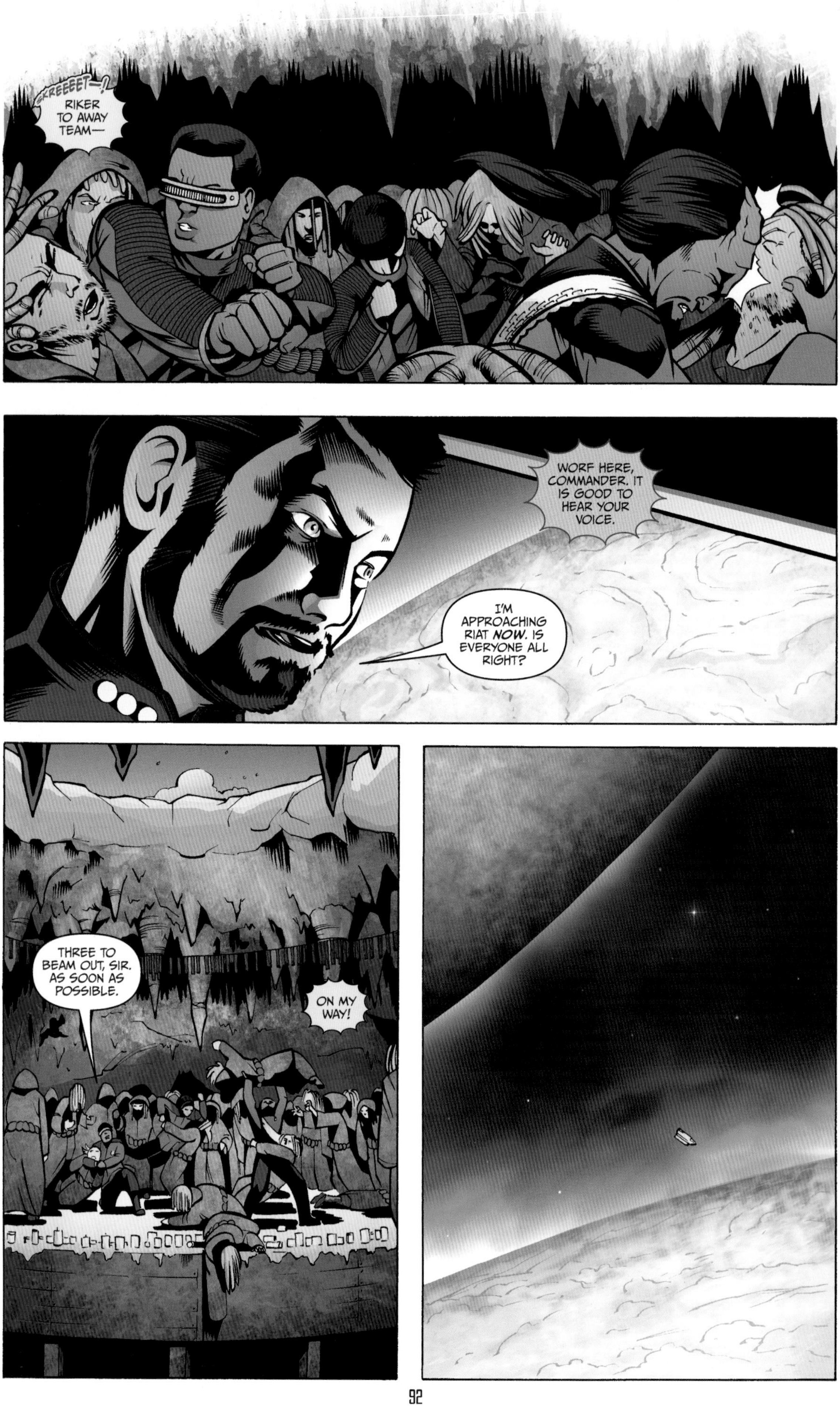
SKREEEEET—!
RIKER TO AWAY TEAM—
WORF HERE, COMMANDER. IT IS GOOD TO HEAR YOUR VOICE.
I'M APPROACHING RIAT NOW. IS EVERYONE ALL RIGHT?
THREE TO BEAM OUT, SIR. AS SOON AS POSSIBLE.
ON MY WAY!

THANK YOU FOR YOUR HELP, GHUD. AND *GOOD LUCK* AT THE TRIAL.

THERE IS NO *LUCK*, PICARD. THERE IS ONLY THE LIGHT.

ENERGIZE.

NHHHNNNHHNNNNNHHH

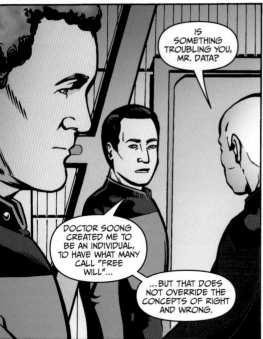

IS SOMETHING TROUBLING YOU, MR. DATA?

DOCTOR SOONG CREATED ME TO BE AN INDIVIDUAL, TO HAVE WHAT MANY CALL "FREE WILL"...

...BUT THAT DOES NOT OVERRIDE THE CONCEPTS OF RIGHT AND WRONG.

TAKING RESPONSIBILITY FOR YOUR *ACTIONS*, DATA, MAY BE WHAT MAKES YOU MOST HUMAN—

SOMETIMES THE *SIGHT* WE SEEK IS MOST *VISIBLE* IN OUR CONSCIENCE.

BUT I CANNOT SEE THE LIGHT.

THANK YOU, SIR.

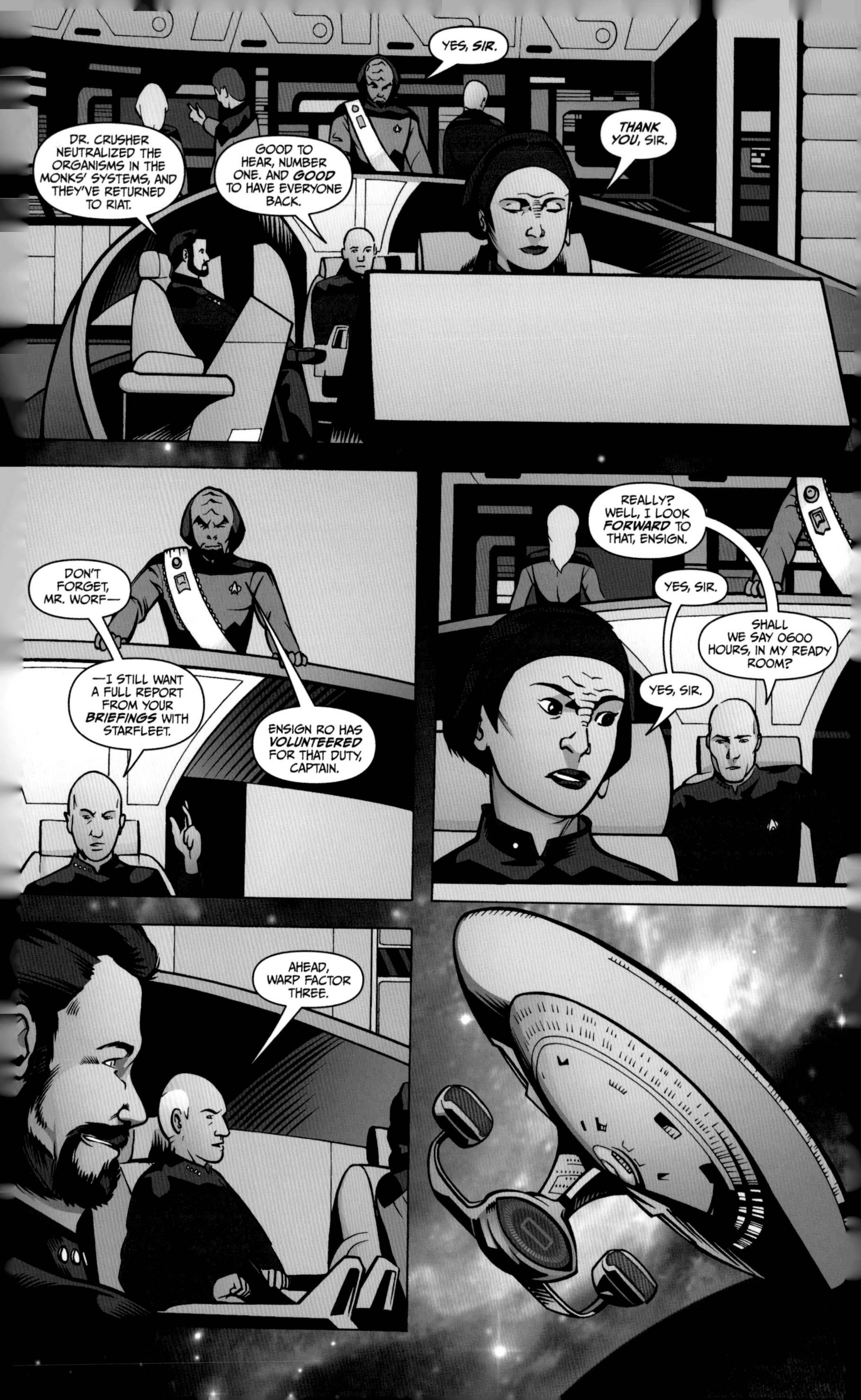
YES, SIR.
DR. CRUSHER NEUTRALIZED THE ORGANISMS IN THE MONKS' SYSTEMS, AND THEY'VE RETURNED TO RIAT.
GOOD TO HEAR, NUMBER ONE. AND GOOD TO HAVE EVERYONE BACK.
THANK YOU, SIR.
DON'T FORGET, MR. WORF—
—I STILL WANT A FULL REPORT FROM YOUR BRIEFINGS WITH STARFLEET.
ENSIGN RO HAS VOLUNTEERED FOR THAT DUTY, CAPTAIN.
REALLY? WELL, I LOOK FORWARD TO THAT, ENSIGN.
YES, SIR.
SHALL WE SAY 0600 HOURS, IN MY READY ROOM?
YES, SIR.
AHEAD, WARP FACTOR THREE.

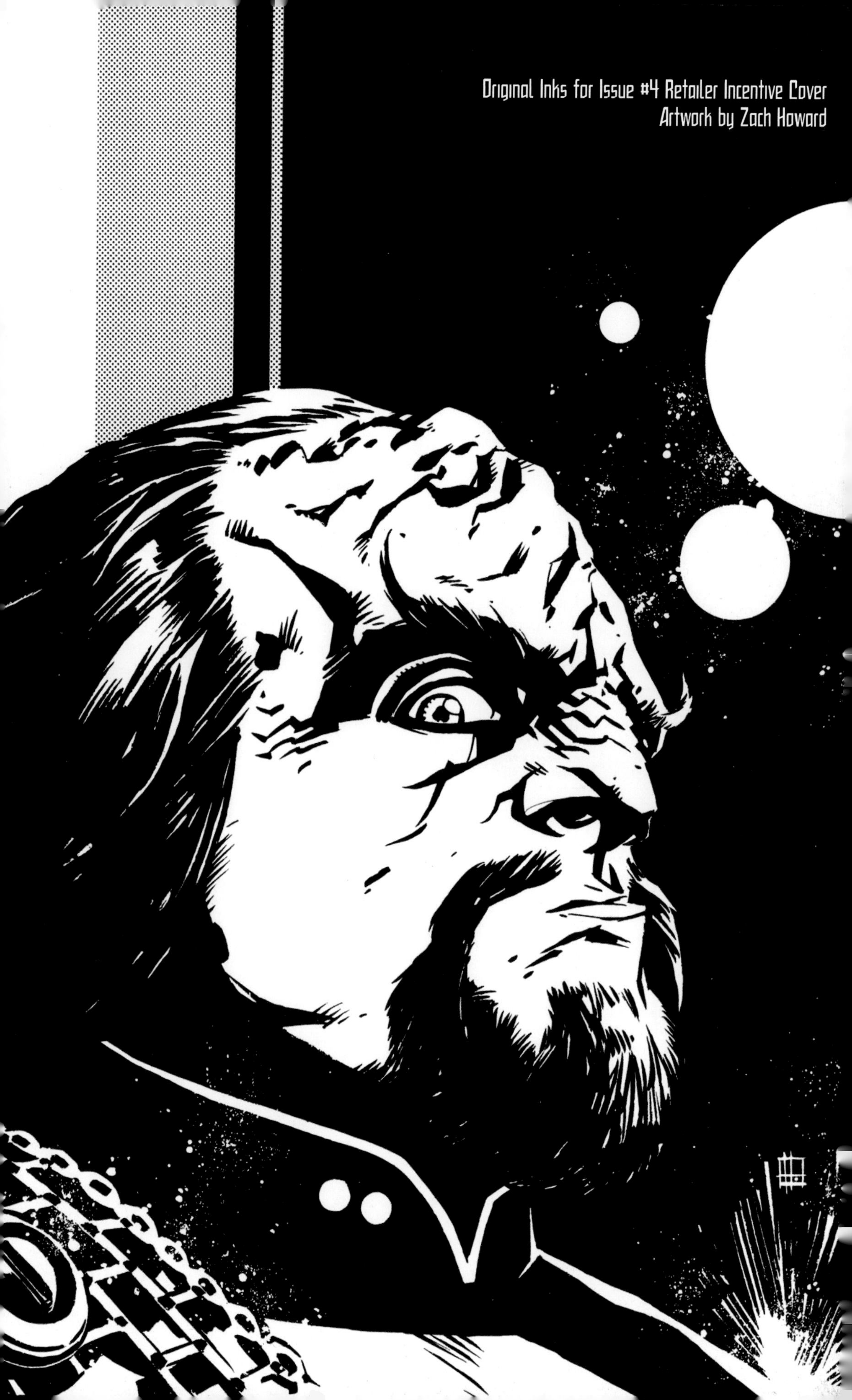

Original Inks for Issue #4 Retailer Incentive Cover
Artwork by Zach Howard

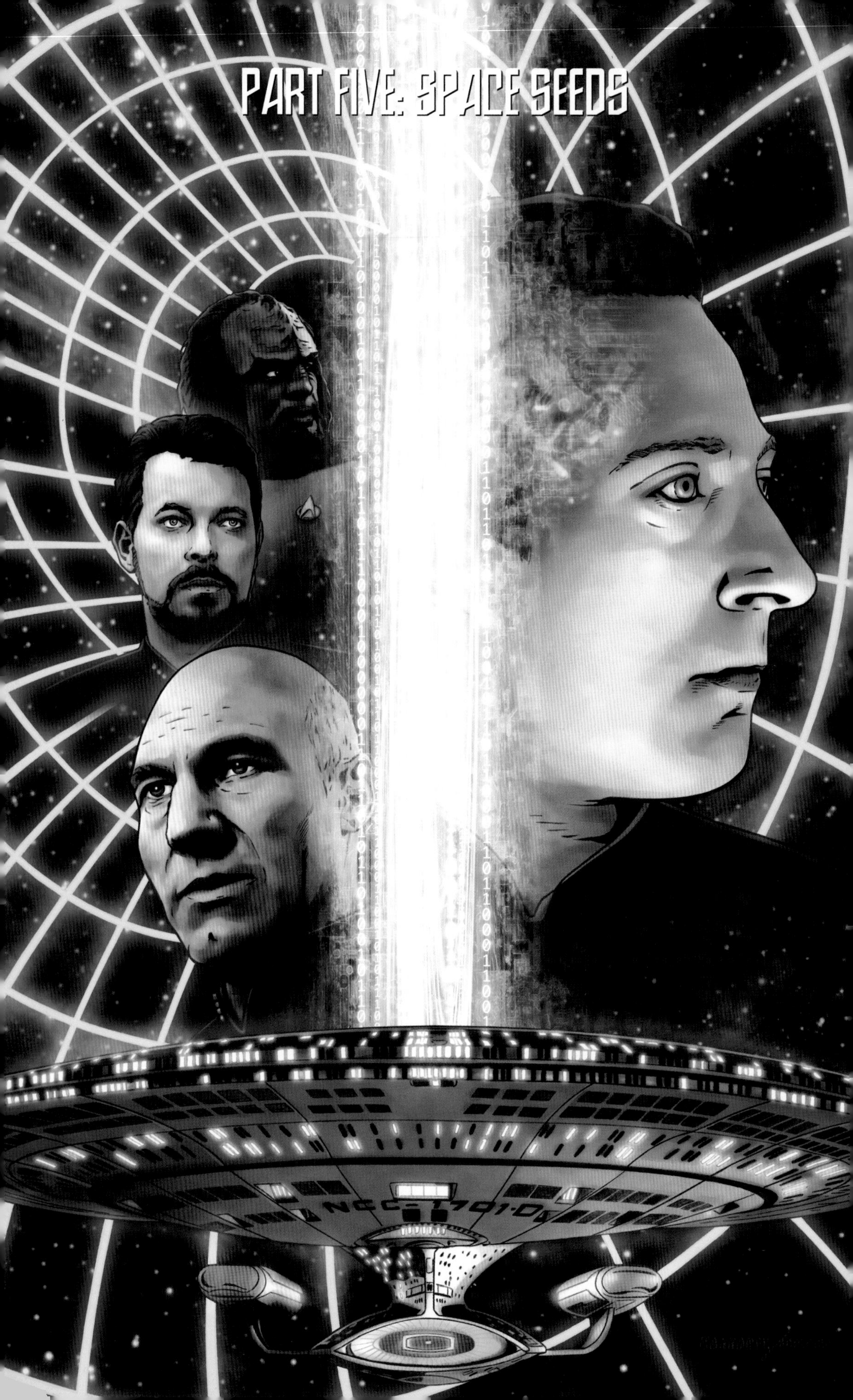
PART FIVE: SPACE SEEDS
NCC-1701-D

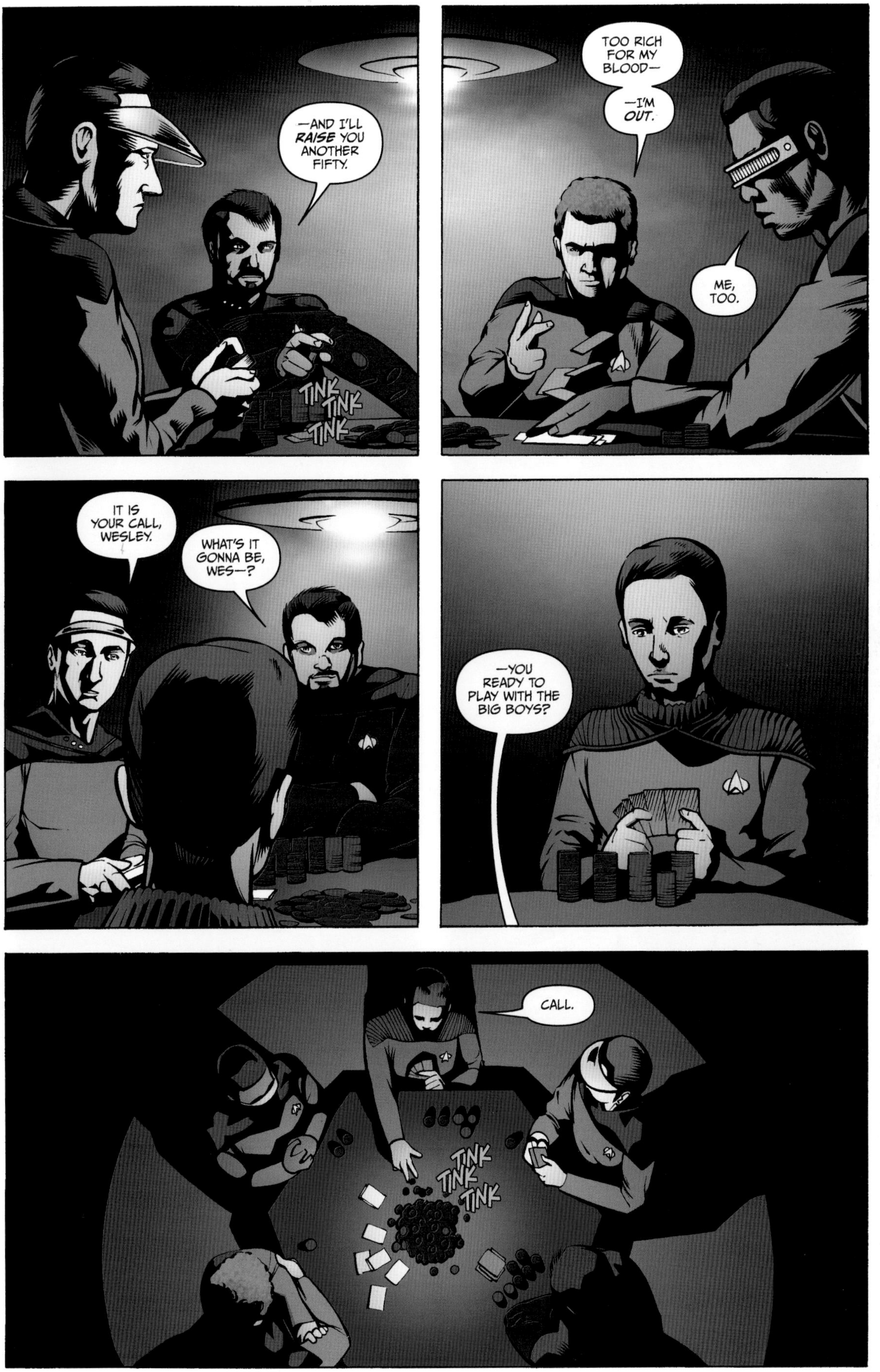
—AND I'LL RAISE YOU ANOTHER FIFTY.
TINK TINK TINK
TOO RICH FOR MY BLOOD—
—I'M OUT.
ME, TOO.
IT IS YOUR CALL, WESLEY.
WHAT'S IT GONNA BE, WES—?
—YOU READY TO PLAY WITH THE BIG BOYS?
CALL.
TINK TINK TINK

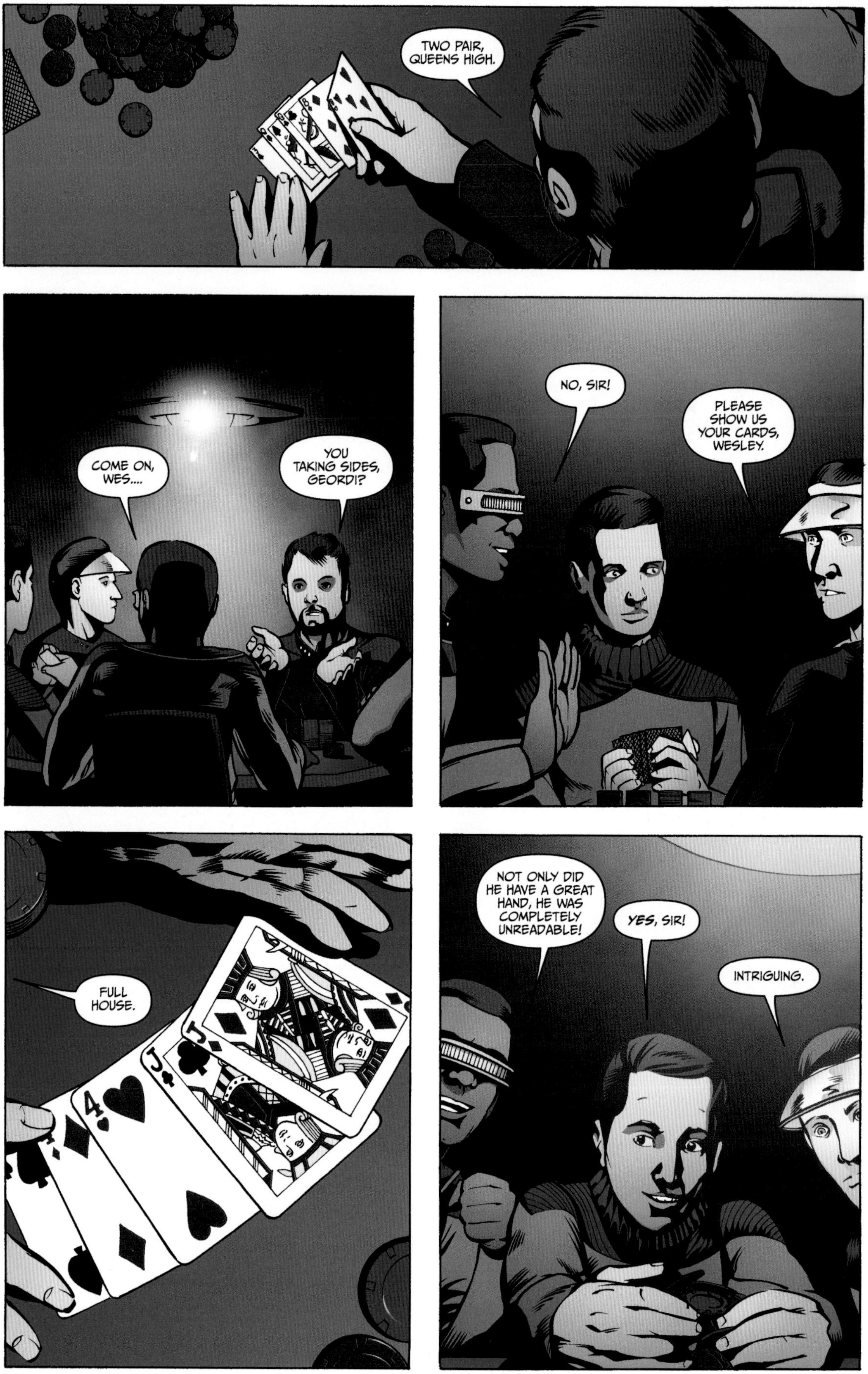
TWO PAIR, QUEENS HIGH.
COME ON, WES....
YOU TAKING SIDES, GEORDI?
NO, SIR!
PLEASE SHOW US YOUR CARDS, WESLEY.
FULL HOUSE.
NOT ONLY DID HE HAVE A GREAT HAND, HE WAS COMPLETELY UNREADABLE!
YES, SIR!
INTRIGUING.

RIKER TO WESLEY CRUSHER—
COMPUTER—FREEZE PROGRAM.
CRUSHER HERE.
WE'VE ARRIVED AT THE ARMADA, WES. MEET THE AWAY TEAM IN TRANSPORTER ROOM THREE.
ON MY WAY.
COMPUTER—END PROGRAM.

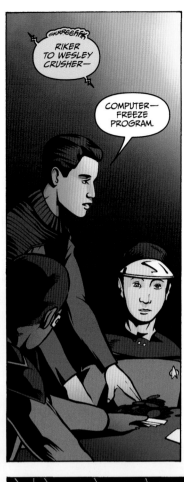

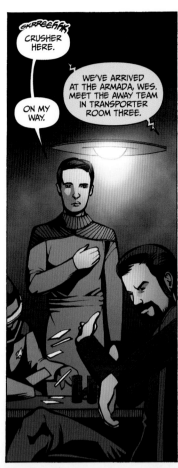

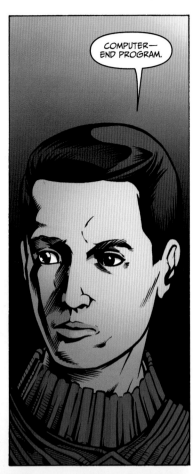

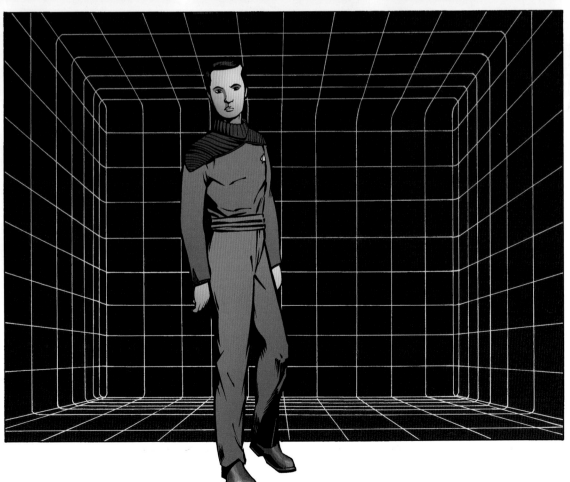

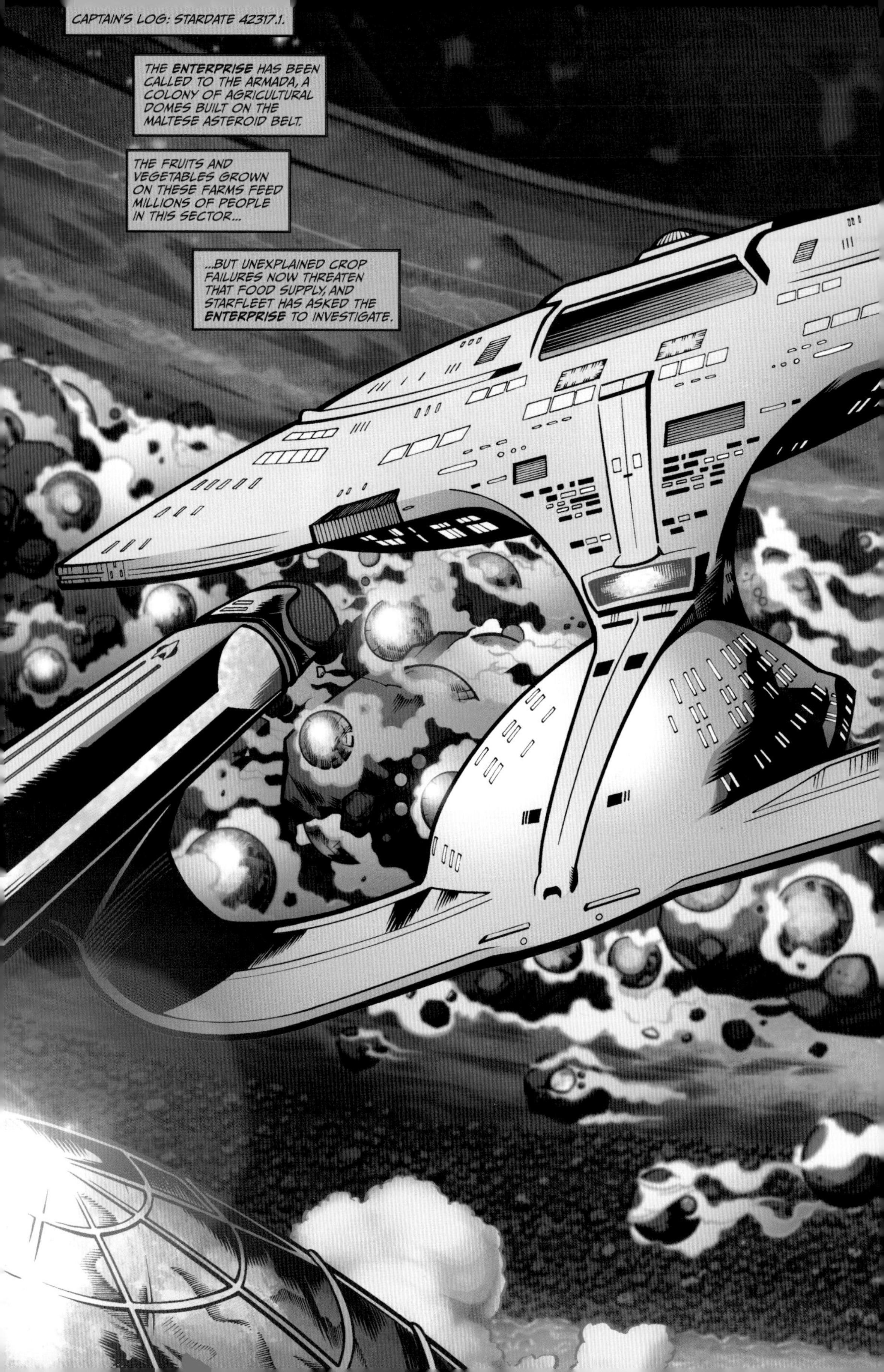
CAPTAIN'S LOG: STARDATE 42317.1.
THE ENTERPRISE HAS BEEN CALLED TO THE ARMADA, A COLONY OF AGRICULTURAL DOMES BUILT ON THE MALTESE ASTEROID BELT.
THE FRUITS AND VEGETABLES GROWN ON THESE FARMS FEED MILLIONS OF PEOPLE IN THIS SECTOR...
...BUT UNEXPLAINED CROP FAILURES NOW THREATEN THAT FOOD SUPPLY, AND STARFLEET HAS ASKED THE ENTERPRISE TO INVESTIGATE.

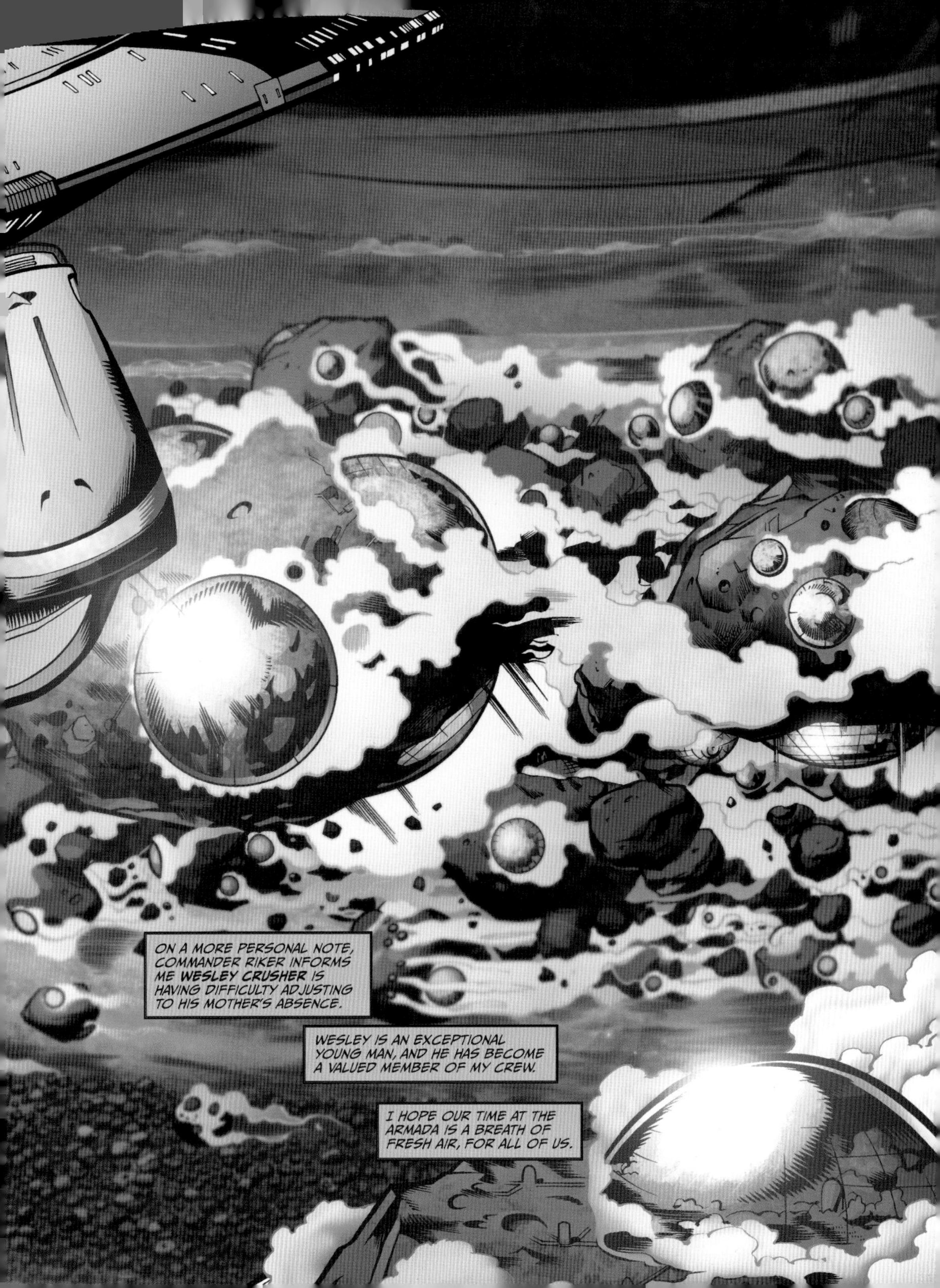
ON A MORE PERSONAL NOTE, COMMANDER RIKER INFORMS ME **WESLEY CRUSHER** IS HAVING DIFFICULTY ADJUSTING TO HIS MOTHER'S ABSENCE.
WESLEY IS AN EXCEPTIONAL YOUNG MAN, AND HE HAS BECOME A VALUED MEMBER OF MY CREW.
I HOPE OUR TIME AT THE ARMADA IS A BREATH OF FRESH AIR, FOR ALL OF US.

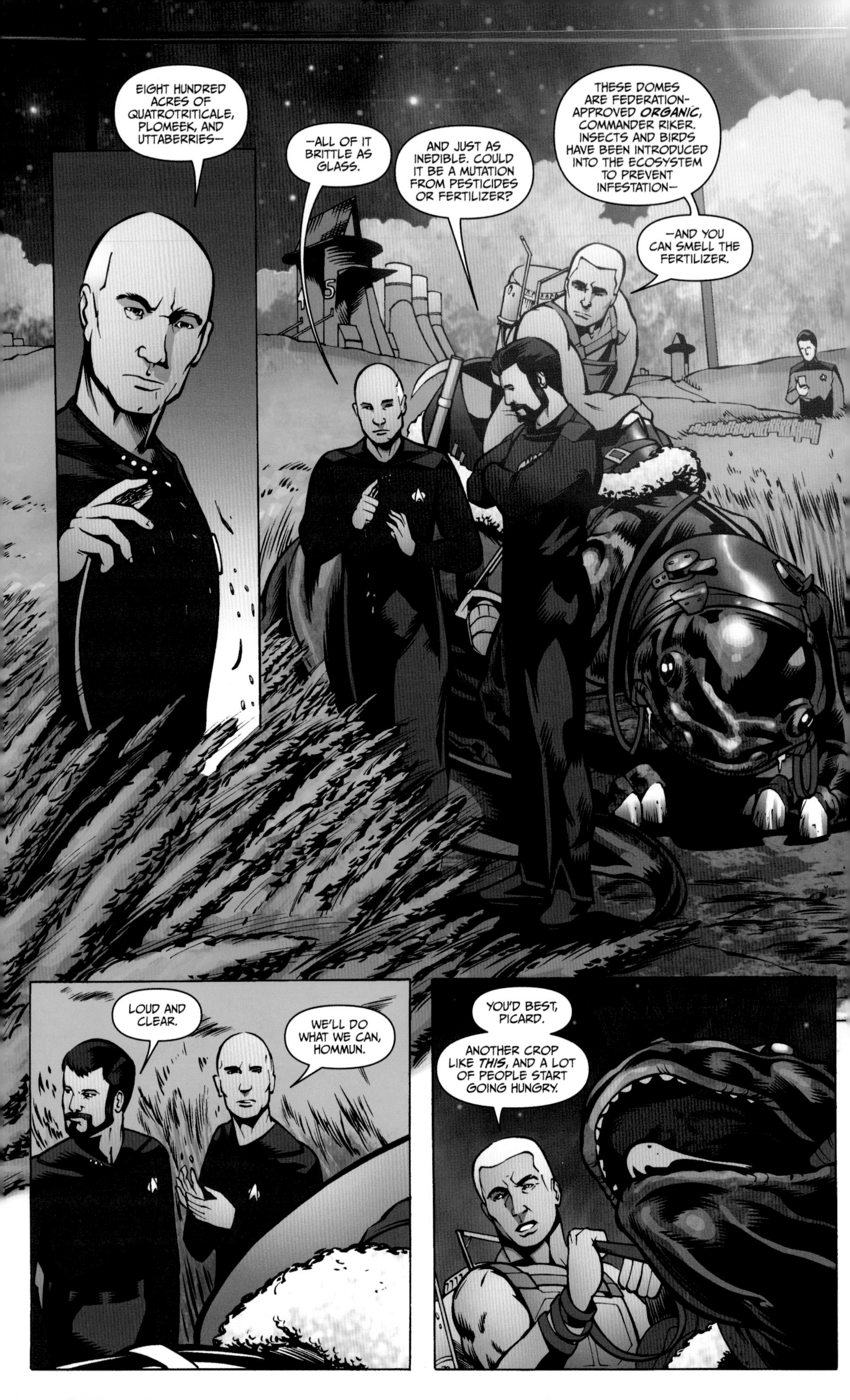
EIGHT HUNDRED ACRES OF QUATROTRITICALE, PLOMEEK, AND UTTABERRIES—
—ALL OF IT BRITTLE AS GLASS.
AND JUST AS INEDIBLE. COULD IT BE A MUTATION FROM PESTICIDES OR FERTILIZER?
THESE DOMES ARE FEDERATION-APPROVED ORGANIC, COMMANDER RIKER. INSECTS AND BIRDS HAVE BEEN INTRODUCED INTO THE ECOSYSTEM TO PREVENT INFESTATION—
—AND YOU CAN SMELL THE FERTILIZER.
LOUD AND CLEAR.
WE'LL DO WHAT WE CAN, HOMMUN.
YOU'D BEST, PICARD.
ANOTHER CROP LIKE THIS, AND A LOT OF PEOPLE START GOING HUNGRY.

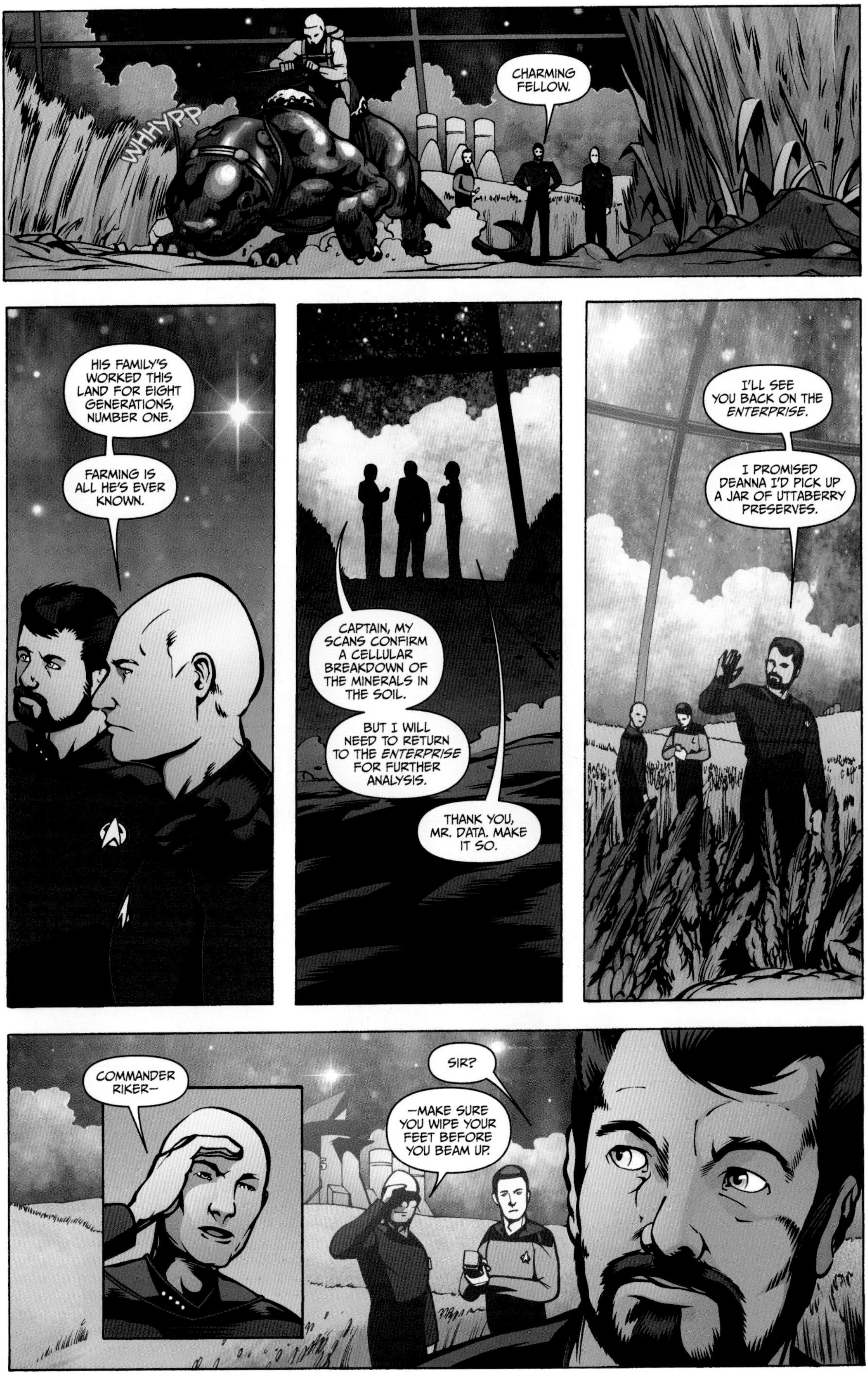
WHHYPP
CHARMING FELLOW.
HIS FAMILY'S WORKED THIS LAND FOR EIGHT GENERATIONS, NUMBER ONE.
FARMING IS ALL HE'S EVER KNOWN.
CAPTAIN, MY SCANS CONFIRM A CELLULAR BREAKDOWN OF THE MINERALS IN THE SOIL.
BUT I WILL NEED TO RETURN TO THE *ENTERPRISE* FOR FURTHER ANALYSIS.
THANK YOU, MR. DATA. MAKE IT SO.
I'LL SEE YOU BACK ON THE *ENTERPRISE*.
I PROMISED DEANNA I'D PICK UP A JAR OF UTTABERRY PRESERVES.
COMMANDER RIKER—
SIR?
—MAKE SURE YOU WIPE YOUR FEET BEFORE YOU BEAM UP.

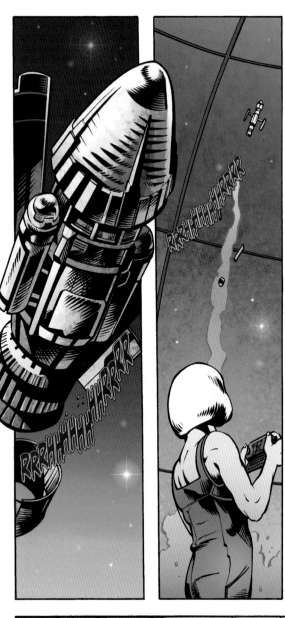

WHAT'S THE POINT?

THE *POINT* IS THAT IT EXPLODES.

WHAT ELSE IS THERE TO DO ON THIS *ROCK*?

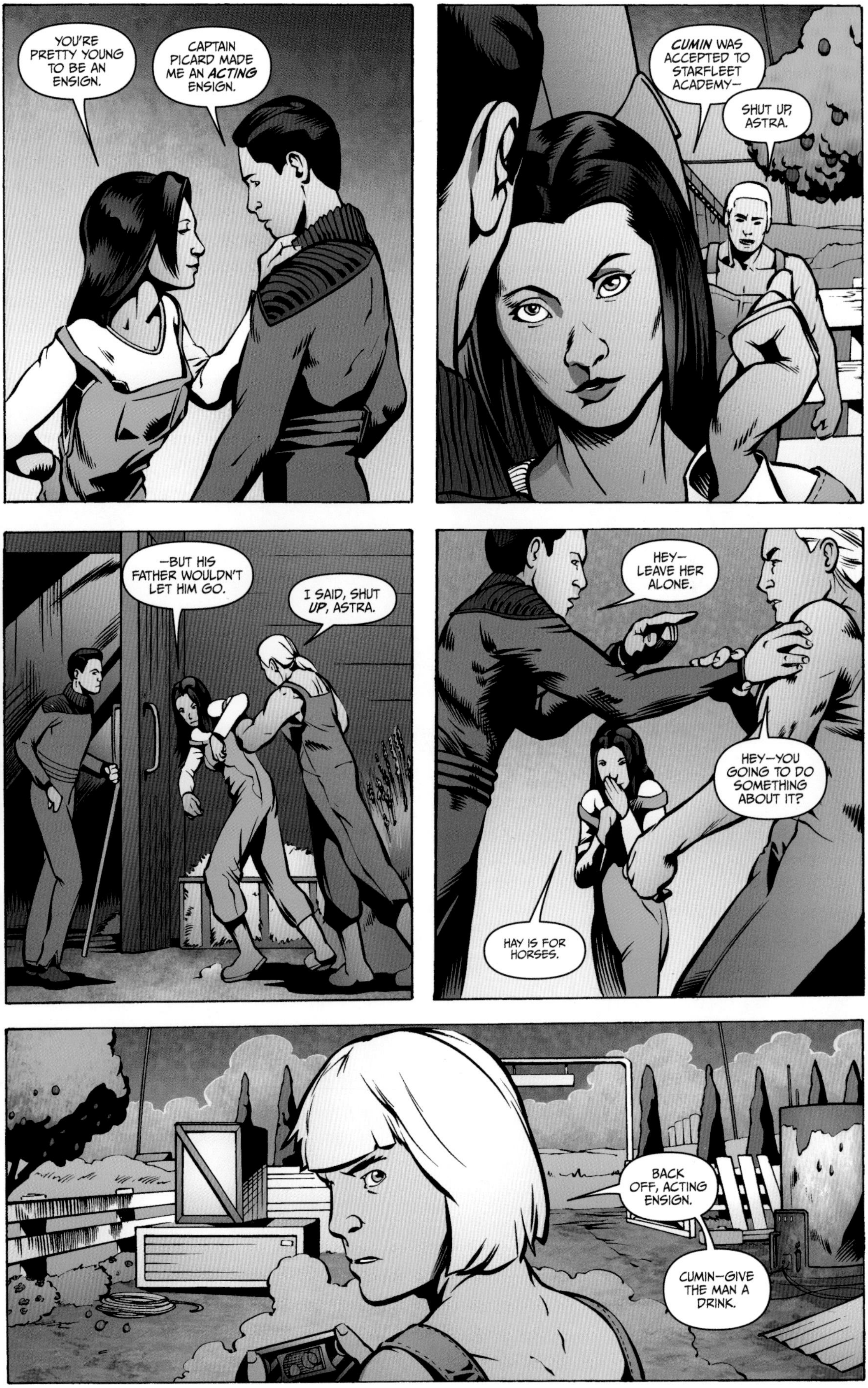
YOU'RE PRETTY YOUNG TO BE AN ENSIGN.
CAPTAIN PICARD MADE ME AN *ACTING* ENSIGN.
CUMIN WAS ACCEPTED TO STARFLEET ACADEMY—
SHUT UP, ASTRA.
—BUT HIS FATHER WOULDN'T LET HIM GO.
I SAID, SHUT *UP*, ASTRA.
HEY— LEAVE HER ALONE.
HEY—YOU GOING TO DO SOMETHING ABOUT IT?
HAY IS FOR HORSES.
BACK OFF, ACTING ENSIGN.
CUMIN—GIVE THE MAN A DRINK.

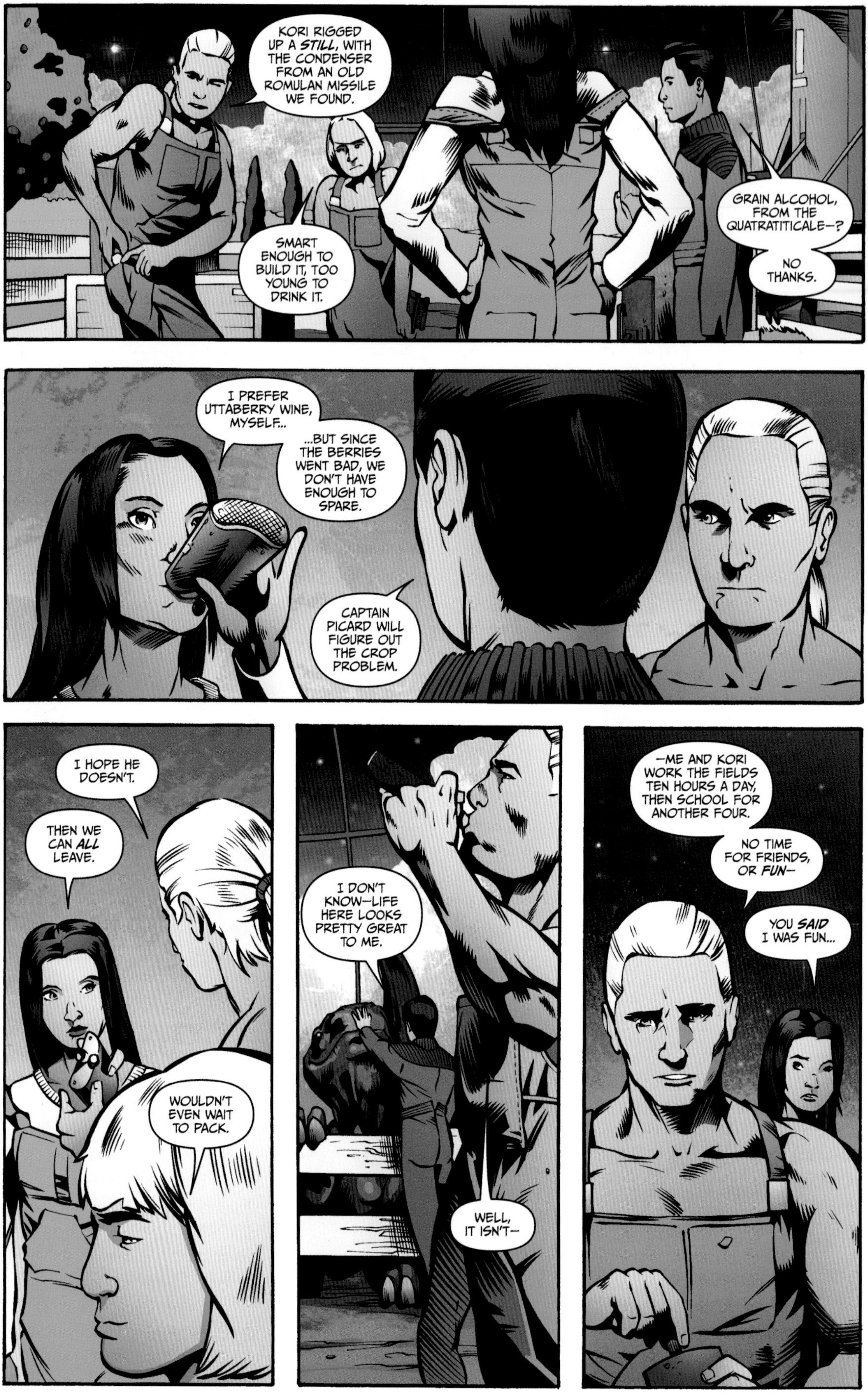

KORI RIGGED UP A STILL, WITH THE CONDENSER FROM AN OLD ROMULAN MISSILE WE FOUND.
SMART ENOUGH TO BUILD IT, TOO YOUNG TO DRINK IT.
GRAIN ALCOHOL, FROM THE QUATRATITICALE--?
NO THANKS.
I PREFER UTTABERRY WINE, MYSELF...
...BUT SINCE THE BERRIES WENT BAD, WE DON'T HAVE ENOUGH TO SPARE.
CAPTAIN PICARD WILL FIGURE OUT THE CROP PROBLEM.
I HOPE HE DOESN'T.
THEN WE CAN ALL LEAVE.
WOULDN'T EVEN WAIT TO PACK.
I DON'T KNOW--LIFE HERE LOOKS PRETTY GREAT TO ME.
WELL, IT ISN'T--
--ME AND KORI WORK THE FIELDS TEN HOURS A DAY, THEN SCHOOL FOR ANOTHER FOUR.
NO TIME FOR FRIENDS, OR FUN--
YOU SAID I WAS FUN...

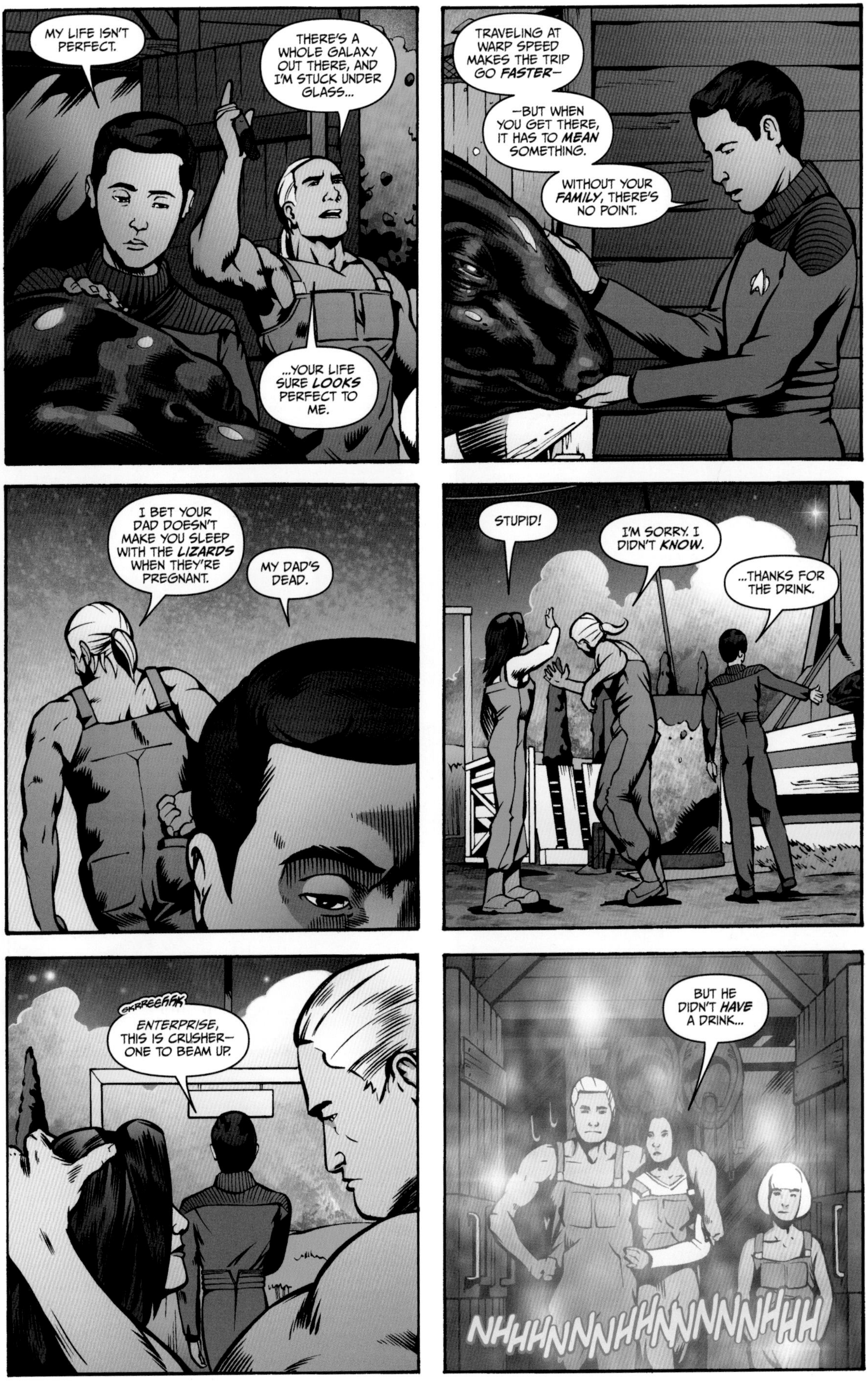
MY LIFE ISN'T PERFECT.
THERE'S A WHOLE GALAXY OUT THERE, AND I'M STUCK UNDER GLASS...
...YOUR LIFE SURE LOOKS PERFECT TO ME.
TRAVELING AT WARP SPEED MAKES THE TRIP GO FASTER—
—BUT WHEN YOU GET THERE, IT HAS TO MEAN SOMETHING.
WITHOUT YOUR FAMILY, THERE'S NO POINT.
I BET YOUR DAD DOESN'T MAKE YOU SLEEP WITH THE LIZARDS WHEN THEY'RE PREGNANT.
MY DAD'S DEAD.
STUPID!
I'M SORRY. I DIDN'T KNOW.
...THANKS FOR THE DRINK.
SKRREEEKK
ENTERPRISE, THIS IS CRUSHER—ONE TO BEAM UP.
BUT HE DIDN'T HAVE A DRINK...
NHHHNNNNHHNNNNNHHH

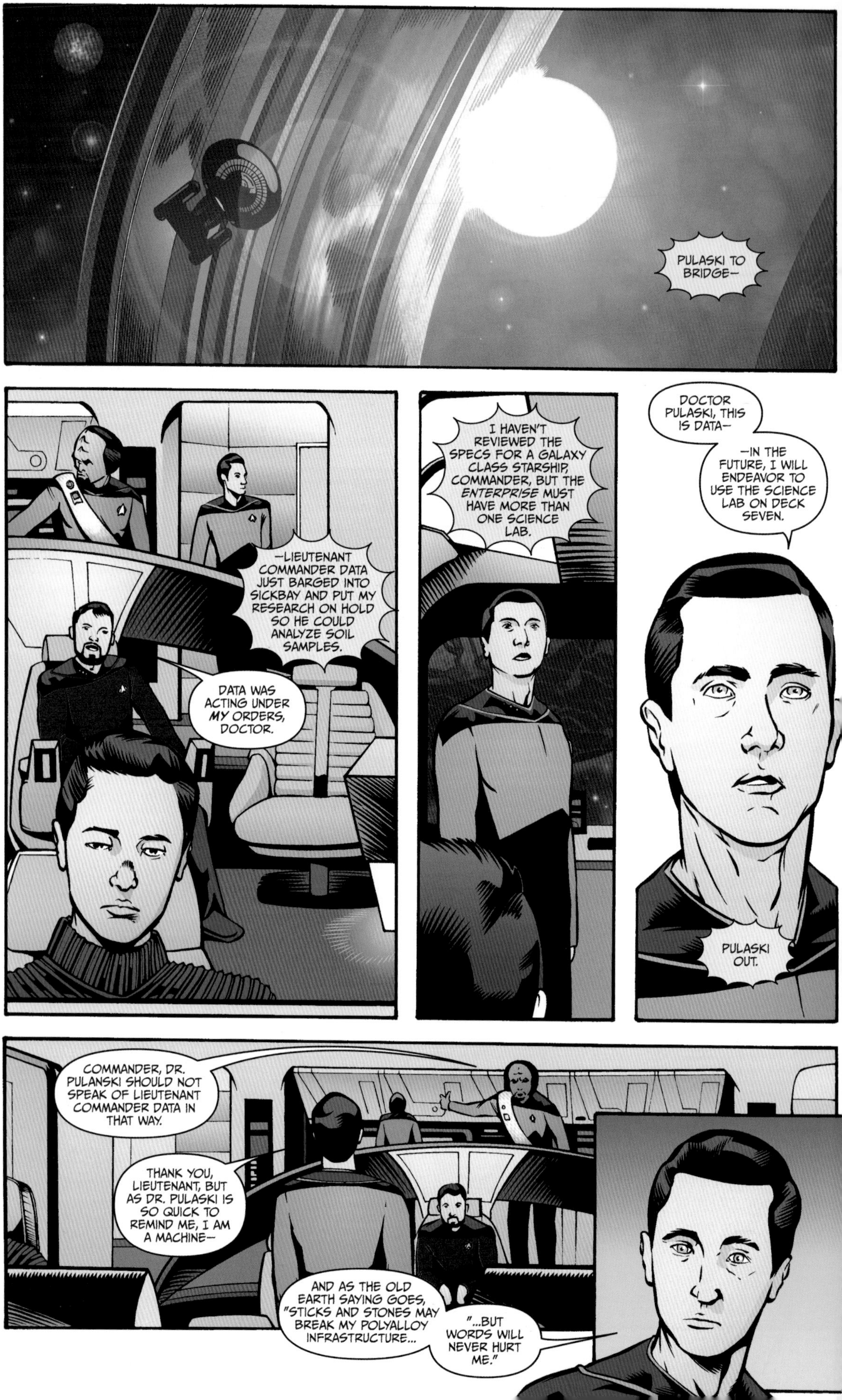
PULASKI TO BRIDGE—
—LIEUTENANT COMMANDER DATA JUST BARGED INTO SICKBAY AND PUT MY RESEARCH ON HOLD SO HE COULD ANALYZE SOIL SAMPLES.
DATA WAS ACTING UNDER MY ORDERS, DOCTOR.
I HAVEN'T REVIEWED THE SPECS FOR A GALAXY CLASS STARSHIP, COMMANDER, BUT THE ENTERPRISE MUST HAVE MORE THAN ONE SCIENCE LAB.
DOCTOR PULASKI, THIS IS DATA—
—IN THE FUTURE, I WILL ENDEAVOR TO USE THE SCIENCE LAB ON DECK SEVEN.
PULASKI OUT.
COMMANDER, DR. PULANSKI SHOULD NOT SPEAK OF LIEUTENANT COMMANDER DATA IN THAT WAY.
THANK YOU, LIEUTENANT, BUT AS DR. PULASKI IS SO QUICK TO REMIND ME, I AM A MACHINE—
AND AS THE OLD EARTH SAYING GOES, "STICKS AND STONES MAY BREAK MY POLYALLOY INFRASTRUCTURE...
"...BUT WORDS WILL NEVER HURT ME."

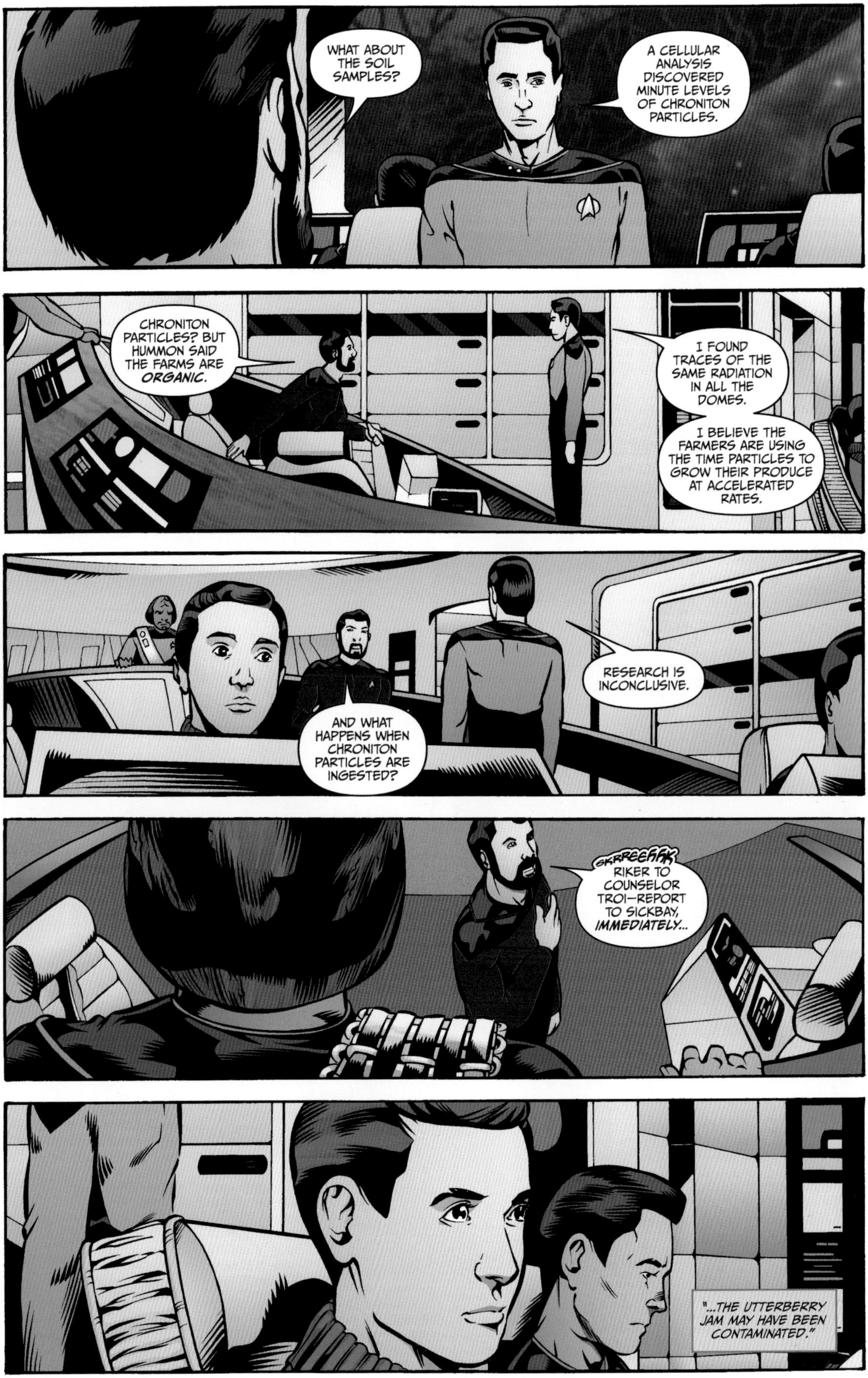

WHAT ABOUT THE SOIL SAMPLES?
A CELLULAR ANALYSIS DISCOVERED MINUTE LEVELS OF CHRONITON PARTICLES.
CHRONITON PARTICLES? BUT HUMMON SAID THE FARMS ARE *ORGANIC*.
I FOUND TRACES OF THE SAME RADIATION IN ALL THE DOMES.
I BELIEVE THE FARMERS ARE USING THE TIME PARTICLES TO GROW THEIR PRODUCE AT ACCELERATED RATES.
AND WHAT HAPPENS WHEN CHRONITON PARTICLES ARE INGESTED?
RESEARCH IS INCONCLUSIVE.
SKRREEAAK
RIKER TO COUNSELOR TROI—REPORT TO SICKBAY, *IMMEDIATELY*...
"...THE UTTERBERRY JAM MAY HAVE BEEN CONTAMINATED."

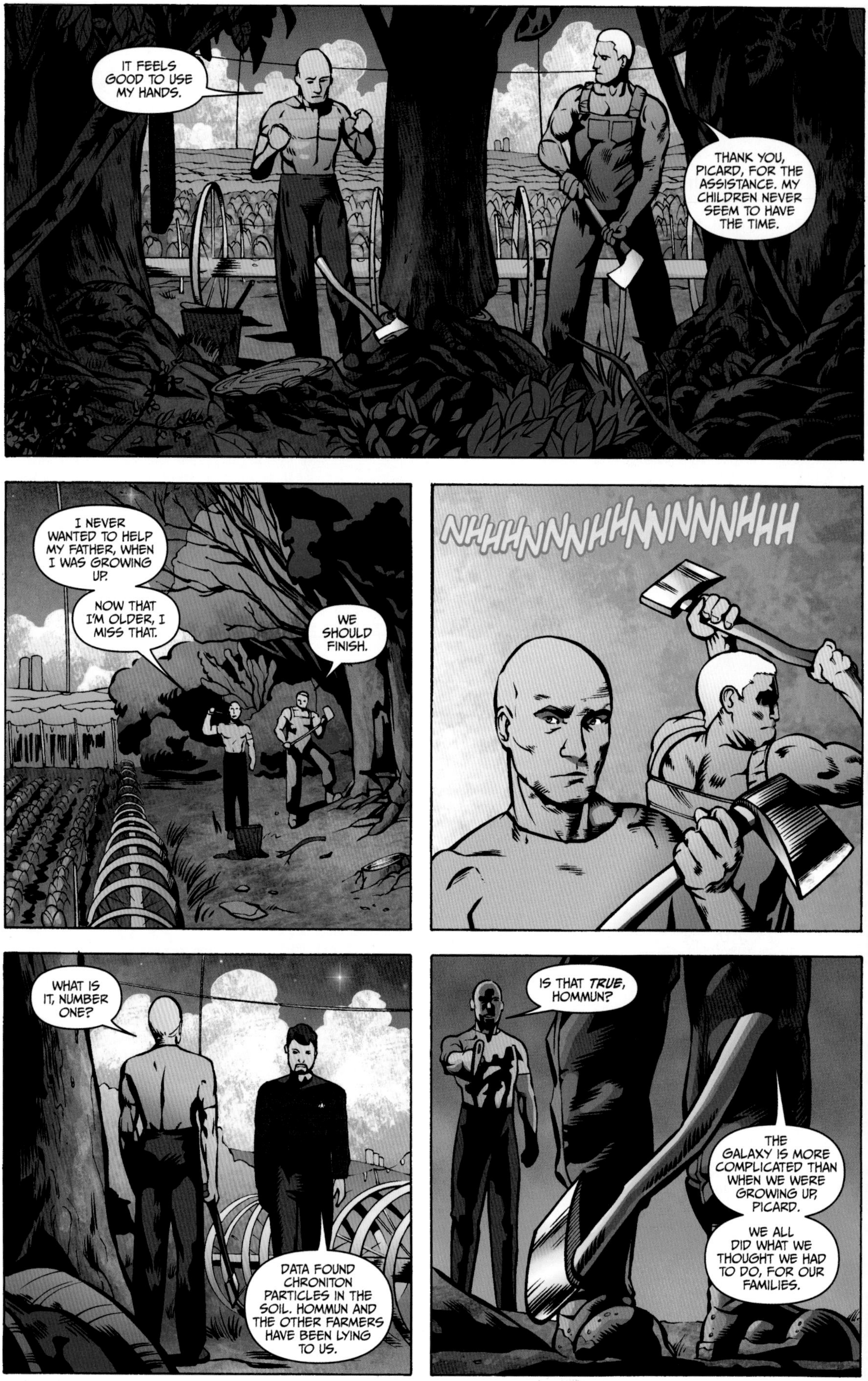
IT FEELS GOOD TO USE MY HANDS.
THANK YOU, PICARD, FOR THE ASSISTANCE. MY CHILDREN NEVER SEEM TO HAVE THE TIME.
I NEVER WANTED TO HELP MY FATHER, WHEN I WAS GROWING UP.
NOW THAT I'M OLDER, I MISS THAT.
WE SHOULD FINISH.
NHHNNNHHNNNNNHHH
WHAT IS IT, NUMBER ONE?
DATA FOUND CHRONITON PARTICLES IN THE SOIL. HOMMUN AND THE OTHER FARMERS HAVE BEEN LYING TO US.
IS THAT *TRUE*, HOMMUN?
THE GALAXY IS MORE COMPLICATED THAN WHEN WE WERE GROWING UP, PICARD.
WE ALL DID WHAT WE THOUGHT WE HAD TO DO, FOR OUR FAMILIES.

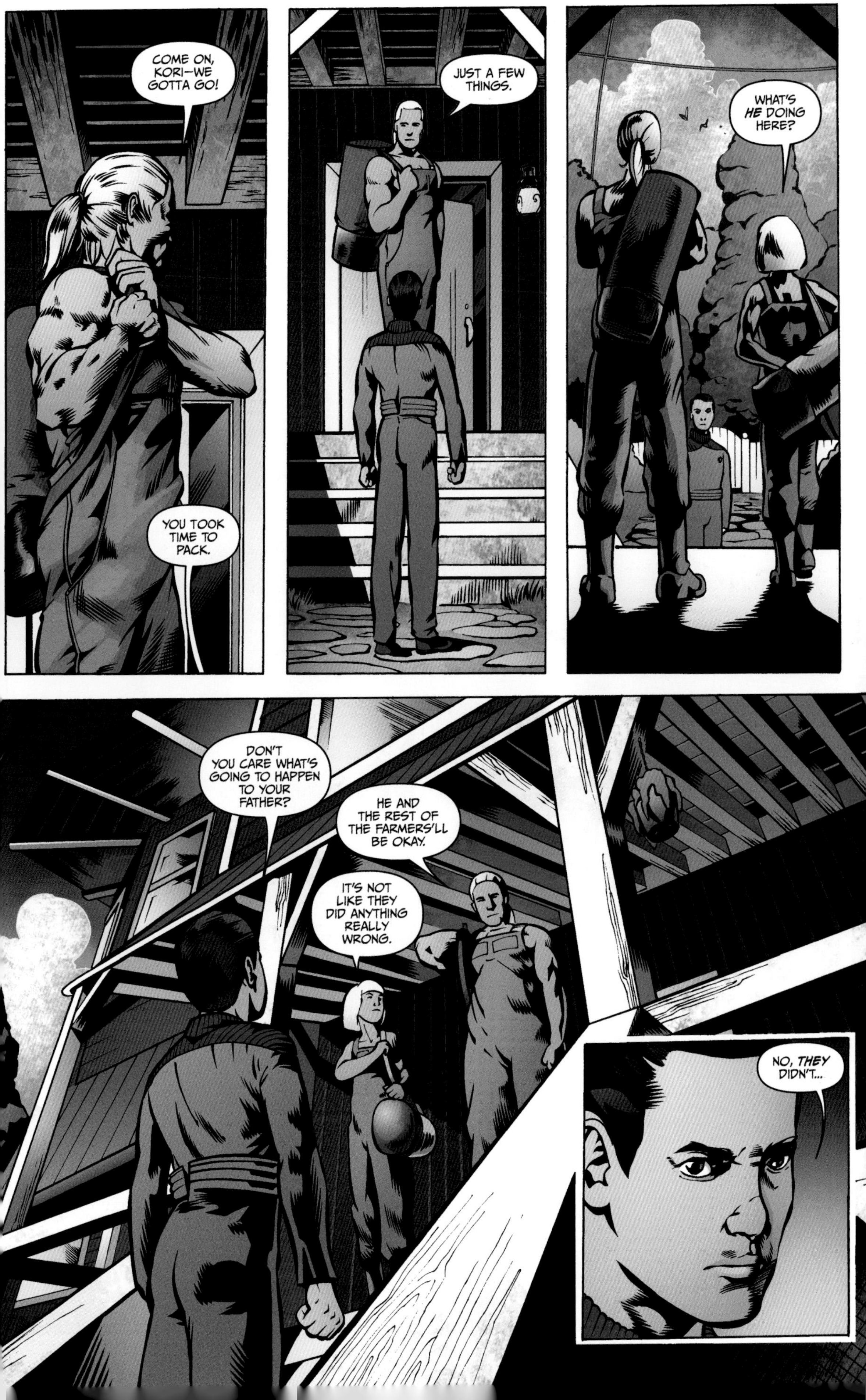
COME ON, KORI—WE GOTTA GO!
YOU TOOK TIME TO PACK.
JUST A FEW THINGS.
WHAT'S *HE* DOING HERE?
DON'T YOU CARE WHAT'S GOING TO HAPPEN TO YOUR FATHER?
HE AND THE REST OF THE FARMERS'LL BE OKAY.
IT'S NOT LIKE THEY DID ANYTHING REALLY WRONG.
NO, *THEY* DIDN'T...

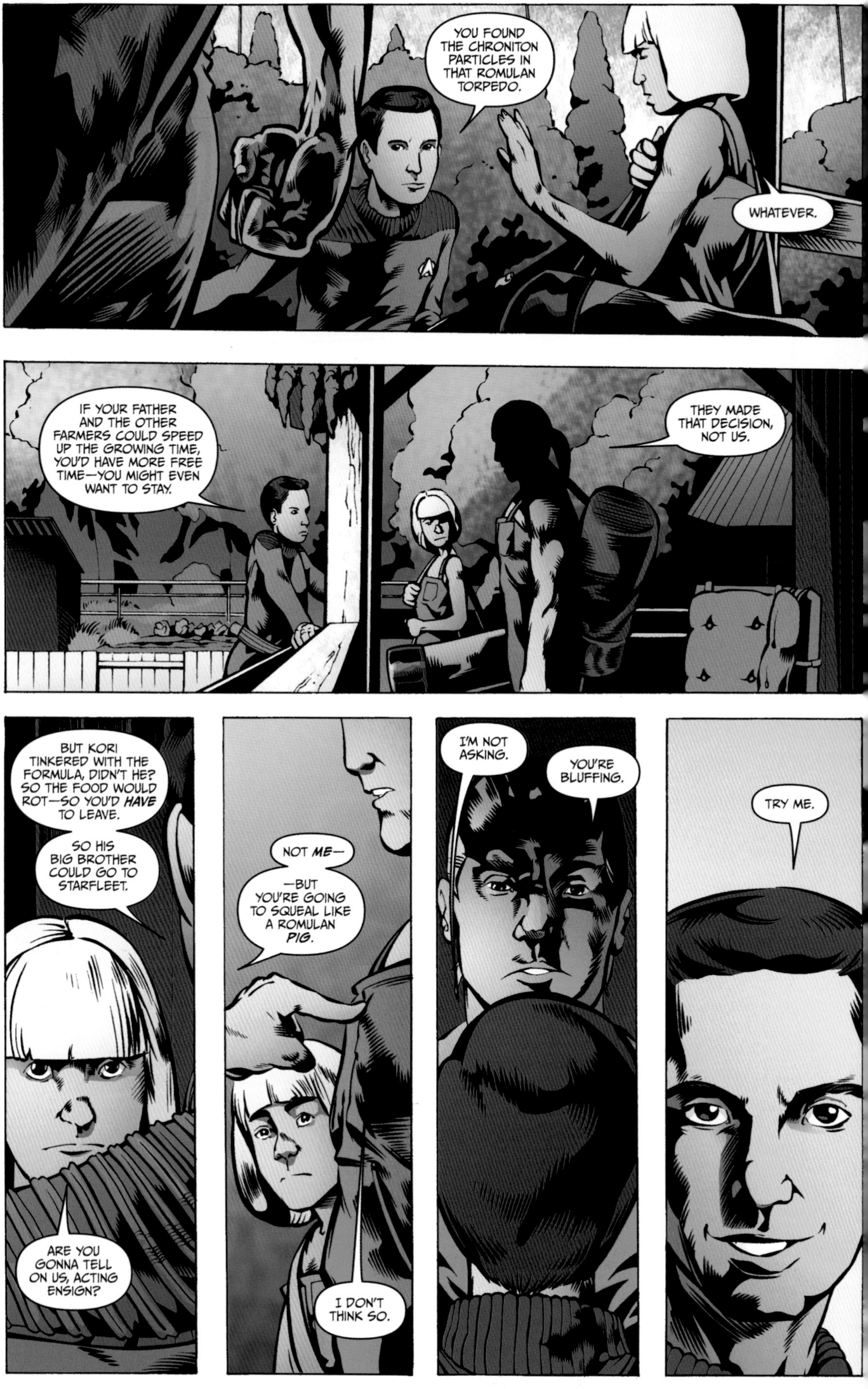
YOU FOUND THE CHRONITON PARTICLES IN THAT ROMULAN TORPEDO.
WHATEVER.
IF YOUR FATHER AND THE OTHER FARMERS COULD SPEED UP THE GROWING TIME, YOU'D HAVE MORE FREE TIME—YOU MIGHT EVEN WANT TO STAY.
THEY MADE THAT DECISION, NOT US.
BUT KORI TINKERED WITH THE FORMULA, DIDN'T HE? SO THE FOOD WOULD ROT—SO YOU'D *HAVE* TO LEAVE.
SO HIS BIG BROTHER COULD GO TO STARFLEET.
ARE YOU GONNA TELL ON US, ACTING ENSIGN?
NOT *ME*—
—BUT YOU'RE GOING TO SQUEAL LIKE A ROMULAN *PIG*.
I DON'T THINK SO.
I'M NOT ASKING.
YOU'RE BLUFFING.
TRY ME.

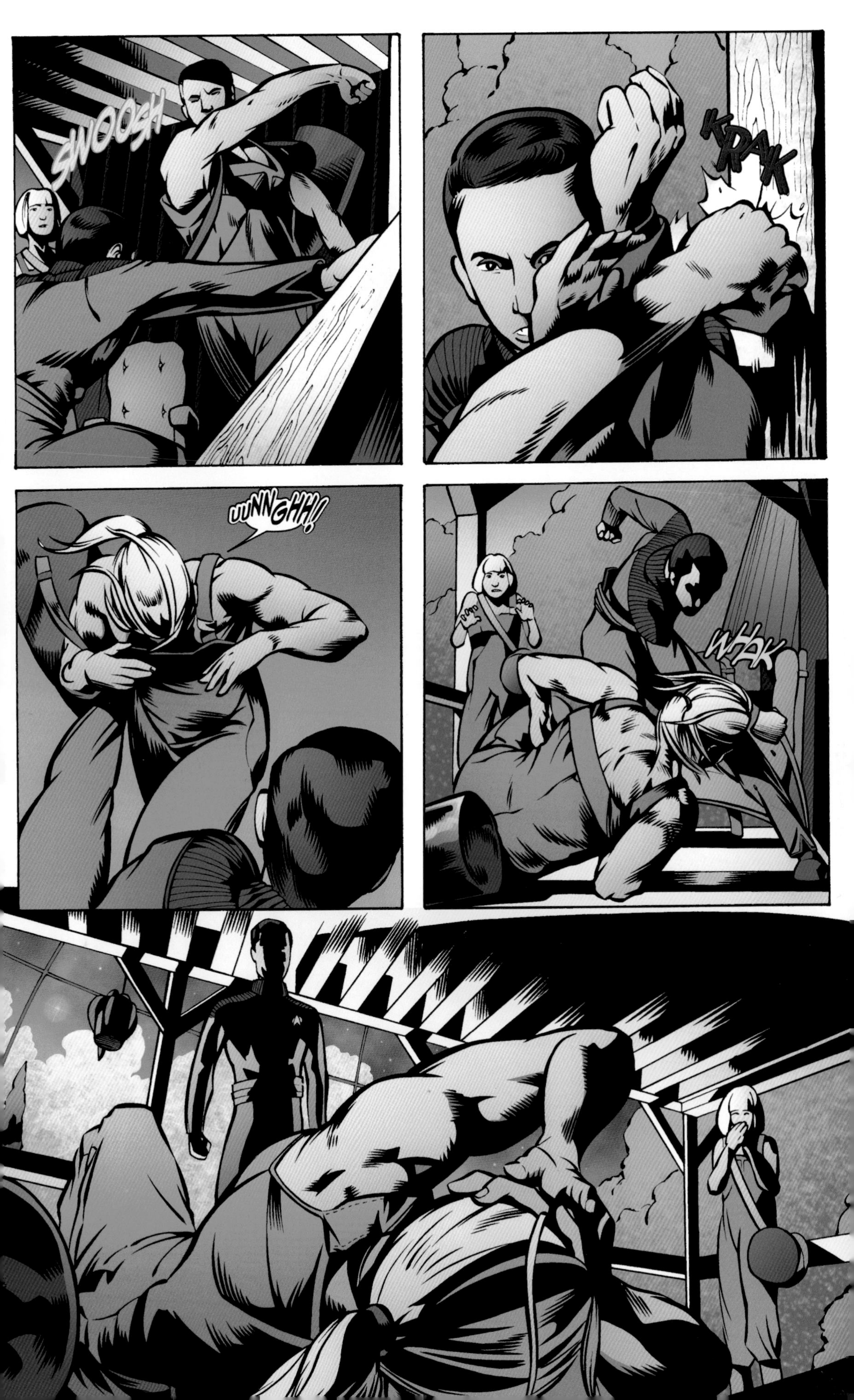
SWOOSH
KRAK
UUNNGHH!
WHAK

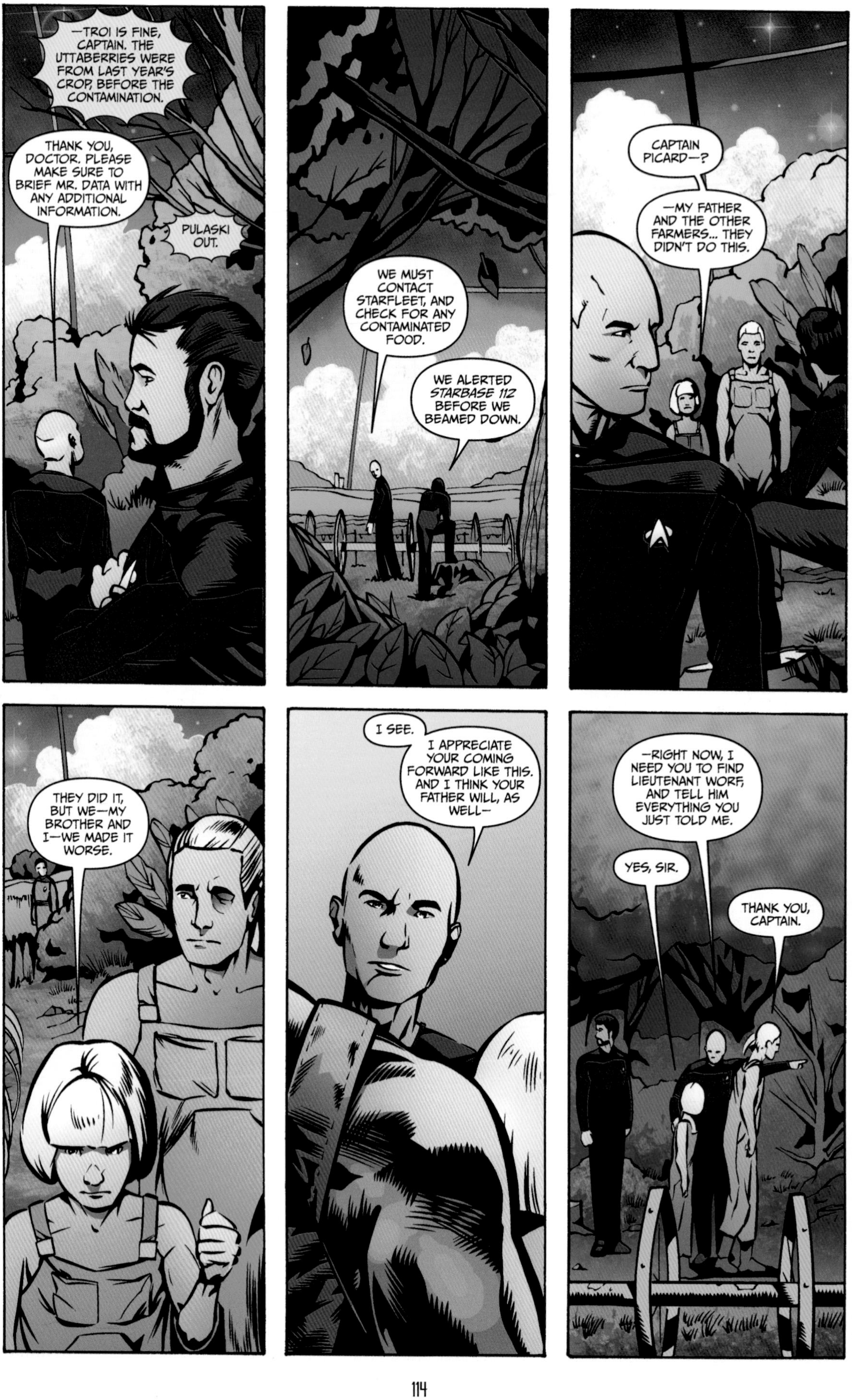
—TROI IS FINE, CAPTAIN. THE UTTABERRIES WERE FROM LAST YEAR'S CROP, BEFORE THE CONTAMINATION.
THANK YOU, DOCTOR. PLEASE MAKE SURE TO BRIEF MR. DATA WITH ANY ADDITIONAL INFORMATION.
PULASKI OUT.
WE MUST CONTACT STARFLEET, AND CHECK FOR ANY CONTAMINATED FOOD.
WE ALERTED STARBASE 112 BEFORE WE BEAMED DOWN.
CAPTAIN PICARD—?
—MY FATHER AND THE OTHER FARMERS... THEY DIDN'T DO THIS.
THEY DID IT, BUT WE—MY BROTHER AND I—WE MADE IT WORSE.
I SEE.
I APPRECIATE YOUR COMING FORWARD LIKE THIS. AND I THINK YOUR FATHER WILL, AS WELL—
—RIGHT NOW, I NEED YOU TO FIND LIEUTENANT WORF, AND TELL HIM EVERYTHING YOU JUST TOLD ME.
YES, SIR.
THANK YOU, CAPTAIN.

CAPTAIN. COMMANDER RIKER.

WES.

IT WAS VERY BRAVE FOR KORI TO COME FORWARD LIKE THAT—

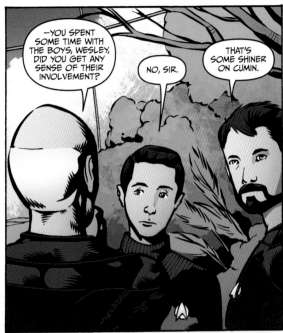

—YOU SPENT SOME TIME WITH THE BOYS, WESLEY, DID YOU GET ANY SENSE OF THEIR INVOLVEMENT?

NO, SIR.

THAT'S SOME SHINER ON CUMIN.

I DIDN'T *NOTICE*, SIR.

IF YOU NEED ME FOR ANYTHING ELSE, I'LL BE ON THE *ENTERPRISE*.

OF COURSE, WESLEY. AND THANK YOU.

THAT'S ODD.

THAT A TEENAGER TELLS THE TRUTH WITHOUT BEING FORCED?

NO— THAT WESLEY IGNORED CUMIN'S VERY *OBVIOUS* BLACK EYE.

IS IT POSSIBLE ENSIGN CRUSHER JUST *LIED* TO US, NUMBER ONE?

I CAN'T BE SURE, CAPTAIN, BUT I WILL SAY THIS—

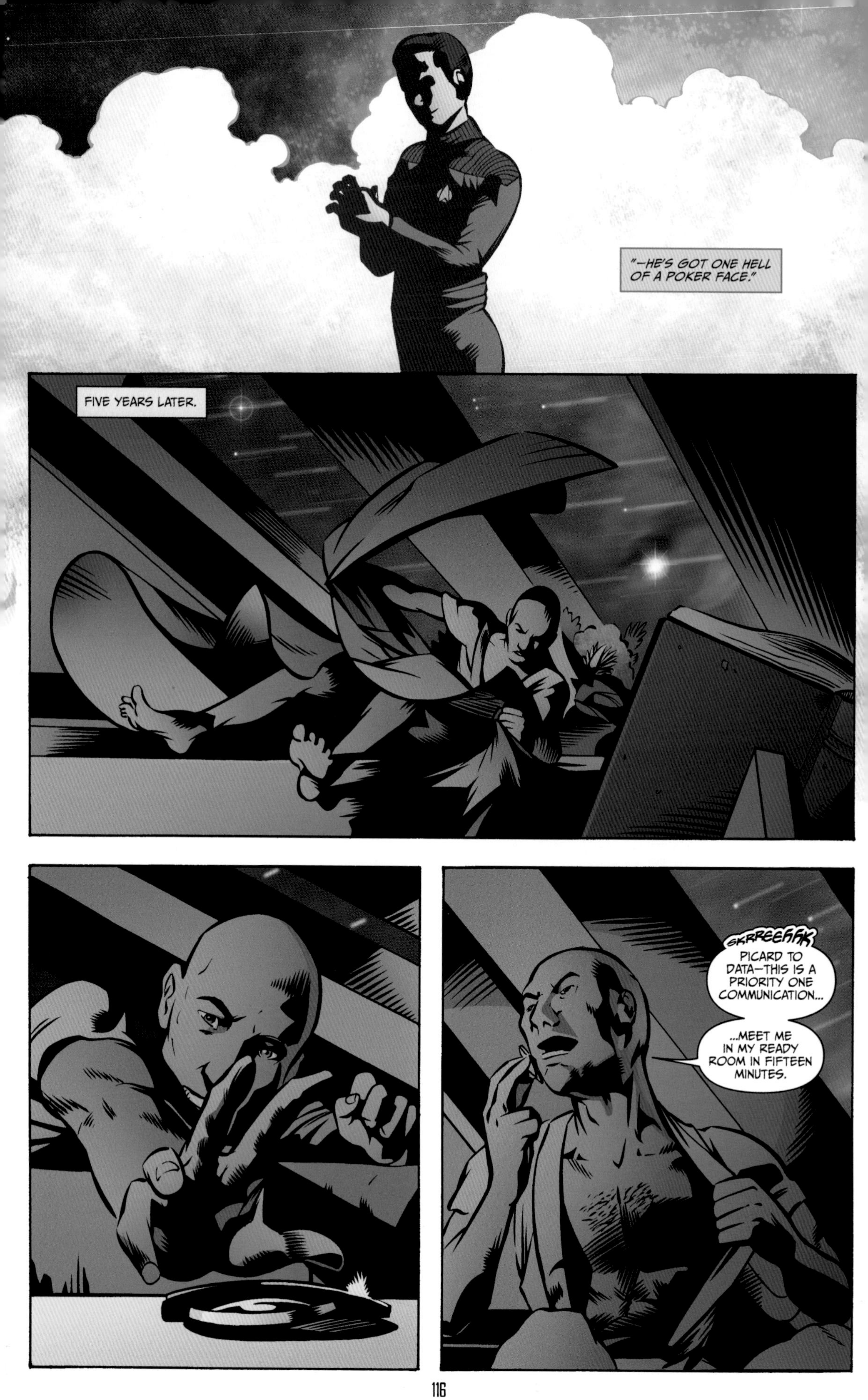
"—HE'S GOT ONE HELL OF A POKER FACE."
FIVE YEARS LATER.
SKRREEKKK
PICARD TO DATA—THIS IS A PRIORITY ONE COMMUNICATION...
...MEET ME IN MY READY ROOM IN FIFTEEN MINUTES.

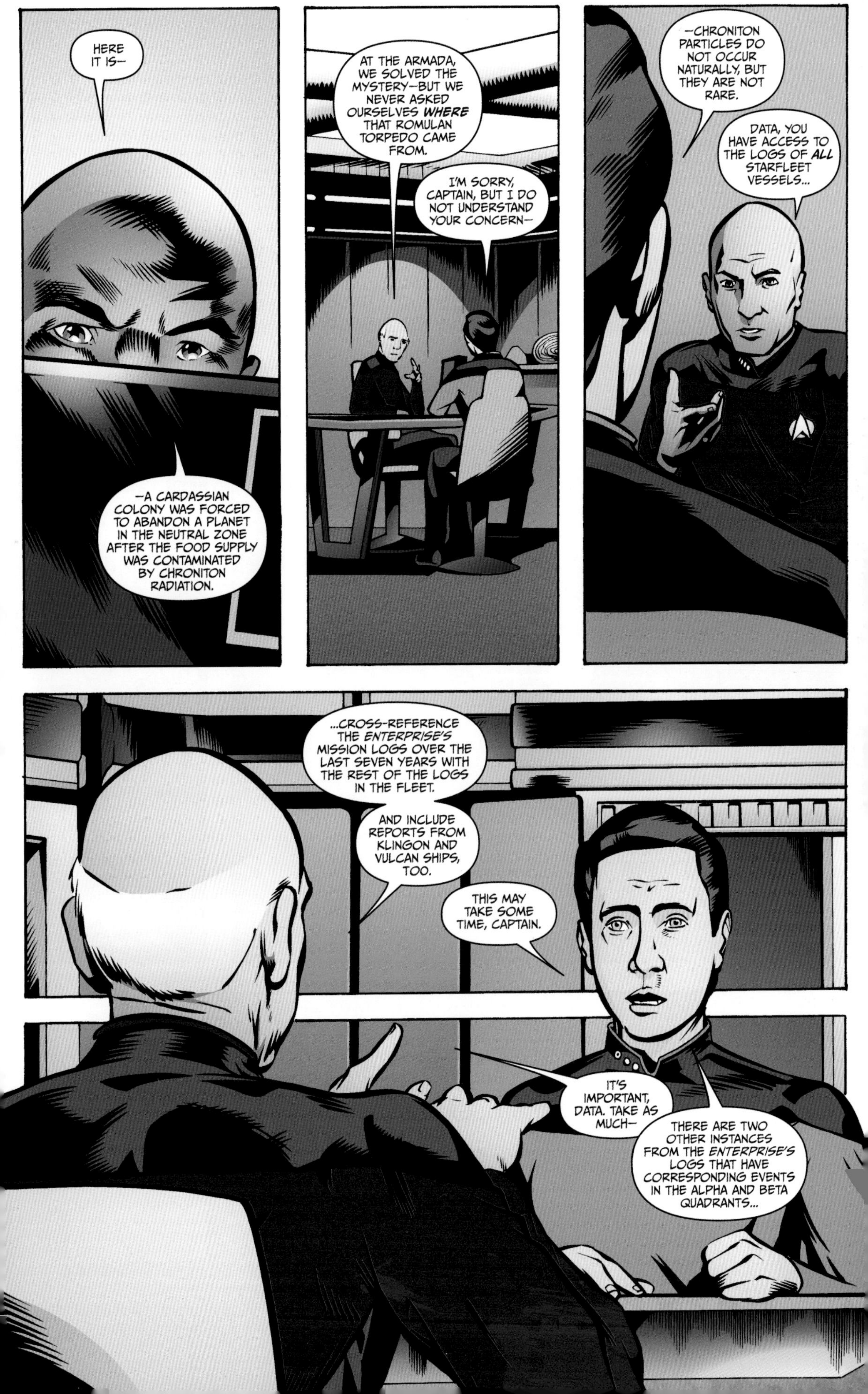
HERE IT IS—
—A CARDASSIAN COLONY WAS FORCED TO ABANDON A PLANET IN THE NEUTRAL ZONE AFTER THE FOOD SUPPLY WAS CONTAMINATED BY CHRONITON RADIATION.
AT THE ARMADA, WE SOLVED THE MYSTERY—BUT WE NEVER ASKED OURSELVES *WHERE* THAT ROMULAN TORPEDO CAME FROM.
I'M SORRY, CAPTAIN, BUT I DO NOT UNDERSTAND YOUR CONCERN—
—CHRONITON PARTICLES DO NOT OCCUR NATURALLY, BUT THEY ARE NOT RARE.
DATA, YOU HAVE ACCESS TO THE LOGS OF *ALL* STARFLEET VESSELS...
...CROSS-REFERENCE THE *ENTERPRISE'S* MISSION LOGS OVER THE LAST SEVEN YEARS WITH THE REST OF THE LOGS IN THE FLEET.
AND INCLUDE REPORTS FROM KLINGON AND VULCAN SHIPS, TOO.
THIS MAY TAKE SOME TIME, CAPTAIN.
IT'S IMPORTANT, DATA. TAKE AS MUCH—
THERE ARE TWO OTHER INSTANCES FROM THE *ENTERPRISE'S* LOGS THAT HAVE CORRESPONDING EVENTS IN THE ALPHA AND BETA QUADRANTS...

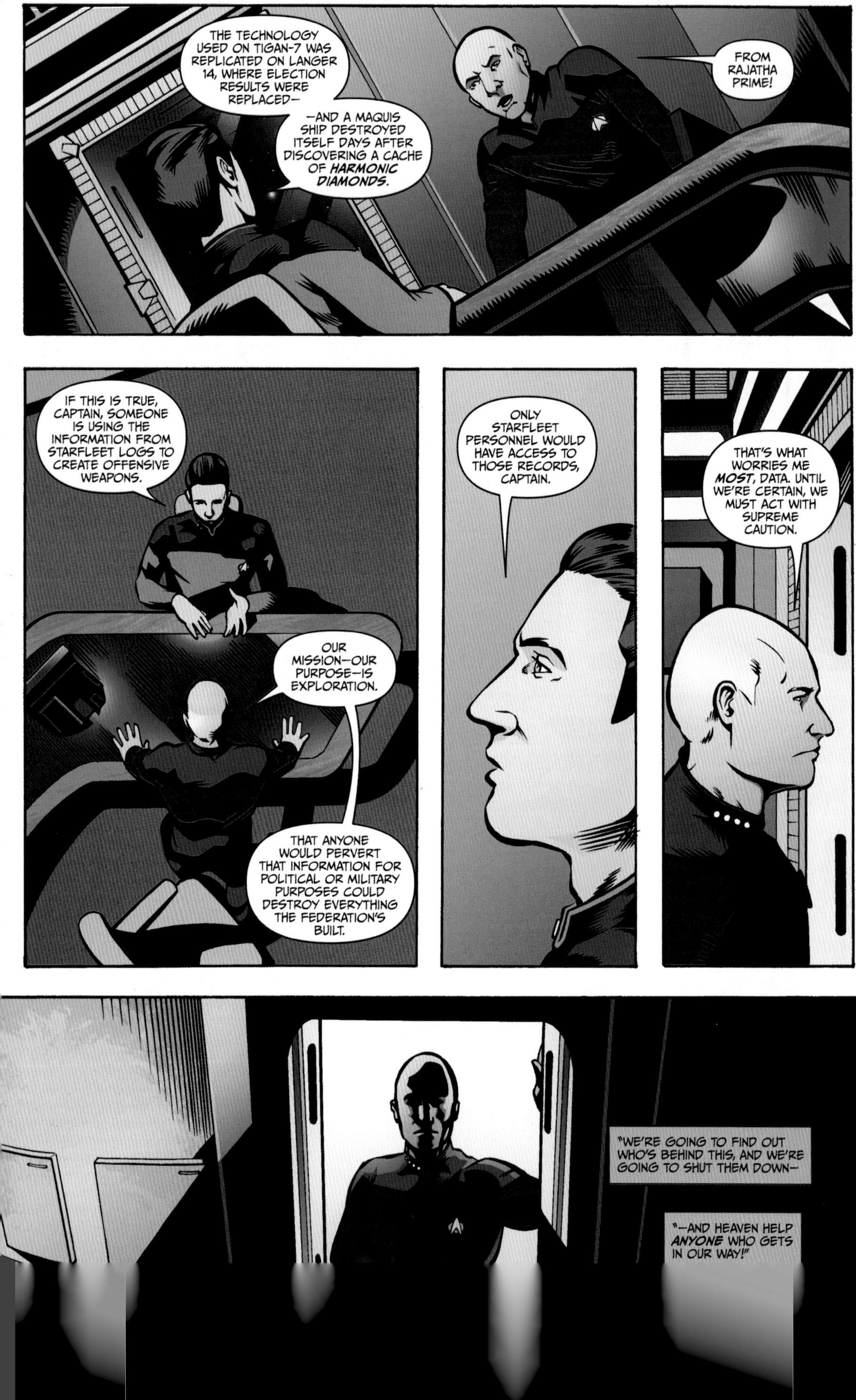
THE TECHNOLOGY USED ON TIGAN-7 WAS REPLICATED ON LANGER 14, WHERE ELECTION RESULTS WERE REPLACED—
—AND A MAQUIS SHIP DESTROYED ITSELF DAYS AFTER DISCOVERING A CACHE OF *HARMONIC DIAMONDS.*
FROM RAJATHA PRIME!
IF THIS IS TRUE, CAPTAIN, SOMEONE IS USING THE INFORMATION FROM STARFLEET LOGS TO CREATE OFFENSIVE WEAPONS.
OUR MISSION—OUR PURPOSE—IS EXPLORATION.
THAT ANYONE WOULD PERVERT THAT INFORMATION FOR POLITICAL OR MILITARY PURPOSES COULD DESTROY EVERYTHING THE FEDERATION'S BUILT.
ONLY STARFLEET PERSONNEL WOULD HAVE ACCESS TO THOSE RECORDS, CAPTAIN.
THAT'S WHAT WORRIES ME *MOST*, DATA. UNTIL WE'RE CERTAIN, WE MUST ACT WITH SUPREME CAUTION.
"WE'RE GOING TO FIND OUT WHO'S BEHIND THIS, AND WE'RE GOING TO SHUT THEM DOWN—
"—AND HEAVEN HELP *ANYONE* WHO GETS IN OUR WAY!"

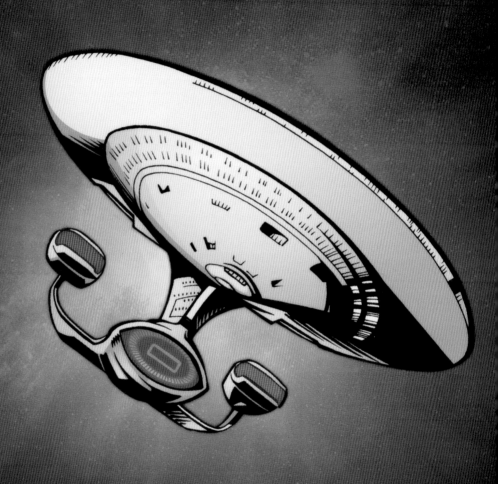

PART SIX: AN INCONVENIENT TRUTH

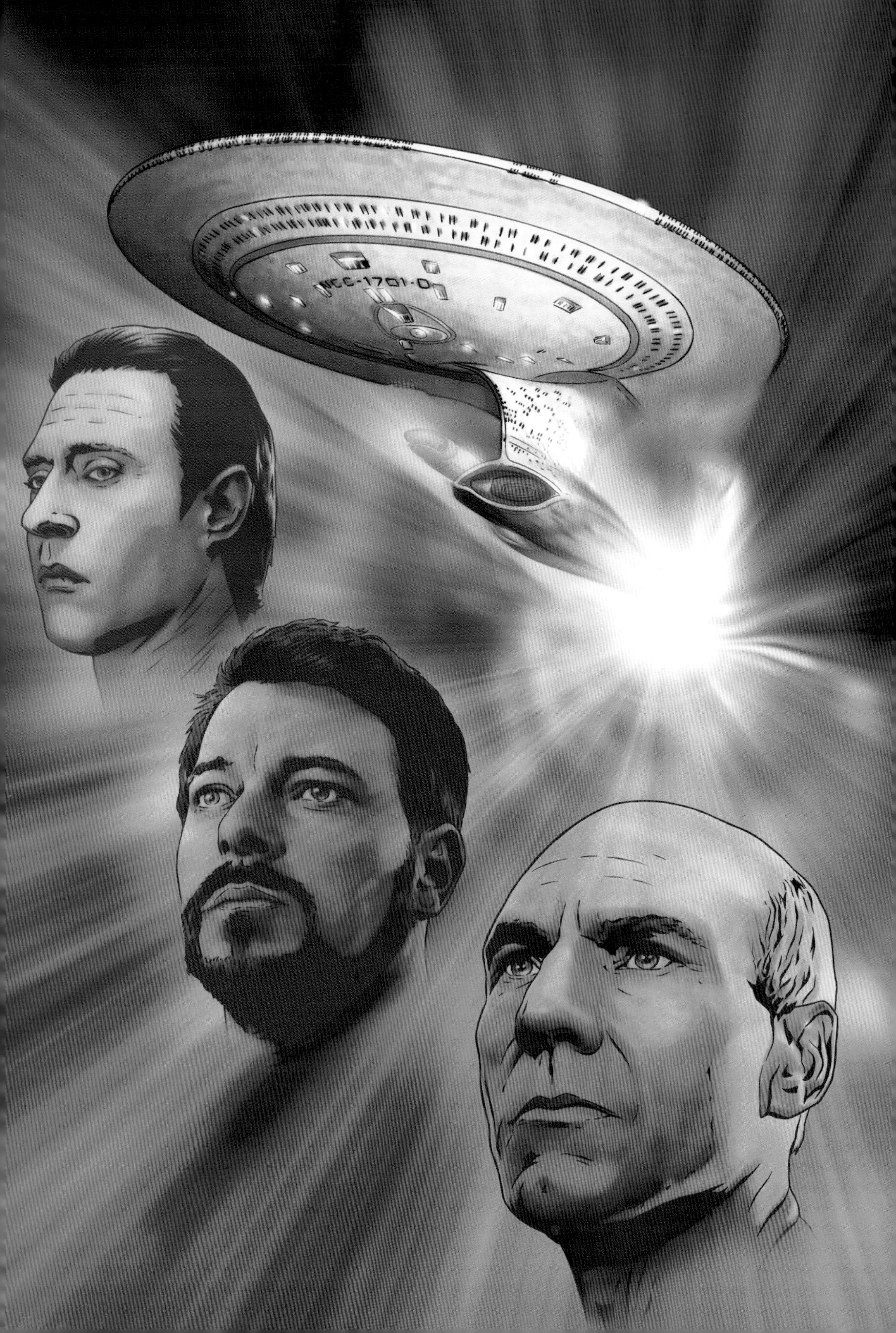
NCC-1701-D

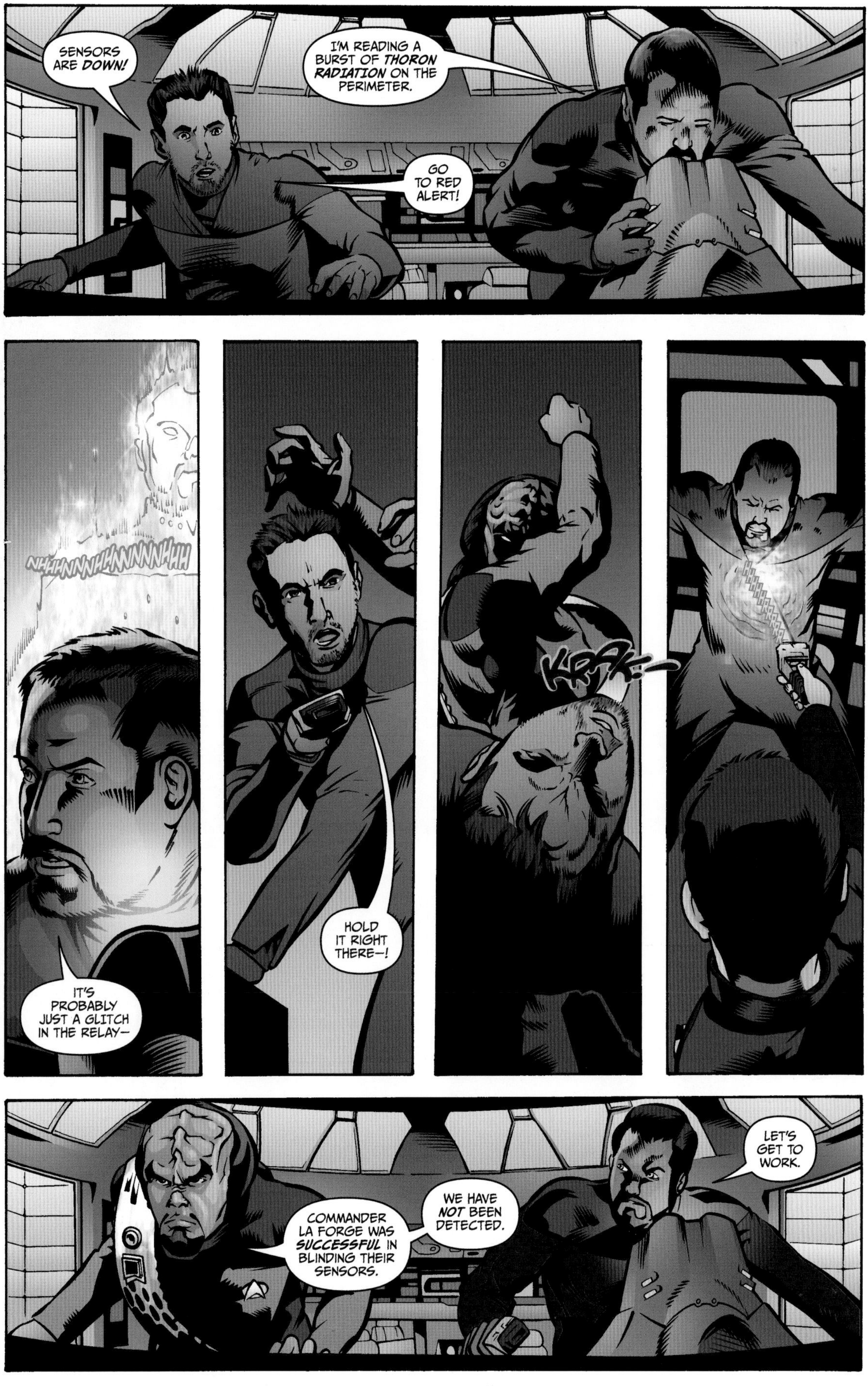

SENSORS ARE *DOWN!*
I'M READING A BURST OF *THORON RADIATION* ON THE PERIMETER.
GO TO RED ALERT!
IT'S PROBABLY JUST A GLITCH IN THE RELAY—
HOLD IT RIGHT THERE—!
KRAK!—
LET'S GET TO WORK.
WE HAVE *NOT* BEEN DETECTED.
COMMANDER LA FORGE WAS *SUCCESSFUL* IN BLINDING THEIR SENSORS.

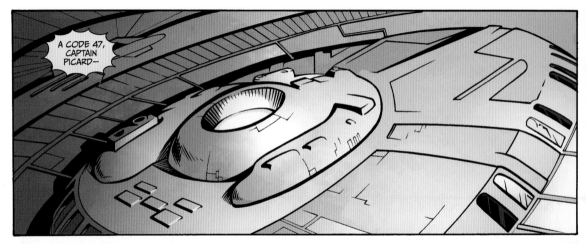

A CODE 47, CAPTAIN PICARD—

—THIS MUST BE IMPORTANT.

INDEED, ADMIRAL.

I RECENTLY DISCOVERED INFORMATION FROM THE *ENTERPRISE'S* MISSION LOGS IS BEING USED FOR *OFFENSIVE* PURPOSES—

—TO FORWARD A POLITICAL *AGENDA* ON SEVERAL PLANETS IN THE ALPHA QUADRANT... AND PERHAPS *BEYOND*.

DID YOU *HEAR* WHAT I—

YES.

WHAT DO YOU PLAN TO *DO* WITH THIS INFORMATION?

THAT DEPENDS A GREAT DEAL ON WHAT *YOU* INTEND ON DOING WITH THIS INFORMATION, ADMIRAL NECHAYEV.

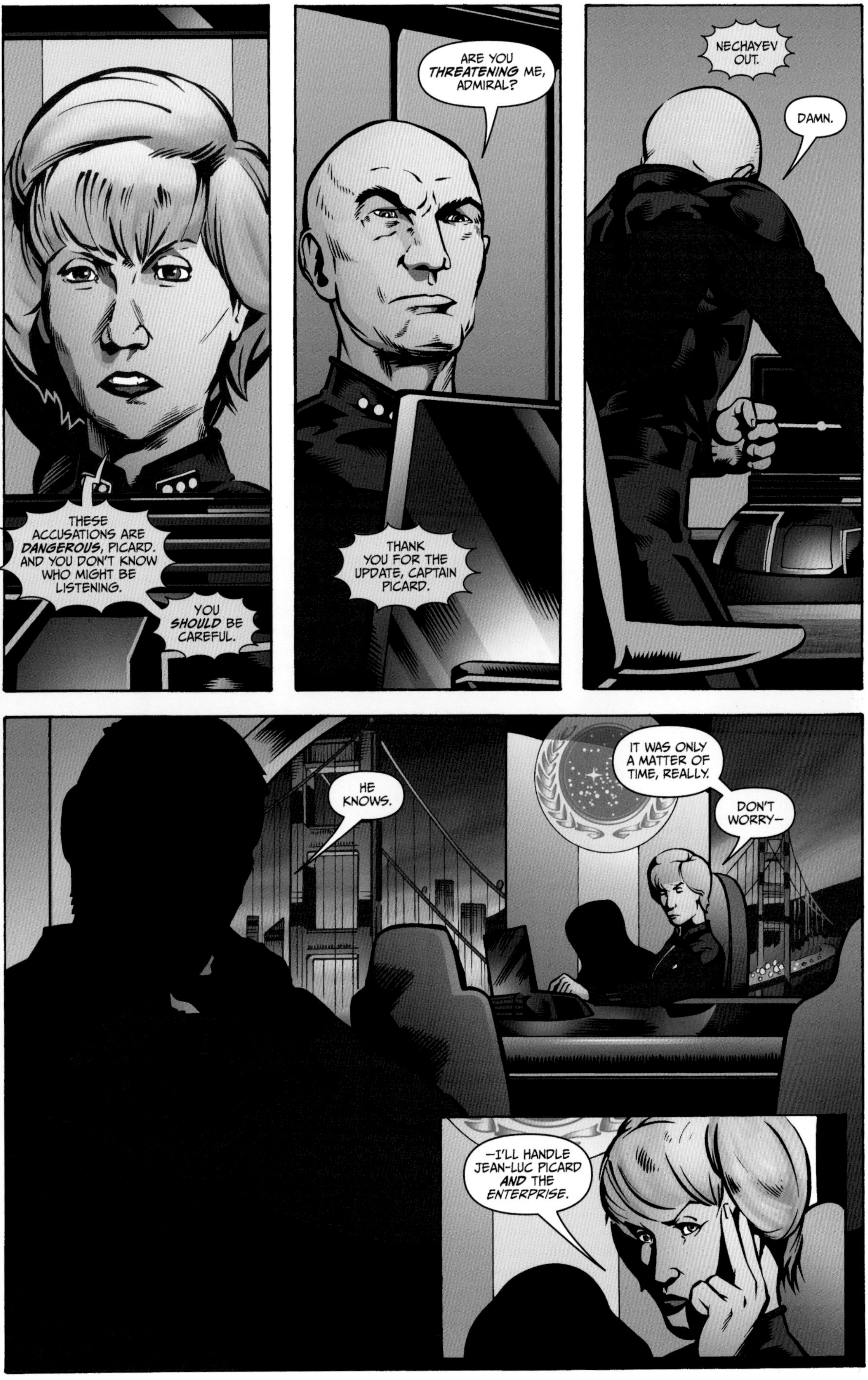
THESE ACCUSATIONS ARE DANGEROUS, PICARD. AND YOU DON'T KNOW WHO MIGHT BE LISTENING.
YOU SHOULD BE CAREFUL.
ARE YOU THREATENING ME, ADMIRAL?
THANK YOU FOR THE UPDATE, CAPTAIN PICARD.
NECHAYEV OUT.
DAMN.
HE KNOWS.
IT WAS ONLY A MATTER OF TIME, REALLY.
DON'T WORRY—
—I'LL HANDLE JEAN-LUC PICARD AND THE ENTERPRISE.

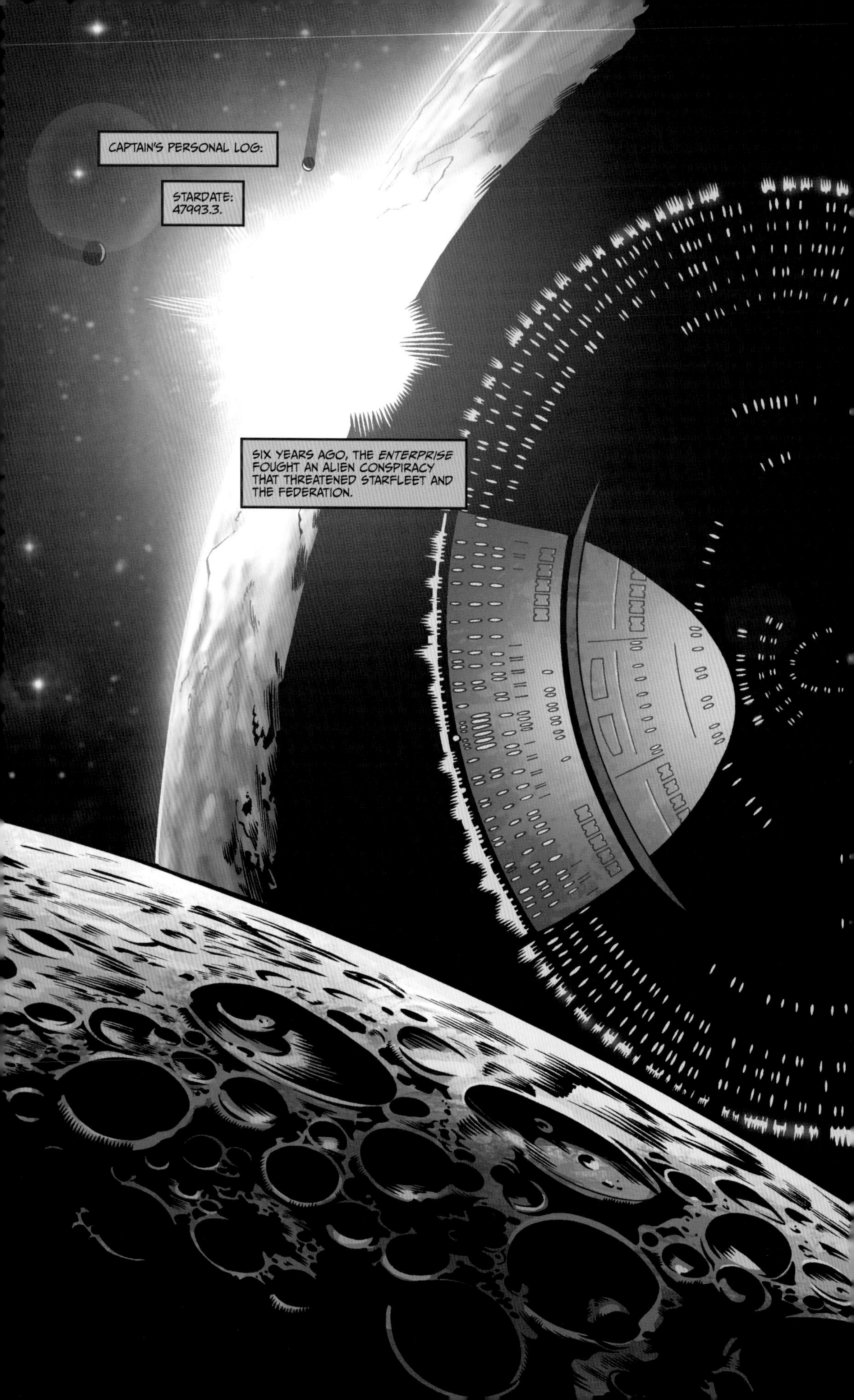
CAPTAIN'S PERSONAL LOG:
STARDATE: 47993.3.
SIX YEARS AGO, THE *ENTERPRISE* FOUGHT AN ALIEN CONSPIRACY THAT THREATENED STARFLEET AND THE FEDERATION.

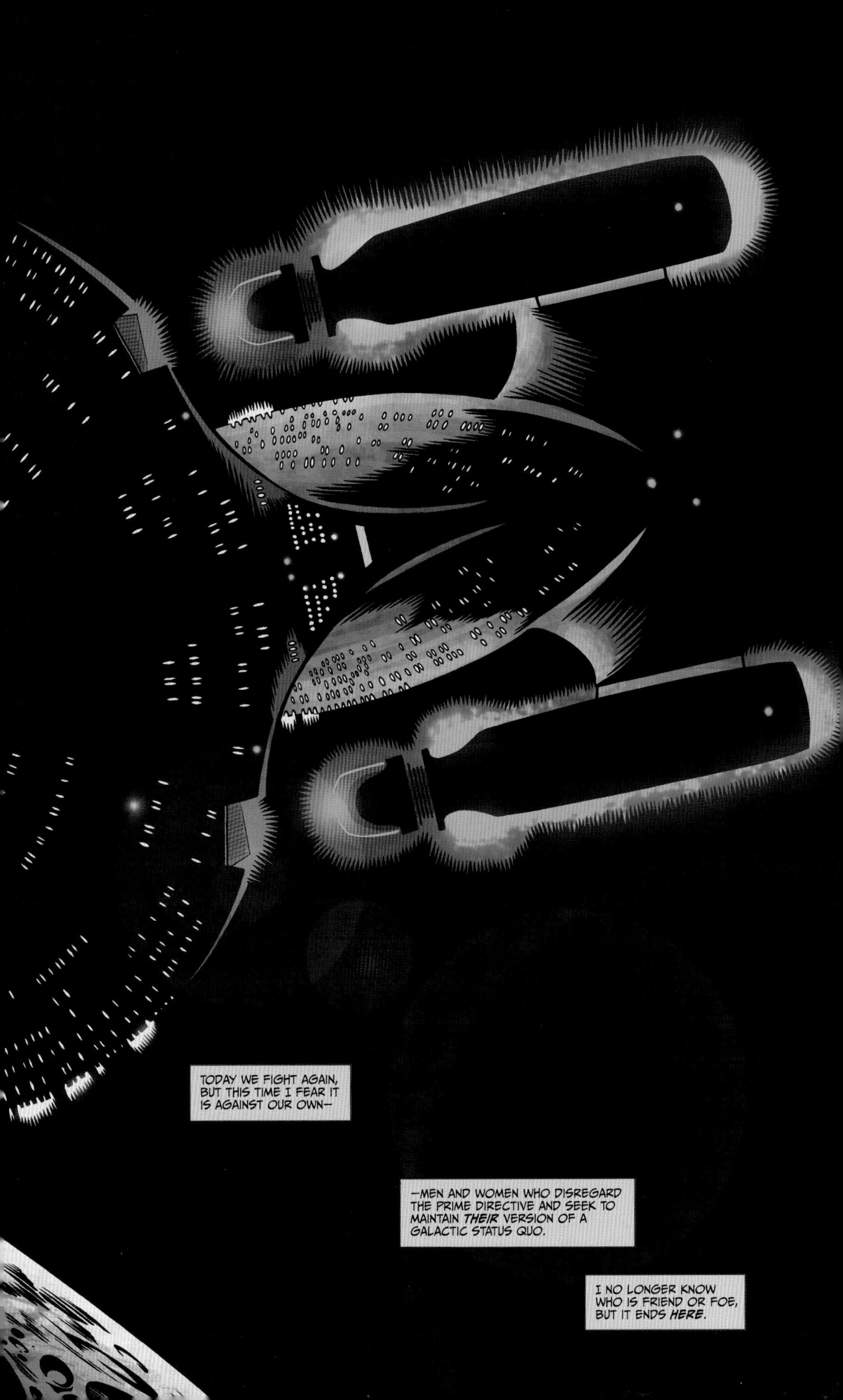
TODAY WE FIGHT AGAIN, BUT THIS TIME I FEAR IT IS AGAINST OUR OWN–
–MEN AND WOMEN WHO DISREGARD THE PRIME DIRECTIVE AND SEEK TO MAINTAIN *THEIR* VERSION OF A GALACTIC STATUS QUO.
I NO LONGER KNOW WHO IS FRIEND OR FOE, BUT IT ENDS *HERE*.

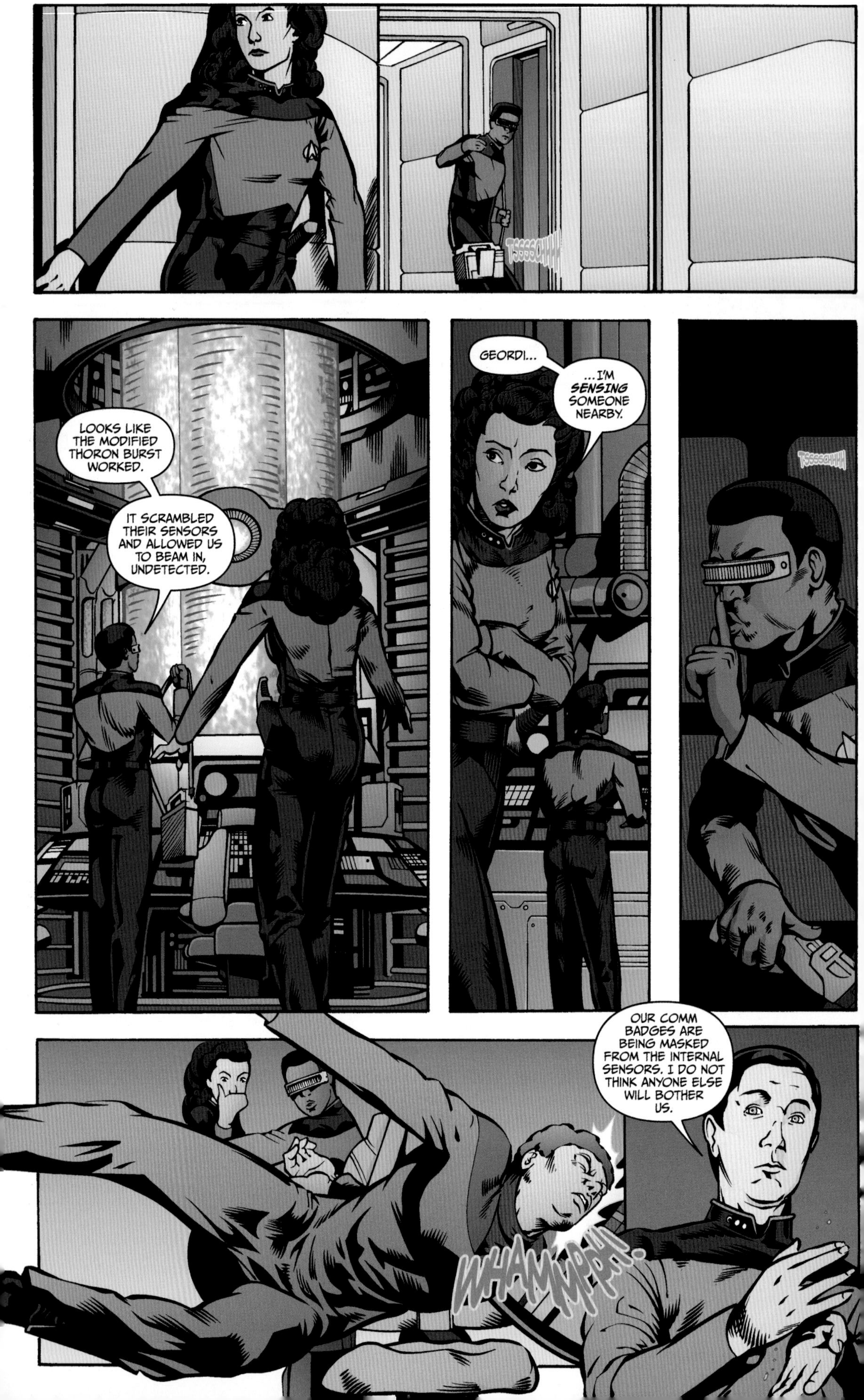
TSSSSCHHH
LOOKS LIKE THE MODIFIED THORON BURST WORKED.
IT SCRAMBLED THEIR SENSORS AND ALLOWED US TO BEAM IN, UNDETECTED.
GEORDI...
...I'M *SENSING* SOMEONE NEARBY.
TSSSSCHHHH
OUR COMM BADGES ARE BEING MASKED FROM THE INTERNAL SENSORS. I DO NOT THINK ANYONE ELSE WILL BOTHER US.
WHAMMPH!

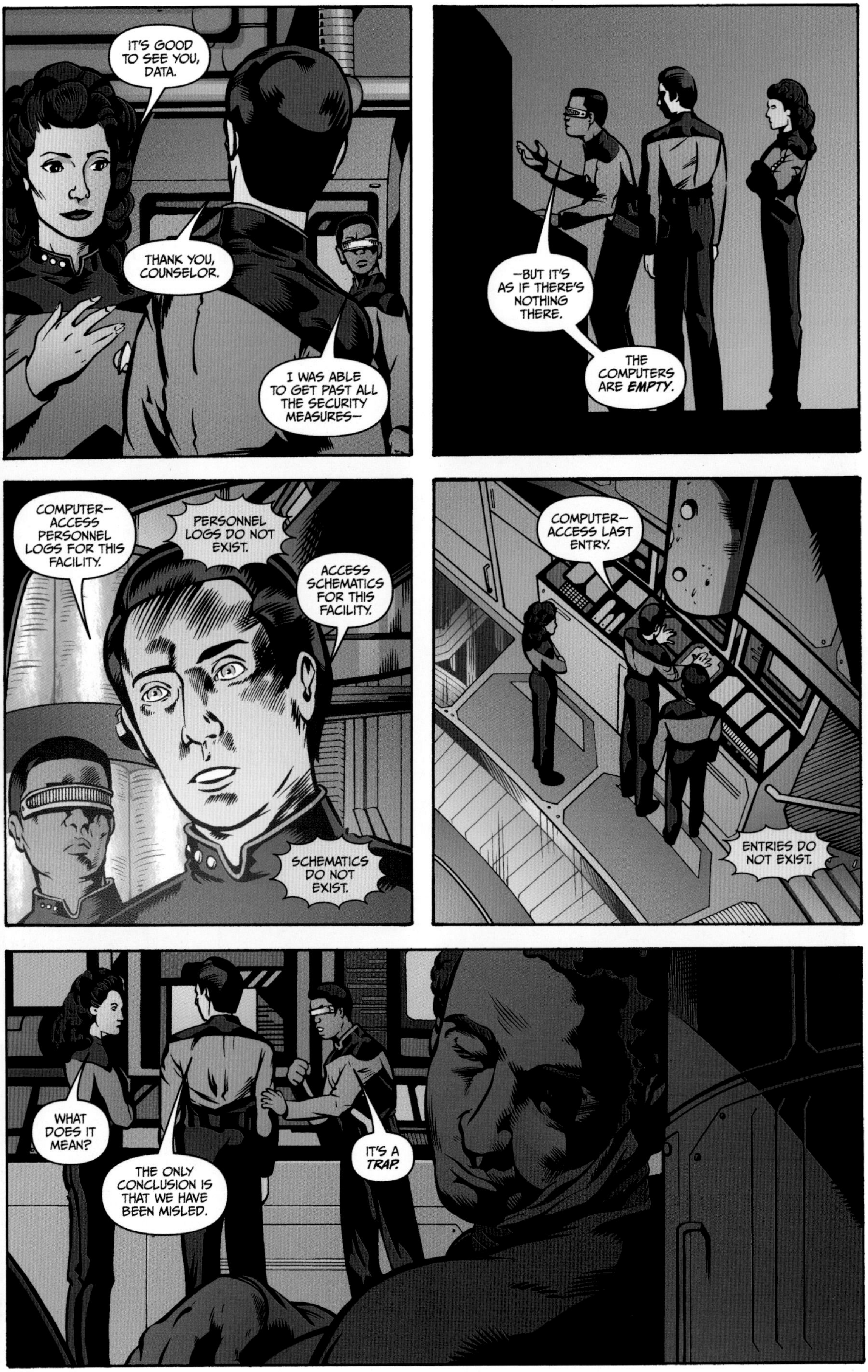
IT'S GOOD TO SEE YOU, DATA.
THANK YOU, COUNSELOR.
I WAS ABLE TO GET PAST ALL THE SECURITY MEASURES—
—BUT IT'S AS IF THERE'S NOTHING THERE.
THE COMPUTERS ARE *EMPTY*.
COMPUTER—ACCESS PERSONNEL LOGS FOR THIS FACILITY.
PERSONNEL LOGS DO NOT EXIST.
ACCESS SCHEMATICS FOR THIS FACILITY.
SCHEMATICS DO NOT EXIST.
COMPUTER—ACCESS LAST ENTRY.
ENTRIES DO NOT EXIST.
WHAT DOES IT MEAN?
THE ONLY CONCLUSION IS THAT WE HAVE BEEN MISLED.
IT'S A *TRAP*.

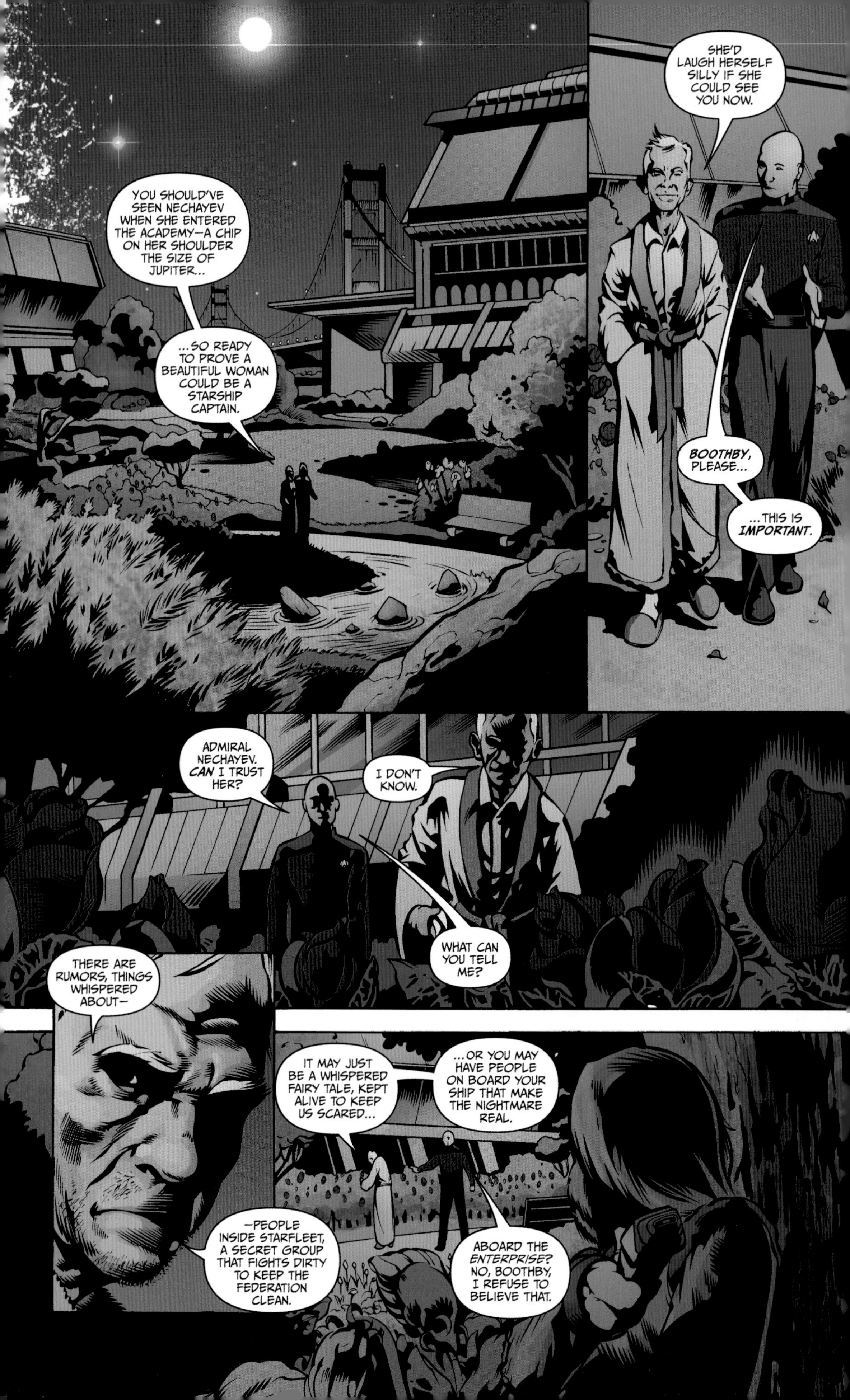
YOU SHOULD'VE SEEN NECHAYEV WHEN SHE ENTERED THE ACADEMY—A CHIP ON HER SHOULDER THE SIZE OF JUPITER...
...SO READY TO PROVE A BEAUTIFUL WOMAN COULD BE A STARSHIP CAPTAIN.
SHE'D LAUGH HERSELF SILLY IF SHE COULD SEE YOU NOW.
BOOTHBY, PLEASE...
...THIS IS *IMPORTANT*.
ADMIRAL NECHAYEV. *CAN* I TRUST HER?
I DON'T KNOW.
WHAT CAN YOU TELL ME?
THERE ARE RUMORS, THINGS WHISPERED ABOUT—
—PEOPLE INSIDE STARFLEET, A SECRET GROUP THAT FIGHTS DIRTY TO KEEP THE FEDERATION CLEAN.
IT MAY JUST BE A WHISPERED FAIRY TALE, KEPT ALIVE TO KEEP US SCARED...
...OR YOU MAY HAVE PEOPLE ON BOARD YOUR SHIP THAT MAKE THE NIGHTMARE REAL.
ABOARD THE *ENTERPRISE*? NO, BOOTHBY, I REFUSE TO BELIEVE THAT.

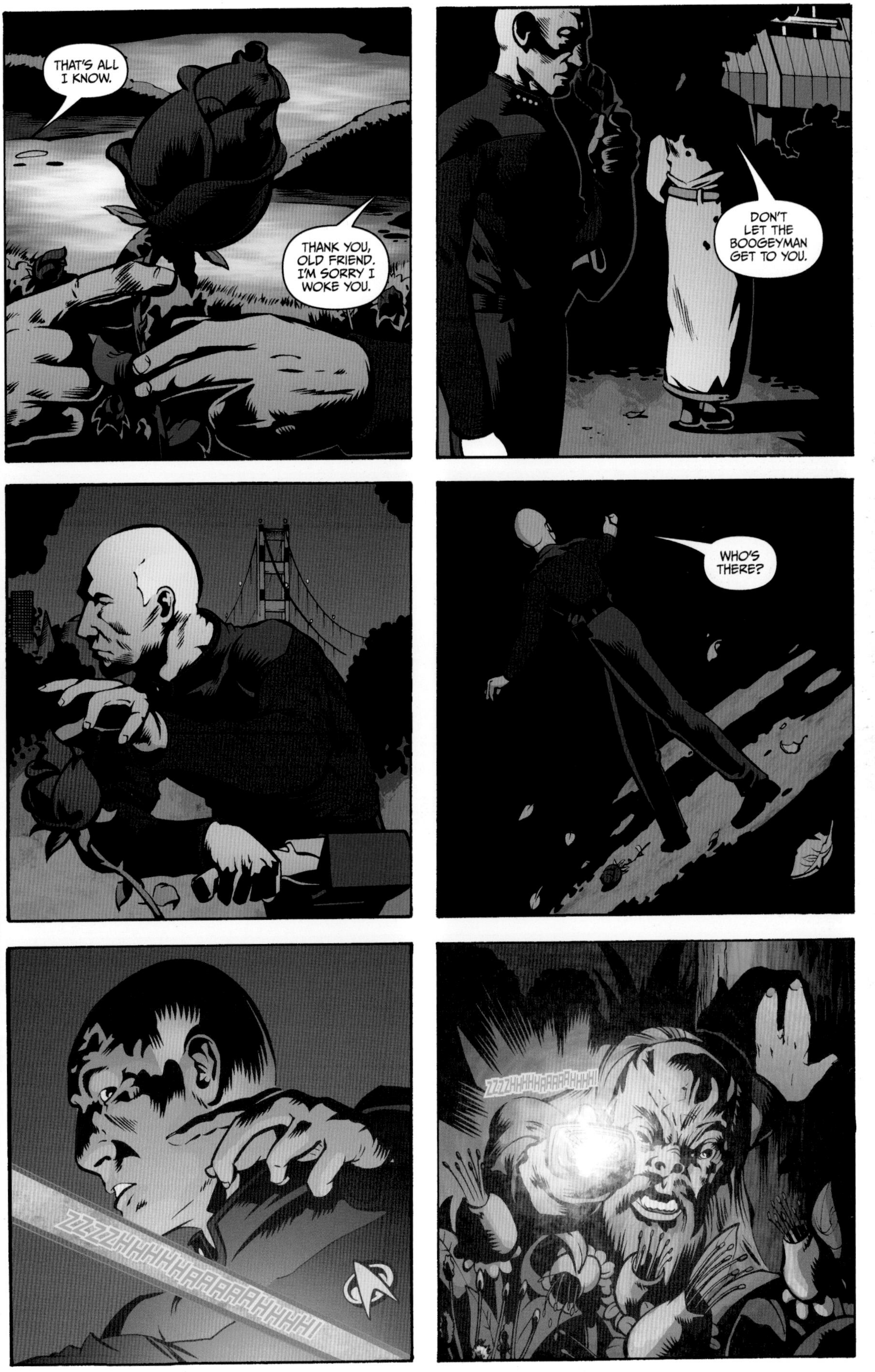
THAT'S ALL I KNOW.
THANK YOU, OLD FRIEND. I'M SORRY I WOKE YOU.
DON'T LET THE BOOGEYMAN GET TO YOU.
WHO'S THERE?
ZZZZHHHHHAAAAAHHHH!
ZZZZHHHHHAAAAAHHHH!

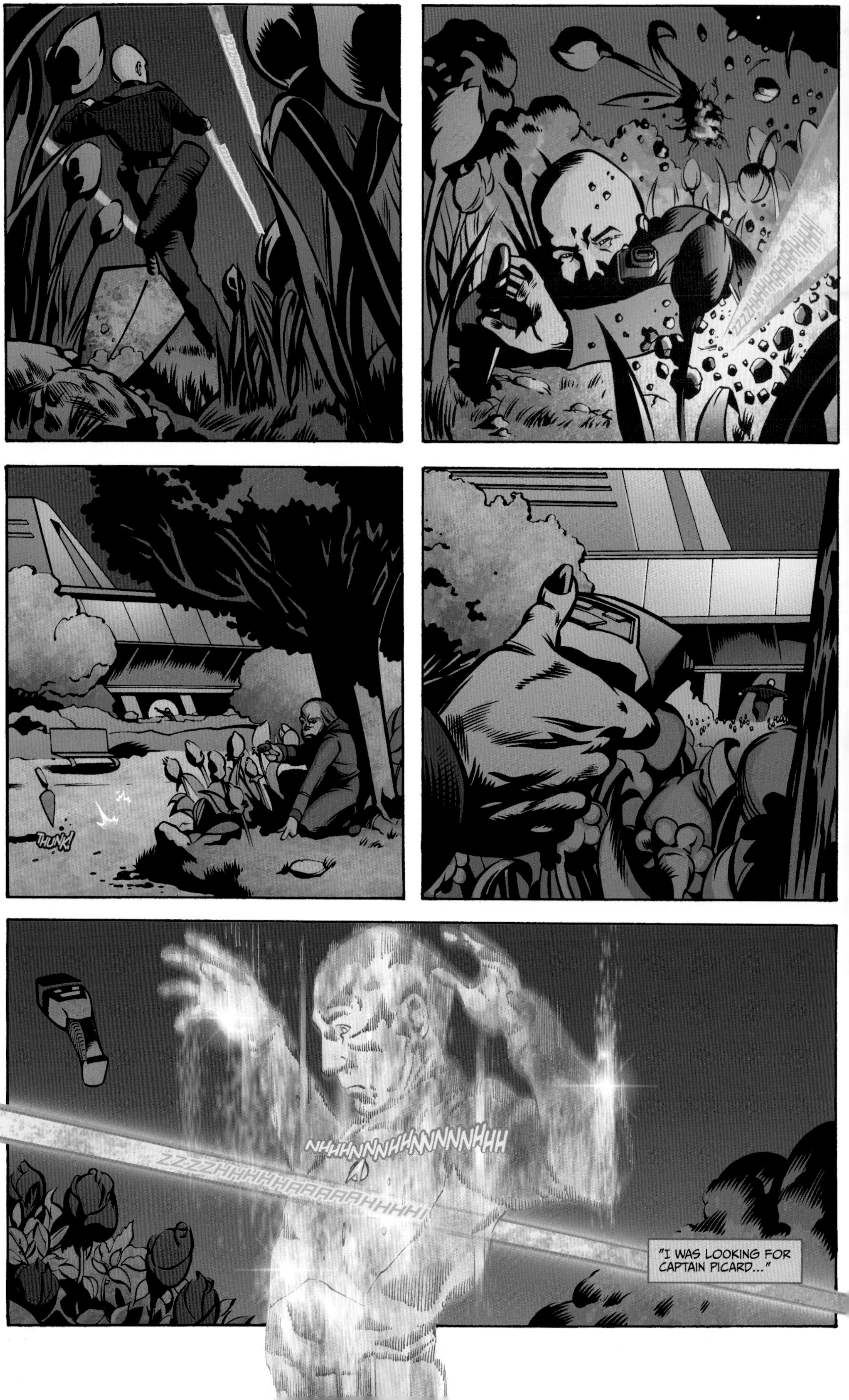
THUNK!
"I WAS LOOKING FOR CAPTAIN PICARD..."

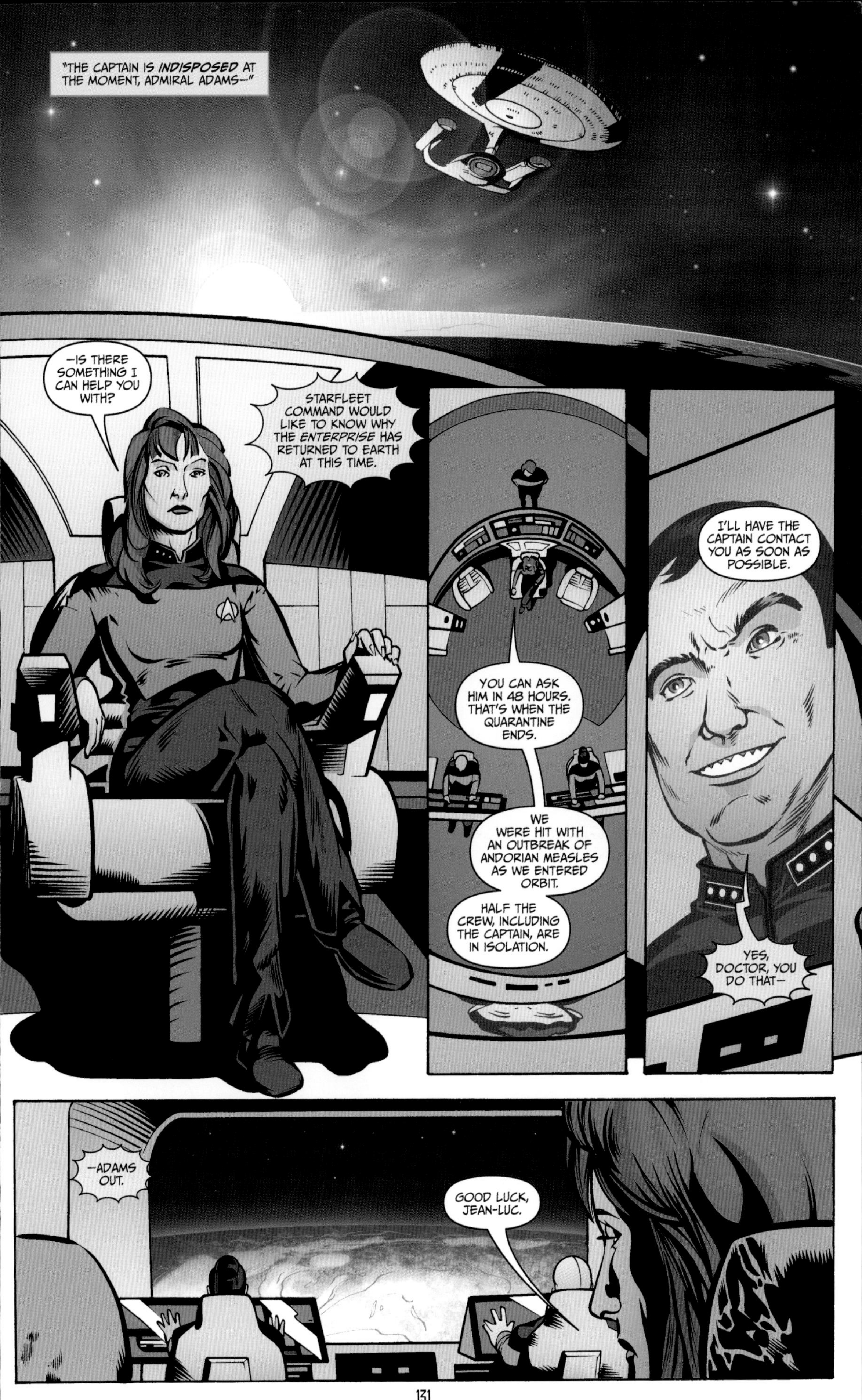
"THE CAPTAIN IS *INDISPOSED* AT THE MOMENT, ADMIRAL ADAMS—"
—IS THERE SOMETHING I CAN HELP YOU WITH?
STARFLEET COMMAND WOULD LIKE TO KNOW WHY THE *ENTERPRISE* HAS RETURNED TO EARTH AT THIS TIME.
YOU CAN ASK HIM IN 48 HOURS. THAT'S WHEN THE QUARANTINE ENDS.
WE WERE HIT WITH AN OUTBREAK OF ANDORIAN MEASLES AS WE ENTERED ORBIT.
HALF THE CREW, INCLUDING THE CAPTAIN, ARE IN ISOLATION.
I'LL HAVE THE CAPTAIN CONTACT YOU AS SOON AS POSSIBLE.
YES, DOCTOR, YOU DO THAT—
—ADAMS OUT.
GOOD LUCK, JEAN-LUC.

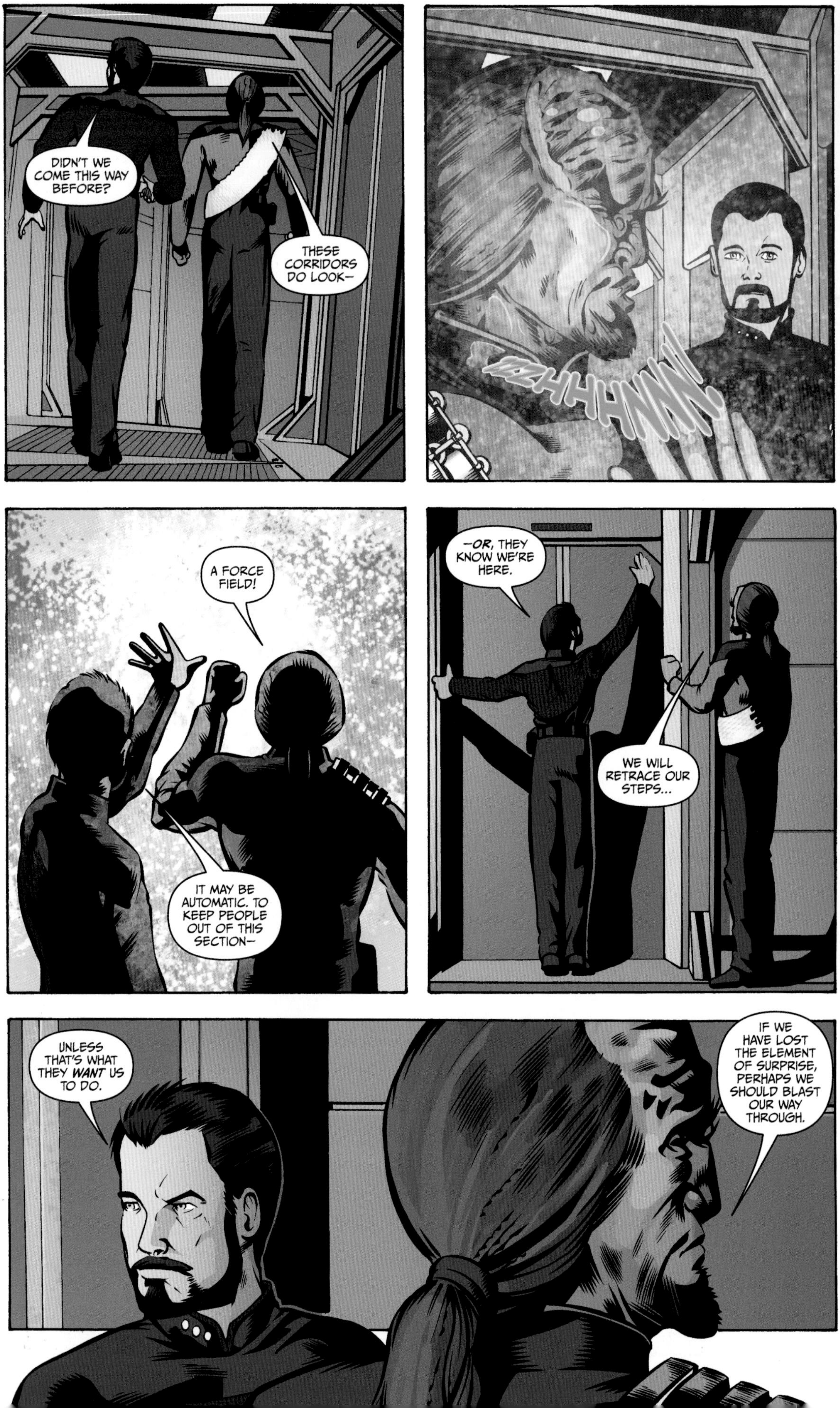

DIDN'T WE COME THIS WAY BEFORE?
THESE CORRIDORS DO LOOK—
ZZZHHHNNN!
A FORCE FIELD!
IT MAY BE AUTOMATIC. TO KEEP PEOPLE OUT OF THIS SECTION—
—OR, THEY KNOW WE'RE HERE.
WE WILL RETRACE OUR STEPS...
UNLESS THAT'S WHAT THEY WANT US TO DO.
IF WE HAVE LOST THE ELEMENT OF SURPRISE, PERHAPS WE SHOULD BLAST OUR WAY THROUGH.

SKREEEET—! TROI HERE.

WE NEED THE SCHEMATICS, DEANNA.

I'M SORRY, WILL. THE COMPUTER FILES HAVE BEEN WIPED CLEAN.

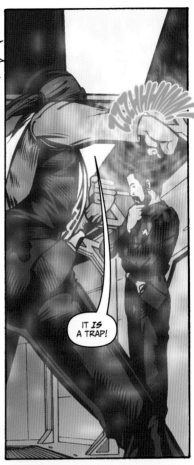

CH-HNNN

IT IS A TRAP!

COMMANDER, PLEASE HAVE LIEUTENANT WORF RECONFIGURE HIS COMM BADGE TO A FREQUENCY OF 13.5 TETRAHERTZ.

THAT FREQUENCY SHOULD BE HIGH ENOUGH TO ESCAPE DETECTION BY THE SENSORS AT THIS FACILITY, BUT ALLOW ME TO GUIDE YOU TO US.

THANKS, DATA.

I WOULD STILL PREFER TO BLAST OUR WAY OUT.

AT THIS POINT, WORF— SO WOULD I.

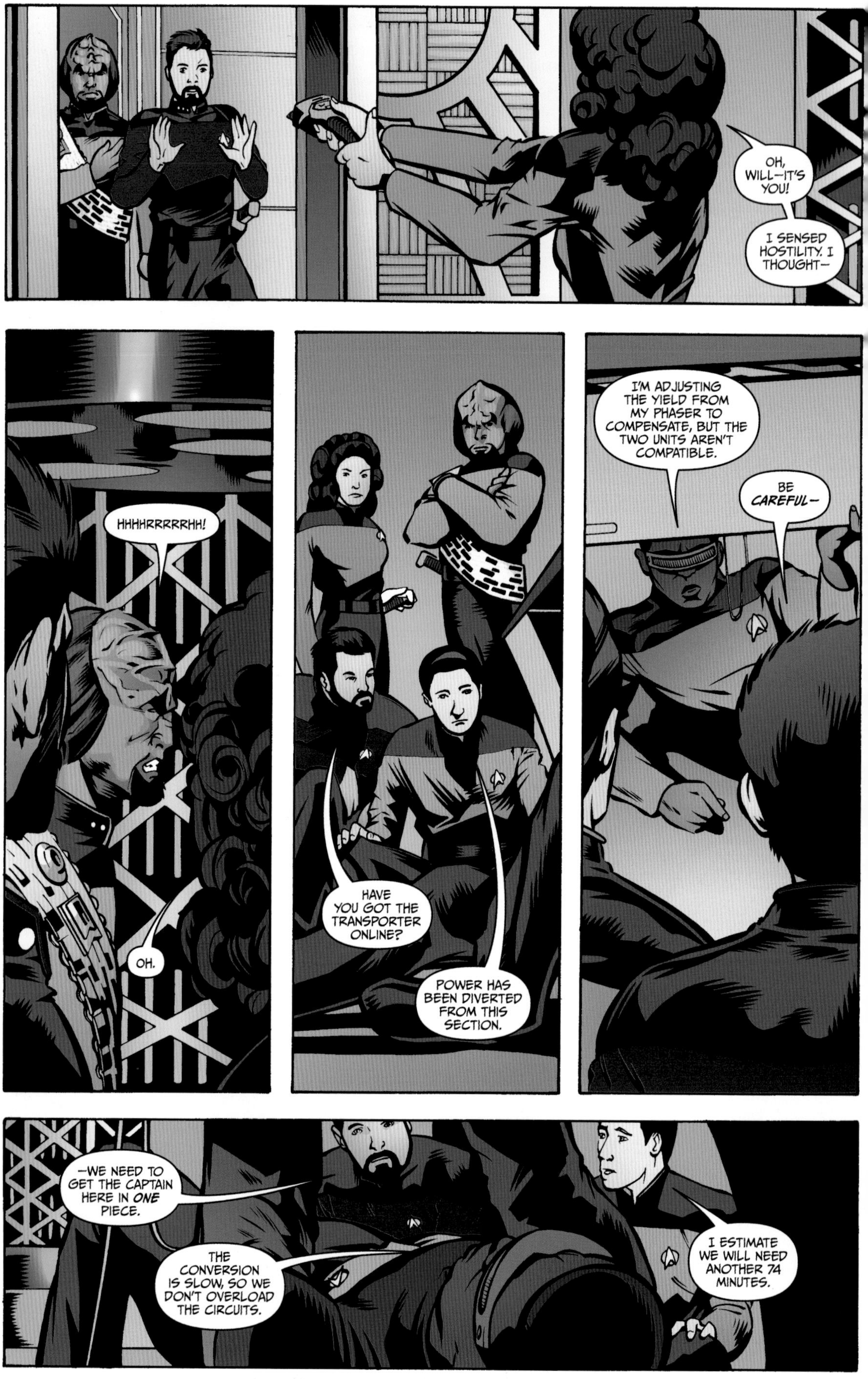
OH, WILL—IT'S YOU!
I SENSED HOSTILITY. I THOUGHT—
HHHHRRRRRHH!
OH.
HAVE YOU GOT THE TRANSPORTER ONLINE?
POWER HAS BEEN DIVERTED FROM THIS SECTION.
I'M ADJUSTING THE YIELD FROM MY PHASER TO COMPENSATE, BUT THE TWO UNITS AREN'T COMPATIBLE.
BE *CAREFUL*—
—WE NEED TO GET THE CAPTAIN HERE IN *ONE* PIECE.
THE CONVERSION IS SLOW, SO WE DON'T OVERLOAD THE CIRCUITS.
I ESTIMATE WE WILL NEED ANOTHER 74 MINUTES.

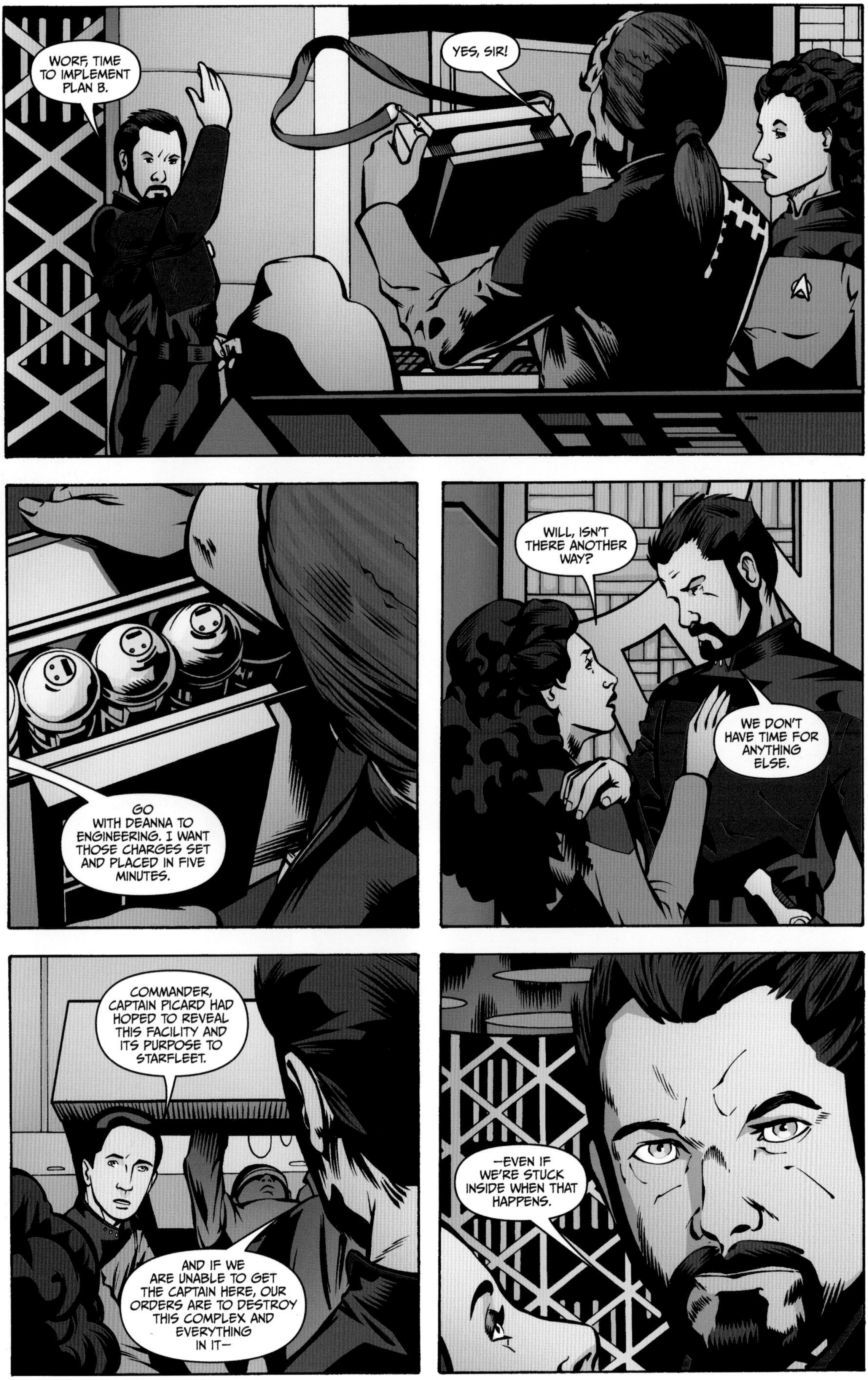
WORF, TIME TO IMPLEMENT PLAN B.
YES, SIR!
GO WITH DEANNA TO ENGINEERING. I WANT THOSE CHARGES SET AND PLACED IN FIVE MINUTES.
WILL, ISN'T THERE ANOTHER WAY?
WE DON'T HAVE TIME FOR ANYTHING ELSE.
COMMANDER, CAPTAIN PICARD HAD HOPED TO REVEAL THIS FACILITY AND ITS PURPOSE TO STARFLEET.
AND IF WE ARE UNABLE TO GET THE CAPTAIN HERE, OUR ORDERS ARE TO DESTROY THIS COMPLEX AND EVERYTHING IN IT—
—EVEN IF WE'RE STUCK INSIDE WHEN THAT HAPPENS.

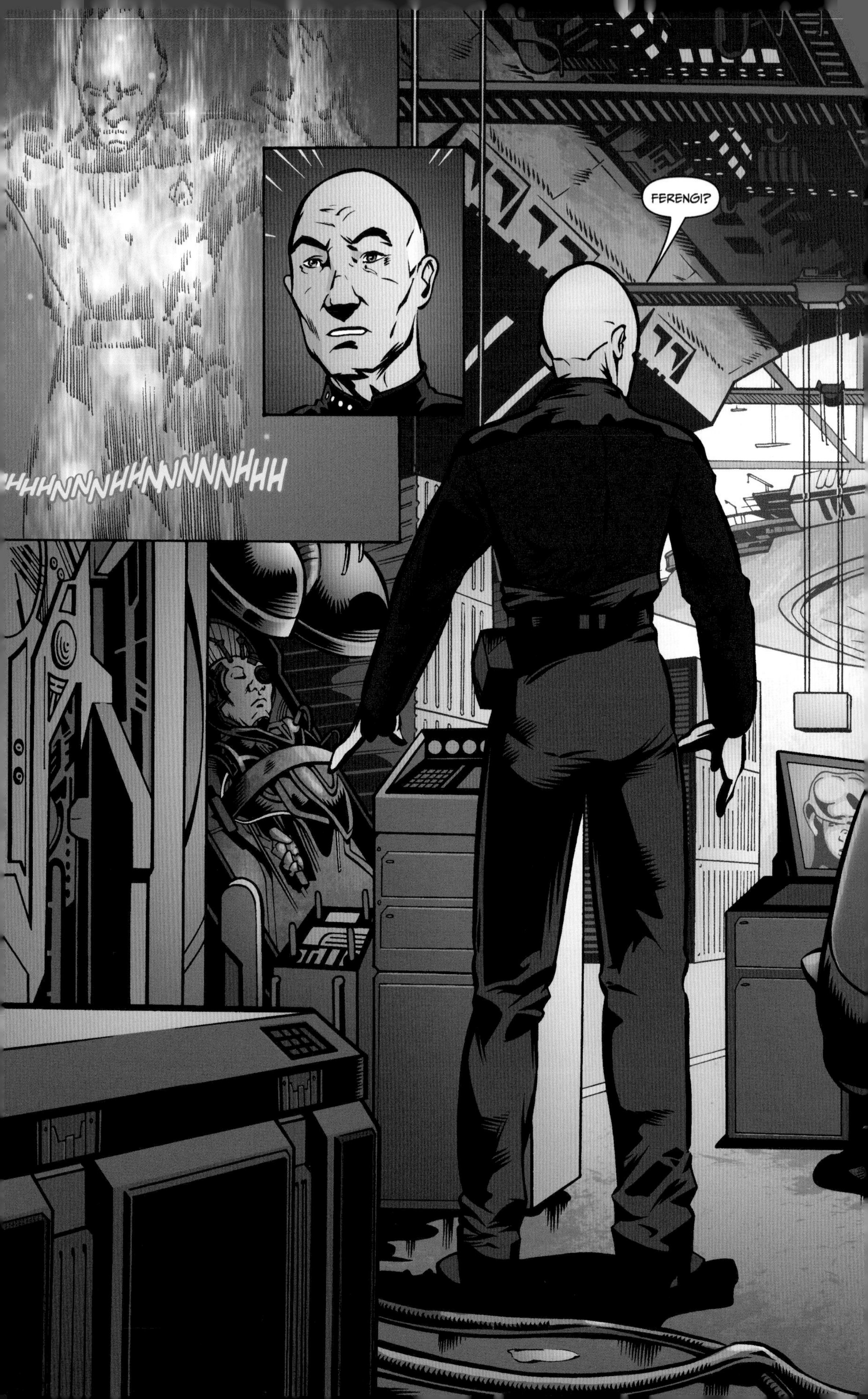
HHHNNNHHNNNNNHHH
FERENGI!?

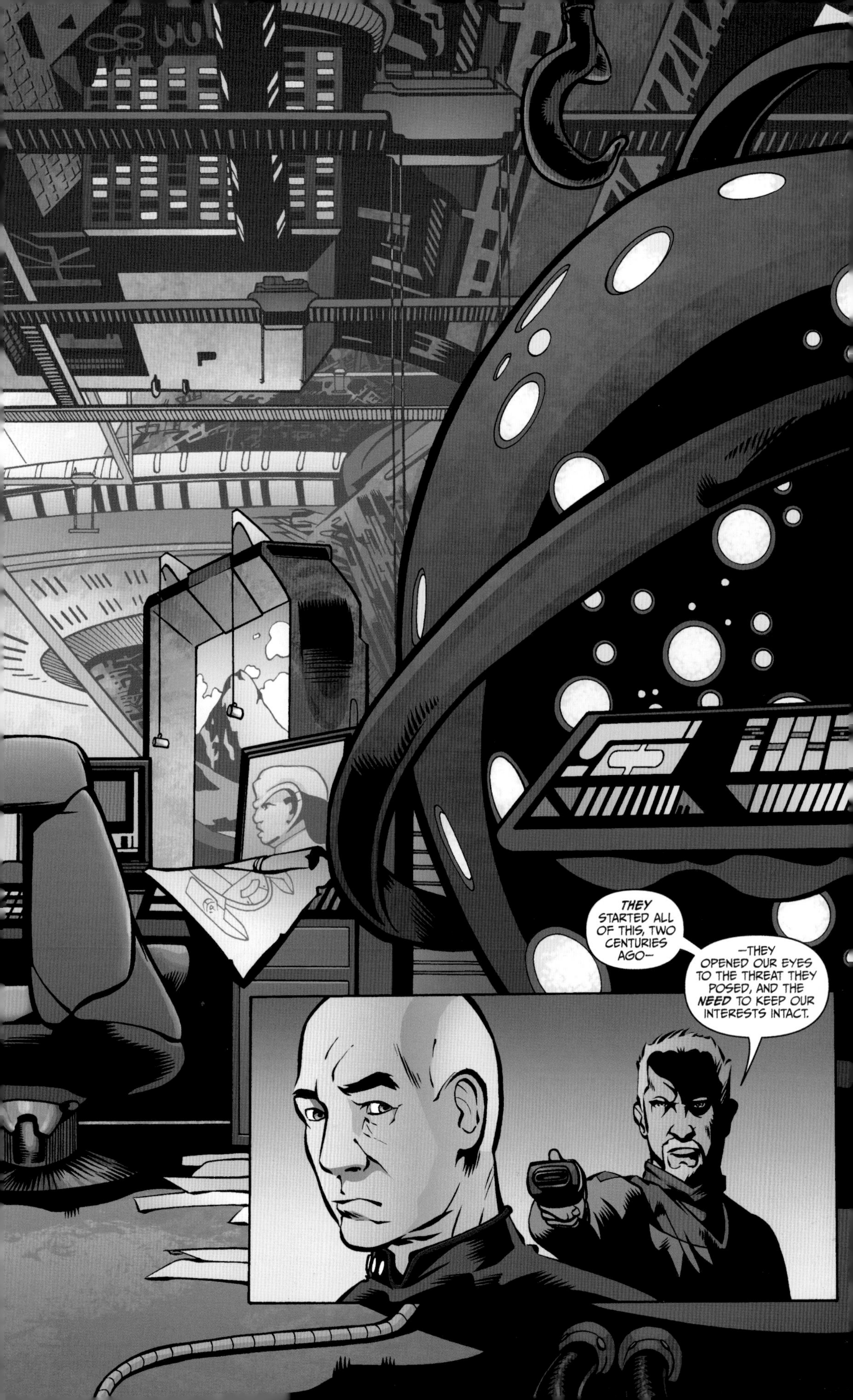
THEY STARTED ALL OF THIS, TWO CENTURIES AGO–
–THEY OPENED OUR EYES TO THE THREAT THEY POSED, AND THE NEED TO KEEP OUR INTERESTS INTACT.

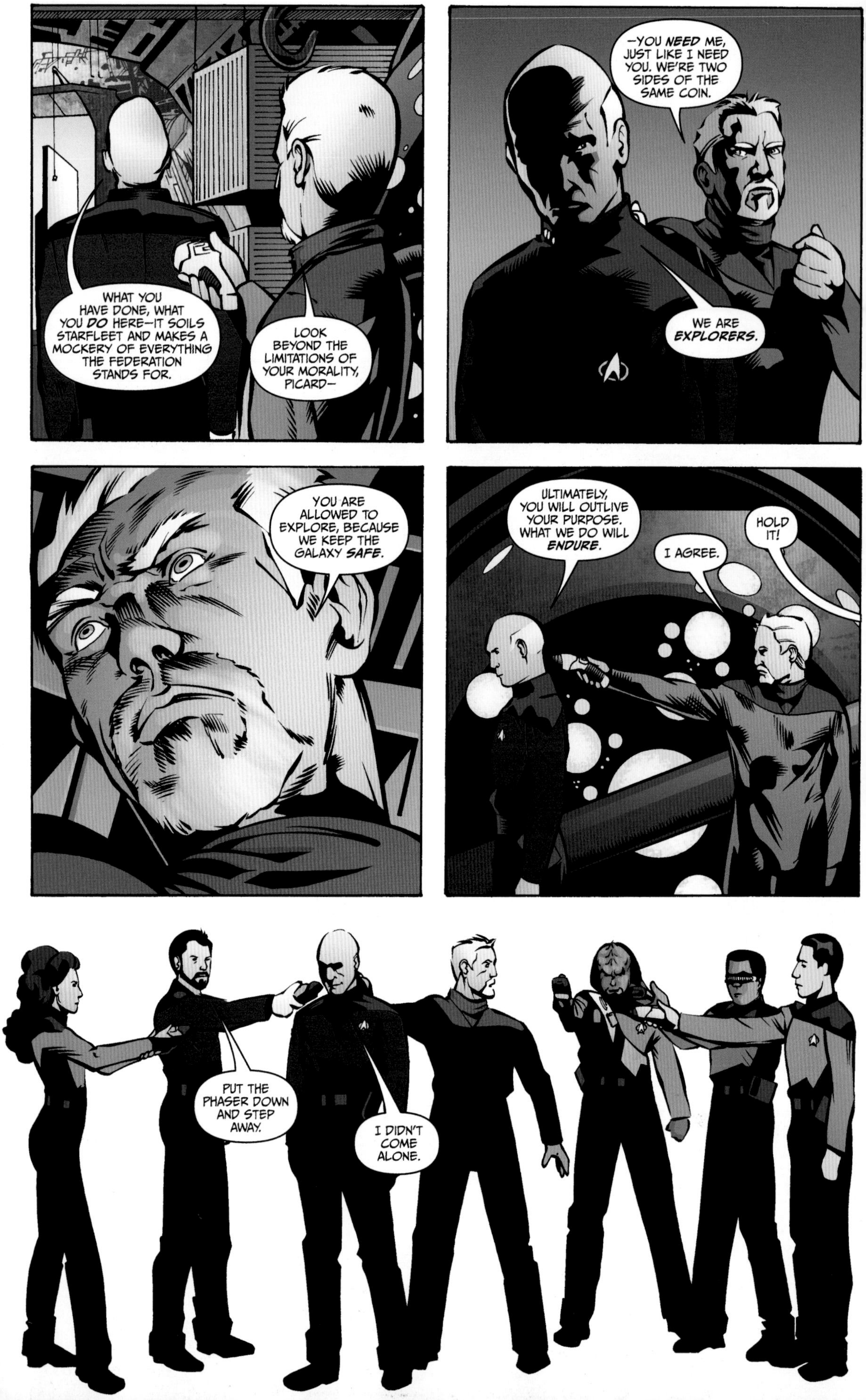
WHAT YOU HAVE DONE, WHAT YOU DO HERE—IT SOILS STARFLEET AND MAKES A MOCKERY OF EVERYTHING THE FEDERATION STANDS FOR.
LOOK BEYOND THE LIMITATIONS OF YOUR MORALITY, PICARD—
—YOU NEED ME, JUST LIKE I NEED YOU. WE'RE TWO SIDES OF THE SAME COIN.
WE ARE EXPLORERS.
YOU ARE ALLOWED TO EXPLORE, BECAUSE WE KEEP THE GALAXY SAFE.
ULTIMATELY, YOU WILL OUTLIVE YOUR PURPOSE. WHAT WE DO WILL ENDURE.
I AGREE.
HOLD IT!
PUT THE PHASER DOWN AND STEP AWAY.
I DIDN'T COME ALONE.

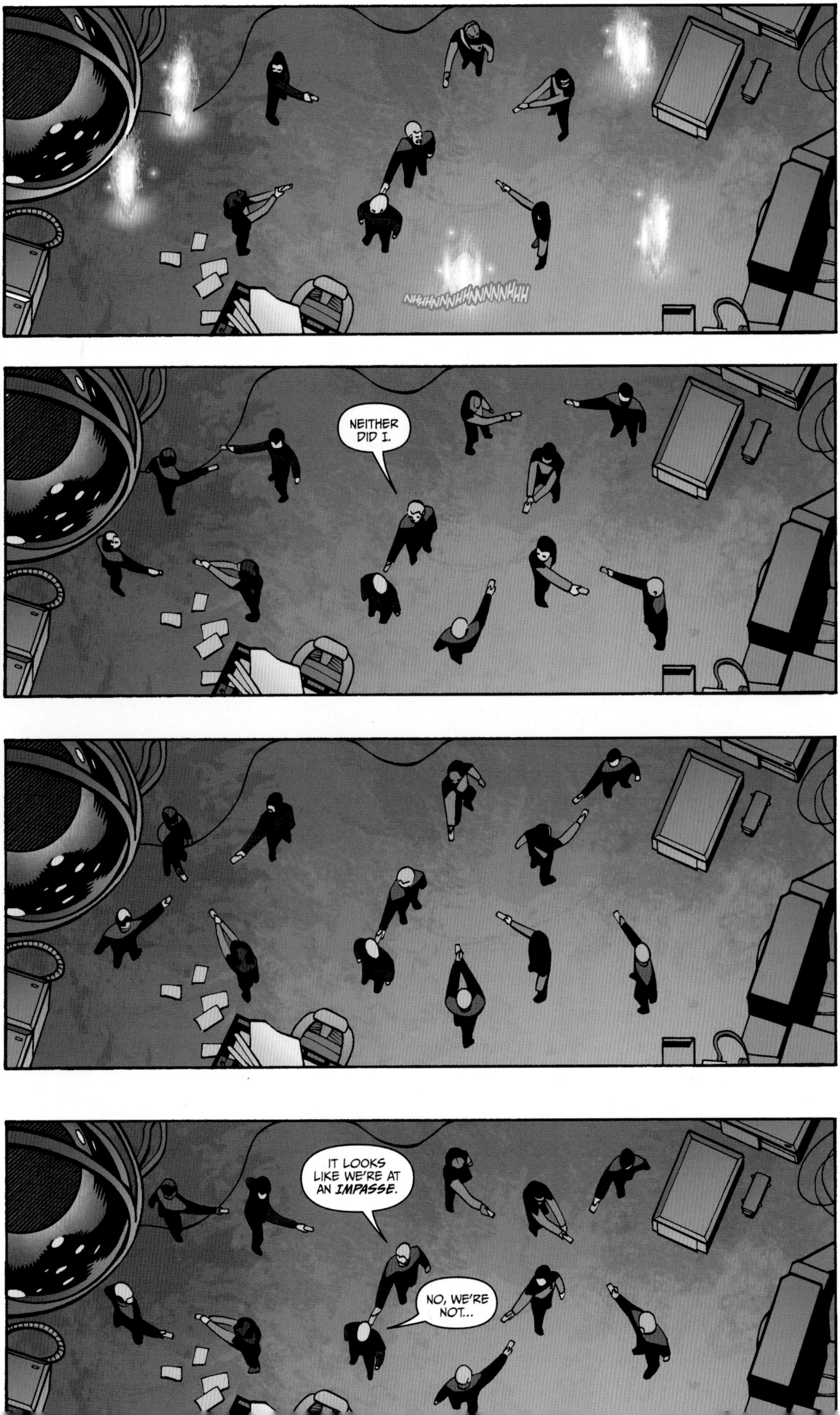
NHHHNNNHHNNNNNHHH
NEITHER DID I.
IT LOOKS LIKE WE'RE AT AN *IMPASSE*.
NO, WE'RE NOT...

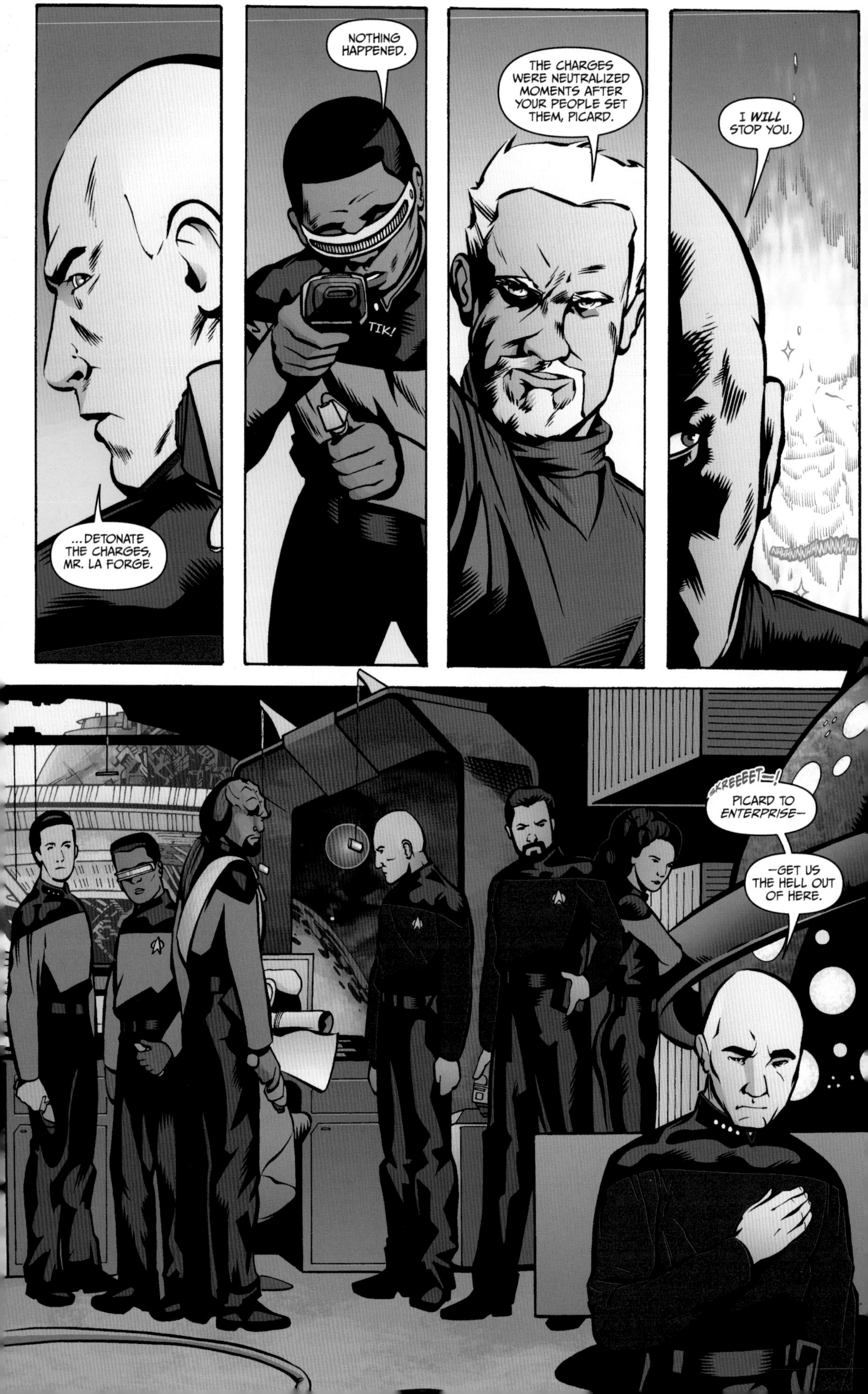
...DETONATE THE CHARGES, MR. LA FORGE.
NOTHING HAPPENED.
TIK!
THE CHARGES WERE NEUTRALIZED MOMENTS AFTER YOUR PEOPLE SET THEM, PICARD.
I *WILL* STOP YOU.
SKREEEET!
PICARD TO *ENTERPRISE*—
—GET US THE HELL OUT OF HERE.

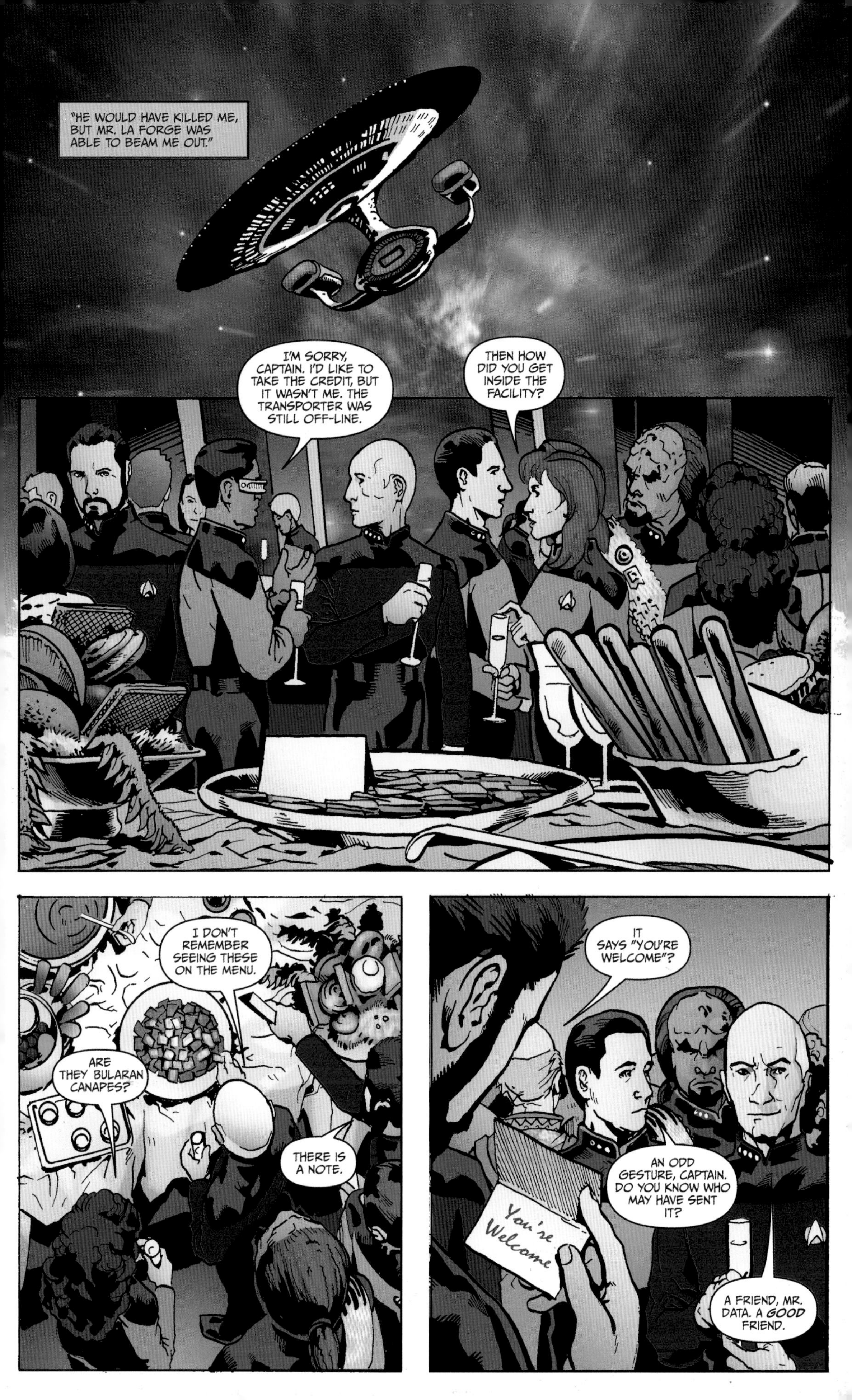
"HE WOULD HAVE KILLED ME, BUT MR. LA FORGE WAS ABLE TO BEAM ME OUT."
I'M SORRY, CAPTAIN. I'D LIKE TO TAKE THE CREDIT, BUT IT WASN'T ME. THE TRANSPORTER WAS STILL OFF-LINE.
THEN HOW DID YOU GET INSIDE THE FACILITY?
I DON'T REMEMBER SEEING THESE ON THE MENU.
ARE THEY BULARAN CANAPES?
THERE IS A NOTE.
IT SAYS "YOU'RE WELCOME"?
You're Welcome
AN ODD GESTURE, CAPTAIN. DO YOU KNOW WHO MAY HAVE SENT IT?
A FRIEND, MR. DATA. A *GOOD* FRIEND.

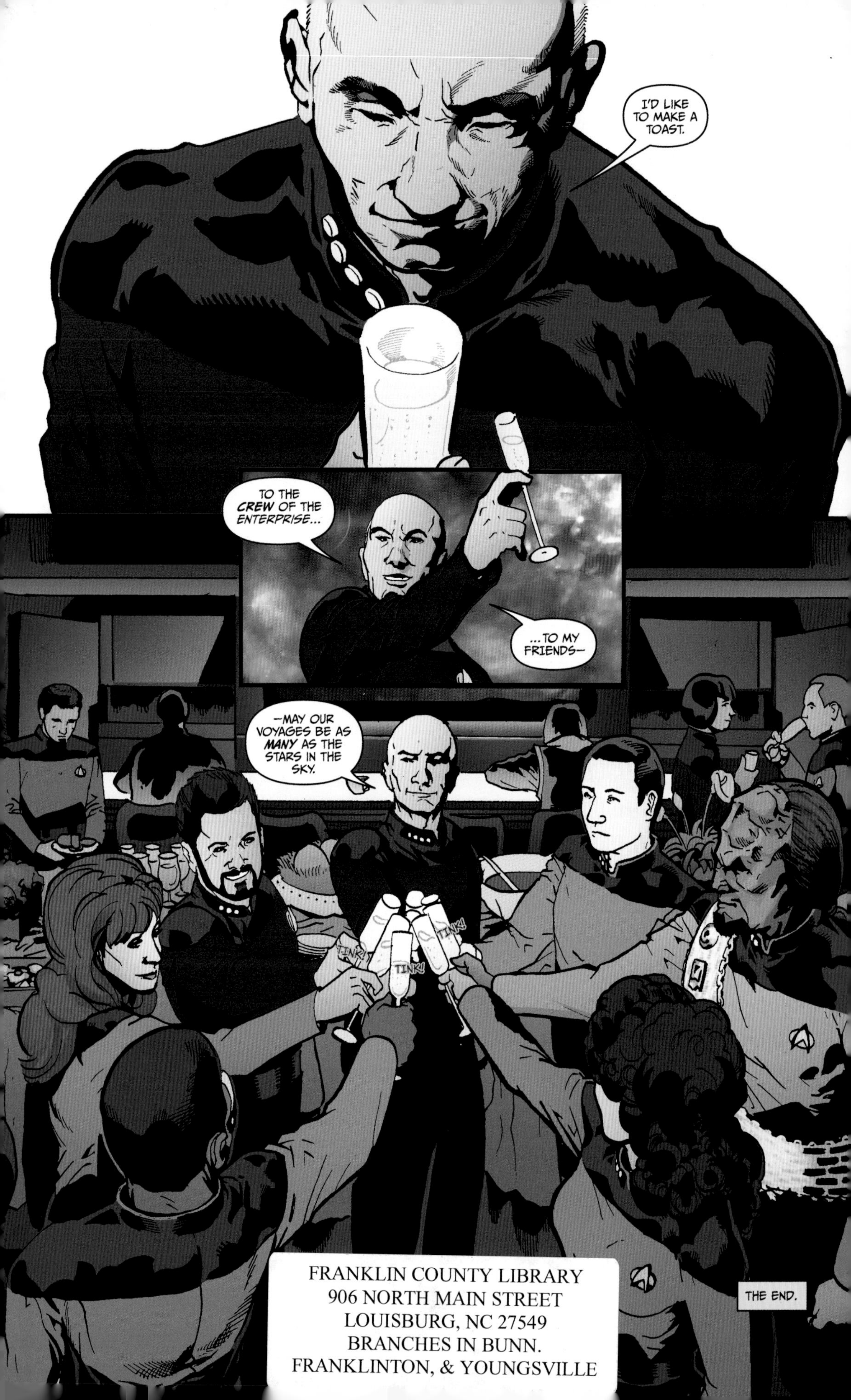
I'D LIKE TO MAKE A TOAST.
TO THE CREW OF THE ENTERPRISE...
...TO MY FRIENDS—
—MAY OUR VOYAGES BE AS MANY AS THE STARS IN THE SKY.
TINK!
TINK!
TINK!
THE END.

VARIANT COVER GALLERY

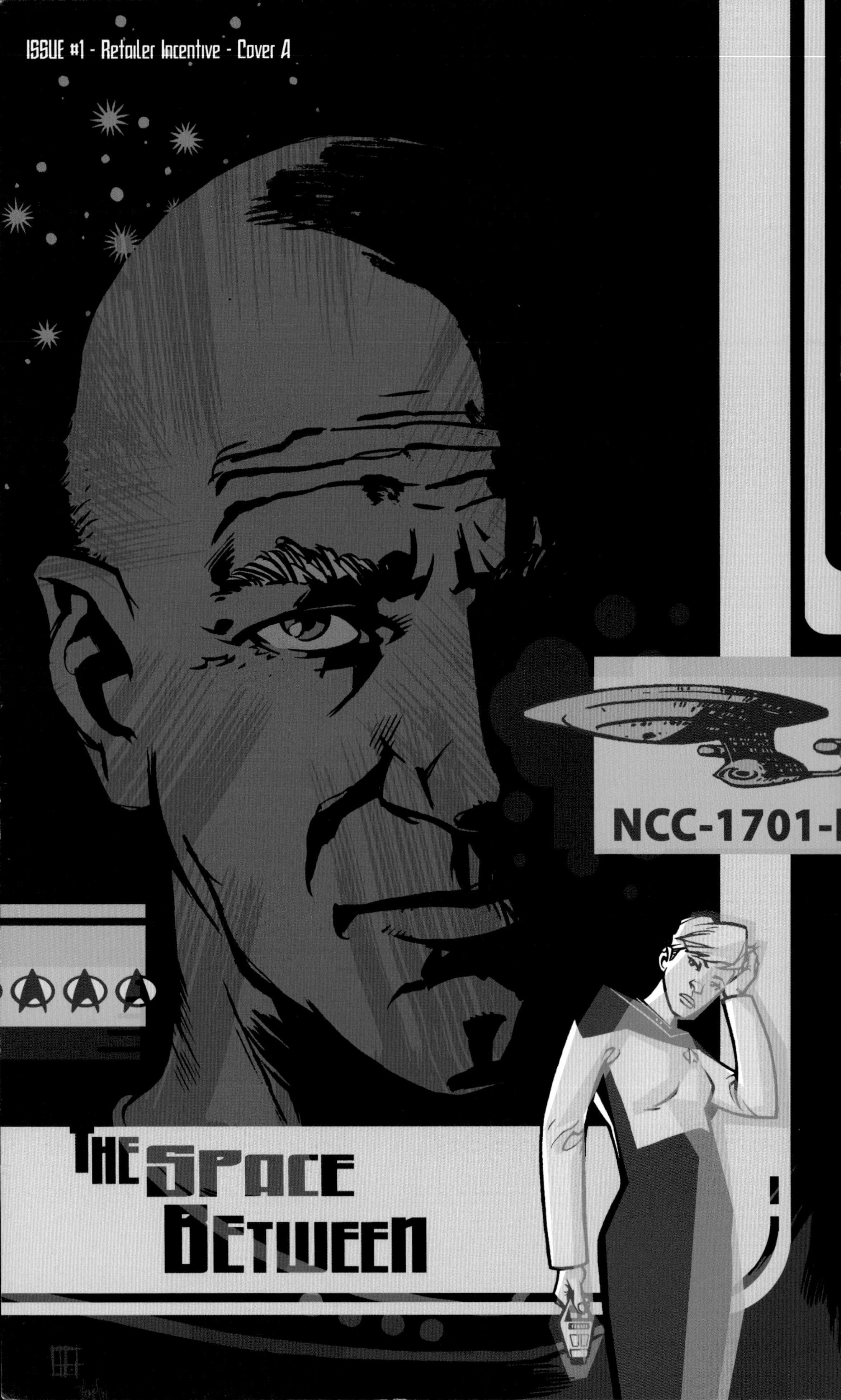

ISSUE #1 - Retailer Incentive - Cover A
NCC-1701-
THE SPACE BETWEEN

ISSUE #2 - Retailer Incentive - Cover A

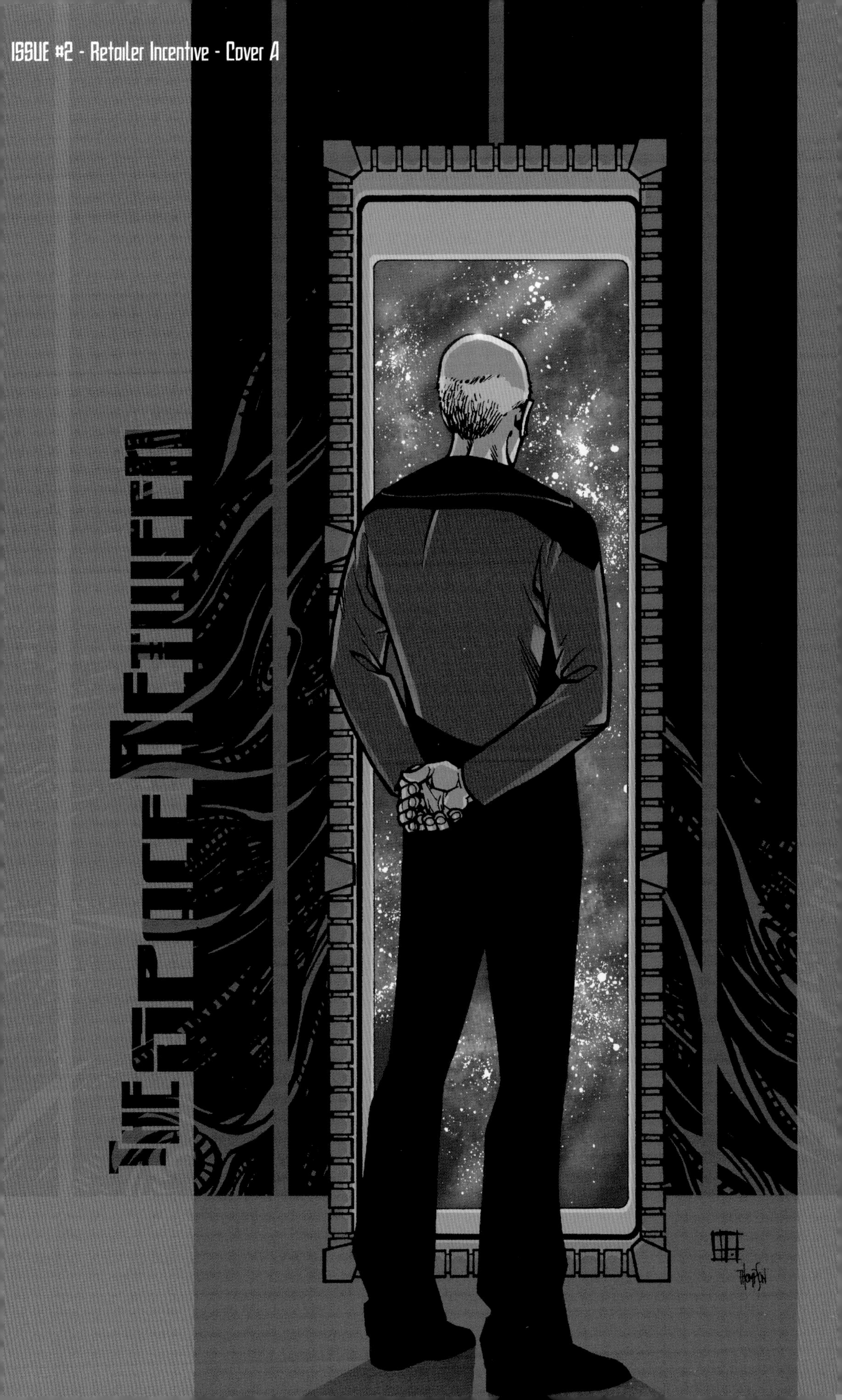
THE SPACE BETWEEN

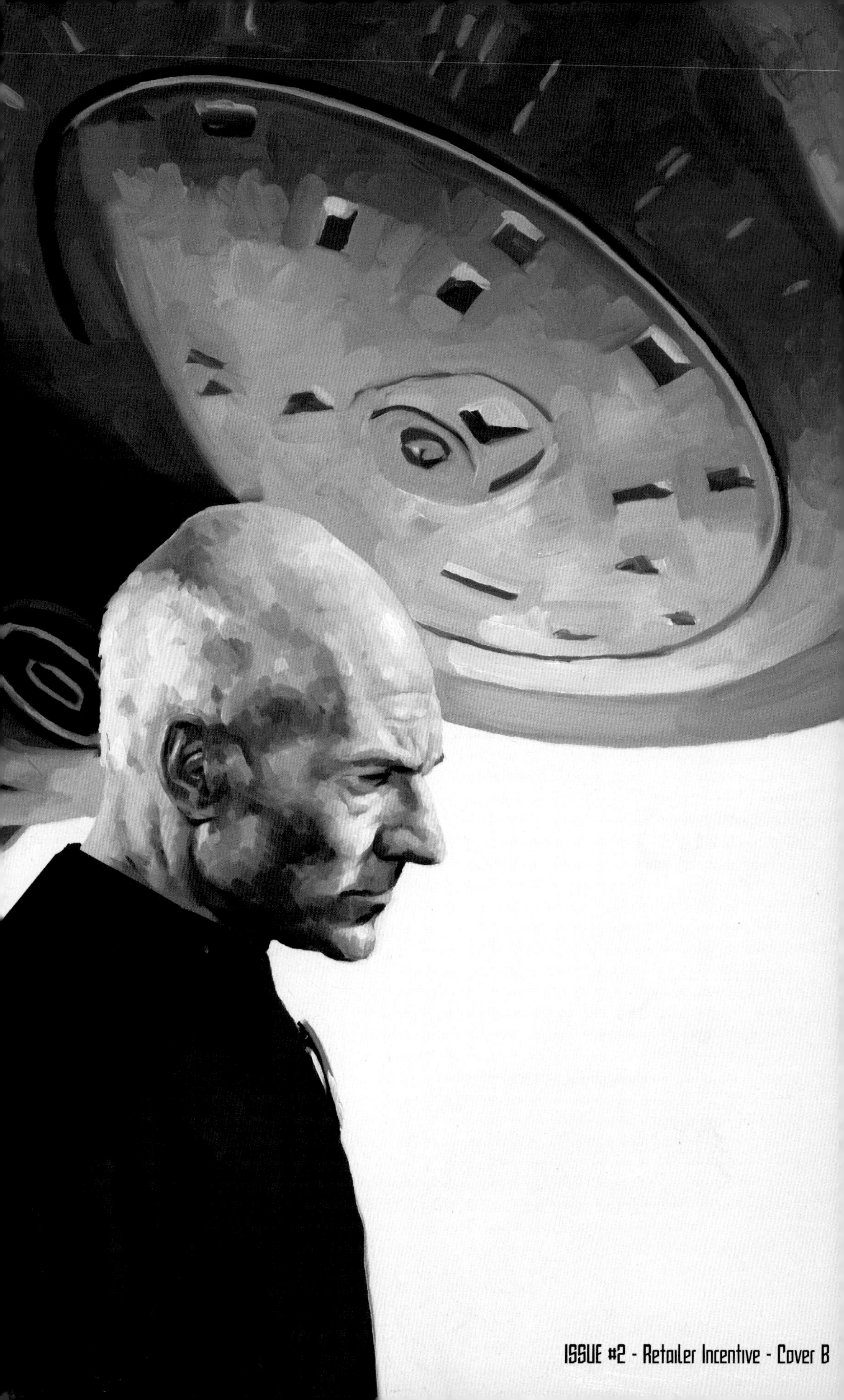

ISSUE #2 - Retailer Incentive - Cover B

ISSUE #4 - Retailer Incentive Cover

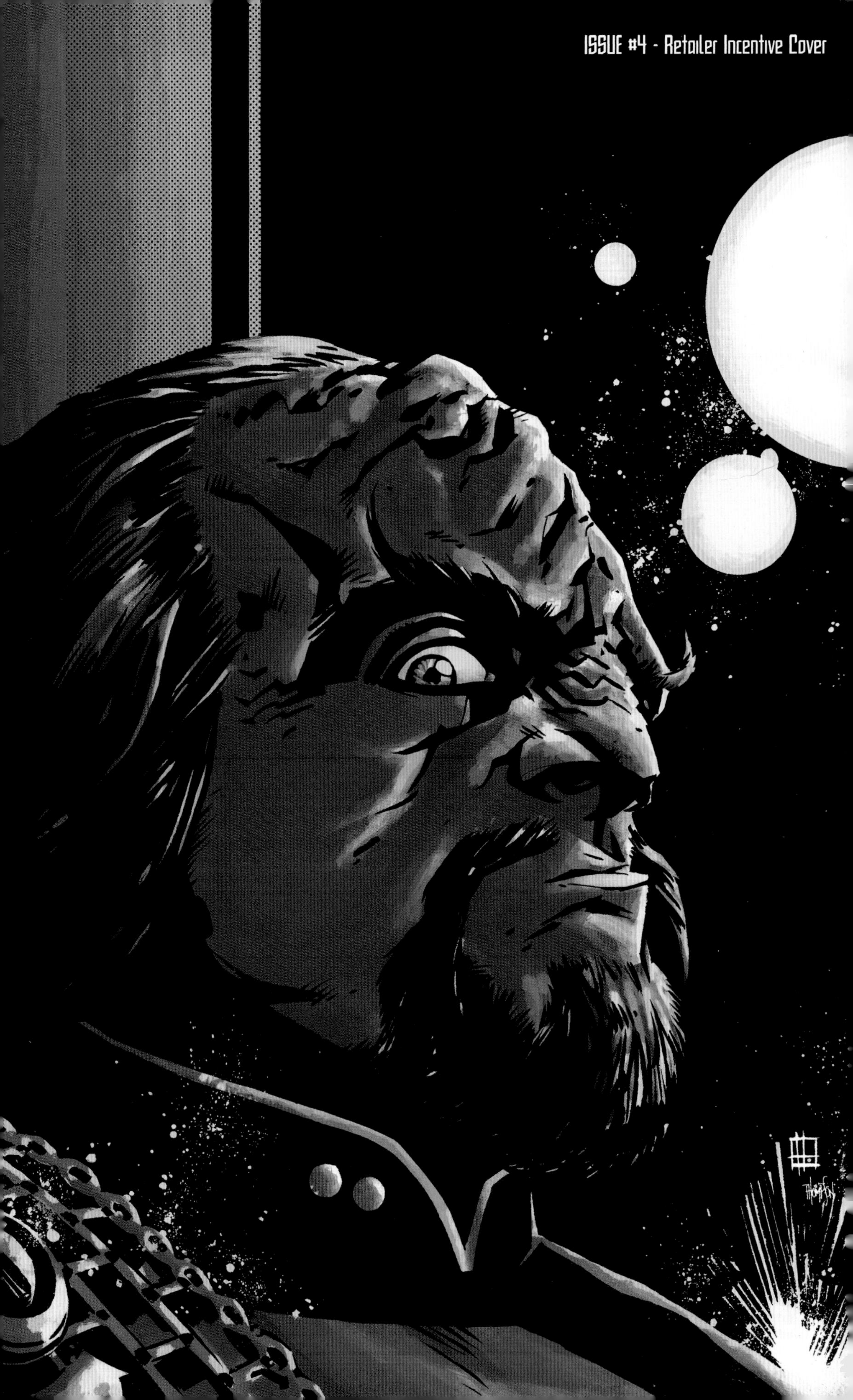

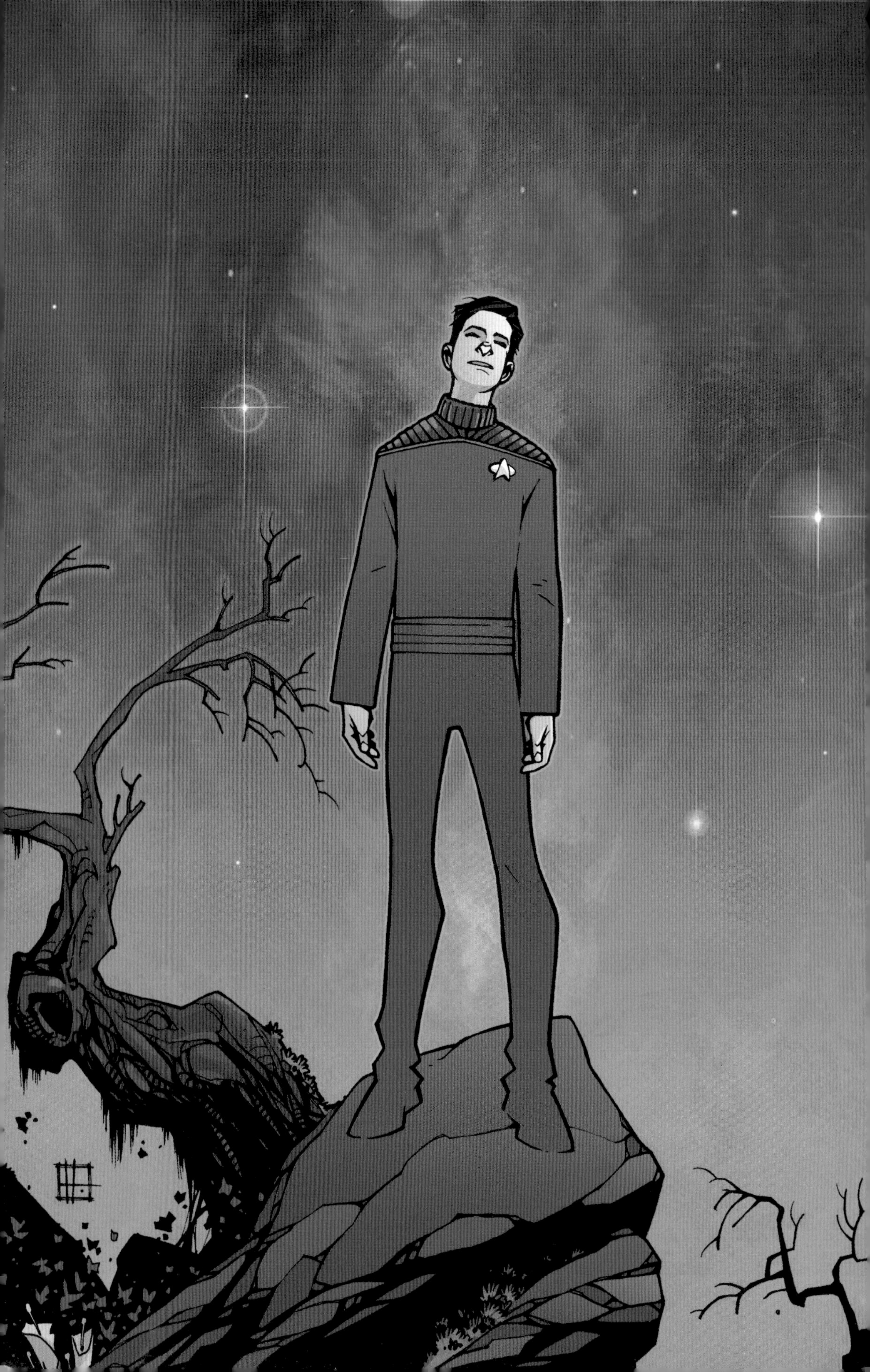

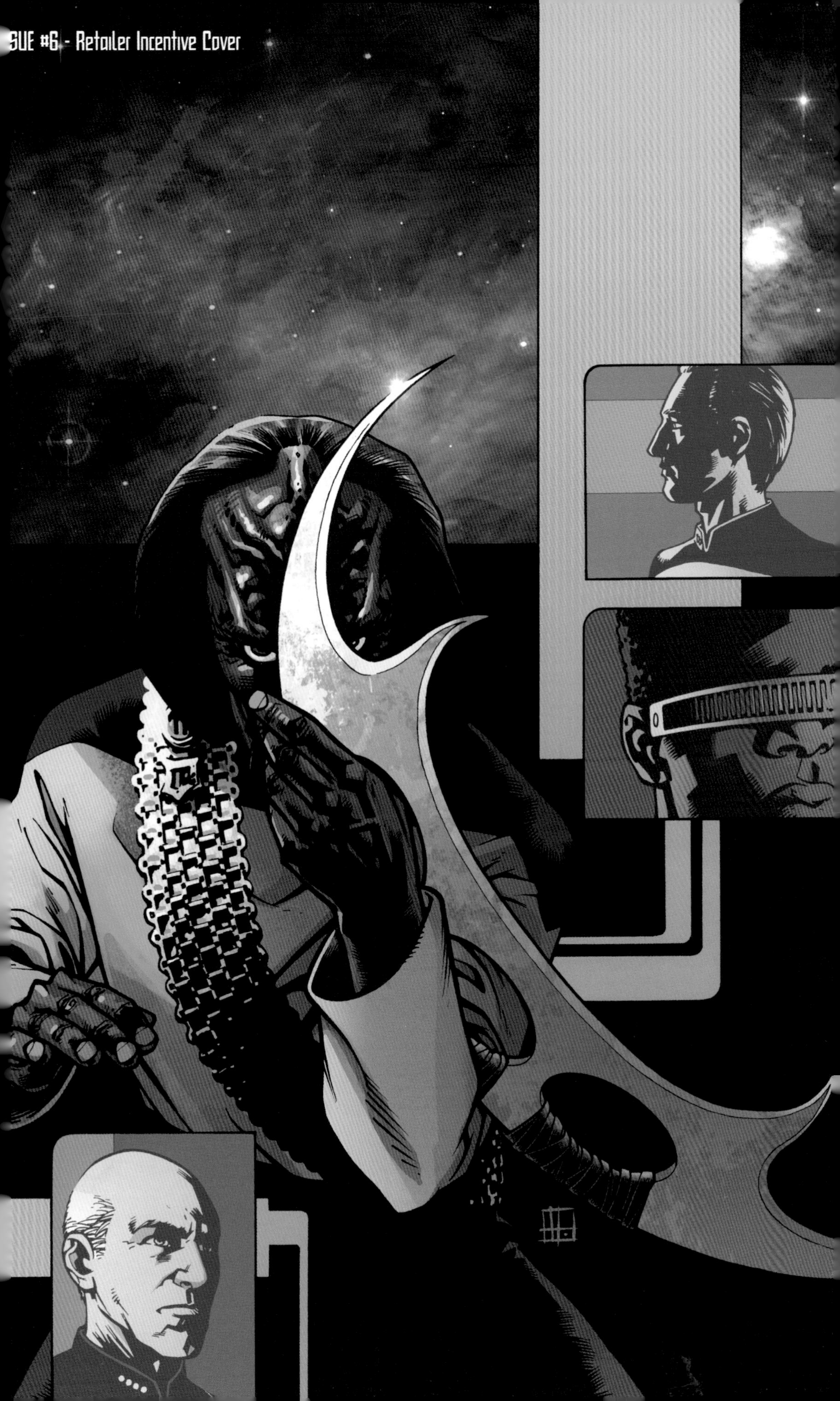

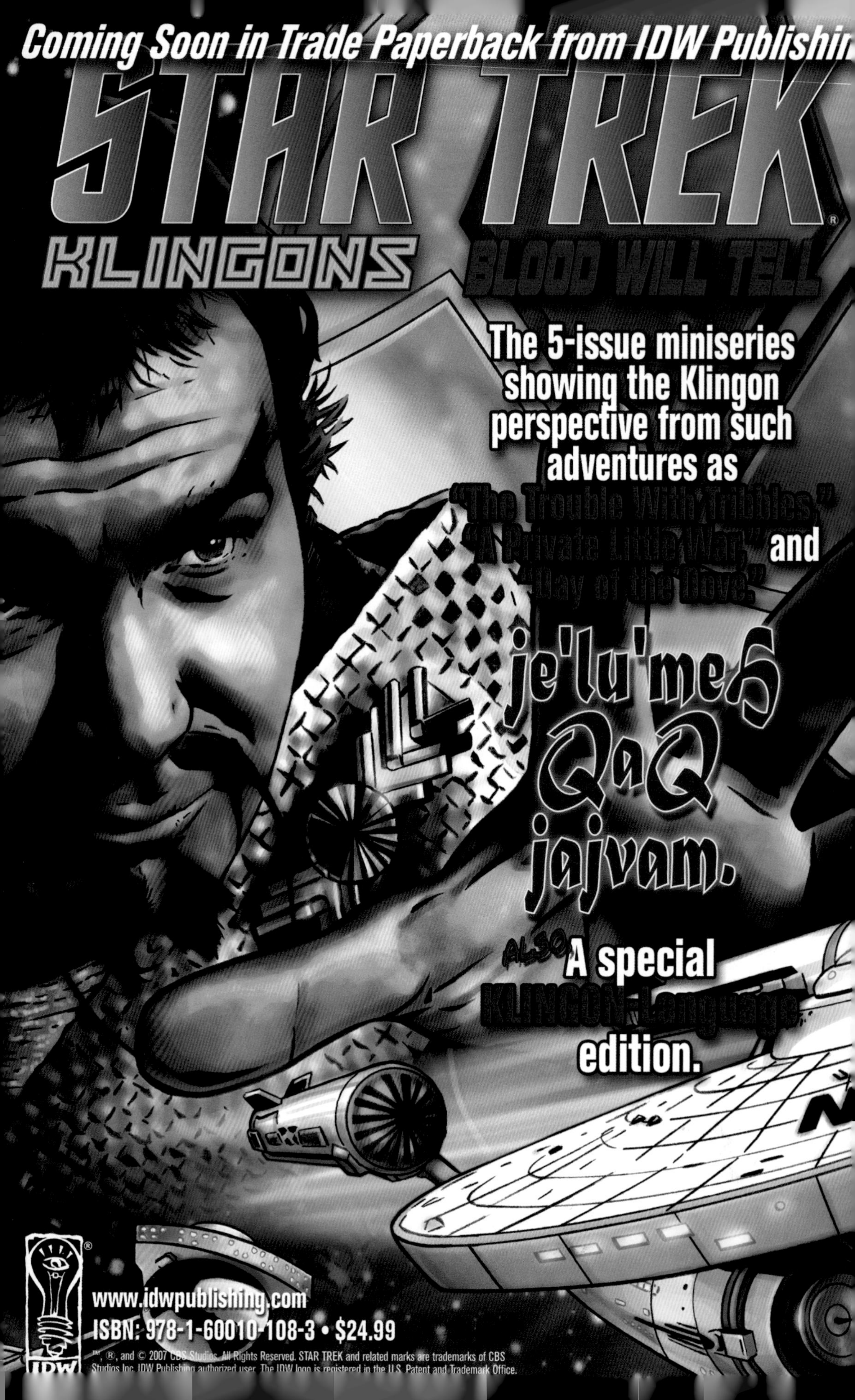

Coming Soon in Trade Paperback from IDW Publishin
STAR TREK®
KLINGONS
BLOOD WILL TELL
The 5-issue miniseries showing the Klingon perspective from such adventures as "The Trouble With Tribbles," "A Private Little War," and "Day of the Dove."
je'lu'meS QaQ jajvam.
ALSO A special KLINGON-Language edition.
www.idwpublishing.com
ISBN: 978-1-60010-108-3 • $24.99
™, ®, and © 2007 CBS Studios. All Rights Reserved. STAR TREK and related marks are trademarks of CBS Studios Inc. IDW Publishing authorized user. The IDW logo is registered in the U.S. Patent and Trademark Office.

IDW Publishing
San Diego, CA
www.idwpublishing.com